Kitiara signaled Raistlin, who was hanging back. He stood ready in his best spellcasting stance.

After a few murmured phrases from the young mage, the surface of Crystalmir Lake began to bubble and seethe. The odd noise captured Bronk's and Dune's attention. Immediately the two bullies lost interest in their private drama. They froze, their eyes riveted to the lake.

"What's that?" Bronk said fearfully to Kit.

Dark plumes of smoke and fingers of flame erupted from the sandy banks. The surface of the water roiled, and a huge shape began to emerge—a thing, a creature, manlike but much larger, with wet tendrils of slimy plants clinging to its sides. Suddenly its empty eye sockets blazed with orange fire, and its upper limbs began to sway, making it appear as if the horrible creature were moving toward shore.

THE DRAGONLANCE® SAGA

CHRONICLES TRILOGY

Dragons of Autumn Twilight
Dragons of Winter Night
Dragons of Spring Dawning

LEGENDS TRILOGY

Time of the Twins
War of the Twins
Test of the Twins

The Art of the DRAGONLANCE Saga

The Atlas of the DRAGONLANCE Saga

TALES TRILOGY

The Magic of Krynn
Kender, Gully Dwarves, and Gnomes
Love and War

HEROES TRILOGY

The Legend of Huma
Stormblade
Weasel's Luck

PRELUDES TRILOGY

Darkness and Light
Kendermore
Brothers Majere

HEROES II TRILOGY

Kaz, the Minotaur
The Gates of Thorbardin
Galen Beknighted

PRELUDES II TRILOGY

Riverwind, the Plainsman
Flint, the King
Tanis, the Shadow Years

ELVEN NATIONS TRILOGY

Firstborn
The Kinslayer Wars
The Qualinesti

MEETINGS SEXTET

Kindred Spirits
Wanderlust
Dark Heart
The Oath and the Measure
Steel and Stone
The Companions

MEETINGS SEXTET

VOLUME THREE

Dark Heart

Tina Daniell

DRAGONLANCE® Saga Meetings

Volume Three

Dark Heart

Copyright ©1992 TSR, Inc.
All Rights Reserved.

First Printing: January 1992
Printed in the United States of America.
Library of Congress Catalog Card Number: 90-71496

9 8 7 6 5 4

ISBN: 1-56076-116-4

TSR, Inc.
P.O. Box 756
Lake Geneva, WI
53147 U.S.A.

TSR Ltd.
120 Church End, Cherry Hinton
Cambridge CB1 3LB
United Kingdom

For Connie and Hank

───────────

My thanks to Jim Lowder for the final care he gave my manuscript; to Mary Kirchoff for her initial leap of faith; and to Pat McGilligan for his patience and well-thought-out, if not always well-received, criticism.

Chapter I

GREGOR'S LEGACY

Kitiara Uth Matar stood in the shade of a lone oak on a small rise that overlooked a shallow valley. It was barely dawn, and mist clung to tall grasses in the meadow that spread before her. She was a long day's journey away from the familiar vallenwoods of Solace, and this was her first chance to get a look at the rolling countryside that stretched far to the west of that comfortable village.

Darkness had fallen by the time they had reached camp the night before, and no welcoming fires had greeted them. The soldiers did not want to risk revealing their position.

Riding into camp, Kit had heard the muffled clank of armor and weapons being put aside and had dimly made out the forms of men and other creatures preparing their bedrolls. She herself felt nothing like sleep. Her senses tingled with a novel, not unpleasant sensation—excitement combined with a frisson of fear. She was about to see her first battle!

Nonetheless, when Gregor Uth Matar swung easily off Cinnamon, his prize chestnut mare, and handed the reins to a waiting squire, Kit scrambled off her smaller mount to keep up with him. She didn't want to get too far away from the protection of this tall, imposing warrior who was her father.

He strode quickly to the one light in the camp, a carefully banked lantern that shone in the tent of the troop's commander. Nolan of Vinses was little more than a dull-witted farmer, according to Gregor, and Gregor had little use for farmers or anyone else whose work didn't involve handling a sword well.

But it was Nolan who headed the five-man militia in the rich farming community of Vinses, and he who had convinced the village's guardians, finally, to dig into their pockets and pay for a mercenary force to defend the residents against a marauding army of barbarians that had been terrorizing them for more than a year. So he was, nominally at least, in charge.

After making a few inquiries, Nolan had learned of Gregor, sought him out, and hired him. Gregor then recruited fifty or so other worthies. He also advised Nolan to send word to Burek, the head of a band of minotaurs based in Caergoth who hired themselves out for combat. If Nolan's desire was to end the rampage by destroying Swiftwater and his outlaw followers, it would be useful to have minotaurs fighting on their side, Gregor had said.

"I have heard tales of this Swiftwater," her father told Kit as they made their way through the quiet camp. "He is a savage, the worst human scum. They say he fights without a brain—without a heart, as well. With such an opponent, the minotaurs are worth the trouble and expense. His wild degeneracy will inflame them, and they will fight to the utmost."

When they reached Nolan's tent, Gregor motioned for

Kitiara to wait outside. She crept as close as possible to the light leaking from the tent's doorway flap, then peered inside. She saw her father standing with his back to the opening, facing a table spread with a large map. Not for the first time did she think Gregor was the handsomest man she would ever see: regal and sturdy, with well-muscled limbs and raven-black hair that curled closely around his head and graced his upper lip with a luxurious mustache.

A blond, clean-shaven man stood opposite Gregor on the other side of the table. He wore a farmer's green tunic and had a sword in its scabbard strapped awkwardly around his waist. His face was grim. Nolan, Kitiara thought.

Looking to the right of Nolan, Kit saw someone step out of the shadows at her father's beckoning. She sucked in her breath. The creature towered over Gregor, who himself stood at over six feet. He wore a heavy leather girdle that flashed with richly colored gems and carried a fascinating array of daggers and other weapons, most prominent among them a huge, double-edged ax. The pair of horns that curved away from his forehead, each at least two feet long, threatened to rip through the top of the tent.

"A minotaur!" Kit whispered to herself breathlessly. She had heard many stories of these fierce and brutish fighters from her father, but never in her seven years had she seen one in her treetop village of Solace.

Burek, the minotaur, spoke in a deep, guttural voice, discussing strategy for the next day's battle. Gregor and Nolan pondered the map. As time went on, Gregor made his own suggestions about the battle plan, some of them seemingly not congenial to Burek. Nolan took Burek's side unexpectedly, and Gregor, shaking with suppressed rage, turned to confront Burek. He pushed up against the minotaur and spoke harshly. Burek did not budge from his point of view. Nor did Gregor back off. The warrior hammered at Burek with his raised voice, his face flushed with anger. Kitiara could see the dots of her father's eyes as they danced above the rise and fall of his extravagant mustache.

"Don't speak to me of hypothetical situations; give me

the iron dice of battle! Anything else is blather! I pledge my life—"

"Pah! I say it is better to wait and watch. Your life means nothing to me. All you humans are in such a hurry to die anyway!"

"If I may say something—"

"NO!"

The discussion grew even more heated. It seemed to go on for hours.

Crouched on the ground outside the tent, Kit must have fallen asleep. She woke to find Gregor hefting her gently in his arms and striding to their bedrolls. He looked peaceful now, as he usually did in that deep time of the night when people—and disagreements—slept. The young girl smiled sleepily up at her father, and he smiled back. Their faces were so alike; their mouths mimicked each other, the right corners rising at a slant, giving their expressions a charmingly roguish caste.

"Tomorrow, my little warrior, you shall see the power and truth the sword can bring," Gregor whispered to Kit as he tucked a blanket around her. She shivered with anticipation, curled up next to her father, and fell back asleep.

It was still dark when Gregor woke Kitiara. The summer night had never cooled off, and before dawn the warm air hung around the camp like a damp, heavy curtain. Kit rubbed her fists into her eyes then rose quickly. She strapped on her prized wooden sword, the one Gregor had brought back for her from one of his expeditions two years ago. Kitiara had shown more than a passing interest in the plaything, and Gregor began drilling her in the warrior arts.

The sword was scaled to Kitiara's size, with an exceedingly sharp point. Gregor had decorated the precious half-toy with emblems and sigils. At home, Kitiara wore it belted at her side from the moment she rose until she tumbled into bed at night. She felt about it as she felt about nothing else.

Only now, surrounded by preparations for a real battle,

Kit suddenly saw the sword as childish. She started to take it off when Gregor, who had been watching silently, stopped her.

"There are men who cannot use a real sword as well as you can wield your wooden one," Gregor told her somberly. "Don't worry. It won't be long before your skill guarantees you the pick of all the swords you could want. After all," he added, his eyes glinting at her, "you are my daughter."

Grinning in return, the seven-year-old girl busied herself checking Gregor's daggers, sword, shield, bow and quiver of arrows, then helped her father adjust his armor. His body armor consisted of pieces of iron held together with leather straps and bronze fittings. The helmet was open in style, permitting him to move and aim with impunity.

Working next to Gregor, Kitiara looked like a tiny version of the striking warrior. Gregor had cut Kit's long hair shortly after he had smuggled her out of the house for this expedition. Now her cap of dark, curly hair, and the slender yet athletic build apparent underneath her leather jerkin and leggings, made Kit look like a young boy. Like Gregor her eyes were brown, and, almost comically so, little Kit had even modeled her purposeful stride after Gregor's.

When other soldiers came up to him, Gregor introduced Kit as "my importunate son," catching her eye and winking when no one was looking. Seven was a young age to bring such a lad into camp, but none of his fellows would have stood for Gregor bringing a daughter along, since girls were seen as little more than a potential burden.

The ruse made no difference to Kit. She didn't long to be a boy. She only felt sorry for people who weren't able to take the full measure of a person because of their sex or what they appeared to be. She never intended to make that mistake.

As they continued preparing for the battle, Kit noticed a commotion at the edge of the camp. In the dim pre-dawn light she thought she saw a cluster of children scatter among the bedrolls.

"Look, Father, perhaps I can practice my sword fighting

with one of those children at the end of the day," she said, motioning toward the distant forms.

"Those aren't children. Those are gully dwarves." Gregor spat out that benighted race's name as if it were an epithet. "It's amazing how they turn up sooner or later, no matter what the danger or where you pitch camp."

As Gregor was speaking, one of the gully dwarves had the misfortune to scurry near and start nosing around their equipment. An unpleasant odor wafted from the smallish creature. Moving a step closer, Gregor swung his foot back and gave the gully dwarf a boot that hurled him halfway across the camp. "Pleasure of your acquaintance!" Kit heard the unfortunate creature cry out as it soared. Apparently unharmed and unfazed, the gully dwarf picked himself up and scampered off in the opposite direction.

Kit smiled to herself. Even gully dwarves added to her pleasure at being part of camp life. She was brought back to more pressing matters when Gregor began outlining the battle plan for her.

Swiftwater's outlaws occupied a heavily wooded ridge at the far end of the valley. The location offered the barbarians a commanding view of the landscape to the east. At their backs, the ridge sloped away steeply, offering little cover except for widely scattered rocks. Potential attackers had few options.

Gregor's forces were within striking distance, sequestered among rocks and trees on a sharp rise to the south. So far, they had managed to remain undetected.

Burek had wanted to wait until the hovering storm broke and provided a distraction, obscuring their attack, Gregor explained. Then, being both proud and impatient, the minotaur had wanted to attempt to lead a frontal assault, hoping to draw out Swiftwater and his group from their sanctuary. Part of the hired troops would also circle around and attempt to besiege Swiftwater's camp from the rear, despite the rough terrain.

Gregor had disagreed, and eventually he won the argument. Scouts loyal to the mercenary leader had reported that the barbarians sent out a large foraging party every morning, often with Swiftwater himself in command. Gregor wanted the minotaurs to split up and creep forward along both sides of the valley, under cover of foliage, to just below the ridge where the outlaw band was camped.

When the foraging contingent emerged into the meadow, the minotaurs would cut in from the rear while Gregor and his reserves attacked from the front. With any luck, Swiftwater would be in the surrounded party. Once he was killed, his immediate troops could be expected to panic and flee into the woods. Some of Gregor's soldiers would be hanging back among the trees to eliminate them.

The plan placed the minotaurs in a difficult position, Gregor acknowledged, since there would be close fighting with members of the foraging party, as well as danger from the rear when those who remained at Swiftwater's camp joined the battle. But Gregor's troops would press the attack from all sides and attempt to draw off fire from the minotaurs.

Burek had conceded the boldness of Gregor's scheme. Valiant race that they were, the minotaurs had accepted their risky assignment with dignity. Before they divided up, Kit noticed that the mammoth creatures, outfitted in all their glittering armament, knelt as a group to exchange hushed vows amongst themselves, secret words that no human would ever be permitted to overhear.

The other mercenaries observed their ritual with respect. The long minutes of silence were almost unbearable.

Then, with Burek in the lead, the nearly two dozen minotaurs rose as one and marched off. After them, with great solemnity, came Gregor and his men. Her father was riding a borrowed steed, a silver-gray charger. He had left behind his precious Cinnamon for Kit, so that she would have a reliable means of escape in the unlikely event of a rout.

Her father did not pay her any attention now. His eyes were trained resolutely on the task ahead, his mouth set in a grim line. This was the first time Kit had seen Gregor riding into battle, and that scene was how she would always think of him—proud, erect, invincible.

Trailing them all, serving as little more than a buffer in the battle, were Nolan and his small volunteer brigade of locals. Unlike the more professional soldiers, Nolan's farmers clutched roughhewn clubs and shovels and odd tools. But these could be every bit as deadly as more sophisticated weapons in the hand-to-hand struggle that would follow the first clash.

From the vantage Gregor had chosen for her, underneath the oak tree, Kitiara strained to see the minotaurs moving through the tall grass, past the brush and occasional trees that lined the valley. But she could see nothing.

Suddenly, Kitiara caught the sound of horses snuffling and snorting in the still morning air. Birds flew out from the underbrush on the opposite side of the valley, and a group of roughly forty barbarians filed out of the woods. They rode a high-strung breed of horses renowned for their speed. Kitiara wondered how the minotaurs, who were afoot, would fare against them.

The barbarians sat easily in their saddles. From a distance, they looked to Kitiara to be wearing leather capes decorated with multicolored feathers. She thought she spied their chieftain, Swiftwater, trotting in the lead, stocky and arrogant. Then another of the horde caught her eye. He alone was shrouded like a wraith, his garb devoid of all decoration or color. From his saddle dangled a multitude of vials and potions. A magic-user, thought Kit.

After more than a year of raiding the countryside virtually unchallenged, the barbarians were careless of any possible threat. Their horses seemed to float through the grass. The riders said little to each other as they rode, though the small dogs trotting alongside yapped and growled occasionally.

As the party moved out into the open sweep of the meadow, Burek and his companions burst from the mists that still clung to the lower reaches of the valley. Their wild bellows caused several of the barbarians' horses to rear up in fright, and at least two of the riders lost their purchase and were trampled in the ensuing confusion.

One of the barbarians put a hollow gourd to his lips and sounded a shrill call for help. Already a few men were scrambling from the dense pine trees on top of the ridge behind the minotaurs, alerted by the commotion. Kitiara could see other fighters move to the edge of the trees and start fitting arrows in their bows, taking aim at Burek and his gallant troop.

As the first arrows started flying, Kitiara heard a shout and saw a brigade of her father's soldiers charge up along the sides of the ridge on horseback, forcing the archers to retreat. At the same time, reinforcements swung up on their horses from behind bushes and trees where they had been camouflaged, attacking the advance guard of barbarians from the front. Swiftwater's men, neatly bisected, recoiled in surprise.

Smoke and flame indicated that the magic-user had managed to cast a spell. Up above the melee rose a garish phantasm that dripped blood and flashed horrid yellow fangs. Kitiara knew that it was an illusion intended to paralyze nerves and terrorize opponents. Gregor, with his wisdom of many battles, had predicted this tactic. He and many of his men had rimmed their eyes with an ointment to counteract the spell.

Fortunately, Kitiara had been forewarned. She, too, had protected her eyes. Otherwise, she would not have been able to fend off the panic she felt inside, even at this safe distance from the ghastly bloodthing.

Dire screams could be heard. Whether emanating from the barbarians' or Gregor's side, Kit could not be sure. Everything was intermingled now.

Kitiara saw one brave warrior—she thought it must be her father—plow into the vanguard and challenge a barbarian on a large horse, one wearing not only a leather cloak, but a mottled helmet covered with feathers. No, she was wrong before; the man Gregor faced, not the arrogant barbarian she had spied earlier, must be Swiftwater. The two men leaned over their mounts, lashing out with their swords.

Kitiara locked her eyes on the two warriors. The smoke and noise were dense now. She willed herself not to lose sight of the pair, for Gregor was hard at it and Swiftwater was matching him blow for blow, giving good proof of himself. Around them, the battlefield was chaotic, full of harsh sound and movement and gore.

Almost unconsciously, Kitiara pulled out her wooden sword and began thrusting and parrying in the thick summer air, imitating the combat on the field. . . .

* * * * *

"Aha! Not bad for a skinny whelp using a wooden sword."

Kitiara was shaken from her daydream by the sound of a voice and a soft thud behind her. She whirled around to confront a tawny-haired man with glittering dark eyes. He wore brown leggings and a close-fitting tunic. One hand held a shiny red apple and the other rested easily on the handle of his sword. He looked like he knew how to use it.

"Where did you come from?" she demanded, humiliated at her wooden weapon and angry at being caught off guard.

"When preparing for battle, never forget to look up to the gods for a blessing, and while your eyes are thus occupied, to check for enemies hidden in the trees. It's an old Solamnic saying. I'm surprised such a stouthearted warrior as yourself isn't familiar with it," said the stranger with mock seriousness. At that he sat down, crossed his legs, and took a hungry bite out of his apple. He flashed her a teasing smile.

In no mood to be ridiculed, however mildly, Kitiara flushed with annoyance before pointing her sword in his direction. "Then, if you are trained in Solamnic traditions, you must know you cannot refuse my challenge to a match without seriously compromising your honor."

"That would presume I have some honor left to be compromised," he said indifferently, taking another eager bite.

With a precocity remarkable for a child of eight, Kitiara

stepped up and deftly knocked the stranger's apple from his hand by slapping the flat of her sword against his knuckles. His smile vanished, replaced by stern, pursed lips. He stood up to face her.

"I am sorry that you are so disrespectful of your elders," he said ruefully. "Someone has neglected to teach you your manners. I shall endeavor to fill the void."

He moved toward her, but Kit scuttled to the left, her sword point outstretched, keeping him at bay. He circled around, a look on his face every bit as resolute as Kitiara's. Though only slightly more than half his size, she was determined to run him through, wooden sword or not.

The stranger dropped his shoulder and made suddenly as if to reach for his sheathed weapon, at which point Kitiara lunged toward him. Unexpectedly, he dropped to the ground and rolled directly toward her, grabbing her by her ankles before she could make a move with her sword. In another instant he had vaulted to a standing position and hoisted her, kicking and screaming, over his shoulders. Her wooden blade fell to the ground.

Carrying her easily, the stranger walked to a stand of trees and gave her a tremendous heave skyward. Much to her astonishment Kitiara found herself tossed like a leaf high up into the air. She landed in the twisted branches of an apple tree, high above the ground. It took a few moments before she got her breath back. Then she looked down to see the stranger peering up at her with an implacable expression.

"Pick out a nice juicy one, if you please," the stranger said.

"I'd sooner die!" she shouted back defiantly.

In a movement so quick that it seemed a blur, the stranger unleashed his sword and thrust it upward, toward Kitiara. Even with his height and long reach, the sword just barely reached her, its tip scraping her bottomside. She scurried to escape its touch, but these were mere apple trees, not mighty vallenwoods, and there were no sturdy branches above her offering an escape route.

Coiling as tightly as she could, Kitiara retreated against the tree trunk. The stranger merely reached a couple of inches higher and flicked his sword point, ripping her leggings.

"Tch tch," he said. "Pants need mending."

She set her chin and determined to say nothing. He stretched a little higher, and she felt the sword point flick again.

"Ouch!"

"First blood," said the stranger merrily. Then his tone altered. "Don't tempt me, little one. Krynn is lousy with children, orphans especially. One less would be a blessing."

A brief, tense silence ensued. There was a rustling of branches, and Kitiara dropped to the ground, holding a ripe apple. Her eyes averted, she held it out to the stranger, who stuck his sword in the ground triumphantly and reached to grab the fruit.

Before he knew it her teeth had sunk into his wrist.

"Ouch!" he yelled and, with a furious oath, cuffed Kit across the face, knocking her roughly to the ground.

She got up very slowly. Rubbing the side of her face, Kitiara looked down at the ground and fought back her tears. She wouldn't cry in front of a stranger.

As for the stranger, he too was nursing his wound, rubbing his wrist with a betrayed air. He looked up and caught Kitiara's eye. To the girl's dismay, the situation suddenly became hilarious. The stranger's face broke into an engaging grin, and rich, throaty laughter began to pour from his mouth.

Kit couldn't help but notice that this curious fellow had an altogether different, more congenial look about him when he smiled. He was like her father in that respect: one way when fighting, another way when at peace. However, she didn't feel the slightest compulsion to laugh with him. She was still smarting with resentment.

With some effort the stranger brought his laughter under control. "Say, at first I thought you were a boy or I wouldn't have hit you. You fight like one. Some day, perhaps, you'll fight like a man."

That was no compliment to her. But when the stranger proffered his hand in the Solamnic clasp, she smiled tentatively despite herself. She gripped his hand firmly in response.

He laughed again, sat down, and took a bite out of the apple Kitiara had picked. From a fold in his cloak, he produced another apple and offered it to her with a mischievous smirk.

She frowned in irritation.

"Oh, don't let it bother you," said the stranger soothingly. "What's your name, half-pint?"

With a show of reluctance she took the apple. "Kitiara Uth Matar," she said proudly.

Was it her imagination, or did some recognition flicker across the stranger's face? Some emotion had registered, some inscrutable reaction.

"Any relation to Gregor Uth Matar?" he asked, keeping a smile on his face.

"Do you know him?" She leaned forward excitedly.

"No, no," he said hastily, shifting his tone. "Heard of him, of course. Heard of him." He seemed to look at Kit differently, more intently, appraising her face. "I'd like to meet a man of such stature—if he happened to be in these parts."

All at once, Kitiara was blinking back tears. "My father doesn't live in Solace anymore," she said stoically after a few moments. "He left home not long after we returned from a battle with some barbarians. That was over a year ago."

Kitiara would never forget that unhappy morning. For once, her father had not been there, smiling at her, when she woke up. There had been no true warning of his departure; he hadn't been getting along with Rosamun, but that was nothing new. And the note he left hardly offered an adequate explanation:

Good-bye for now. Take care of Cinnamon. She's yours. Know that your father loves you. Think of me. Gregor.

He had left behind his favorite horse and ridden off on a

freshly bartered one. Kitiara had crumpled the paper and cried intermittently for days, even weeks. Now she wished she still had the note, if only as a memento.

Nobody in Solace could say for sure which way Gregor had gone, on which road in which direction.

"Have you heard news of him?" she asked the stranger eagerly.

"Hmmm. I seem to remember hearing something about some escapades in the North," he replied vaguely, preoccupied now with standing up and slipping his sword into its scabbard.

"His family hails from the North," Kit said, keenly interested.

"Or maybe it was in the wilds of Khur to the east. I'm not certain."

"Oh." Kit's voice fell.

"A man like that would never stay in one place for long," he continued.

"What do you mean?" Kit asked a little defensively, " 'a man like that'?"

Looking up, he saw the apprehension that animated Kitiara's face. "I have to be on my way, little one. If I run into your father, can I give him a message?" he inquired, not unkindly.

Kitiara weighed what she could tell this stranger who in some ways reminded her of Gregor, though he was neither as tall nor as handsome. "Just tell him that I've been practicing," she said finally. "And that I'm ready."

They were standing just out of sight of Kit's home, in a clearing below the elevated walkways between the vallenwoods where Kit often came to practice her swordplay. The stranger was preparing to take his leave when Kit thought to ask his name.

"Ursa Il Kinth, but you can call me Ursa if our paths cross again."

"Wait!" Kit cried out almost in desperation as he turned to go. "Take me with you, Ursa. All I need is a real sword or dagger, and I could help protect you during your travels. I wouldn't be any trouble. I have relatives in the North, and they can help me find my father. Oh, please, please, take me with you!"

"You, protect me?" Ursa snorted. "I should hope it would be a few years before I need the protection of a child!"

Again he erupted into laughter, this time more derisively. "If it would be any child it would be you, little Miss Kitiara," Ursa said over his shoulder as he took a few steps away from her. He gave a sharp whistle between his teeth, and a muscular gray steed burst from the woods. In a minute he had mounted her and was riding off, still chuckling.

A fiercely determined Kitiara had started to run after him when she heard sharp cries from the direction of her home.

"Kitiara! Kitiara! Come home! I need help!"

Kit stopped and looked resentfully in the direction of the summons.

"My labor has begun! Hurry!"

Sighing, with one last look at Ursa's back, Kitiara clambered up the nearest vallenwood. Halfway up the tree, she climbed onto the walkway that would take her home, where her mother was ready to give birth.

Chapter 2

The Birth of the Twins

RUNNING IN FROM THE SUN-DAPPLED WALKWAYS, KIT momentarily lost her bearings as she plunged into the cottage. It was midday, but almost no light penetrated through the shutters. Rosamun had managed to close them somehow, in the interest of modesty, when she went into labor.

As her eyes adjusted to the dim light, Kit heard more than saw her mother, who was breathing heavily. Rosamun was squatting on the floor to one side of the common room, next to the big bed. She looked up frantically when she heard Kit enter.

"Oh, Kitiara! I . . . I didn't want to keep Gilon from his day's work this morning, but—" Here Rosamun stopped. She fixed her eyes on a point somewhere over Kit's head, twisted the bedclothes in her hands, and started a low moan that built to an unholy screech. Kit was already backing up toward the door when the sound ebbed and Rosamun slumped against the side of the bed.

"Please, please, get Minna," Rosamun gasped.

Terrified, Kit bolted out the door and raced along the elevated walkways between the giant vallenwoods toward a local midwife's house, heedless of the people she jostled. Her encounter with the roguish stranger and thirst for adventure momentarily forgotten, Kit felt suddenly not a moment older than her eight years. Oh, if only Gilon hadn't gone off to chop wood today . . . If only Rosamun could manage on her own . . . If only there were someone else to help besides Minna!

Kit paused to catch her breath for a second before opening the gate to the midwife's front walk. Kit thought, as she always did when passing Minna's house, how the elaborate gingerbread cottage nestled between two giant vallenwood limbs resembled its owner—prim and haughty.

Kit knocked on the door. The moment Minna opened it, Kit grabbed her arm and started tugging her outside. The short, plump midwife was wearing her trademark muslin apron that, if it were not always so clean and starched, Kit would suspect she wore even to bed. Her wispy auburn hair was elaborately coiffed and beribboned.

"Hurry up! We have to hurry! It's my mother, she's gone into labor. You must come right away," Kit said as she pulled.

Minna tugged right back, easily freeing her arm from the child's grasp. The midwife paused and collected her dignity around her. As Kit stood by the front door, shifting impatiently from foot to foot, Minna busied herself around her home, gathering potions, herbs, and vials, which she placed carefully in a large leather sack while nattering away at Kit.

"My dear, you look flushed. Catch your breath. I must find my aspen leaves. Aspen leaf juice really makes the best clotting drink, you know. It's quite rare in these parts. I have Asa—you know Asa, that funny, black-haired kender who appears in town every now and then?—I have Asa collect the leaves for me specially whenever he is near Qualinesti or Silvanesti. Of course, he's not all that reliable as a gatherer. Although I'm sure if he says they are aspenwood leaves, then they probably are. . . ."

Glancing in a mirror as she patted her hair in place, Minna caught a tense look from Kitiara, who was barely able to keep from shouting at the midwife to shut up and get out the door.

"Is anything wrong dear?" Minna asked, peering at Kit concernedly with her small, olive eyes.

"Yes, yes!" Kit declared, stamping her foot. "I told you! My mother has started having her baby. She needs you!"

"Well, there's no need to be rude, I'm sure. There's enough of that in Krynn these days," Minna said with an injured air. "People have been having babies since the beginning of time. I'm sure your mother is doing just fine," she added, checking her leather rucksack full of whatnot one more time before pulling it closed. "Ah, here are the aspen leaves. I shouldn't worry. I suppose your father is home with Rosamun?"

The query seemed innocent enough, but Kit, always thinskinned when it came to questions about fathers, mistrusted Minna's reasons for asking. The midwife made it her business to know all the gossip there was to know in Solace, and everything she discovered through her snooping she passed on to dozens of acquaintances at the morning market. Kit knew that Rosamun was one of her favorite topics.

Rosamun intermittently suffered strange trances and was chronically abed with fever and imagined ills. After Gregor had left her, things had only grown worse. Kitiara supposed Rosamun blamed herself for Gregor's going. Well, she should. She had practically driven him away with her homebody concerns.

It was difficult to understand what Gregor had seen in her mother in the first place. Maybe she had been pretty once, Kit admitted grudgingly. She was a good enough cook. Yet whatever Rosamun once was, more and more in recent months she had become the kind of sickly, indoors drudge that Kit planned never to be.

Rosamun didn't have very many friends or people sympathetic to her sick spells. That's where Minna came in. Kitiara had to admit that Minna tended to her mother as best she could. And she never pressured Gilon to pay her mounting bill.

Even so, Kitiara detested the bossy busybody.

"*Gilon,*" Kit emphasized the name, since he was not her father, "is cutting wood in the forest. I don't know where, probably miles away. Otherwise I'd run and get him. My mother has been feeling well enough lately, and I didn't want to ask him to stay home even though we knew it was close to her time. Can't you hurry?"

Kit looked out the window and wished she were anywhere but in this house, anywhere except perhaps her own cottage. She couldn't forget the anguished sounds that Rosamun had made, and the look of fear on her face.

"Well, who's in a hurry now, young lady? Do your best to keep up."

With that, Minna swept past Kitiara and out the door. Kit would have liked to kick her in the behind. But the thought of Rosamun at home, in the throes of childbirth, made her repress the impulse.

Indeed, Kit practically had to run to keep up with Minna, who moved along the walkways with quick strides.

When they reached the cottage, Kit saw that her mother had climbed back onto the bed, where the blanket and sheets were already soiled and bloodstained. As they rushed to her, Rosamun uttered a low groan and her breathing quickened with the beginning of another contraction. This time, she seemed nearly too exhausted to scream. Her long, pale blond hair was plastered against her skull with perspiration. Her delicately boned face was drawn. When Rosamun's lips parted, only a strangled moan escaped as her body curled forward. After the contraction crested, she collapsed back against the sheets.

Minna hurried up to feel her forehead. The contractions were speeding up. Rosamun's bed was almost soaked.

"Good, your water has broken," Minna declared. But the midwife frowned slightly when she noticed the greenish stain on the bedclothes.

Minna unceremoniously pulled up Rosamun's smock and checked on the labor's progress. "Put some water on to boil and get the clean cloths ready. The baby will be coming any time now. That green water means there might be trouble," she said meaningfully.

Never a deft hand with household chores, Kit awkwardly helped Minna slip clean sheets onto Rosamun's bed. She gathered what clean cloths she could find, then lugged in a bucket of water from outside and put it in a pot to boil on the fire.

By now Rosamun was so consumed by her struggle to give birth that she barely acknowledged the presence of either Kitiara or Minna. Her gray eyes were glassy, her body buffeted by the painful contractions that came relentlessly.

Minna pulled a small pouch out of her birthing bag and ordered Kit to bring a clean bowl filled with hot water to the bedside table. She poured the contents of the pouch into the bowl and wrung out a cloth in the brownish liquid. Minna used the cloth to wipe Rosamun's brow and, occasionally, pulling up the smock Rosamun wore, to bathe her swollen stomach.

"What is it?" Kit ventured to ask.

"Secret ingredients," responded Minna smugly. "Don't know myself, actually." She tittered. "Buy it off that kender I was telling you about, Asa. He calls it his 'Never Fail Balm.' "

Kit had to admit her mother breathed a bit more easily after these ablutions.

Minna kept Kit busy. She ordered her to bring a chair to the bedside, to find more blankets, to brew a pot of tea, to get some more wood for the fire. Kit knew Minna did not like her and had counseled Rosamun that her young daughter was too headstrong and should be reined in a bit. Now Kit chafed under the midwife's orders, realizing how much Minna gloried in her authority over Kit in this emergency.

Rosamun's groans and screams kept the two of them pre-occupied, however. Her agony was terrible for the child to witness. At times Rosamun's eyes rolled up into her head and her body went rigid as she endured the repeated contractions.

As the labor dragged on, Kit secretly longed for Gilon's calming presence and wondered when her stepfather would return. But she realized forlornly that it was only about midday, and that, typically, Gilon did not return until dusk.

About an hour after Minna's arrival, Rosamun's breathing slowed dramatically. The midwife thrust her hand under Rosamun's smock and gave Kit a nod. "Push the baby out, Rosamun," she commanded.

Kit looked at Minna in surprise. Rosamun, pale, delirious, and drenched in sweat, seemed barely able to turn her head on the pillow, much less push anything. Nonetheless, at Minna's urging, Kit climbed onto the bed and helped Rosamun to sit up. She then placed her small back against her mother's sweat-stained one and braced her feet against the wooden headboard, thus propping up Rosamun while Minna again exhorted her mother to push.

"Push!" cried Minna. "if you want it over and done with, push!"

An hour after that, nothing had changed except that Kit's legs felt like logs and Rosamun's head had lolled back against her daughter's as if she had lost consciousness. Minna had sat down, strands of hair falling over her sweat-beaded brow. Though exhausted, the midwife methodically urged Rosamun to keep pushing.

Then, finally, with one drawn-out moan, Rosamun gave birth.

To Kit, the baby looked like a reddish-purple monkey covered with blood and a white, cheeselike goo. A lusty cry that seemed to shake the windows in their frames immediately established the child's virility.

"A boy!" Minna crowed. "You have yourself a fine, healthy boy, Rosamun!" she said as she expertly wiped down the infant, diapered him, and swaddled him in a clean blanket. "Why he must weigh ten pounds! He's a giant!"

The information was lost on the baby's mother. Rosamun's eyes fluttered open, then closed as Kit slipped out from behind her, letting Rosamun sink back, exhausted, against the pillows.

Almost instantly, a sharp intake of breath wrenched Rosamun fully awake, her eyes huge and startled.

"Just the afterbirth," Minna muttered to herself, glancing at Rosamun. But the midwife quickly thrust the swaddled infant at Kit and turned back to the mother. Gazing at her intently, Minna reached for her birthing bag at the foot of the bed. She dug through its contents and pulled out another small pouch, this one with a double clasp. As the midwife carefully opened it, Kit, who stood near Minna, could have sworn that a light glowed from within!

Minna drew out a pinch of something. Turning her back on the bed, Minna tossed a sprinkling of particles into the air while chanting a few words Kit didn't understand. The light in the room seemed to shimmer. An instant later, Kit felt a sense of well-being descend on her. The infant in her arms even stopped bawling. More amazing still, Rosamun smiled, heaved a deep sigh, and sank back against the pillows. In that split second, Kit's mother seemed to fall serenely asleep! The girl could not believe the evidence of her eyes.

Then almost as quickly as it had come, the peaceful aura evaporated.

Rosamun's breathing quickened. Her eyelids flew up, but the eyes had rolled up into their sockets again. Minna leaned over Rosamun worriedly, patting her cheeks.

Only the baby seemed to have received some lasting benefit from Minna's hocus pocus. Kit held the infant stiffly away from herself as she edged over to the cradle Gilon had lovingly crafted. Luckily for everyone present, Kit's new brother forgot his initial irritation at being pushed out of the warm comfort of the womb. Immediately after Kit laid him in his new bed and set the cradle rocking, he fell asleep, cooing.

Minna yanked up Rosamun's smock and firmly placed two hands on her swollen stomach. She took what looked like a small drum out of her medicinal bag, only it was a drum whose bottom tapered to a narrow neck, then flared out into a flexible cup.

"A listening drum," Minna said to no one in particular—certainly not to Kitiara. She placed the cup end on Rosamun's bulging stomach and inclined her ear against the drum covering. As Rosamun began to whimper, Minna pulled her head away decisively. Sure enough, it was the start of another contraction.

"There's another baby in there," Minna declared with amazement.

A drawn out, guttural "No-o-o-o!" escaped from Rosamun's pursed lips.

"Another baby!" Kit exclaimed. "How can that be? Why didn't you know that before? What are we going to do? My mother can't survive another childbirth."

"Listen here, young lady. Don't you sass me." Minna whirled on Kit with surprising ferocity, her patience almost gone. Her beehive of hair was badly mussed, and her usually tidy uniform was disheveled. Her sharp eyes pinned Kit down.

"I don't need advice from a stripling. These things happen. I can't be expected to know everything, to fix everything—"

Whimpering from Rosamun sent them both scurrying.

Once again Minna began searching through her birthing bag. Practically shouting, the midwife directed Kit to put a fresh kettle of water on the fire and to fetch more clean blankets. Suddenly Kit, who had been up since sunrise and had missed eating lunch, was swept by fatigue. Her knees buckled, and she nearly swooned.

Minna reached over and grabbed the girl before she fell, shaking her violently by the shoulders. "You've got to bear up now, Kit," she said fiercely. "Don't go sissy on me. I need you. Rosamun needs you." She gave Kit a push toward her duties.

The girl could barely keep her eyes open as she trudged around the room, doing what Minna had asked. The afternoon had grown awfully warm, and with the fire that had been kept burning to heat the water, the inside of the cottage seemed hotter than a dwarven forge. Kitiara felt as if she were suffocating.

"Pour some over your head," advised Minna.

"What?"

"The water, over your head," the midwife repeated.

"Oh," said Kitiara, scooping cold water out of the bucket and splashing it over her head so that her face and clothes were soaked. It felt good. Refreshed, she dashed out to get another load.

"Idiot girl," Minna murmured under her breath.

Rosamun was likewise fevered, and Minna did the best she could to keep her cool, sponging her constantly with water. Looking limp and lifeless, Kit's mother faded in and out of consciousness, her store of energy all but exhausted. The contractions persisted. What should have been a short labor dragged on interminably.

"I don't understand. That baby should slip right out," Minna said in a low voice to Kit.

Feeling around underneath Rosamun's covering, Minna muttered an oath as she discovered the reason. She drew Kit aside.

"This baby is coming out feet first," she confided ominously, "not head first like most babies are born. It's a breech birth. No telling how long her labor will last. It's not normal."

Kit digested Minna's report numbly. She looked over at the first baby, who was still sleeping, eyes shut peacefully. "Can you do anything?" she asked hopefully.

"I can try," said Minna plainly, "but Paladine is going to have to help."

Hours passed as the birth dragged on, until it was almost sundown. At one point, Rosamun's eyes began to blink uncontrollably. Her face flushed a bright pink and her body writhed restlessly. When Kit touched her mother's hand, it was burning hot.

"She has a high temperature. You have to do something," cried Kit, almost accusingly.

Minna, clearly worried, ignored the girl, except to ask for more heated water to mix a new batch of "Never Fail Balm." She had been bathing Rosamun's stomach with it continuously since after the first birth.

Rosamun was unconscious most of the time now. Kitiara had to hold her mother up as best as she could from the back. Minna didn't even bother asking Rosamun to push.

Finally, there was some progress, and Minna perked up. "A toe, I see a toe. Now, if only I can get both feet coming out together, we might be able to see this stubborn twin born."

Eventually both feet did emerge, then the legs, then the hips—it was another boy. Still wedged against her mother's back, Kit listened to Minna's excited reports on the progress of the second birth. Over her shoulder she could see her mother's eyes were lidded. Rosamun's breathing came in weak spurts. At last, just past dusk, the baby's head started to slip out. Kit heard Minna curse.

"By the gods! He's not breathing, and blood is running out of your mother like a river."

Acting swiftly, Minna took a small knife from her bag and severed the umbilical cord, then lay the baby across the foot of the bed. Now her attention turned to the infant's mother, who was unconscious, drenched in sweat and blood. One hand massaged Rosamun's stomach to stimulate the afterbirth contractions that would help stem the bleeding. The other hand stirred crumbled aspen leaves into a cup of water to make the clotting drink.

"I've got my hands full with your mother now. You'd better try to help your second brother," Minna told Kit. "Rub his feet. Try to get some breath into his body. Do something!"

Kit slid out from behind Rosamun and climbed onto the bed next to the baby. Fighting panic, she grabbed several clean blankets and began rubbing his small body, as she had seen Minna do with the first baby. At last, a rasping noise came from this one's chest as he spit up a small amount of green liquid and drew in a few pitiful breaths. After a minute, his ragged breathing stopped.

"Minna, what should I do? He doesn't seem to be breathing very well," Kit asked the midwife urgently.

Minna was cradling Rosamun's head and, through a dropper, easing some of the aspen leaf liquid into her mouth. The midwife looked up only briefly before turning back to Rosamun, who herself was barely holding onto life.

"Take him over to the fire and just keep rubbing him, especially the bottoms of his feet. If that doesn't work try pinching his cheeks. Blow in his ears, softly. Anything. But mind you, the second twin is like an afterthought and often weak-spirited. Maybe he's a lost cause."

At that comment, Kit's head snapped up and she glared at the stupid midwife, but only for a second. Her thoughts quickly focused on saving her half-brother, and she rushed to the hearth. Using her foot to kick more logs onto the blaze, she threw herself into rubbing the frail baby with an intensity she usually reserved for practicing moves with her wooden sword. After a tense silence, the infant's breathing resumed.

Finally the baby let out a few mews of dissent at his rough treatment. His color began to look slightly more pinkish than bluish to Kit. But when she tried stopping his vigorous massage, the infant's breathing slowed again. So the therapeutic rubbing continued. Kitiara was as determined to prove Minna wrong as she was concerned for the welfare of her second-born half brother.

She stole a glance at the first twin, snug in Gilon's cradle. That baby boy, chubby and cherubic by comparison, slept soundly. How unalike they were! Yet as Kit continued to gaze at the older of her new brothers, she had the impression that he was breathing in unison with his weaker twin. She could pause in her rubbing now. The second baby was breathing more easily and had drifted off to sleep.

Across the room, the midwife relaxed. She, too, had succeeded. Rosamun's bleeding had stopped. Kit's mother lay in an exhausted slumber, looking like a wan corpse.

"Well," sighed Minna, pulling a sheet and blanket up around Rosamun, "about as close a call as I've ever had. Not that I was worried. When you're as experienced in these affairs as Minna, child . . ."

Kit, sitting on the hearth, cradling the baby, was hardly paying any attention. She looked up to see Minna standing over her, her face flushed, her stack of auburn hair now lop-sided.

"Someone needs to rouse your mother every two hours and give her a generous sip of tea made from the aspen-wood leaves," said the midwife with crisp efficiency. "You or Gilon will have to go out tonight and find some goat's milk. Your mother is in no condition to nurse those babies, and goat's milk is the best thing for newborn humans. Goats have kids, too, you know."

Studying the look of obvious dislike on the girl's face, Minna decided Kitiara needed to learn some common cour-tesies. The girl glanced away, peering intently at the second-born twin, gauging the effects of her diligent massage. The baby made a congested sound. Kit went back to massaging him.

"I don't know that I'd get my hopes up," Minna said brusquely. "You'd be better off using that energy to take care of your mother. I told you, second twins are notori-ously short-lived. We may have to dig a grave for that one come morning."

All the fear and helplessness and frustration of the past hours welled up in Kit with Minna's unfeeling remark. An-ger surged through her small frame, pulling her to her feet. Without actually deciding to do it, Kit reached up and slapped the midwife across the face as hard as she could.

"Don't say that again!" Kit screamed.

Shocked and infuriated, Minna grabbed Kit roughly by the shoulder, almost jostling the infant from her arms. Dis-tracted by a sound near the door, first Minna, then Kit turn-ed to observe Gilon standing there, his face solemn. A slight gust of wind blew into their faces.

"Did you see that, Master Majere?" Minna let go of Kit's shoulder and hurried over to Gilon, bobbing with outrage. "Did you see that? She struck me! You can't allow her to get away with it. I demand an apology, and I claim the right to strike her in punishment. Unless that child is properly disciplined, she's going to end up just like her father—worthless!"

Gilon looked from the midwife to his stepdaughter. His weary brown eyes showed not fury, but sadness. He put his ax down inside the door and slowly took his jacket off. His big dog, Amber, who always accompanied Gilon on wood-cutting forays, sensed something amiss and trotted away. The stolid Gilon ran his fingers through his thick, brown hair and took a long time before speaking.

Without saying a word in her own defense, Kit had resumed rubbing the baby. Bone-tired, she despised the tears pooling in her eyes. She bent her head close to the baby, refusing to look up.

"Talk about morning burials," the stocky woodcutter said at last, "isn't welcome at a birthing. I'd say you two are about even." His words carried a quiet authority. His face was impassive.

Kit kept her eyes on the baby, but inwardly she exulted.

"Well!" Grumbling to herself, Minna quickly moved around the cottage, throwing her belongings unceremoniously into her bag. She dangled a pouch of aspenwood leaves and threw it conspicuously on the bedside table. "I'll check back tomorrow!" she snapped, before flouncing out the door.

Kit looked up finally when she heard the latch click. She and Gilon exchanged a rare smile.

Gilon hastened over, peering anxiously first at Rosamun's bed, then at the cradle, then at the infant in Kit's arms. The look on his face blended pride with confusion.

"Twins, is it twins? How is Rosamun? How are they doing? What can I do to help?" Plaintively he gestured with his big, clumsy hands.

"You have to go out and get some goat's milk, right away," Kit advised. "Minna said it was the only thing the babies could drink, and I think we have to credit her on that one. Then we have to wake Mother—"

"Just a minute. Just a minute," Gilon interrupted, still anxious. "I don't even know about my children. Are there two?" he repeated. "Twins?"

"Yes, two boys." Kitiara surprised herself by saying it with as much satisfaction as if she were the mother.

Again Gilon walked over to the cradle, beaming down at his first born, who was beginning to stir. Then he came to Kit, who continued to rub and comfort the second infant.

"Shhhhh," she cautioned. "This is the weaker one."

Outside, it was dark. Inside, the only light came from the dying fire. Hurriedly, Gilon lit two oil lamps, which cast huge, dancing shadows on the cottage walls.

"We had a hard time of it," Kit confessed, covering up her relief that it was over with a matter-of-fact tone. "Mother lost a lot of blood. I think she'll be all right. The first baby, he's strong. But this one, he will have to be watched closely."

Gilon moved to Rosamun's bed and tenderly sat next to her, taking her hand. Her face was drained of all color. She lay still, breathing shallowly. When he brushed her forehead with his lips, she didn't stir. Baby sounds of grunts and snuffles drew Gilon away from his wife's side to the cradle.

"I'd better go get that milk before we have a rebellion on our hands." He pulled on his jacket, then came to stand next to Kit, putting his hand on her shoulder. Kit reacted hesitantly. She and her stepfather rarely touched. Gilon gave her shoulder a gentle squeeze before turning to leave on his errand.

He paused at the door. "Rosamun and I had decided on Caramon as the name if we had a boy," he told Kit, almost apologetically. "It means strength of the vallenwoods. It was my grandfather's name. A good name, don't you think?" After a pause, he smiled and added, "But we're going to need some ideas for the other boy. Why don't you see if you can think of a name to help us out?"

Pleased as a kender at a county fair with being asked to participate in the naming, Kit felt the color rise to her cheeks. She replied solemnly that she would give it some thought.

* * * * *

Gilon returned with the goat's milk to find Kit jiggling one infant in her arms and using her foot to rock the cradle, whose occupant had started issuing piercing, hungry-sounding cries. He made two bottles from slender jars fitted with the skin from the teat of a dead ewe. Picking up the squalling baby Caramon, the new father held him as he sucked at the bottle vigorously.

Kitiara wished her charge were half as energetic. She had to coax the second-born twin to take the nipple, and he had a difficult time keeping milk down. Breathing seemed to sap most of his energy. What with spitting up and fussing, Kitiara worried that he barely seemed to get any of the milk into his system at all.

Eventually, both infants drifted off to sleep. Kit was still holding the smaller one. "I have a name," she ventured.

"And what do you recommend?" Gilon asked, matching Kit's serious tone.

"Raistlin."

"Hmm. Raistlin," Gilon repeated. "I like the sound of it, Raistlin and Caramon. But what does it mean?"

"Oh, nothing really. I mean, I don't know for sure. I must have heard it somewhere."

Kit didn't tell Gilon that Raistlin was the name of the hero in the made-up stories Gregor sometimes told her at bedtime. Most of Gregor's stories were true ones about himself, or epic legends of the fabled figures of Krynn. But there was one tale he liked to tell that Kit believed her father had made up. Its installments went on and on, and Gregor had never finished telling it, probably because there was no ending. And because he had left.

The Raistlin of her father's stories was not the bravest or

the strongest warrior, but he was clever and had a will of iron. Over and over he used his wits to best superior opponents.

If Caramon's name meant strength of the trees, Raistlin's would stand for cunning and will power, Kit thought.

Gilon pondered the choice. Once again he roamed to Rosamun's bedside. Kit's mother had yet to open her eyes. He realized that it might be some time before Rosamun could voice an opinion. Gilon smiled at Kit as he uttered his verdict.

"Raistlin . . . I think that will do nicely."

An hour or two later, Kit was still by the hearth, holding Raistlin, while Gilon was just finishing the long, involved job of giving Rosamun a sponge bath, then changing her bedding and clothes.

The town watch had called midnight long ago. Out the window, Lunitari, the red moon, had risen high in the sky. It shared the night canopy with Solinari, which was in its arc of descent. Sitting up with Raistlin by the fire, Kit must have dozed off. She woke with a start when the baby Raistlin drew a particularly harsh breath.

"Time to give Mother her tea," Kit said, so tired she slurred the words.

Gilon, sitting on the edge of Rosamun's bed, looked over at the girl and suddenly realized how exhausted she was. Her stepfather took Raistlin and sent her off to bed.

Kit's legs felt so heavy she could barely climb the ladder that led up to her bedroom above the rear of the common room. It was really just a small space she had fashioned for herself in the grain storage loft tucked under the roof of the cottage.

Behind burlap sacks full of grains and other dry goods stood her cot and small dresser. The single window, low under the eaves, offered a splendid view of the crisscrossing vallenwood branches. In the summer, Kit could look out and feel like she was floating on a cloud of leaves. She endured the extra summer heat and the coldness under the eaves during the winter because of the luxury of privacy her loft space afforded her in the cramped cottage.

Once she got up to her room, Kit went to her dresser and pulled it away from the wall, then felt behind it for the hidden shelf.

Carefully, Kitiara drew out a worn piece of parchment. Unrolling it, she gazed at an ink drawing of what she knew to be the emblem of a Knight of Solamnia. In the pale stream of moonlight that came through her window, Kit saw hawk talons, an arrow, and an eye-shaped orb.

After some minutes, Kit re-rolled the parchment and put it away. She fell onto her cot, clothes and all, and collapsed into a deep sleep.

That first night, Caramon slept peacefully in his cradle. Gilon kept Raistlin on the bed, tucked in between him and Rosamun, hoping their body warmth would help the baby. Kit never heard the many times her stepfather rose in the night to care for his beloved wife and newborn twins.

*　*　*　*　*

The following day, Gilon was preparing a pot of porridge over the fire and Kit was holding Raistlin in one arm while attempting to give a bottle to Caramon in the cradle, when someone knocked on the door. Without waiting for an answer, Minna entered with her sister, Yarly.

Yarly was a younger variation of Minna—every bit as short, stout, and starchy. Both of them were wearing their aprons, and Yarly's hair was swept under a headpiece. Obviously she had been instructed by her sister to say little or nothing. They both looked cross, but Yarly had a thick, protruding lower lip that even in the best of circumstances made her look sullen.

Minna pointedly ignored Kit and bestowed only a cool nod on Gilon as she crossed the floor to Rosamun's bedside, with Yarly in tow.

Rosamun had yet to regain full consciousness, though today she slept more comfortably and breathed more easily.

"How are we doing?" Minna asked while feeling and

prodding Rosamun's stomach.

"Not so well," Gilon responded with obvious concern. "She still has a fever, and she hasn't even really opened her eyes. She's too weak to eat."

"Mmmmm. The poor thing lost a lot of blood. She'll get better, I warrant, though it could be weeks before she's well enough to care for her new babies. Don't worry about the eating. Just be sure she drinks a lot of the medicinal tea I left with you. And be sure she's not disturbed by any wild playing," Minna added, with a meaningful glance in Kitiara's direction. "I would move her into that small room there, if I were you. Give her a little peace and quiet."

At that moment, Kit, trying to juggle the two infants, looked more like a harried homemaker than a potential troublemaker. She turned her back on Minna, shielding baby Raistlin from the midwife's prying eyes.

The room Minna pointed to was the only other room in the cottage besides the common living space. Branching off the north wall, it was a small space that had been used by Rosamun periodically over the years as a place to work on the sewing she sometimes took in to make extra money for the household. Gilon saw the wisdom of Minna's advice, and assented with a nod.

"You know my sister, Yarly, don't you? She'll be checking in on Rosamun for the next few days so I won't have to bother you with my opinions. After that I reckon you can get by on your own."

Minna had sidled over so that she could peek around Kitiara's shoulder at Raistlin. Kit turned so that she faced her, staring fiercely at the meddling midwife. Pointedly Minna looked down at the frail baby, sniffed sympathetically, then cast a glance over at the robust one contentedly sucking on his bottle in the cradle.

Raistlin's complexion was still pale, his grip on life hardly secure. All morning Kit had tried not to think of what Minna had said about weak-spirited second babies.

"Hmph," said Minna, turning away

Pulling Gilon aside, she brought something out of her

bag. Briefly, she showed him how to fashion a leather sling that would hold one of the babies next to his body while freeing hands for another chore. After that, Minna said a brusque good-bye, and she and Yarly went away.

"Well, now," said Gilon, after an inconclusive moment of silence. "It was nice of her to stop by."

Kitiara muttered something under her breath in response.

"And this is a handy contraption," Gilon added good-naturedly, holding up the leather sling. "Let's see if we can fit it onto you."

*   *   *   *   *

For the next three weeks, Kit wore the sling constantly, using it to keep Raistlin near her at all times. The baby's breathing improved, but still it was not strong or steady. At any given moment, Kit might have to drop everything to rub the bottoms of his feet in order to stimulate his breathing and circulation.

Most nights, Kit dropped fully dressed into bed, stone tired. Most mornings, she woke up still wearing Minna's sling and ready to take Raistlin out of Gilon's tired arms and begin the routine again.

On the morning of the first day of the fourth week, Kit woke up realizing she had overslept. Jumping out of bed, she climbed down the ladder and looked around. Caramon was kicking energetically in his cradle, but Raistlin was still sleeping, curled up in another wooden cradle that Gilon had hurriedly carved and assembled.

Kit glanced in the direction of the small adjoining room and saw that her mother, too, was still asleep. Rosamun had remained bedridden since her difficult childbirth, barely stirring on most days, unable to speak on many others. She had to be watched as conscientiously as Raistlin. Turn your head for a minute, and Kit's mother would be sitting straight up, eyes open, wailing in fright. She had begun pointing to things nobody could see and speaking absolute gibberish.

Next to her big bed was a straw pallet on which Gilon usually slept. It had become his job to make the cups of strong tea that sometimes helped calm Rosamun. Even with the soothing tea, however, there was no telling how long one of her wild trances might last. Kit's stepfather looked at his wife more and more sorrowfully these days, for the gentle woman he had once loved had been replaced by an unpredictable stranger.

Today his pallet was empty, and Gilon had already gone. In the weeks since the twins were born, he had been staying home from the forest too much. The household could ill afford the loss of his income as well as of the meager sums Rosamun earned from mending and sewing. Kit had insisted to Gilon that she was more than willing to devote herself to taking care of the twins if he went back to work.

With Caramon, the job was easy. As long as you didn't let his diaper get too wet, he was fine. Loud, restless, perpetually hungry, but fine.

Raistlin was a different story. Kit had to watch him closely, be alert to his breathing and coax him to eat. The young girl found that those tasks were not nearly so exhausting as the time she spent thinking of the infant, willing Raistlin with all her might to grow stronger.

As she began making breakfast this day, Kit heard a slight noise and looked around. To her amazement, Rosamun was standing—wobbly, but standing—in the doorway of her room. If Kit hadn't looked into her eyes, she would have thought her mother was fine. But Rosamun's gray eyes were eerie, out of focus.

When Gilon returned home well before dusk, Kitiara greeted him at the door. They had agreed that upon his return Kit would be allowed an immediate escape from the confines of the cottage. Rather than sitting down to eat supper right away, the eight-year-old girl played outside until total darkness descended, usually practicing her swordplay with a furious intensity, as if cramming her childhood into a few short hours.

"Mother wandered around the cottage a lot today," Kit

informed Gilon this day as she got ready to leave. "I had to tie her to the bed at one point."

Gilon raised his eyebrows in surprise, then looked into the small adjoining room. Wearing stained bedclothes, Rosamun was sitting in the rocking chair in the corner, moving her hands as if she were knitting, only she had no needles or yarn.

"I don't know what the twins made of their mother, but she didn't pay any attention to them," Kit told Gilon with some satisfaction just before she shot out into the warm summer evening.

* * * * *

When the twins were six weeks old, Kitiara came home from her evening's play to find Rosamun seated at the kitchen table, holding Raistlin and cooing down at Caramon in his cradle. While Gilon must have helped her to bathe and dress herself, Kit's frail mother still looked like a wraith after weeks of illness. Yet her face was shining, as was that of Gilon, who stood nearby, observing the scene with proud pleasure.

Rosamun turned away from the twins when she heard Kit at the door and warmly beckoned her daughter toward her. She set Raistlin down in his cradle so that she could put her blue-veined hands on the girl's sturdy shoulders. Rosamun attempted to pull Kit toward her, but her daughter held back.

"I want to thank you for all that you have done. Gilon says you have been . . . indispensable," Rosamun said while gazing at the raven-haired young girl with a mixture of love and uncertain respect.

Kitiara looked down at the floor, confused by her own feelings of gratitude and resentment. As she started to pull away, Rosamun stood up and put her thin arms around her daughter in an awkward embrace. Kit held herself stiffly, then broke for the door the minute she felt her mother's grasp loosen.

Rosamun sank heavily back into her chair, while Gilon hovered nearby, not knowing what to say. Rosamun's eyes clouded with tears as she watched her daughter race back into the summer night.

"Your father would have been proud of you," Rosamun whispered after Kit's retreating figure.

Chapter 3

Red Moon Festival

Thanks to Gilon, there was always plenty of good, slow-burning oak ready to heap on the overnight fire. But the flames usually died down in the middle of the night, and especially on the worst, most forbidding nights, no one wanted to get up and tread across the cold floor to replenish the blaze.

Kitiara preferred to sleep in her own quarters, though they were farthest away from the heat. Up a ladder and divided from the rest of the cottage by a thin muslin curtain, the loft at least gave her some privacy. The price for that privacy could be a bit high. More mornings than not in the long winters, she woke up curled into a tight ball and shivering.

Gnomes had a saying about Solace winters, which were

notoriously harsh: "Three layers not enough, and noses always stick out." The winters seemed neverending, yet practically overnight, when everyone felt at the breaking point, spring would arrive, catching even the most vigilant of the Solace citizenry by surprise.

On this particular morning, twelve-year-old Kitiara was still sleeping. She wasn't curled up—a good sign of the weather to come. In fact, she was stretched out luxuriously across her straw mattress. Her feet hung over the end of it, an indication that she was outgrowing her little nook. Her face in repose was childish, almost gentle, quite unlike the cool, practiced expression she had already adopted, if not always convincingly, as part of her armor against the world.

The softness evaporated as something blunt and unwelcome poked her in the side.

Out of Kit's mouth came some rather imaginative muttering, and, without opening her eyes, she turned on her side against the wall, pulling the quilted blanket tightly over her. After a pause, the poking resumed, this time in the small of her back.

"Go away, Caramon," she murmured sullenly.

Poke, poke.

Slowly she faced the obnoxious intrusion, still more than half asleep, her eyes bleary.

Oh. Her eyes opened with mild surprise as she made out the diminutive form of, not Caramon, but Raistlin. Thin and pale, an oval face framed by wisps of light brown hair, the four-year-old was standing at the edge of the bed. He was smiling mysteriously. Smiling was out of the ordinary for Raistlin, an unusually preoccupied little boy.

"I woke up early . . ." he began reedily.

"Uh-huh." By now Kitiara was unfortunately wide-eyed and knew she was not going to be able to steal any more sleep. She propped herself up on one elbow and regarded her odd little brother, whom she loved enough, yet would just as soon strangle breathless some days—no, *most* days—particularly right now.

A glance downstairs told her that his more high-spirited brother, Caramon, was still fast asleep, lying on his back, his toes pointed in the air, snoring lightly. The twins had small beds alongside each other, but Caramon was usually sprawled at an angle over both of them. Kit knew Caramon had been up late the night before, practicing, under Gilon's tutelage, how to whittle. He was applying his newfound expertise to creating his first wooden dagger.

As was his wont, Raistlin had gone to bed shortly after supper, and Kitiara must have fallen asleep in front of the smoldering fire. Good, reliable Gilon would have lifted her up the ladder and into bed.

Kitiara sighed. How early was it anyway?

Poke, poke.

"Will you stop that, Raist?"

He still had that vague smile. What was he so smiley about today?

"I was saying," he said unnecessarily, now that he had renewed her attention, "a bird was talking to me. . . ."

Kitiara lifted one eyebrow suspiciously. The story did not seem very likely—but with Raistlin, you never could be sure. The child had a peculiarity about him, a singularity. Since he didn't talk much to other children, he might as well talk to birds. But did birds talk back to him? What birds were there anyway, this time of year, in Solace?

"What kind of bird?" she asked in exasperation.

"Brown bird," replied Raistlin, shrugging as if this was unimportant information. "Wings got white tips," he said, almost as an afterthought. "Just passing through on its way somewhere else."

"Well. What did the brown bird say?" persisted Kitiara, beginning to roll into a sitting position.

"Said it was going to be an extra-special day."

"Oh," she said, unimpressed. "Extra-special good, or extra-special bad?"

"Hmm," Raist said thoughtfully. "Probably good. He sounded happy." His older sister began to pull on her boots. "Of course with brown birds," he added authoritatively, "you never know. They think every day's special. It doesn't take much to convince them."

"Optimists," Kit said drily.

"Uh-huh," Raist agreed.

She stopped and gave him an appraising look. His expression was certainly ingenuous, almost angelic. Well, Raistlin was the imaginative twin.

She yawned as she grabbed a tunic and pulled it over her head. Caramon—he was the predictable one. If he saw a brown bird, he wouldn't try to talk to it; he'd try to catch it with a net or whack it with a stone. Listen for the rowdy mischief, there was Caramon.

Weary to the bone after almost five years of trailing after the twins, of taking care of them and worrying about them, of teaching them as best she could—of being their mother, practically—Kitiara felt as if she could sleep for an entire month. Her body ached and her mind often felt dulled. She hated the thought of what she would feel like after five more years of such duty.

Her mother had never really recovered from the trauma of the twins' birth. Nothing seemed to be actually wrong with Rosamun, not physically at least, but she was more often in her bed than out of it. For five years she had eaten little and had wasted away to gauntness. Her pale blond hair had turned a ghostly white. In Rosamun's shrunken face, her gray eyes were immense, spooky, and pegged beyond the horizon. Beyond this world.

For a short time after the twins were born, Yarly had tended to Rosamun. But Yarly was even less skilled and less accommodating than her sister, Minna. It wasn't long before she was counted a nuisance even in Gilon's eyes. They still owed the two midwife sisters a pile of money, and not a week went by that Minna didn't stop by to mention it. Good-hearted Gilon was paying the debt a little at a time.

Yarly had been unable to do much to alleviate Rosamun's mysterious malady, in any case. So for a long time now, the family had made do with the resources of the local healer, a fat, well-intentioned man with appalling horsebreath, name of Bigardus.

Bigardus had known Rosamun for many years and seemed to have a genuine fondness for her. A simple—Kit would be tempted to say simple-minded—healer, he had none of Minna's airs or "never-fail" pretensions. He admitted he did not have the slightest idea what was wrong with Rosamun, and he did not boast about cures. But he kept the Majere family stocked with various pouches and vials of exotic medicines that were arranged on a small stand next to Rosamun's bed. They seemed to ease her recurring pains. Bigardus came periodically now, to check on Rosamun or to observe one of her spells. Kit liked him. She could almost say she looked forward to his jolly visits.

Rosamun would drift in and out of a half-sleep for months at a stretch. At times, she seemed almost serene, watching everything so quietly with her big eyes that one almost forgot she was nearby. Sometimes she would surprise everyone by suddenly sitting up in bed and calling the twins to her to hear a story. This usually marked the start of one of those rare periods during which Rosamun appeared almost normal. She might get up to bake her special sunflower seed muffins that Caramon and Raistlin loved. Sometimes she even ventured out to go shopping, or for a walk in the woods, as long as Gilon was by her side.

During these normal-seeming periods, Rosamun devoted most of her precious energy to the twins and Gilon. Rarely—Kitiara felt certain she could count the times on one hand—did Rosamun make any effort to spend time with her daughter. It was as if she were uncertain how to act toward this self-sufficient girl who most of the time functioned as the surrogate mother of the household. At first Kit had been hurt by what she took to be her mother's indifference, but no longer.

Rosamun's interludes of normalcy would disintegrate without warning. Kitiara or Gilon or one of the boys would find her crumpled on the floor and endeavor to help her into bed. Then, for brief minutes or weeks on end, Rosamun went into one of her spells, suffering agonizing and horrifying visions that mystified everyone.

In fact, only Bigardus called them "visions." What they consisted of, what her mother actually envisioned, Kit could hardly guess. The spells came upon her without warning. All of a sudden Rosamun's face would twist and contort, her arms would begin to flail. She might even leap out of bed with astonishing energy and roam about the room, knocking down furniture and breaking objects in a strange fury. The words that poured from her mouth were jumbled, without meaning. Warnings screamed at Gregor, at the twins, at Kitiara herself. Nonsense warnings.

Once, in her befuddlement, Rosamun had seen Kitiara brandishing her wooden sword and mistaken her daughter for the girl's father. She had bolted upright, stretched out her hands, and cried out in pathetic joy, "Gregor, you have come back to me!"

Kitiara scoffed to herself in thinking it over. Gregor had been gone without any word for six winters.

If Rosamun grew too agitated, they might have to tie her down to the bed. And when her mother came out of one of her spells—after hours, days or weeks—she would have no recollection of what had transpired. She would lay back on her pillow, drained of all spirit and vigor, her white hair soaked with sweat and plastered around her face. After one of these spells, Kitiara had learned from experience, her mother became even more useless and even more irrelevant to the daily life of the family.

Kitiara had taught herself everything—how to cook, how to sew and mend, how to watch and instruct the boys. Aside from cooking, she may not have done these things well, but, by the gods, she did them. And Kitiara was proud of what she had done, proud of surviving, even while she despised the homemaking skills she had learned.

Kit remembered, long ago, feeling something like love for her mother. It must have been love. What else could it have been? But nowadays she felt nothing but pity for her. Pity and growing distance.

"A bird!" exclaimed Kitiara, startled back to the present

moment. She looked again at Raistlin, who was peering at her from atop the ladder, as if trying to discern her thoughts. She reached over and cuffed him affectionately on the ear. "You were talking to a bird! That means . . . "

She lunged past him and hurtled down to the ground floor. Crossing the room, Kit threw one of the shutters open. Sunshine streamed through the window.

Spring! Sunshine, blue sky, fragrant air—and yes, birds, birds everywhere.

"Spring!" She leaned contentedly on the narrow sill.

"That's what I've been trying to tell you," said Raistlin earnestly, following her. "What do you think I was talking about?"

She gazed out the window. The snow, there in patches only the afternoon before, was practically all gone. The ground was wet, and buds and blossoms were peeking out. There was a brightness and color all around. From a ways off, she could hear music and laughter, the augury of a celebration. Then she remembered this was the first morning of the annual Red Moon Fair.

Eagerly, she stooped to lace up her boots and leggings. Gilon, she noted, was already gone, out chopping wood no doubt. Every morning her stepfather rose at dawn and went out to do his work accompanied by the faithful Amber. Gilon was solitary and secretive about his woodcutting, like a fisherman guarding his favorite trawling spots. Kitiara had never been asked to come with him, though she was thankful for that. Alone among the siblings, husky little Caramon had been invited to tag along once. When he came back from the day of chopping wood, he didn't say much. "Lot of work," he confided to Kit and Raistlin. "Boring."

Swiftly, Kitiara crossed the room, followed by Raistlin. She peered through the homespun drape Gilon had hung across the doorway of the small area that served as his and Rosamun's private space. Her mother was still sleeping, Kitiara saw with an apprehensive glance. Good. Let her sleep. She motioned Raist to be quiet.

She crept to where Caramon was still blithely snoring.

Raist followed her, as he always did. Caramon didn't even stir at their approach. That little imp could sleep through a rock slide, Kitiara thought.

She got a good grip on his pillow and leaned over to position herself close to his ear. As Kit yanked the pillow out from under her little brother, she gave a wild shout, "Surrounded by enemies!"

Caramon's eyes flew open as his head thunked down on the headboard. The next instant, he sprang off the bed into a boyish fighting stance. His dazed look turned to a sheepish one when he saw Kitiara sprawled on the floor, clutching her sides and trying to muffle her laughter. As for Raistlin, a smile tugged at the corner of his mouth.

"Aw," said Caramon, "I was in the middle of a dream."

"Maybe you dream too much," said Raist blandly.

Caramon shot him an offended glance.

"First day of spring!" announced Kitiara. "The fair is on." She had already scrambled to her feet and was heading toward the door, Raistlin in tow.

"What about Mother? Shouldn't we wait for Father?" asked Caramon plaintively.

But Kit and Raist were already out the door, and Caramon, pulling on his clothes, had to hurry if he wanted to catch up.

* * * * *

By midmorning the sun was hot in the sky, and all memory of winter had been banished. For someone stuck in Solace through the cold months, not to mention those stuck there for their whole lives, this first festival of spring was the happiest time of the year. It was a day when the proverbial small-town door opened and the whole rest of the world seemed to step in and gaudily introduce itself.

The town's activity had moved completely from the elevated walkways between the vallenwoods to the spaces below, where the town square and smithy lay. Townspeople milled around the green, hailing friends and forming groups that set off for the Northfields on the outskirts of town where the Red Moon Fair set up. Kitiara and her two brothers scouted out the square before joining those headed for the fairgrounds.

When the dense vallenwoods ended and the Red Moon Fair began, Kit and the boys stopped for a moment to drink it all in—the sights and sounds and strangers.

Merchants who spent their entire lives journeying from fair to festival in Ansalon had set up tents with bright pennants. Booths offered dry goods and tapestries, glass vessels and ornaments, quills and precious spices, bulk commodities, medicinal herbs, copperware and shoes, linen and garments—anything and everything. Notaries stood ready with wax and parchment to seal contracts; groups of music-makers spun through the press of people; there were shows by stunt animals and rope dancers. Everywhere were crowds.

It was a veritable honeycomb of humanity, and some who were decidedly not human. Among the long lines of travelers who had arrived for the occasion were many kender and some elves, dwarves who kept to themselves mostly, and even a lone, haughty minotaur, hulking and sullen, who, wherever he chose to stroll, was given a wide berth among the people.

Caramon had stopped to gaze enviously at some metal wares. He listened to the craftsman extol the virtues of his handiwork as he hawked the items to several listeners. Safely below the man's line of vision, Caramon reached up to finger the elaborate buckles and spurs.

Kitiara and Raistlin waited patiently for him, some paces off. Kitiara was feeling a little hungry by now, and in vain she searched her pockets for some coins. Skeptically, she looked up at a booth with a sign that offered fried gull or hare, and a green drink that mixed chopped dittany, rue, tansy, mint, and gillyflowers. No coins. No matter. Her chin was in the air, and she was breathing in deep draughts of the smells of cooking all around.

Her attention was drawn to a group of men in motley

regalia, standing on the fringes of the grounds. A saddle fell off one of their horses, and a member of the group, a thick, muscled fellow, swatted the head of his squire. But the swat was a good-natured one, and the other men laughed boisterously as the squire hastened to set things right. The men paid no attention to the hurly-burly of the fair. They were on their way to more important adventures.

For a moment Kit wondered if she might approach them and ask about her father, whether they had heard news of Gregor Uth Matar or actually met him on their travels. They looked like rogues who had been around. But she reacted too slowly, and they were already on their way, still yelling and laughing to one another, before she got up the nerve.

Immersed as she was in everything that was going on around her, Kitiara at first did not hear the noises and raucous gaiety coming from the gaggle of youths directly behind her. But now she became aware of some of the comments.

"If it isn't little Miss Woodcutter!"

"Kind of the motherly type!"

"Not much in the beauty department, that's for sure!"

She turned slowly to observe a pack of boys and girls, her own age and older. A few of them she recognized, elbowing and jostling each other, from school days, though she hadn't seen them in a while. With household chores and caring for the twins, Kitiara had found little time for school. In fact, she had little enough time to herself, barely enough to daydream for a few moments or practice her beloved swordplay. This last winter, she told Gilon she would not go to school any longer. Her stepfather knew better than to object when Kit told him something with her hands placed on her hips like that and her mouth set in a thin line.

One of the boys, the beefy one with the pink face swimming in brown freckles, she knew well from past encounters—a bullying lad named Bronk Wister. Bronk was a born troublemaker, the son of a tanner whom Gilon sometimes bartered with. Bronk's father always smiled gently at Kit, but the son had gotten it into his mind that he was superior to her. He liked to taunt her with slurs about Gilon and Rosamun and the twins. To get back at him, Kit called him Speckleface, for the obvious reason.

"If it isn't Speckleface," she responded, placing her hands on her hips in characteristic fashion. At her side, little Raistlin watched the persecutors warily.

"Chop any good trees today?" Bronk's sneering laugh was harsh and dissonant, like a braying donkey.

"Break any mirrors with your ugly face lately?" she retorted.

The crowd of young people jeered. They were spoiling for amusement and didn't care who the butt of the joke might be. Bronk stepped forward, a contemptuous look on his face, and pushed up his sleeves. "I've been meaning to teach you a lesson. What you need is a good pasting. Same as any boy."

Raistlin glanced nervously over his shoulder, but couldn't spot Caramon. Instinctively he took a step back, out of the line of fire. At the same time, by impulse, Kitiara stepped in front of him, shielding her little brother.

Kitiara's smile was a cunning one. Whipping Speckleface in front of his dumb friends would just about make her morning perfect. Win or lose, she had no doubt that the fight would be worthwhile.

The boys and girls cheered encouragingly as Bronk shuffled forward, his fists circling like small shields in front of his eyes. Kit planted her feet and awaited his attack.

Suddenly Kit felt a bump from behind, and as she lost balance she was shoved aside. A new protagonist had gallantly substituted himself for her.

"Leave my sister alone!" shouted Caramon, his not-quite-five-year-old fists threatening fancifully. Clutched in one of them was a stout branch at least as long as Caramon was tall. Her little brother barely reached Kitiara's chest, but he had some girth—and pluck—for his age. His brown eyes, half-hidden by unruly golden brown hair that tumbled over his brow, flashed angrily.

The crowd liked the fresh attraction. They erupted in new laughter, taunts, and yelling. As for Bronk, he stared in disbelief. "Aw, she has to have help from her little baby brother. Isn't that cute!"

"Pssst!" whispered Kitiara, and not much of a whisper at that. "Back off, Caramon. This is my fight."

"It would not be honorable," intoned Caramon solemnly, trying to sound baritone and warriorlike. The sturdier of the two Majere brothers waded forward to meet Bronk, who had paused with uncertainty as to who, or how many, he was going to have to fight.

There was another push from behind, and this time Caramon went sprawling head over heels, jolting a nearby vegetable cart and tipping it precariously. The owner, who was interrupted in the middle of a promising sales pitch, shrieked a curse. He picked the boy up by the nape of his tunic until Caramon's legs dangled off the ground. This the swelling number of onlookers thought the funniest thing yet.

"I'll let you know what's honorable, and what's not, little brother," scolded Kitiara. "Especially where my honor is concerned."

Caramon broke away from the vegetable man and, with dignity, dusted himself off. He glared at Kit balefully.

"I was trying to be chiv . . . chiv . . ."

"Chivalric!" muttered Raistlin half to himself, before sitting down on an outcropping of stone. His watery eyes did not look as fascinated as the rest of the crowd's.

"Chivalric!" exclaimed Caramon, with a look of gratitude at his brother. He marched up to Kitiara, nose to chest, his look determined and fierce.

"Try being chivalric somewhere else," said Kitiara tolerantly. She pushed him off.

"Ingrate!" Caramon said, stepping forward again.

"Squirt!" she retorted, a glint in her eyes.

By now the crowd had forgotten Bronk, and the troublemaker had safely melted—with some relief—back into the throng. All eyes were trained on Caramon as he made the first move, bringing his stick up and whacking Kit hard on her right arm. He followed that swift assault with another one, which caught her across the knees. She bent over, wincing.

Up rose a huzzah from the spectators—now as many adults as young people—as they gathered in a half-circle around the two squabbling siblings. Caramon somehow managed to leapfrog over Kitiara's doubled-over form while delivering a backblow with the knob of his amateur weapon. For such a youngster it was an impressive display of agility.

But even as Caramon turned to grin smugly at the crowd, Kit straightened up and whirled toward him, grabbing the boy by the waist and hoisting him over her shoulders like a bag of potatoes. She spun him in a circle, then tossed him through the air to land on his back in the brackish water of a nearby trough.

The crowd erupted with glee. Their cries were cut short when Caramon sprang out of the trough and, dripping water and sediment, hurled himself at his sister with what he believed to be a Solamnic war cry. It was something Caramon dimly recalled hearing once, which was really more a kender insult cry.

Whack! This time Kitiara blocked his swing with an outstretched arm, another with her hand, so that Caramon had to spin around—Where did he learn to do that? Kit wondered fleetingly—in order to deliver a shot to the back of her shoulder.

Kitiara rubbed her shoulder ruefully, amused in spite of her pain. They had wrestled like this many times in the forest. Good thing that stick was not particularly thick or heavy, she decided. That Caramon was sure getting feisty, though. "Ouch!" she yelped as something caught her on the ear. "Now that stung!"

"Sorry," said Caramon, panting. He was grinning like a drunken kender and plainly having fun, too.

Kitiara flipped around, dove to the ground, and grabbed the upstart by the feet. As Caramon rained blows on her head, Kit thumped him to the ground. He dropped his stick, and she managed to kick it away. In doing so, she pinned him down, got a hold on one of his legs, and bent it back toward his head. But at the same time he was able to reach behind him and grab her head in his hands. They were all pretzeled up together, grunting and sputtering, she twisting his leg, he bending her by the neck.

"Give up!" Kit demanded, pulling his leg so close to his back that the crowd groaned in sympathy with the pain.

"No way!" Caramon roared.

The crowd signaled its approval of the defiant standoff. Kit bent Caramon's leg back even farther; she could almost hear the bones popping. In reply, he tightened his hold on her head. While his face was being pressed into the ground, hers was being bent back to face the sky.

"Give!

"You give!"

"I won!"

"I won first!"

"Let Raist be the judge!"

Pause. "OK."

"Raist? Raist?"

Kitiara managed to swivel her head enough to see that Raistlin had vanished. Caramon's twin had observed this entertaining spectacle a few too many times in his short life, and he was quickly bored by the variations on it. Raist had given up and wandered away.

Kitiara jumped up. "Raistlin!"

Caramon jumped up too, rubbing his face. His tunic was ripped in places. Kitiara's ear was showing a drool of blood. "Aw c'mon," muttered Caramon, "where can he have got to now?"

Kitiara wheeled on him vehemently. "How many times do I have to tell you? You're his brother! He's your responsibility as much as mine!"

Caramon looked not only somewhat beat up but contrite. "Aw, why do I have to look after him all the time? You're his big sister, aren't you? Anyway, I—"

Kitiara practically spat out the words. "You're his twin brother, his *twin* brother. You're two halves of the same whole. And he's not as strong as you. You know that. I'm not going to babysit the two of you for the rest of my life. So go find him, and hurry up about it!"

She aimed a kick at Caramon but missed by a narrow margin. He had taken her words to heart and was already dashing away to locate his missing twin.

In exasperation Kitiara sank to the ground. Realizing the fun was over, most of the onlookers had moved off into the larger crowd. Nobody seemed to be paying any attention to her anymore. Kit felt her ear and reached over to adjust one of her boots that had somehow almost wriggled off.

"You should have let him best you!"

She looked up to see a girl her age, with blue eyes and strawberry blond hair that fell in ringlets over her shoulders. Aureleen Damark, the coquettish daughter of a local furniture-maker, was one of Kit's few friends. They were practically opposites, but Kitiara had to admit that Aureleen made her laugh.

"Who, Caramon?" Kit scoffed, as she flashed a welcoming grin at her friend.

"No, Speckleface!" answered Aureleen earnestly. "Why do you think he's always picking on you, anyway?"

"Probably just mean and dumb," said Kit flatly.

Aureleen sat down beside Kit and spread her gangly legs out. "Not at all," scolded Aureleen. "Although I won't argue with you that he's dumb." She giggled. "He likes you!"

Kitiara looked sternly into the eyes of her friend, finding it hard to believe Aureleen wasn't kidding. "Speckleface?"

"He's not so ugly really," said Aureleen decidedly, arranging her pink and white dress so that it spread out around her like a coral shell in the dirt and dust. With her rosy cheeks and long-lashed eyes, Aureleen was the picture of femininity. "Guys like a girl who acts tough, Father says. Although," she paused and thought for a moment. "Mother says they prefer one with a soft heart. Hard outside, soft inside. What does your father say?"

Kitiara sighed. She could never keep up with the line of Aureleen's prattle. "Did say . . . *did* say. I haven't seen my father in almost six years, Aureleen. You know that."

"Yes, I do," said Aureleen reprovingly. "I mean Gilon—your *step*father, if you want to be technical. What does he say?"

"He doesn't say much, thank the spirits," said Kitiara. She glared fiercely at her friend. "Life isn't just about getting a man anyway," she declared.

"Oh, I disagree," said Aureleen, fluffing out her hair prettily. "My point is that Bronk likes you because you act strong and tough. But it would be better to let him win if it comes to wrestling or fighting. Men have their pride, and boys are worse."

With that, she reached into a fold of her skirt and brought out a thick square of fruit bread, broke it in half, and offered Kitiara a share.

Kit had to smile. Soon the two girls were whispering and laughing as they ate the treat. The fairgoers simply walked around them; the Red Moon Fair was casual if nothing else.

"Miss Kitiara . . ."

This time Kit looked up to see Minna, her mother's former midwife, staring down at her with a most calculating expression. Kit hadn't seen the old biddy in several months. Aureleen jumped to her feet politely, and Kitiara reluctantly followed suit.

"How's your dear mother been?" Minna asked.

"Fine, thank you," Kit said in a low voice.

"I haven't seen her about much lately," continued Minna, her eyes narrowing to slits.

No, and you won't you old witch, Kitiara thought to say, but her tongue was tied and her eyes cast to the ground.

"Why, she's right here, enjoying herself at the fair," piped up Aureleen in an ingenuous tone.

"What? Here?" Minna looked thrown by this report.

"Yes 'm," said Aureleen pertly. "She accompanied us here, and then . . . you know how it is, she had to go off with those two rascal boys somewhere. They were pulling her

---

53

arms and legs—it was very funny to see—and she laughing and enjoying herself so very much."

"Where? Where did they go?" Minna gazed over the heads of the crowd, avid for a new piece of gossip.

"Oh, you might look for them over by the games, if you just want to say hello, ma'am," said Aureleen innocently.

"I might just do that," Minna replied, suspicious.

She peered intently at Kit, but Kitiara's mask of politeness betrayed nothing.

"If you do, please tell her we're dawdling behind," said Aureleen.

"Yes, yes. I will," said Minna busily, looking over her shoulder at them as she hurried off through the crowd. The midwife was certain she had been gulled, but just in case, she would try to track Rosamun down.

When Minna was out of sight, the girls collapsed on each other. They were laughing so hard they could hardly stop for several minutes.

"That was royal," said Kit finally, catching her breath.

They giggled some more. "Yes'm, laughing and enjoying herself so much, she was!" Aureleen mimicked herself.

Kitiara stopped suddenly and drew an intake of breath. "Oh, I've got to find the twins!" she muttered.

"Don't worry," Aureleen reassured her, "they'll be—"

"I'd better," said Kitiara, turning to go.

"Oh, all right," grumbled Aureleen, following her. "Darned nuisances, both of 'em."

* * * * *

While Kitiara was tussling with Caramon, a tall, thin man with piercing feline eyes, frosted eyelashes, and a dry, leathery face weaved through the crowd near Raistlin, handing out cards. Instinctively Raist reached out his hand, and the man put one of the cards in his tiny palm. On it was a weird inscription. The little boy could not read so very well yet, but he could decipher a symbol on the slip of paper—one of the many iconic symbols for a traveling magician.

When the man moved off, Raistlin got up and followed. In liquid motion the man threaded his way through the crowd, past this booth and that stall, around a patch of rocks and trees, down a path where people were clumped around, eating their lunches, to a small clearing that had been set aside for a presentation. The shambling man nodded at Raist conspiratorially and continued on his way, handing out cards. The crowd seemed to divide for him, then to swallow him up.

Raistlin looked to the center of the clearing. There, a circle of people had begun to tighten around a man preparing a show. When the man looked up for a moment, Raistlin had a flash of recognition. He looked behind him, to where he had last glimpsed the man with the cards, and then back at the other. The man setting up the show was almost identical to the one he had been following, except that this man was dressed in a yellow robe of somewhat faded grandeur.

Twins! thought Raistlin to himself, like me and Caramon. Intrigued by the coincidence, the boy moved closer. Soon he was only one of the dozen or so people who stood around, talking amongst themselves and waiting for the traveling magician to begin his act.

The man was arranging containers and scrolls and small objects on a stand that he had unfolded. As he did so, he murmured and cackled, seemingly to himself, but with some winking and nods to members of the crowd. One of the audience, a young maid with long, braided hair and a peach complexion, seemed to interest him particularly. When he cleared his throat to begin, for a moment his eyes rested on her.

Plucking a small coin from the recesses of his garment, the magician held it up to his audience, and then, with a flourish, carried it to the edge of the clearing and placed it against the forehead of a bowlegged farmer who stood gaping at him. "Think. Think hard," intoned the illusionist. "Think of something important to you. One word or two. Don't try to fool a clever old magician. . . ."

The farmer fretted his brow intensely, the job of thinking

apparently every bit as arduous as that of plowing soil. "New cow," proclaimed the magician with a flourish, and the farmer's face flushed with an astonished expression that indicated the magician had got it right.

The magician moved down the row and came to the maid he had been eyeing. More gently, he held the coin to this one's forehead, looking deeply into her fresh face. Her expression, unlike the farmer's, was carefree. The magician seemed to ponder thoughtfully before crying out, "A young man named . . . Artis!" She clapped her hands in delight as he continued, a slight frown on his face as if he were a little disappointed at what her thoughts revealed.

Raistlin was startled to see the mage's hand with the coin in it stretch out toward him. As he watched the man intently, the magic coin was planted against his own perspiring forehead. "Now, a child. Children's minds are easy to plumb," exclaimed the magician, bending over as if to listen with one ear to the message of the coin. Raistlin's face was terrified. He squirmed a bit, but he stayed rooted to the spot, awaiting the revelation.

Probably no one but Raistlin noticed the surprise that flickered over the man's face as he strained for the insight that did not come. The yellow-robed magician bent closer, and so did the crowd as it listened for what he would say. There was a suspense of nearly one minute.

"Candy!" declared the magician, straightening up with an impressive gesture. The spectators cheered and applauded. "Candy," repeated the magician, turning back to his array of objects and stealing another furtive glance at the pretty young girl.

Nobody paid much attention to Raistlin. "I wasn't thinking of candy," he said irritably under his breath. But he had to admit the old professional was a crowd-pleaser. The boy moved closer, for the illusionist was already in the middle of his next stunt.

The man was waving his hands gracefully now, chanting a few words. He opened drawers and doves flew out, opened pockets and discovered sparkling trinkets, tore and shredded colored paper and then reconstructed the scraps. Raistlin knew, somewhere inside of himself, that it was only hocus-pocus, not very difficult, certainly not very meaningful magic. But in his almost five years, the boy had never seen such a wondrous show. The crowd watched in respectful silence. Raistlin himself was mesmerized.

"There you are, Raist!" Caramon came up beside him, huffing with importance. "Kitiara asked me to find you and bring you back right away." He looked over his shoulder, a little disoriented. "Although I'm not quite sure where 'back' is right—"

"Shhh!" Raistlin gave him a stern glance, and then paid his brother no further attention.

Caramon looked up just in time to witness the climax of the traveling magician's performance, probably the apex of the man's knowledge and skill. As far as Caramon could tell, the tall, thin mage was juggling several balls of light in the air. Big deal, he thought. In all, Caramon was about as fascinated by magic feats as Raistlin was by his twin's wrestling matches.

Caramon was glancing over his shoulder, looking for Kitiara, when a huge hurrah went up from the crowd. He looked back, but he was too late. The finale was over, and the mage was packing up his stuff. Another man—almost a ringer for the magician, Caramon thought with a frown—had begun passing a basket for donations.

"What did he do?" Caramon asked Raistlin. "What did he do?"

But Raistlin said nothing, and the expression on his face was almost beatific.

"There you two are!" said a hearty voice, and one hand clasped each of them on the shoulders. "You should be home. And where's Kitiara?"

It was Gilon, Amber yipping at his heels. He gave both his sons a squeeze and hoisted Raistlin easily to his sturdy shoulders. "C'mon!" he shouted to Caramon. "Where's Kit?" he asked again, looking around hesitantly.

"Uh," said Caramon, looking behind him. "Back there.

Or back somewhere. We got separated because Raist—"

Gilon scolded Caramon affectionately. "You've got chores to do, and you shouldn't leave your mother at home alone. You know that." He looked round again. "Well," he shrugged, "Kit will catch up."

Gilon set a vigorous pace. Caramon had to run to keep up. Raistlin, bouncing on his father's shoulders, twisted his head to get a last glimpse of the magician in the faded yellow robe. But he and his look-alike had already vanished.

Peeking out from behind a tent, Kitiara and Aureleen observed their going. Aureleen pondered the situation, biting the nail of her thumb.

"I should really go," began Kitiara.

Aureleen held up one of her decorated pouches and shook it so that Kitiara could hear the coins jingling inside. "I've got enough for both of us," she said invitingly. "They're selling sausage sticks and custard pies and . . ."

Kitiara frowned, feeling the tug of her family responsibilities.

"And over there," Aureleen pointed out slyly, "they're setting up the sports and contests. Girls can enter too!"

Kit didn't need much convincing. "Well, just for a few hours!" she said.

* * * * *

More than one teenage boy was dismayed that spring day in Solace when a girl who was several years younger than many of them took first place in the vine climb, barefoot sprint, and wiggleboat races—juvenile category.

Aureleen, her cheeks flushed, once again tried to explain to Kitiara that she ought to get in the habit of letting a man beat her occasionally, if she ever wanted to attract someone when she grew up and get happily married. But Kit was in a good mood. Aureleen could not faze her.

Bronk Wister was hanging around with his little brother, Dune, just watching the games. They jeered whenever Kit's name was announced. Aureleen—because, after all, she was Kit's booster—got in the spirit by cheering her friend on from the sidelines.

Afterward, they shared a prize-bag of chits from Kit's victories that could be swapped for food and trinkets. They stuffed themselves with sugary sweets until their stomachs ached. Then they played a couple of the games of chance run by unsavory characters inside tents, but they had no luck. Aureleen thought the games were probably rigged.

They browsed the traders' booths where Aureleen bargained for a shiny copper bracelet and Kit bought a pouch of magnets whose geometric shapes pleased her.

After several hours, low on energy, they sprawled on the grass in one corner of the fairgrounds, idly watching the crowd. A sign on a small striped tent she had not noticed before caught Kit's eye: "Futures Foretold, The Renowned Madame Dragatsnu." A stout, important-looking man left the tent with a satisfied expression.

Kit was intrigued, but when she counted up the tickets in her hand, she realized that they only had enough for one fortune-telling.

"Go ahead," said Aureleen, gesturing wearily. She had guessed Kit's mind. "My future is right here for the moment."

When Kit ducked under the tent flap, she came face to face with Madame Dragatsnu, a small, swarthy woman, ancient, with salt-and-pepper hair and whiskers sprouting from her nose and chin. Sitting on a woven rug, wearing a simple brown dress, the fortune-teller appeared rather unimpressive. Glancing around, Kit saw none of the mysterious paraphernalia she associated with the job of fortune-telling—no crystal sphere, cup of bones, jars of leaf crumbs, or the like.

"Sit down, child," said Madame Dragatsnu, some irritation in her thick voice. Kit could not place her peculiar accent.

Kit settled herself with crossed knees in front of the fortune-teller. Madame Dragatsnu's glistening eyes seemed to reach across the space between them and rake her over.

"It's not for me," the girl said softly, looking down, suddenly abashed. "The fortune, I mean."

"Your boyfriend then?"

Kit looked up defiantly. "No." She put down the chits she had been clutching and pushed them over to the old woman, who nodded.

"You have something that belongs to this person?"

Kit reached into her tunic and brought out a carefully folded piece of parchment—the Solamnic crest from her father. She had brought it along today in hopes of seeing people from that region who, if she showed the crest to them, might be able to give her information about Gregor or his family.

"It's—"

"Your father," said Madame Dragatsnu, cutting her off.

Kit watched the fortune-teller hopefully. Madame Dragatsnu turned the parchment over and over in her hands, feeling its surface in an almost sensuous way, as if the paper were a rare textile. While doing so, she gazed, not at Gregor's Solamnic symbol, but at Kit herself. The impassive look on Madame Dragatsnu's face didn't tell Kit anything, but oh how her eyes burned!

"I was hoping," Kit said, softly again, "that you might be able to tell me where he is."

"I don't reveal the present," said Madame Dragatsnu sharply. "*Futures* foretold. That's what the sign says."

Kit flushed. "Can you tell me anything about his future?"

"Shush!"

Several minutes of silence ensued while Madame Dragatsnu continued to finger the parchment's surface and stare at Kit, who was finding it difficult not to fidget.

"How long has it been since you have seen him?" the fortune-teller asked unexpectedly. The question wasn't as surprising as the manner in which it was asked. Madame Dragatsnu had dropped her businesslike tone and allowed an unmistakable note of sympathy to surface.

"More than five years."

"Ummm. I cannot tell you very much. I think, North.

Yes. Somewhere in the North."

"He has family in the North, I think, in Solamnia," Kitiara said excitedly.

"Somewhere else," Madame Dragatsnu declared. Another long spell of silence followed as she traced Gregor's crude ink drawing of the crest with her finger. "A battle," she continued in a trancelike voice. "A big battle, many men—"

"Will he be in danger?" Kit could hardly contain herself.

"Yes."

Kit drew in her breath sharply, her heart pounding. Gregor in danger!

"But not from the battle," said Madame Dragatsnu with finality. "He will win the battle."

"How then?" Kit asked urgently.

Madame Dragatsnu paused. "Afterward."

"When?" demanded Kit. "When?"

Madame Dragatsnu stared at her. "Soon. Very soon."

"What can I do? What more can you tell me?" Kit felt like screaming into the old hag's face.

The fortune-teller was imperturbable. She took a long time to respond, and before she did, she carefully re-folded Gregor's sketch, handing it back to Kitiara.

"Nothing. The answer to both of your questions is, nothing."

In a rage, Kit leaped up and dashed outside the tent. She took refuge behind a tree some distance away, her eyes brimming with tears. It was all some kind of filthy fortune-telling charade. She knew that. At fairs these soothsayers were as common as horseflies. The old hag didn't have a clue as to Gregor's future. That was just a wild guess, when Madame Dragatsnu had said that the ink sketch had to do with her father.

It took Kit some time to convince herself, calm down, dry her eyes, and return to Aureleen, who had fallen asleep on her back and was dozing with a smile on her lips.

"Any good news?" inquired her pretty friend after Kit woke her.

"A charlatan," Kit said firmly, with a shake of her head. "A waste of good tickets. C'mon, it's late. I have to get home."

* * * * *

Well past sunset, Kit eased open the door to the cottage and slipped inside. Her face was tired and dirt-streaked, her clothes torn and mussed. But she had blocked the fortune-teller's prediction from her mind and was more than usually happy. It took her a moment to adjust her eyesight, from the darkness of night to the strange light of the interior.

"Shhh!" Gilon grabbed her arm and pulled her down next to him where he sat on the floor.

"Where have you been?" Caramon demanded to know. He was sitting next to his father.

Before she could answer, Gilon whispered, "That's OK." With his hand he gently brushed back Kit's black hair. "Watch!"

Now she could see what was going on. Raistlin was in the center of the room, doing some kind of show. Magic tricks? Yes, Raistlin was doing magic tricks.

"I don't know how he learned them," Caramon leaned over to confide, "but he's been doing them all night. He's pretty good!"

The look on Raistlin's face was solemn, intense. The boy held his hands aloft. Suspended between them—somehow, Kitiara couldn't figure out how—was a ball of white light. Raist's hands were moving slightly, fluttering, and out of his mouth came a low chant of words that were mostly indistinguishable, if they were words at all. After a moment, Kit had the uncomfortable realization that they sounded like Rosamun's gibberish during one of her trances.

Raistlin moved his hands, the ball of light separated into several balls of light, and he began to juggle them. He made a rapid movement. The balls separated again, this time into dozens of smaller spheres of light. One more movement, and they became hundreds of tiny globes, shimmering snowflakes, pulsing and throbbing as if alive, moving in an artfully conceived pattern.

Finally, as Kitiara watched, Raistlin's words and gestures slowed. The lights, too, slowed in tandem, almost to a halt. Gilon, Caramon, and Kit were silent, watching Raistlin's face, which now carried a look of almost painful concentration. Abruptly Raist murmured something and did a quick, elaborate charade with his hands.

The globes of light began to spin, to expand and glow with deep, bright colors. Then, more rapidly than could be distinguished, the globes exploded into tiny shapes: fireflowers, shell blossoms, comet butterflies. There was a fusillade of tiny popping noises, climaxed by an explosion of white light that left all of them momentarily stunned and blinded.

"What's going on? What's the trouble?" asked Rosamun, her voice shaking with terror. She was clinging to the door frame of her small room, her face twisted with anxiety.

Gilon rose hurriedly to take her back to bed and reassure her.

All was back to normal now. Raistlin came and sat down. He held out his arms to his sister and brother, and they each took him by the hand. Kitiara and Caramon laughed with joy, and, most extraordinary, Raistlin laughed with them.

Chapter 4

The Mage School

Gilon wrapped up some cheese and bread for the trip while Kitiara looked over Raistlin one last time. Hands and face—clean. Tunic and leggings—darned at the knees and elbows, but presentable. Kit stretched and yawned. The early spring sun had not been visible in the sky when Gilon had roused her to prepare for the day's outing.

Raistlin watched her solemnly. Kit knew by how still he held himself just how excited Raist was to be going to the mage school today. Faced with a similar outing, Caramon—and most six-year-olds—would be bouncing up and down uncontrollably, asking a million questions.

Not Raist. Always quiet and watchful, he grew even more so when anticipating his audience with the master mage.

"I'll never be as tall or strong as Caramon, will I? No matter how much gunk you rub on my legs?" he had asked Kit the night before, as she was getting him ready for bed by spreading some foul-smelling ointment on his legs and arms. It had been part of his nightly ritual ever since the last visit of the healer, Bigardus. After treating Rosamun that day, Bigardus had stared at the spindly arms and legs of little Raistlin and made a tch-tch face. He then rummaged around in his bag of palliatives and produced some wortwood salve, telling Kit to rub it over Raist's limbs every night, to strengthen them. Well, Kitiara had thought skeptically, maybe the ointment was worth trying.

Last night, looking forward to his trip to meet the master mage, Raist had protested at the smelly routine.

"This stuff isn't going to change the way I am," he said sincerely. "I'll always be small and weak. I know that. It doesn't matter. You can stop thinking you'll always have to look out for me."

Kit had leaned over, giving her little brother a quick hug while wondering at his perceptiveness. Not a day went by, truly, that she didn't think about ways she could stop being her younger brothers' caretaker—not just Raistlin, but Caramon, too. She was almost fourteen. She longed to set out on her own, to see the world, perhaps even to track down her father. She was bone-tired of doing everything Rosamun should have been doing, if it weren't for her stupid trances.

Raist had pushed her away and sat up straight in bed, flushed, his eyes glittering.

"Once I become a mage," the little boy vowed, "nobody is going to have to take care of me! I'll be the one who takes care of Mother and Father and Caramon. And I'll take care of anybody else, any way I see fit."

"Big talk," Kit said fondly, mussing his hair and putting the rest of the ointment away. "Just like your brother."

"Yeah, big talker," piped up Caramon sleepily from his bed.

"You'll see," Raistlin said.

"Go to sleep, both of you. Tomorrow's a big day."

Always exhausted by the end of the day, Raist had fallen back against his pillow, pale and glistening with sweat from his defiant declaration. His eyelids fluttered, then he fell into a restless sleep.

Kit had watched Raist for a few minutes to make sure he would stay asleep. That was a habit she had developed during his infancy, when she'd watched over him, sometimes staying up with him all through the night to make sure his breathing didn't falter.

In contrast, she never had needed to check on Caramon. He already snored contentedly on the small wooden bed next to Raist's along the wall opposite Rosamun's and Gilon's bedroom. For all his energy, Caramon usually preceded his twin brother into slumber.

The morning of Raist's visit to the master mage, Caramon still lay in bed, all tangled up in the bedding, as if he had been dreaming about wrestling with a serpent. He had protested when Gilon told him he would be staying behind, but his arguments had died quickly when Rosamun promised they would bake sunflower seed muffins.

Rosamun was in the midst of one of her longer periods of good health. She had begun to dress up a little, to comb her hair regularly, and to set it off with beads and flowers. For weeks her face, usually so tense and lined with worry, had been more relaxed and almost happy.

Kit's mother stood by the kitchen table now, preparing tea for the trio of travelers. Kit avoided her mother's solicitous gaze as she went over to take a warm mug. When Rosamun turned to tend to the fire, Gilon, who had just emerged from the bedroom, drew Kit aside.

"Caramon knows to run and get Bigardus if Rosamun . . . if . . . you know . . ." he trailed off, looking at Kit anxiously.

"If she goes off her head, you mean," Kit said bluntly, ignoring the look of hurt that crossed Gilon's face. "Yes. Caramon may not be able to do anything else for Mother, but he certainly knows how to run.

"And," she added, seeing Gilon's anxiety mounting, "it

wouldn't take him much time to get to Bigardus's and back, as long as he doesn't run into one of his dumb friends and—"

"Perhaps we shouldn't go," Gilon said. "I mean, if you think your mother won't be all right or that Caramon can't manage without us . . ." He lifted his hands questioningly.

It had been Gilon's idea to pay a visit to the mage school today. Kit's stepfather had spent two long evenings at the kitchen table, laboring over a letter to the master mage asking for permission to enroll Raist. He had searched his brain for the right wording, the proper tone. But he was not satisfied with any one of his dozen drafts, and at the end of the second night he had stood up and crumpled his latest effort into the fire.

"Letters are so cold," he had declared. He would go himself to make a plea for his youngest child. Then the master mage could see for himself what a gifted pupil Raist would make.

The mage school was mysteriously situated on the outskirts of Solace, its location a source of rumor and gossip, and Kit did not know anyone who could make a credible claim to have actually been there. Yet Gilon, with his simple, stubborn nature, was determined to go. Kit knew Gilon wanted to get Raist's future "settled" as much as she did, if for different reasons.

"No, no. Caramon can manage fine. It's Rosamun who can't. We'll just have to keep our fingers crossed," she reassured Gilon—without comforting him much.

During this whispered exchange, Caramon had woken up and trudged sleepily over to the table, where Rosamun was coaxing Raist to eat some porridge. Kit watched her mother turn toward Caramon with a loving smile and hug him before serving up a generous bowl of porridge. Caramon dug into his portion eagerly, asking, with his mouth full, what else there was to eat.

Both boys watched their mother avidly, obviously delighted to have her up and about. Rosamun glanced up from her duties and met Kit's judgmental gaze.

"Kitiara, won't you have something to eat before you leave? You have a busy morning ahead, and who knows what hospitality you will find at your destination," Rosamun said kindly.

"Don't worry about me, Mother." Kit must have put an edge on the word that caused Rosamun to flinch. "I've packed some bread and cheese, enough for me, Gilon, and Raist. I know how to fend for myself—I've been doing just that for years. Don't start worrying about me now."

Flushing, Rosamun turned back to the twins. Caramon, busy shoveling porridge into his mouth, hadn't paid any attention to the exchange, but Raistlin, ever observant, had been listening with a frown.

Gilon stepped in from the outside, breaking the tension. "Hurry up, Raist. We want to arrive early enough so that the master mage will have time to see us. Kitiara, are you ready?"

Raistlin slipped off his chair, had his face wiped by Rosamun, and joined Gilon at the door. Kit tied a rope around the sack of food she had prepared and slung it over her shoulder. Gilon planted a gentle kiss on Rosamun's forehead, then hesitated, obviously torn about leaving her and Caramon for the day.

Rosamun, looking the very image of a typical, if slightly disheveled, homebody, shrugged off his concern affectionately. "Go on," she urged. "We'll be just fine."

As they filed out the door, Caramon had already pulled out a mortar and pestle from the kitchen cabinet and was kneeling on a chair next to the eating table, determinedly grinding sunflower seeds while his mother looked on, beaming with approval.

The last to leave, Kitiara took in the domestic scene before closing the door, gripped by envy as well as resentment. She hated the way the twins and Gilon doted on Rosamun during her "normal" periods. If her mother had ever spent any special time with Kit, it was so long ago she could not remember it.

* * * * *

The trio descended along the ropeways and ramps between the vallenwoods toward one of the paths that wound through the trunks of the giant trees and to the southern outskirts of Solace. Kit, who had not helped herself to any breakfast back at the cottage, pulled a piece of black bread and cheese from her pack and began munching as she walked.

Dropping back alongside her, Gilon spoke to Kit in a lowered voice, out of Raist's earshot. "Though I have never been there, I judge it to be a good hour's walk to where the master mage is said to keep his school. Will Raist be all right? Should we rest halfway? We don't want him to be too tired once he gets there."

Kit eyed the slight figure walking dutifully in front of them. His curious eyes roamed the sky, the treetops, the side of the path, picking out things that intrigued him. He paid no attention to Kit and Gilon and imagined himself the bold leader of their little expedition.

"If he looks like he's tiring, we can take turns carrying him on our backs," Kit said, adding under her breath, "it won't be the first time." Though Raistlin resembled his sister, especially his deep brown eyes, he had none of her wiry strength.

The early morning was warm, with the songs of birds returning from their winter migrations carried on welcome breezes. Kit felt her spirits lift as she headed toward the ancient bridge that spanned Solace Stream. They soon veered off the road. Gilon knew a shortcut through the forest that lined the edge of Crystalmir Lake, one that would help them reach their destination more quickly.

Before long, the three of them emerged from the shadows of the vallenwoods into less wooded, hilly country. Raist continued to trod ahead of Kitiara and Gilon, showing no signs that his energy was flagging. He really must be excited about this, Kit thought to herself.

Three quarters of an hour passed with very little conversation between them. Single file, they followed a narrow, pebbly path that snaked through the tall yellow grass and wildflowers that heralded spring. Little crawling creatures scuttled across the path in front of them, and wild game flew up out of nowhere. The land was beautiful, and its natural harmony had a blissful effect on the travelers.

Kit was daydreaming about her father when a loud declaration from Raist jolted her back to the present. Raist was skipping between Kit and Gilon, tugging at their sleeves and exclaiming as he pointed. "Look, look, there it is! The school!"

A rocky outcropping had risen out of the contoured landscape the same way a small island seems to appear, without warning, out of the sea. A moment before, they hadn't seen it. The glare of the sun meant they had to shade their eyes. The rocks formed a steep hill, its dimensions lost in the haze of the sun. It was bleached of color, its sides littered with limestone boulders, its top obscured from view. Kitiara had to blink to be certain of what she was seeing.

"That's it! That's it! Can't you see?" Raist demanded with obvious exasperation.

Coming closer, Kit and Gilon saw what Raistlin meant: the pale stonework facade of an entrance so artfully blended in with its surroundings as to be almost invisible to passers-by. With such subterfuge, the master mage both ensured his school's exclusivity and protected his students against potential acts of ill will from a local population that, like most sensible people on Krynn, viewed magic with skepticism, mistrust, or plain hostility.

Gilon's upturned face showed how impressed the woodcutter was with the unusual site. For his part, Raist betrayed no awe. If anything, the child wore a smug expression, as if nothing would surprise him about this place.

The mage school was built into the hill, camouflaged by rocks and the sparse vegetation that clung to them. Parts of the edifice could be glimpsed, close up, between the boulders and scrub. Kitiara looked up and saw something that made her wonder how she had missed it before. At regular intervals, ducks and other water fowl were alighting on top of the rocky hill, which led her to think there must be some sort of concealed pond there.

As they stopped a few yards away, they heard a low rumbling and, with amazing fluidity, the massive front door swung open. Someone had opened it without the slightest signal from them! Following Raist inside, Kit had to elbow Gilon, whose mouth was impolitely agape. The door boomed shut behind them.

They found themselves at the head of a corridor sided with smooth alabaster that gently spiraled upward in a clockwise direction. The corridor had no obvious light source. Illumination seemed to emanate from the pale, gray stone itself. Raistlin was already walking ahead. Gilon and Kit hastened to keep up. The winding hallway was lined with iron doors, all tightly shut, but Raistlin passed them by without so much as a glance. He seemed certain of his destination.

They continued up the spiraling corridor for ten minutes, passing twenty-seven doors by Kit's reckoning. At last they came to the top—or at least to the end of the curious hallway. In front of them stood an impressive set of double iron doors, the black metal decorated with runes and elaborate scrollwork.

Kit found herself holding back and drawing closer to Gilon. Her little brother had reached the doors first, but seemed reluctant to knock. He stood in front of them, leaning forward slightly, straining to perceive what waited for him beyond. It was left to Gilon, who stepped up next to his son a few seconds later, to knock forthrightly.

Kit waited, fidgeting impatiently, no longer out of any nervousness, but because she was getting annoyed at whoever or whatever was putting them through this rigmarole. It was all quite obviously designed to intimidate visitors.

The three of them—a roughly dressed, burly woodcutter; a young, undersized six-year-old; and this slender teenager with her dark cap of curly hair—waited with varying attitudes, but with one feeling in common, impatience. For a long time the inner door, unlike the outer, showed no response to their presence.

Finally the iron hinges creaked and the double door swung inward. Gilon, Raist, and Kitiara stepped forward into a large circular room without any windows or lamplight. Every inch of the walls was lined with shelves, and the shelves groaned with books—hundreds of portentous, leather-bound tomes; hundreds more ordinary volumes with numerical indices; one entire wall of slim pamphlets and sheaves of neatly ordered essays; another wall of yellowed, crumbling manuscripts, stacked and tied neatly in ribbons; and rows upon rows upon more rows of diaries and journals.

Hazy light filtered in through a translucent, domed ceiling. Not until she gazed upward and saw a pikeshead swim by outside, tailfin wiggling, did Kit realize that this room lay beneath the pond at the top of the camouflaged hill.

An immense wooden table stood in the center of the room, a hooded figure seated behind it, waiting. The hood that shadowed his face was the color of the bleached boulders strewn over his hill, which as any youngster on Krynn knew, was a sign that the master mage was aligned with the forces of good.

Abruptly the mage slipped off his hood, revealing steel gray, close-cropped hair and beard. Black eyes glinted at the visitors.

"I am Morath. I ought to bid you welcome to my humble repository of learning, except that you have arrived without invitation and—" here Morath sighed, wearily flicking one of his hands "—I have no idle time to waste on uninvited guests. So instead I bid you state your business and go."

Gilon squared his shoulders and stepped forward.

"If you please, sir, I am Gilon Majere of nearby Solace. I wish to enter my son, Raistlin Majere, in your school of magic, whose reputation is well known in this vicinity. I know he is rather young, but he has already shown both interest and aptitude for your art. When he was not quite five, he was able to learn and copy the tricks a traveling magician performed at the Red Moon Fair."

Gilon's confidence had soared as he gave his little speech. By the end, he was fairly glowing with fatherly enthusiasm.

"Well!" With noticeable sarcasm, Morath hurled the word in Gilon's direction, ignoring the small child standing near his father. "Copied some roving trickster, did he? A prodigy, is he? No, I think not. I beg to differ. Mere sleight of hand has nothing to do with true magic. A ready pupil would know that."

The master mage had turned his gaze on Raistlin's pale, oval face. Unflinching, Raist returned the stare. Kit admired her little brother's temerity.

Raistlin had been chattering about magic off and on over the past year, asking questions Kit often was unable to answer. He had brought the subject up with anyone within earshot, even his mother. Kit knew Raistlin felt proud of the simple illusions he had managed to pick up. She knew that he was fascinated by the possibilities and power of greater magic. And she despised this mage for treating him like a clod.

As she had once fought to save his life as a newborn, now Kit concentrated on mentally supporting her little brother in this uneven contest of wills. She couldn't be sure, but she thought she detected a hint of curiosity in Morath's stern expression as Raist refused to back down and continued to meet his piercing gaze.

"Even if it were proof of anything," Morath went on matter-of-factly, "I require all applicants to be at least eight years of age and to be able to read difficult and obscure texts with ease. This is not a school for reading fundamentals. This boy is too small. Too young. He would lag behind the others, some of whom are already, in many ways, young men."

Gilon was about to respond, when Raistlin piped up in his own defense. "I can read," he said simply. "I can read anything."

Morath looked annoyed. He rose from his seat and strode to a nearby shelf, pausing for a moment before pull-

ing out one of the larger, more auspicious tomes. He handed
it to Raistlin, who staggered briefly under its weight. The
six-year-old sat down on the floor, crosslegged, with the
book straddling his lap. Then he looked up at the master
mage for instructions.

"Turn to the third chapter," Morath commanded, "and
start reading the fourth paragraph down. Proper enuncia-
tion, please."

With some difficulty, Raistlin opened the musty book
and turned to its lengthy table of contents. Completely absorbed in his task, he ran his finger down the table, located
the chapter's page number, and turned to it. Again he used
his finger to find the paragraph, then began reading in his
reedy voice.

"*A mage turns his body into a conductor of energy
streams and currents from all zones of existence. Through
correct incantations, he is able to draw in certain forces or
combination of forces, and then to reshape and redirect
them as he wishes . . .*"

Morath watched Raist intently. Kit thought the master
mage was contriving to conceal his reaction. The ranks of
mages were thin enough these days; she imagined he could
ill afford to turn away any pupil. Yet magic-users were notoriously arrogant and did not act out of necessity or logic.
Morath's criteria would have to be met. Resolutely, Raist
read on.

"That's enough," Morath said curtly, snatching the book
out of the boys hands and replacing it on the shelf.

Interrupted in midsentence, Raist looked up, startled. His
eyes were wide with irritation, Kit could tell. She knew her
lookalike eyes betrayed the same reaction. Gilon was off to
one side, his big hands dangling awkwardly at his sides, silent and unsure as to how to act.

Morath circled the wide room, his face fraught with annoyance. He fingered certain books as he brushed up
against the shelves. Deep in concentration, he virtually ignored the three visitors who tensely awaited his next move.
Kit and Gilon looked at each other uncertainly.

The filtered sunlight from above bathed the master mage in a golden glow as he passed Kit. For a moment, before his stern features came under shadow again, Kit had a less fearsome impression of Morath.

"Answer me this," the master mage said suddenly, turning to address Raistlin who was still sitting crosslegged on the floor. Raist stood expectantly. "What do you suppose is the nickname of this place, a name I am not supposed to know but which is used, familiarly, by all the aspiring mages behind my back?

A sliver of a smile, not altogether unfriendly in its effect, played on Morath's lips as he bent in Raistlin's direction.

"Why it's the mage school, that's all," blurted out Gilon.

Kitiara shot her stepfather a withering glance. Gilon's face wilted, realizing he had blundered.

"No, no," said Morath contemptuously. "Let the boy answer."

A moment of silence followed, as Morath's eyes met Raistlin's. Again, the little boy did not flinch, but withstood the master mage's direct gaze.

"There's nothing fancy about it, nothing secret," said Morath with mock congeniality. "But only those who are privileged to study here learn of it. Concentrate, boy. Take a guess. Or do you give up?"

Old Hilltop, Kitiara guessed to herself.

Raistlin took his time before responding. "Hilltop would be the obvious choice," he said finally, speaking slowly, "and—"

"Wrong! Wrong!" cackled Morath, straightening up. He was a trifle obvious in his glee.

"You didn't let me finish!" snapped Raistlin, raising his voice most disrespectfully. Gilon winced. Kitiara had to repress a smile.

"And that is why, I was saying, they probably invented some name like Poolbottom or Drywater. I don't see why it's important, or much of a test," Raist finished sulkily.

"It's not important!" Morath snapped back, raising his voice and baring his teeth. "I didn't say it was important!"

The master mage swirled his robe and retreated to the double iron doors with an angry flourish. "You may leave now," he commanded.

Their faces glum, the three trooped toward the entrance, but Morath stepped in front of Raist, who was last, blocking his movement.

"Not you," he said decisively. When the others looked at him for some explanation, Morath said with obvious pique, "It *is* Poolbottom. Poolbottom! Stupid name. If a six-year-old can guess it, then it may as well be Dungdeep!"

With a shrug, the master mage yanked a pullcord that hung next to the doors. One of the massive bookshelves swung open like a sluice gate to reveal an annex tucked behind it, rectangular and sparsely furnished with a modest table and two ordinary chairs. Paper and writing implements rested on the table, along with a couple of books.

Morath turned Raistlin around and gave him a push toward the small interior room. He turned back to Gilon and Kit, who were boggle-eyed.

"I need to conduct a more detailed examination," Morath announced authoritatively. "Return at dusk." Unceremoniously, the master mage slammed the double doors in their faces.

Kit was fuming. "Who does that gully dwarf of a wizard think he is? I don't think we should leave Raist here."

But most of this was muttered helplessly, for Gilon had firmly grasped his stepdaughter by the arm and steered her down the winding corridor and out of the mage school called Poolbottom at a rapid pace.

"It will be a good thing for Raistlin to learn this ancient art," Gilon said gently, letting go of her outside. "It means a lot to him. To that end we can afford to ignore Morath's inhospitality. Let's use this time to visit the fair back in Solace."

Kit glared around at nothing in particular before shrugging. In truth, spending half a day on her own would be a treat. Her mood started to lift the minute she put one foot in front of the other, walking toward Solace and this year's

Red Moon Fair.

At a small rise, she paused and turned back to look at the mage school. She was not surprised that she could barely make out the shape of the white, rocky hill, which was almost invisible under the glare of the late morning sun.

Kit looked at Gilon, standing alongside her, not speaking. He was not at all like her real father. Despite that, and despite the fact she had no respect for woodcutting and no liking for the humdrum life Gilon lived, Kit appreciated her stepfather's solicitude for the twins. And she appreciated the fact that he had never tried to boss her around. Gilon was not, when all was said and done, entirely stupid.

Sighing deeply, Kit said, in pinched tones that perfectly mimicked the mage's, "Poolbottom! Might as well be Dungdeep!"

Kit turned her roguish grin on Gilon, and they both started laughing.

The day was perfect. The outlines of trees stripped bare by the winter winds were already feathered with a faint, pure green. Kitiara and Gilon kept a companionable silence as they headed for the fairgrounds on the north edge of Solace. The sound reached them first, like the energetic hum of some elaborate gnome creation. Then they topped the crest of a hill and saw the brightly colored flags and tents.

The festival grounds started just off the road about a mile beyond the foot of the hill where they stood. It spread out from there like a small town, with grassy promenades lined with tents and booths instead of houses. Scattered throughout were small clearings where the various demonstrations and entertainments took place.

As she and Gilon started down the road, Kit scanned the crowd approaching the grounds, ever hopeful that she would spot a dark, curly-haired man who stood a head taller than most, and who, when he saw his daughter after all these years, would beam with paternal pride.

Instead, she spied a black-robed mage gliding through the throng, easy enough to spot given the way people made way for him. She saw a kender family, the father puzzling over a map, the mother watching her little girl with pride. Kit smiled to herself as she observed the little one, who was jumping up and down and clapping her hands at every new sight, picking up stones, pieces of paper—and a shiny bauble here and there, whether or not it was somebody else's property.

Complex, savory smells wafted from several nearby booths. It was not yet midday, but the early morning trek had left Kit with a gnawing hunger. Her growling stomach distracted her from the sights and sounds. When she stopped to search her pack for any leftover crumbs of bread or cheese, Kit realized Gilon was no longer at her side. A minute later, he reappeared, carrying two steaming bowls of goat meat stew.

"I thought you might be hungry," Gilon said simply, handing her a bowl. Kit smiled at him in thanks, and they made their way out of the stream of people to a bench that sat in the shade of an oak tree.

"I thought I'd find you at the festival, but I expected it would be at the sword-fighting exhibition, not lazing under the shade of this old tree."

The voice at her back was good-natured, teasing. Kit looked over her shoulder to see Aureleen, well-turned out as usual, wearing a flowing petal-colored gown. Her figure had blossomed over the last year, and she was no longer a mere girl, but practically a young lady. As different as their natures were, Kit was always glad to see her friend.

"Hello, Master Majere," Aureleen said, smiling prettily at Gilon.

Kit watched as her stepfather rose a little awkwardly, obviously charmed as well as discomfited.

"Er, would you like to join us?" Gilon asked. "Can I get you a bowl of stew?"

"Oh, no. I really don't have much of an appetite," Aureleen said, shaking her strawberry blond curls. "I don't know where Kitiara puts all that food she eats."

"The same place you 'put' those fried doughwheels you

buy at the baker's every day," Kit muttered under her breath, just loud enough for Aureleen to hear. The two girls burst out laughing, joined in a minute by Gilon, who didn't quite comprehend the joke, but was enjoying the high spirits.

Kit had already finished off her goat stew. Now she stood.

"Aureleen and I are going to go off and find some, er, jugglers," Kit said to Gilon abruptly. A look of conspiracy crossed her friend's face. "I'll meet you at the crossroads outside the festival in four hours, to go back and get Raist. OK?"

Gilon, chewing a mouthful of stew, could only nod good-naturedly and wave them away.

"Mmmm, jugglers. Ah, yes, now where could those exciting fellows be?" Aureleen teased, smiling over her shoulder at Gilon as the two girls strolled off, arm and arm.

They hadn't gone far, sauntering through the crowd and laughing, when another familiar voice brought them up short.

"Aureleen! We were supposed to meet at the dressmaker's booth an hour ago." Aureleen's mother, hands on her hips, stood in front of the two friends. Unlike Aureleen, she was a homely woman with brown wavy hair and a downturned mouth. While her daughter wore finery, she usually dressed in plain household smocks.

Kitiara thought, as she often did when she encountered Aureleen's mother, that her best friend must have gotten her looks from her father's side of the family. He was a hard worker with a handsome, craggy face and an omnipresent twinkle in his eye.

"Oh, hello, Kitiara."

Kit recognized the edge of coolness in the greeting. Aureleen's mother had never fully approved of her daughter's friendship with Kit, offspring of "that irresponsible warrior and his poor, crazy wife—before he left her."

Aureleen shrugged and winked at Kit almost imperceptibly, before turning to placate her mother. Grasping the older woman by the elbow, she began steering her through the festival-goers toward the dressmaker's booth. "I was coming to meet you, Mother, when Kit and I ran into Minna. You know what a talker she is, but you did teach me never to be rude to adults. Anyway . . ."

As they moved out of Kit's hearing, Aureleen turned and gave Kit an apologetic little wave.

Now she was truly alone for the day. Well, good. Kit had little enough solitude.

On her own, Kit drifted away from the noise and crowds of the festival toward the commons adjacent to the fairgrounds, where the hundreds of itinerant visitors traveling to Solace for the event pitched camp. The grassy area was dotted with tents, lean-tos, boarded wagons, bedrolls, and hammocks. People congregated in groups, talking and laughing loudly, sharing drinks and food—peddlers and merchants, wandering minstrels, honest as well as dishonest tradesmen, illusionists, hucksters and the occasional warrior whose only allegiance was to the highest purse.

Kit moved away from a gaunt cleric who was standing on a tree stump and declaiming loudly to anyone who would listen about the power and omnipotence of the new gods. Few were listening to him, and Kitiara always gave clerics a wide berth.

She walked aimlessly around the perimeter of the commons, searching people's faces and clothing for clues as to where they came from and where they were going.

The people here were more interesting to Kit than the wares and amusements of the festival. She realized she was in a part of the campground where more drink was imbibed than food eaten, and fairgoers had to be careful of their purse and their person—or risk finding themselves with a cracked skull and empty pockets. But Kit already had empty pockets and was confident she could take care of herself in a tight situation. At the very least, she could run.

Kitiara was about to turn around when the sound of a harsh laugh and muffled argument caught her attention. To her right, between two storage tents, Kit saw four persons huddled together, talking heatedly. Some sixth sense told her to sneak closer and eavesdrop on their conversation.

Creeping forward, Kit made her way inside one of the tents until only a thin sheet of canvas separated her from the group. Through a tear she could see there were four men, mercenaries by the looks of their clothing and weapons. One of them, whom she could only glimpse from the side, seemed distinctly familiar.

"I say we don't kill him. We kidnap him and later ransom him back. That way we can double the payoff."

"No! Forget the ransom. We're not supposed to kill him and we're not supposed to kidnap him. I tell you, the payroll will be plenty. Plenty for all of us, and no complications, nothing to regret."

The first voice was a whiny one. The second—Kit knew she had heard that voice before, but where? She shifted her position, but couldn't get a good look at any of their faces, which were turned in a narrow circle toward each other. And she could only catch some of the words because the men spoke in low voices.

"How far is this spot?" asked a third man, his voice deep and mellifluous.

"About six days to the north," replied the familiar voice. "I have the directions, but we have to keep off the roads. I figure six days, at least, which will give us time to set the trap. According to our informant—"

A guffaw of laughter from the whiny one made everyone pause.

"According to our informant, Gwathmey's son has to make the delivery himself, on time and according to contract. So there will be no deviation in the schedule or the route."

"I still say, if we ask for ransom, we'll double—" began the whiny voice.

"Forget it, Radisson," said the deep-voiced conspirator with some authority. "Ursa is right. We do it his way."

Kit's heart leapt. Of course! It was the rogue she had met that long-ago day when Rosamun gave birth to the twins—

Ursa Il Kinth. What was he up to?

Obviously the third voice had cast the deciding vote.

"Then it's agreed," Kit heard Ursa say. "We will gather at midnight three days hence, out beyond the oak tree grove on the north side of town. We will ride an hour or two by moonlight, until we are safe beyond the town and farms. After that, we can make camp."

Another pause followed, then Ursa concluded, "Now break up, keep away from each other, and until then, stay out of trouble."

After some grumbling from the whiny-voiced one, Radisson, the group split up. Kit crouched behind a crate, giving them some time to scatter. Then she dashed outside the tent and glanced around frantically. The others had melted into the crowds and campsites, but she was lucky enough to catch sight of Ursa's broad back and tall shape some distance away.

Racing after him, Kit trailed Ursa for several minutes as he weaved through campsites without speaking to anyone. She had to be sure Ursa was alone. At last, when she was sure, she caught up to him and fell into step.

After thirty paces or so, Ursa finally noticed the little female figure in the green tunic and brown leggings walking alongside him. Nodding curtly in her direction, Ursa quickened his pace. Because of his long legs, Kit had to jog to keep up. After a minute they had reached the far south fringe of the commons, where there was a makeshift stable. Few other people gathered in that area.

Deciding that the risk was minimal, Kit called out his name, a bit breathlessly. "Ursa Il Kinth."

He turned slowly, legs apart, hand on the hilt of a dagger in his belt, to confront this strange girl.

"You must be mistaken," he said warningly. "I don't know you."

"I have no apple to offer you today, but I have something better," Kit bantered with a grin.

Ursa stared at her uneasily, as if recognizing someone he hadn't expected to see. He recovered his composure quickly and let out a bark of laughter. "You!" He reached over and gave Kit a "friendly" cuff on the ears. "Why you've grown up—some anyway!"

"I've grown up a lot," she said, bridling.

He laughed, his eyes appraising her. "So you have," he said. "But what could Gregor Uth Matar's daughter have to interest me?" he asked. His tone was dismissive, though his eyes were friendly.

"Quick-witted help."

"I have all the wits I need. Thank you, young *lady*." Ursa drew out the word mockingly.

"You may, indeed, but what about your three companions? Robbery and kidnapping are serious business, and it might do to have someone along with brains as well as fighting skills."

Ursa grabbed her by the arm, all traces of amusement vanished from his face. "My three friends have brains enough not to shout out their plans in a busy campground," he snarled at her, looking over his shoulder to see if anyone had overheard.

He dragged her closer to the roped-off stable, then leaned into her face threateningly. "What do you know?" Ursa demanded, maintaining his rough grip on her.

"Little enough, and that's the truth," she said furiously, trying to shake off his grip and staring back at him in kind. "But I know you'd have to be a fool to turn me down. I've got skill with a sword and I'm no dunce like, like . . . Radisson!"

He glared at her in outraged silence.

"Make me part of the gang," she insisted.

Ursa snorted. "My partners are greedy. They would not look kindly on dividing the pot with one more person, especially—" he ground out the word "—a *girl*. Forget what you heard. Forget Radisson. And I'll do you the favor of forgetting we had this little chat."

His eyes softened slightly. "Ask me again the next time we meet," said Ursa, stepping back from her. "They say the third time's the charm. Until then, farewell, Kitiara."

Ursa gave a shout. His horse, the same muscular gray that Kit remembered from years earlier, detached itself from a cluster in the roped-off pen, easily leapt over the makeshift fence, and trotted up to the mercenary. Ursa swung smoothly up onto the horse's unsaddled back—just like before—and was gone.

Kit stood for a minute looking after him, rubbing her arm ruefully. Unlike the last time they'd met, she knew where to find Ursa now, and when. Clenching her hands at her sides, she slowly turned back toward the fair, toward the crossroads where she was to meet Gilon.

Chapter 5

Raistlin's Examination

FOR CARAMON, IT WAS A GOOD DAY. ALL MORNING HIS
mother baked batches of sunflower seed muffins, and he
helped. Well, sort of. He attached himself to Rosamun,
chattering like a monkey, and every time she was through
with a mixing spoon or bowl, he licked it clean. His face
and little tunic were splotched with batter; there were
streaks of the honey-brown stuff in his hair. And when the
muffins were done, he helped out by eating twelve or seven-
teen of them. Caramon wasn't keeping track—he wasn't so
good at counting anyway.

After this major effort, his stomach started to feel
stuffed.

"Owwwww," he said, rubbing his round belly. "Mother,
don't you think going outside and playing might make me

feel better?" He grinned at his frail mother, who smiled back sunnily. Rosamun was in the best possible mood.

"Fine, dear, just don't wander too far. I have a little sewing and straightening up to do, and I don't think that would help your stomach at all."

Remembering his vow to look after her, Caramon glanced over his shoulder to make sure his mother was fine before heading out the door. Rosamun was humming to herself as she cleaned up the pots and utensils that were scattered around the kitchen.

Outside, the six-year-old climbed down a rope ladder to the area just below their cottage, where he and Raist sometimes played, within earshot of home. Nobody else was nearby, although the occasional wayfarer could be spotted through the vallenwood trunks on the main road. Stomping around, Caramon kicked away sticks and stones and cleared a space for digging.

He hunted around and found several big sticks that he judged suitable for use as picks and wedges and makeshift shovels. He knew he needed a good supply, because they tended to break.

For about an hour Caramon was thoroughly happy digging for buried treasure (he had been told by his father that treasure could be located, sometimes, in the most unlikely places). After which time the little boy stood, sweat-drenched and covered with scratches and dirt, up to his waist in a hole that was almost two feet deep. He surveyed his work with satisfaction. He hadn't found any treasure, but he was still optimistic.

Just as Caramon was going to resume digging, a horde of little boys his own age, some of whom he knew from school, went running and shouting by on their way to somewhere.

"Where you going?" called Caramon to one he recognized.

"Crab apple war!" replied the boy, a freckled lad of eight, taking the opportunity to stop and catch his breath. "Come on!"

"Yeah! But don't bring that droopy brother of yours!" added another boy, who screeched to a halt, almost bowling the first one over.

Caramon scampered up the rope ladder to check on Rosamun. He found her on the small porch outside the cottage, sitting in a chair next to a pile of clothes, basking in the sun as she hemmed a dress. With a smile on her face, his mother waved him off unconcernedly.

He hurried to catch up with the gang of boys, who had gathered around a little thicket of trees some ten minutes away from Caramon's home. Tiny, firm green crab apples hung from the low-slung branches, and the boys had picked and collected dozens of them in piles on the ground. They stuffed this "ammunition" into their pockets and pouches and backpacks, while carrying as many as possible in each hand.

"There you are Caramon. Hurry up! You be commander of our side," shouted one group of the boys, who had divided up into two armies.

Caramon, who was greatly liked—as opposed to his twin brother—and greatly feared in war games, was chosen over a number of eight -and even ten-year-old candidates. Indeed, the other "general," a hulking ten-year-old named Ranelagh, was two heads taller than Caramon.

Taking up their positions at opposite ends of the crab apple thicket, the two sides rushed each other at the agreed upon signal. Caramon was in the forefront of his army, which numbered about a half-dozen boys, yelling and directing them.

"Willem, you go around that way. Lank, watch your backside. Wolf, take some of those crab apples and get up in that tree."

He led the charges, throwing the little crab apples as quickly and hard as he could. Caramon had a good arm, and he nimbly dodged the hail of apples that hurtled in his direction. The object was to land as many of the missiles as possible, and then to retreat before being whacked on the shoulder, shins or, worse, noggin. It was not a game for the fainthearted.

The crab apple war went on most of the afternoon. There were occasional defections, when a boy had to quit and go home, and occasional time outs when everyone took a break and sprawled around, taking bites out of the sour fruit. But mostly it was attack, retreat, attack, retreat, attack, retreat, over and over, until the sun was waning.

Caramon had proved himself a worthy and brave tactician. More than the other boys he was dotted with bumps and bruises from well-aimed crab apples, not to mention pieces of pulp and gobs of juice. During the time outs, the commander had sampled a few too many of the crab apples, so his stomach was kind of hurting again.

He and Ranelagh, who had a good-sized, bloody bulge on his forehead owing to one of Caramon's better throws, decided that the war was a draw. They shook hands on a truce.

"It was a good fight. May we do battle again some day," said Caramon with the gravity he imagined a real warrior would feel at the end of a fiercely fought combat. Then he let out a whoop, setting off loud cheers by survivors on both sides.

Realizing that it was almost suppertime, and that he had been gone for a good part of the day, Caramon tried to hurry along toward home, half skipping, half running. He was sore and tired and, in truth, getting a little hungry again. His clothes were torn; shaggy, golden brown hair was plastered against his brow. Dried cookie batter, dirt, crab apple sludge, cuts, scrapes, and purple bruises told the tale of his eventful day.

As Caramon came around a bend within sight of the high vallenwood that bore his home, he heard a distinctly feminine scream for help. He immediately thought of his mother, but the cry came from another direction, near a clump of smaller trees, not from his cottage.

Running over, he saw a girl about his own age, standing and looking up toward the higher reaches of one of the trees. She was cute and dimpled, but her face was marred by tears. Looking up, too, Caramon saw that a small tabby was lodged in the branches near the very top of the tree.

"My kitty!" the girl said, pointing upward for Caramon's benefit. "My kitty is stuck in that tree!"

Caramon looked up again, a frown on his face. He was awfully tired, and the tree looked awfully high.

"It's such a tall tree," the girl continued, turning to give Caramon the full benefit of her pleading expression. "I would climb it myself, except that I can't reach the branches to get started. My kitty's name is Cirque. I'm afraid he's going to be stuck up there forever." She started to wail, then quieted to a few sobs and sniffles. Caramon stood there awkwardly, wanting to comfort her but not knowing what to do.

"You look like a good climber. Do you think you could get him?"

Caramon puffed out his chest a bit, his hunger and tiredness fleeing in the face of her appealing gaze. He looked up at the mewing tabby again. Then the little boy hitched his pants manfully, got a good grip on one of the bottom branches, and began to haul himself upward.

* * * * *

After Kitiara and Gilon had left, the master mage followed Raistlin into the small, spartan annex and bade him sit in one of the chairs. Then Morath summoned a young man, dressed in simple workman's clothes, who took instructions that the master mage not be interrupted for the duration of the morning. The man, evidently some sort of servant, nodded and left, closing the door to the library as he did.

From behind that door, Raist occasionally heard the muffled comings and goings of Morath's students, who availed themselves of the library's resources. Their conversations were whispered. Doubtless they were not anxious to disturb the master mage. Raistlin guessed that most of their studies took place in the rooms that lined the long, winding corridor.

The room Morath and Raistlin occupied was as nondescript as could be—limestone walls, with no windows, color, or decorations. The strategy, even little Raist realized, was to minimize distractions and to focus concentration. Morath interrogated him for several hours, until well past midday. His questions seemed to be, not tricky, but openended and philosophical in nature. Perhaps there were no right answers.

In any case Morath appeared every bit as interested in Raist's reaction to the questions as he was in what might be the correct response. The master mage's black eyes bore into the small boy relentlessly. Raistlin, who had gone without lunch, grew increasingly dizzy and hungry, but he fought to stay alert.

"For a mere child, you speak well," Morath said grudgingly at one point, "but let us talk some more about good and evil. A mage must study and understand both. Not only the obvious—the differences—but the similarities, as well. What is the kinship between them? How would you, Raistlin, define evil?"

Any other six-year-old would have been out of his element in such a discussion; certainly Caramon would have scratched his head in bewilderment. But Raist was a solitary boy, physically weak and wary of playmates, and he had spent many hours alone, pondering just such matters. Especially since last year, when he had first observed and learned some rudimentary magic at the Red Moon Fair.

At first the little boy had imagined that he would become a good wizard, battling villains and dread creatures run amok, using his mind and his abilities the same way Caramon so easily mastered athletic and fighting skills. Mages dedicated to neutrality intrigued Raist, though at this point in time he knew little enough about them. Certainly he had thought a lot about evil, as the enemy of good.

"I think it would be a mistake to define evil too precisely or simply," said Raistlin thoughtfully, his voice thin and tired-sounding, despite his best efforts. "But whatever else it is, it is the opposite of good, and so to know it, we must also know good."

"A clever and sensible reply," said the mage tersely. "But tell me this, how would we define it in the absence of good?"

"Well," said Raist with a frown, "there can be no true absence of good, nor of evil really. One cannot exist without the other. They are in a kind of balance, counterpoint, with each other at all times. One might be dominant, the other dormant, but never truly absent."

"Can you think of no example of evil?" asked the master mage.

"No pure example . . . except, of course, the gods of darkness," the boy added hastily.

Morath looked satisfied. "Then how do we recognize evil?" he persisted.

"Its disguises are infinite."

"Yet a mage must strive to recognize and identify evil, both in himself and his magic, and as regards others."

"Yes," agreed Raist. "One must study its manifest forms. More than most—" he paused and searched for the proper words "—a mage does learn to recognize evil. One who wears the white robe would identify it as anathema. A black robe would know it as an ally."

"And a red robe?"

"Hmm," said Raistlin, his voice pitifully weary. "I'm not sure. I guess I would say that a red robe ought to know it as part of himself."

For the past several minutes Morath's eyes had narrowed, intrigued. Indeed, the master mage had stopped pacing and taken a seat on the other wooden chair for the first time since the hours of questioning had begun. Now he leaned forward and emitted a short, barking laugh.

"Hah!" Morath exclaimed. "Very clever. Superficial, I should think, but exceedingly clever for a six-year-old boy!"

Raistlin seized on the brief moment of amity to ask for a break. He was eager for Morath's approval, but sensed he did not have it. "Please sir," Raist asked respectfully, "may I have some water and eat my lunch now?"

Immediately Morath's harsh demeanor returned. He stood up briskly and moved away from the table. Then he turned, folded his arms, and glared at the small, hungry boy.

"Mages must be able to devote hours at a time to their studies, whether they're hungry or not," Morath advised. "If you cannot bear up through one day of simple tests, then you are too young, too much of a child, to begin your studies."

Raist, sitting there all shrunken up with fatigue and hunger, his little-boy face wan and pinched, his eyes watering, refused to apologize. "If that is your answer," he said petulantly, "then let us proceed. I assume you won't penalize me for the mere asking."

In fact, Morath was a little hungry himself, though he hated to admit it. He usually broke at midday and ate a modest lunch in the company of his favorite students. But he had found himself determined to confound this little boy who had an answer to every question. Even if the answers were sometimes unusual, the master mage had to admit they were well considered. He was as impressed as he was irritated by the boy's gravity and defiance, his self-control and refusal to knuckle under.

"Perhaps this would be a good time to break," Morath relented finally. "I will have a tray brought in to you, supplementing whatever you have carried with you on your trek from Solace. In the meantime, I must leave you alone and go check on my students."

The master mage opened the door into the library and, before leaving, hesitated and turned to Raistlin. "You have ten minutes," he said. "No more."

* * * * *

Raistlin ate his lunch quickly, barely managing to wash it down with the cool, foamy drink brought by the young man in workman's garb, before Morath returned.

The master mage stood in the doorway and harrumphed, then with a gesture indicated that Raistlin should come into the library proper. Following Morath into that vast circular room with its poolbottom light and shelves of books after spending hours in the cramped annex, Raist felt revitalized and excited.

His heart thumped wildly against his rib cage. This wondrous library, so different from anything he had known in Solace—how he longed to read all of these books, to study the ancient arts here! Raistlin gazed at the books as another child might gaze longingly at a plate of sweets.

Morath pointed Raistlin toward a chair. He went to a shelf and picked out several tomes, three of which he set before Raist. One other, an ancient leather-bound volume, he placed next to his own chair, across from Raist.

"Open that gilt-embossed book in front of you and turn to page twenty-five."

Raistlin was disappointed to see that the book in question appeared to contain basic numerical equations. Dutifully, he began to read. The minutes stretched on. Morath said nothing, merely sat across from the boy, watching him closely. When Raist peeked over the top of the pages, the master mage seemed almost to be dozing. At least his eyes were hooded.

A discreet knock on the door interrupted Morath's reverie. Muttering a few words under his breath, the master mage stood and bade whoever it was to enter. The door swung open, although how it operated, whether mechanically or magically, Raist could not be sure. In any case, the boy was not supposed to be paying any attention. He was supposed to be reading, so all of his looks were furtive ones.

A plump boy about Kitiara's age, dressed in the gray robes of an apprentice mage, came in. Obviously one of the students, the boy seemed very much in awe of the master mage as he struggled to find his voice.

"Master," the boy began tentatively. "Alekno is having, er, trouble with the invisibility spell. He has been able to make his legs disappear, but unfortunately that is all. Now it seems that he cannot make them re-appear. We have tried to aid him, but cannot tell what he is doing wrong. Would you advise us?"

"Alekno's habitual failure to pay attention during his instruction results in just this sort of difficulty," responded Morath snappishly. "He is fortunate not to be facing a horde of combative minotaurs or some other situation where he might really need to disappear. I am tempted to let him stay half-invisible, if only for a day or two. Teach him to listen next time."

The plump boy shifted uneasily on his feet, uncertain of how to respond, a plaintive look on his face.

"Oh well," said Morath with irritation. He rose and headed toward the door, muttering and grumbling. At the threshold he turned back toward Raist. "Continue. I expect to be back shortly."

As instructed, Raistlin kept going. Laboriously the boy turned the pages, reading with his finger from top to bottom, left to right, doing his best to understand and remember the tables described in the text. These included basic arithmetic and measurements, as well as sophisticated equivalents, angles and degrees, and component breakdowns. Raistlin continued reading until almost an hour had passed, and still the master mage did not return.

All the rote mental exercises made the boy drowsy. Understanding numerical configurations would be helpful for certain spells and situations, Raist supposed, but he had to yawn as he turned the last page of the book and closed its gilt cover.

Still there was no sign of Morath, nor any echo of noise from the other side of the library door where he had disappeared. The late afternoon sun seeping in from above was no longer so pleasant, and the light in the library had grown amber and murky. Reinforced by the silence, it was almost eerie in its effect.

With a sigh, Raistlin reached for one of the other two books that the master mage had set aside for him, the one with a wrinkly cover and crumbly pages. Immediately he realized it was a geography tome, studded with detailed maps of the many familiar as well as obscure regions of Ansalon. There were crude climate charts, topography and elevation references, and soil descriptions, all of it painstakingly hand sketched and coded in colors.

Although not nearly as thick as the numbers book, this one, too, was hard slogging, and Raist turned the pages ever more slowly as time went on, and still the master mage did not return. By the end of another hour, Raistlin had finished the second book. After glancing around the room, which had become latticed with shadows, Raistlin diligently reached for the third and last book in front of him.

This one had a heavy cowhide cover that was banded with iron, and Raist had to use both hands to open it up. Inside, the vellum was very thin, its texture very fine, and upon it someone had transcribed an early history of the Silvanesti nation in tiny, elegant script. The penmanship crowded the margins, and the long, meticulous chronicle was divided into three equal and successive columns on each page.

The bleary-eyed little boy began to read the ancient history. Raist grew interested. He knew little about the tragic history of the elven race, and there were not so many pages really. But the writing was so minuscule and the ink so faded that he had to strain his eyes against the dying light. It wasn't long before his brave energy wilted and his head sagged down on the table. He was asleep.

Damp, clinging mists swirled up around Raist's chair. He was no longer in the library. Voices seemed to be whispering, just out of his hearing. Suddenly his mother appeared. "Come with me, dear," invited Rosamun. "I will be your guide"

The boy reached out eagerly to take her extended hand. The instant their fingers touched, however, Rosamun was transformed into a terrifying slime-covered creature that sucked Raistlin to its chest with an irresistible force. Panicked, he was enveloped in ooze. Desperately he fought against the suffocating sensation, struggling for air, gulping mouthfuls of the sickening stuff. He was drowning in slime!

Just as suddenly it evaporated. Now Raistlin was back home, perched on his mother's bed. He was in fact sharing her body, seeing with her eyes, breathing her tremulous breaths.

Kitiara was getting dinner ready. Caramon was idly flipping twigs into the fireplace. Gilon came in. Only it wasn't Gilon. This creature had horns and a huge head. It towered over Kitiara, brushing against the ceiling. A minotaur, Raist realized with a shudder.

It stormed to Rosamun's side. She screamed and tried to fight the beast-man off as he neatly trussed her—and Raist, in her body—in sheets. Kit and Caramon didn't appear to care or even to notice. While Rosamun screeched in protest, the minotaur carried her under its arm to the front door and heaved her to the ground.

Abruptly Raist was outside his mother's body and pulling himself up by the window ledge to peer inside the cottage. He saw the minotaur and Kit nod to each other conspiratorially. Looking more closely at his older sister, Raist saw that she looked different, changed. She was covered in armor made up of shimmering blue scales. When she opened her mouth, flames shot out. Around her waist was a scabbard with the wooden sword her father had bequeathed her. Only when she drew it forth, it was wooden no longer. The solid metal gleamed in the firelight. With her fearful sword, Kit advanced on the oblivious Caramon.

Raist clung to the window ledge, fascinated, unable to act. Finally he began pounding at the window with one arm, yelling a warning at his twin. Caramon didn't look up as Kit raised the sword above his head. Rosamun's shrieking could be heard behind him still. With horror, Raist watched Kit bring the sword down, slicing off Caramon's head. The bloody thing rolled toward the window, its eyes finally gaping at Raist. Calmly, with sorrow not rancor, Caramon's head asked, "Brother, why didn't you warn me?"

The words pierced Raistlin's heart. He collapsed on the ground, sobbing.

Raistlin jerked awake. He had fallen asleep! Flushed with humiliation, Raist's eyes swept the room, seeing with some relief that he was still alone.

It must be nearly suppertime, when Gilon and Kitiara would be coming back to get him. At least three hours had passed without a clue as to the whereabouts of the master mage. Where could Morath have gone for so long? And what was Raist supposed to do now?

All was silence. The library was virtually dark now, only a pale glow of light fell from above, illuminating the center of the room, slanting westward across part of the table. Opposite from where Raist sat, near Morath's chair, the light shone on the book that the master mage had picked out and set aside for himself.

Eyeing that book, Raist wondered what wisdom it contained. Drumming his fingers, the little boy reached across the table and, after standing on his chair, managed to tug the book closer to himself so that he could make out the words on its cover.

The History of the Present Up to the Moment, As Set Down by Astinus, said the auspicious lettering on the front.

The history of the present! Raist wondered how that could be and what this unusual book might say. He wondered about it so much, he was practically on fire with curiosity. But he sat there for another ten minutes without moving in the slightest.

Then, hearing and seeing nobody, Raistlin stood on the chair again and leaned across the table, touching the cover. He fingered the spine of the book, felt the raised lettering of its title, and caressed the crisp edge of its pages. His face had a intense, almost rapturous expression, as if he was concentrating on receiving some message through his fingertips.

"Ahem."

Raist was startled by the voice behind him and whirled to see the master mage standing there, frowning. Raistlin had not heard the library doors open and close, or Morath come

in. The master mage carried with him a flickering globe that
bathed the library in dancing yellow light. He glided
around to his chair and sat down, putting down the globe,
then pointedly reached across to bring the *Present History*
back to his side of the table.

"What have you been doing?" Morath demanded.

"Well," began Raist uncomfortably, sliding back into his
chair and looking up into Morath's fierce black eyes staring at
him. "I finished the book with all the numbers and equations
in it about two hours ago, so I started to read the other two
books you brought out for me, the ones about geography and
elven history. I finished them, too, and then—" Raist's voice
faltered "—I think I fell asleep for a few minutes."

"Asleep!" Morath boomed indignantly.

"For a few minutes," Raist repeated softly.

There was a long ominous silence while each waited for
the other to say something else.

"I think," said Raist, after a long pause, "that I managed
to memorize a good deal of all three books. I suppose I can
answer almost any question that is taken from them. If that
is the object of the task . . ." His voice trailed off, losing
confidence under Morath's stare.

"No," said Morath, cutting him off harshly. "I mean,
what have you been doing with this book?" He gestured angrily, indicating the chronicle by Astinus. "This most precious volume is intended only for far-seeing eyes and
deep-thinking scholars—not for students, certainly not for
children. This book was not offered to you because it is
mine alone."

Morath's eyes stayed fixed on him, and little Raist, for
once cowed, lowered his.

"I did not open it," said Raist apologetically.

"You were reading it!" accused Morath.

"I was not," said Raist, looking up, surprised.

"Come, come, boy. What were you doing then?" asked the
master mage sarcastically. His eyes were watching Raist.

"I was feeling it, touching it," said Raist, once again holding his gaze level.

"Feeling it, touching it!" derided Morath.

"Yes," said Raist, more confidently. "Touching it!"

"May I ask why?"

A pause. "I don't know why," Raistlin said at last. "I knew that you had set it aside for yourself and that I shouldn't read it, but I wanted, at least, to feel it and touch it. I didn't see the harm."

"You had no business," declared Morath.

Raist bit his lip, angry and overcome with frustration. After all the hard work and long hours, to fail at this, this unexpected test of restraint! It was all he could do to keep from breaking down and crying. But like his sister Kitiara, Raist would not cry, not in front of this hardhearted master mage. Raist wouldn't give Morath the satisfaction.

"All right, boy, the day is done. Your father and sister are here. I'll thank you not to waste any more of my time."

*　*　*　*　*

"Yes, your son is gifted, but I question whether his constitution can withstand the rigors of our program here. Indeed, the boy was so exhausted after the lessons of the afternoon that he fell asleep at his books."

Morath spoke firmly. He and Gilon were at the table in the library, which was now quite dark and lit only by the flickering globe in front of the master mage.

Gilon steeled himself. "He may not be strong in body," Raistlin's father replied steadfastly, "but he is strong-willed, and this is what he truly wants. In all honesty, the lad would not be fit for a vocation that demanded physical prowess. Yet for him, magic is no whim. If you do not accept him, we will go elsewhere and try to find someone who will tutor him. I have made inquiries, and I understand that a mage named Petroc runs an excellent school near Haven."

This was half a bluff on Gilon's part, but a shrewd one. He judged Morath would not want to turn his back on the possible reflected glory of training an exceptional pupil, even such a young one.

A rustle of turning pages interrupted the conversation. Raistlin was in a dark corner, sitting crosslegged on the floor in front of one of the bookshelves, with a slim volume on his lap. Morath started when he saw what Raistlin was doing.

He crossed the room quickly and snatched the book from Raist's hands. "Young man, I thought you had learned a lesson about playing with books that were not given to you, especially spellbooks!"

Raistlin looked up at him coolly. "I wasn't playing with it. I was reading it."

A shocked silence filled the room.

"I was reading the 'Spell for Changing Water Into Sand'," the boy continued defiantly, satisfied at the look of amazement that crossed Morath's face. "You can reject me as a pupil. But I won't miss this opportunity to read one of your precious spellbooks!"

Morath flushed an angry shade. Gilon, in a rare display of temper, pointed toward the door. "That's enough, Raist. Go wait outside with your sister."

When Gilon turned back, the master mage had controlled his rage. Morath was leafing through a richly embroidered book, small in size, and scanning various hand-inked lists and schedules.

"He can start at the beginning of the new week," said the master mage matter-of-factly, taking up a feather pen and formally inscribing Raistlin's name on the roll of students.

Gilon's mouth gaped. No matter Raistlin's certain abilities, his father had come to think he wouldn't be able to gain a place in this vaunted school. His jaws worked but no words came out.

"How will you pay?" asked Morath, scarcely noticing Gilon's struggle to speak when he looked up after inscribing Raistlin's name on the ledger.

Pay? This was something the woodsman could fathom.

"Well, your lordship," said Gilon, not certain how to address a master mage, but certain he didn't want to insult him. "I am a woodcutter by trade, as I mentioned earlier today. And our means are modest. I was hoping that I could keep up with any, er, tuition, by bringing you cut wood for use here at the school. Or I might provide other such services, in fair trade. People in town will tell you that I am honest with my barter, and my accounts are always paid."

"Pah!" snorted Morath. "What do I want with bundles of firewood? I can snap my fingers like this—" he lifted his hands and demonstrated "—and have all the wood I need. Not just local wood, but rare and exotic varieties from all over Krynn. Wood!"

The master mage glared at Gilon, whose face was flushed. Once again the woodsman found that his mouth was not working very well while his arms felt useless dangling at his sides.

"Pah!" repeated Morath, turning back to his book and scribbling something further next to Raistlin's name. "I will carry the boy on scholarship for a while," added the master mage irritably. "And we will see if he is worth the bother."

Before Gilon could think how to respond, Morath had swept out of the room, slipping behind a door that the woodcutter had not noticed before, behind one of the towering bookshelves. Because he had taken the flickering globe with him, instantly the library was plunged into gloomy darkness. A little dazed by everything that had transpired, Gilon backed toward the double doors that led to the long entrance corridor, bowing once or twice in the direction of the vanished mage, just in case.

* * * * *

Little Raist was so worn-out that Kit could not tell, from his drained expression, whether he at all understood what Gilon, bursting with smiles, told him. Indeed the aspiring mage could not walk and was fast asleep in his father's arms before they had traveled several hundred yards away from Poolbottom toward Solace.

Home was more than an hour's hike away, but Gilon carried his burden stoically, his heart light with relief. It was a clear night, a momentous occasion, and neither Kit nor Gilon felt like speaking and breaking the mood.

In truth, Kit was elated, too. Her bad temper had been whisked away by the news of Raist's acceptance. As she trudged along, herself weary, her thoughts raced.

Raist never woke up that night, and Kit skipped the supper Rosamun had prepared and kept warm. Up in her niche, the young girl stayed awake, thinking. She knew now what she would do—catch up to Ursa and convince him to take her with him. Raist's acceptance into the mage school meant that she did not have to worry about him as much any more. About Caramon, Kit was confident in his abilities as a warrior. In short, she was free to leave.

Kitiara decided to say nothing to Gilon or Rosamun about her planned departure, nor, after thinking it over, to Caramon either.

The next morning, talking over the previous day's events, Kit told Raistlin where she was going. But she made him promise not to tell anyone, even after she had gone.

It was as if Raist knew before he was told. "Will you come back?" he asked. The six-year-old's voice was steady, but Kit could see tears glistening in his eyes. She felt as if a hand were squeezing her heart.

"I imagine," she said noncommittally, "I'll have to come back and see how my little brothers are doing!" His eyes accused her. "I have to do this, Raist. I can't spend my life in this cottage, this town. I won't. You understand."

Two nights later, with light from Solinari and Lunitari flooding the cottage, Kit crept quietly down the ladder from her loft. The usual night sounds greeted her as she surveyed the common room. Gilon's gentle snoring and Rosamun's occasional moan or sigh came from their chamber.

She tiptoed over to where the twins slept. Caramon, imitative of his father, snorted as he dreamed. Raist, his face almost serene in repose, lay quietly. Fighting her feelings, Kit tucked the bedclothes up under each twin's chin.

Kitiara did not look back as she walked across the floor and opened the door into the shimmering, moonlit night.

Chapter 6

The Mercenaries

*Kitiara caught up with the four men at their rendez-*vous point after midnight and easily followed them at a distance. They made camp an hour later, off the road. The next day Kit was ready for them when they headed out, pursuing them at a steady interval.

Their two-sectioned caravan had been progressing like that for three days now.

By day the sun burned brightly in the sky, casting a glow of warm color on the trees and rocks and earth. After sundown everything turned black and forbidding, and there was nothing to see except the shadows cast by the twin sentinels of the night, Lunitari and Solinari. The third moon, Nuitari, was invisible to all but the foulest evil creatures.

Ursa and his little band were obviously skirting the main

highway, avoiding all towns and settlements while following a northeast course that was taking them toward the Eastwall Mountains. The open fields gave way to a dark fir forest as the land ascended. Gradually the foliage and pitch of the terrain had increased so that they could not cover more than twenty-five miles in a day.

In any case, Ursa and his men did not seem to be in much of a rush. They rode as steadily as they could during the late morning and afternoon, but camped early and never hurried to rise and get moving at first light.

One of the men rode a mule laden with pots and assorted supplies. The one called Radisson rode a common bay. The third, whose features were cloaked by a cowl, sat on a striking white stallion with a black muzzle. Ursa straddled his familiar gray.

Kit soon realized they were heading in the general direction of Silverhole, a shanty town of dwarven miners and itinerant workers. Yet they were maintaining an eastward drift that would place them below the town, in open, low mountain country. She could think of nothing in that area, only the occasional fief or landed estate. What could they be after near Silverhole? Although it was a mining center, there were no riches there, for the dwarves who specialized in such arduous jobs were said to be cutting stone and clearing the way for a mountain road. At the Red Moon Fair, Kit had overheard the mercenaries debate the kidnapping of a nobleman's son, but surely the miners counted no royalty among them.

Kitiara pondered what Ursa and his band were up to during the long hours she followed them. It was child's play to do so without being found out. Kitiara was a skilled rider, and she had ridden bareback practically since she could walk. Cinnamon, the chestnut mare that had once belonged to Gregor, had been his final gift to her when he absconded. Though she was the only horse the family had, there had been no thought of selling Cinnamon even through all the hard times. She had always—since Gregor left—been Kit's horse, and Kit rode her now.

Cinnamon was a veteran of forest trails and had an instinct for avoiding low branches, nickering a warning so that Kit might duck any that swung down across her path. Obviously, Kit thought, my quarry has no idea they are being tracked. They were as plain as a pack of gnomes, their passage littered with trampled foliage, discarded foodstuffs, and the dregs of their fires.

The mountain forest was different than the familiar landscape surrounding Solace. The smell here was unusually sweet, the air moist, the tapestry of colors dark and rich and mesmerizing. At first Kit had been intoxicated by the newness of everything, attentive to strange varieties of plants and flowers, curious about tracks and droppings, alert to the noises of insects and birds and the multitude of small, unseen creatures all around her. She took immense delight in the small things that she noticed: the blue frost on early morning leaves; a peculiar animal with a long snout and curled ears, staring at her from inside a bush, before it hopped away quickly on all fours; a pear-shaped fruit with prickly points whose juice was sour.

But after a while everything began to look the same in front of her as well as behind, one blurred blue-green vista. After a while Kit wished they would arrive at their mysterious destination. She began to wonder if she should risk coming out into the open and revealing herself.

Kitiara marked her route with notches cut in the trunks of trees, discreet ones below ordinary sight-lines. She was not afraid of getting lost. Gregor had taught her some essential survival skills, and she had made it her business to learn more in the years since he had left, gleaning knowledge from Gilon and even Bigardus, the well-intentioned healer. She knew enough so that she could find her way back to Solace on foot, without supplies, if necessary.

Kit knew how to forage for nuts and berries. She knew how to bank a fire to keep the wind out and the heat in. She knew how—for warmth and protection—to dig a shallow ditch at night and cover herself with leaves and branches. There was plenty of fresh water in the many streams that crisscrossed the mountainous terrain.

Her shoulder pack contained the only things she had chosen to bring along and the only things she might need: meatsticks, a length of rope, a bone whistle, warm under-woolens, and a small, heavy carving knife taken from Gilon's workbench. That was the only weapon she had been able to put her hands on. The blanket Kit sat on when she rode came off at night to serve as her bedding.

At night she remembered the few times she had camped out with Gregor, staying up around the campfire. Her father's eyes would hypnotize her as he spun tales of his and others' exploits. His deep brown eyes glistened then, like water in the moonlight. It was at night, particularly, that Kit remembered things her father had said to her.

"The day can start out sunny and grand," Gregor liked to say, "and betray you in an instant. Start out in the morning cheery as a friend, and turn out to be your enemy. The night is more constant—dangerous and dark, 'tis true, but constant. You can depend on danger in a way that you can never depend on a friend.

"Some people are one way by day, another by night. But night is the true form, for darkness illuminates a man better than sunshine, whose glare can fool the eyes.

"For instance, I knew a knight once who traveled with a young squire. By day this knight, whose name was Sarne, was one of the stalwarts of Krynn. A boon drinking companion and a fierce swordsman. Yet by night this very fellow turned pussycat, and his squire, just a jot of a boy called Winburn . . ."

Kitiara rarely heard the end of Gregor's stories, which seemed to go on forever as she was falling asleep. Now, as she faced another lonely night on her first true adventure, she wondered what had become of her father. The solitude, the sounds and the darkness of this forest brought her not fear but strange comfort, as if somewhere Gregor Uth Matar was also awake in the night and thinking of her.

By the end of third day she estimated they had traveled more than seventy-five miles, still weaving through the forest in the general direction of Silverhole. At first, Kitiara had remained several hours behind Ursa and his men, but by the fourth day she was growing impatient. Heedless of being discovered, she picked up her pace so that she was following them less than an hour behind.

Under cover of dark, Kit made the further mistake of creeping close to their campsite to eavesdrop in hopes of learning some new piece of information about their destination. She felt proud of herself as she picked her way slowly around rocks and trees toward their huddled shapes. Ursa and another of the men, both draped in blankets, had their backs to her. The short, weaselly man named Radisson faced her direction and was speaking vehemently; she recognized his voice from the fair. A fourth, tall and stooped with a sad face, stood at the smaller man's shoulder, listening intently. Once in a while the sad-faced one said something indiscernible, apparently in assent.

Their tone was low and conspiratorial, and Kit had to inch closer than was wise to catch any of the words. The weaselly one was laying out some strategy. She could only hear occasional, garbled words such as "considerable fortune" and "the odds will be favorable." These clues to their mission whetted Kit's appetite for more. She crawled forward on hands and knees until she could almost jump up and spit on the them.

All of a sudden, something big and heavy dropped on Kit's back, knocking her to the ground. For several seconds her breath was taken away. When her head cleared, she found herself hoisted off the ground, nose to nose with Ursa. The look on his glowering face was one of disgust mixed with astonishment.

"You again!" cried Ursa, holding her by the collar. Kit was too dazed to do anything but feebly kick her feet in an effort to get down. As Ursa gripped her firmly, someone else yanked her hands and tightly roped them together behind her back. Kitiara managed to twist around to see the fourth man.

This one was somewhat taller than Ursa, more sinewy,

with skin the color of obsidian. His hair was black, down to his shoulders and so curly that his skull appeared to be covered by writhing snakes. In the moonlight, Kit was struck by the gleaming whiteness of his fearsome grin and a single gold hoop that dangled from his right ear. The color of his skin and the billowing striped pants he wore made her think he must be from the far east island of Karnuth. That race boasted intriguing powers, she recalled hearing, and its denizens were rarely seen in these parts because they were said to be afraid of long sea voyages.

"Ouch!" Kit exclaimed, more to see what reaction that might get than because she was in very much pain.

"Aw, you're hurting her," said the Karnuthian, not unsympathetically. Kit remembered his voice from overhearing the conspirators at the Red Moon Fair—deep, mellow, but with a hint of menace.

"I don't care," responded Ursa, tightening his grip. He was not smiling in the slightest.

"Who is it, El-Navar?" asked another voice. "What's the game?"

The other two mercenaries hurried over to gawk at Kit. The Karnuthian, the one whose name was El-Navar, had found the knife in her boot and now held it up to Ursa as if to say I-told-you-so, before nonchalantly guiding it into his belt. His grin was oddly beguiling for one with so fierce an aspect.

"Splendid performance, Radisson," said El-Navar to the weaselly-faced one. "You learned a few things in your days as a stroller."

"Who is she?" hissed Radisson. The look on his pale, creased face was plainly hostile.

"Didn't I tell you someone was following us?" gloated El-Navar. Every time he moved, his gold ear hoop trembled in the moonlight. The others nodded their approval.

Ursa, meanwhile, had set Kit down and upended her pack, emptying its modest contents on the ground. Finding nothing of interest there, he replaced the belongings and handed Kit's bag to his tall, stooped cohort with the sad face, who clutched it stolidly. That one had not said a word.

Then Ursa began to push Kitiara toward the campsite. When she resisted, he grabbed the rope around her wrists and tugged harshly, so that her shoulder blades were twisted. She practically tripped over her own feet as she was dragged backward, but she did not protest. Kitiara wouldn't yield that satisfaction.

The other three followed, the looks on their faces as different as their personalities: El-Navar, curious, even amused; Radisson, cold and suspicious; the sad-faced one, dismayed. When Ursa reached the campsite, he gave Kit a shove that dumped her unceremoniously to the ground. She rolled over in the dirt and struggled to a sitting position against a stump. Glancing around, Kit took in the cut branches holding up the blanket-shapes in front of the fire. Stupid, that night age-old trick! Her eyes gleamed with fury, as much at herself as at her captors.

Ursa sat down on a nearby rock. Radisson and the tall morose one followed suit, a little farther away, their eyes narrowed on Kit.

"Her horse is a mile back, I daresay," said Ursa.

His tone had leveled, become more matter-of-fact, but showed no hint of warmth. He reached over to stir the embers of the fire, whistling thoughtfully to himself. Almost imperceptibly his eyes scanned the treetops.

"I'm quite sure she's alone," he said after completing his survey.

The other two were obviously waiting for Ursa or El-Navar to make a decision as to Kitiara's fate. But Ursa said nothing more and El-Navar, standing near the fire to warm his hands, now showed little interest in the matter. Each seemed to be waiting for the other to act.

"What do we do with her?" whined Radisson, fed up after a few minutes of this.

"She doesn't know anything," said Ursa emphatically.

"Why was she following us then?" questioned Radisson.

The wind picked up, scattering leaves in a circle at the edge of the campfire. Somewhere, far away, a creature howled. Kit could tell that the four men were spooked, particularly Radisson, whose eyes darted around inside their sockets.

Ursa put his hands in his pockets to warm them, continuing to whistle his strange little tune, not answering. He seemed to pay no attention to Radisson, but his eyes met Kitiara's. He was scowling.

"Any half-brain could follow you," snorted Kitiara contemptuously. "A woolly mammoth travels less conspicuously. You leave a mess and obvious clues everywhere. You have no respect for the forest."

Radisson's face tightened up. His hands fingered the knife at his waist nervously. In a surprising movement he stood and crossed to her, then backhanded Kit across the face so swiftly that she felt the blow even before she realized it was coming. Immediately her mouth puffed up and started to bleed. Kit struggled against her bonds, clenching her teeth to keep from crying out.

"Watch your lip," said the weaselly one.

The Karnuthian seemed to think that was the funniest thing of all, and he bent over laughing. But when he straightened up, his face was somber. El-Navar took a handkerchief out of his pocket and with surprising gentleness wiped the blood from her mouth and chin. Ursa's eyes followed him closely.

"There, there, Radisson," said El-Navar heartily. "No need to be so manly. She's not much more than a girl after all, not more than twelve I figure."

"Thirteen," said Kitiara sulkily. "Almost fourteen."

"A rather pretty thirteen at that, I'd say," added the Karnuthian. He grabbed Kit a little roughly by the chin and tilted her face upward. Ursa and Radisson were quiet, and there was a sudden air of tension among the group

"Let's have the truth, girl," El-Navar continued more sternly. "What is your name? Why were you following us?"

"Kitiara Uth Matar," said Kit stonily. "You could have asked him if you wanted to know," she added, indicating Ursa.

"You know her?" asked the Karnuthian, turning to Ursa, surprised.

"I met her once," said Ursa in pointedly neutral tones, "when she was just a child. . . ."

Kitiara looked spitefully at him.

"She recognized me in Solace and came up to me. I gave her the brush off."

"She knows our faces, El-Navar," said Radisson weakly. "What else does she know?"

"She doesn't know anything," repeated Ursa harshly. "I say we let her go. What could she say against us?"

El-Navar said nothing. Whether he or Ursa was in charge, Kitiara couldn't tell. Radisson, however, was clearly waiting for one of the two to make up his mind.

Alone among them, the tall, sad-faced one was paying little attention to the problem. Slouched on the ground, he had taken out a dog-eared book and seemed to be studying it intently by the firelight, his lips moving soundlessly. A trail of drool fell steadily from his mouth, wetting the pages. The others, no doubt used to his eccentricities, paid him no heed.

El-Navar bent down on his knees so that he was peering into Kit's eyes. "How about it, Kitiara?" he asked. "Why were you following us?"

His tone had softened, but his eyes glittered with a diamond-hard light. The gold hoop swayed as he leaned forward.

"I wanted to join up," she said vaguely.

"What?" asked Radisson brusquely. Ursa's face was impassive.

"Join up. I wanted to join up," Kit repeated, this time more strongly.

El-Navar let go of her chin and stood up, shaking his head and chuckling to himself. This seemed to break the tension, and, in spite of himself, Ursa managed a tentative smile. The sad-faced reader, slouched over his book, continued to ignore them. Only Radisson looked confused and irritated.

"What are we then, some kind of volunteer fire brigade?" asked El-Navar.

"No." Kitiara hesitated. "I wanted to help take care of Gwathmey's son," she ventured boldly.

The smiles vanished. Even the reader heard this and looked up anxiously. Ursa stood and drew El-Navar aside, speaking to him in a whisper. Radisson glared at Kit. El-Navar looked over his shoulder, then nodded in agreement to something that Ursa had said. He broke from Ursa, who sat back down.

"How much do you know?" asked El-Navar tersely.

"Too much! Now we've got to kill her!" exclaimed Radisson.

"Try it!" Kit dared. Again, with startling swiftness, Radisson lunged toward her, but El-Navar was quicker this time and blocked his movement, shoving the smaller man aside. Radisson looked daggers at him, but there was nothing he could do against the bigger man whose charismatic presence—if not his actual size—commanded respect.

"Don't be so hasty, Radisson," admonished El-Navar. "Think with your head. This girl is no match for you, even though she is your equal in other respects. A ringer in size, for example, which might have its value."

Although Kit didn't understand why, something that El-Navar said, something about his tone of voice, sent a message to Radisson. Instead of getting angrier, the weaselly one paced over near where Kit sat. He gazed at her, his expression altered and thoughtful.

El-Navar also circled Kit, studying her. "I say we take her along," he declared after long moments had passed. "Let her . . . as she says, 'join up.'"

Ursa looked at Kitiara and back at El-Navar. Although his face was a tightly controlled mask, he shrugged to indicate his indifference. Still unsmiling, he stared at Kit with his dark, mercurial eyes.

"Maybe," said Radisson stubbornly.

"Look at her," El-Navar said to Radisson. "She's just about your size, isn't she? And she has pluck. It would minimize the risk to us and put you where you're needed most."

After a long hesitation, Radisson shrugged a reluctant agreement. Kit noticed that nobody bothered to consult the fourth member of the party—Droopface, as she had begun to think of him.

"Is that a good horse you're riding? Can you ride fast, Kitiara?" asked El-Navar.

"Fast enough!" she said excitedly.

He cut her bonds. "Then you're one of us," he declared, clapping her on her shoulder.

Kitiara rubbed her wrists ruefully and looked at the four faces staring at her. Although she didn't feel entirely confident, she forced a smile.

"Well . . ." said the weasely man.

"C'mon, Radisson!" boomed El-Navar. "Don't be a jackass. Shake hands with our new partner!"

* * * * *

They continued riding northeast all the next day and the day after that.

Except for Radisson, who maintained his wary demeanor toward her, the others appeared to accept Kit. However, where they were going and exactly what they were going to do remained a mystery. At least Kit could extract no further details, no matter how hard she tried. "Be patient," said El-Navar whenever she brought up the subject. "All in good time."

El-Navar was most enigmatic. Like the people Gregor had once told Kit about, by day he seemed one person, by night another. When the sun was out, El-Navar disappeared into his cowl; indeed he seemed to disappear from the group. He became sleepy-eyed, almost somnambulant, with little of the extroverted personality that he displayed after dark. He kept up with the other riders, but rode slumped over, saying very little.

Under the sun, Ursa was definitely the leader. But after a long day's ride, after making camp and eating supper, Ursa was usually so tired that one feared he would not make his watch. At just around that time, the Karnuthian grew exuberant and full of energy. There was obviously some understanding between Ursa and El-Navar, and neither sought the upper hand.

The tall, sad-faced one continued to say very little to anyone. His responsibilities included the horses and the meals, cooking the small game they managed to trap or shoot along the way. Kit had asked him his name and been told. It was Cleverdon, a name she had a hard time remembering in connection with such a strange character. So Kit called him "Droopface." The others were so amused by this that the nickname stuck.

Much to Kit's annoyance, Ursa continued to treat her coldly. She decided to be grand about it and tried to bolster their friendship by riding alongside him and drawing him out. On the first day she could barely get him to nod in her direction.

On the second, she had better luck. Ursa smiled when she rode up. Surprised and pleased, Kit decided to ask him about Gregor, who was much on her mind these days, or rather, nights.

"Ursa, that day we first met you said you had heard of my father. Have you heard of him since?"

Ursa looked away. "No," he said shortly when he glanced back in her direction.

"I remember you told me that Gregor was in the north, the last you heard," she persisted. "Was that anywhere near where we're going? Do you think there's any chance our paths will cross?"

Despite her best efforts to remain in control of her emotions, Kit knew she sounded plaintive.

"Kitiara, that was a long time ago and very far from where we are bound. Let me give you some advice. If Gregor Uth Matar chose to go so far away, either he doesn't want to be found by you—" here Ursa paused "—or he is dead."

"Dead! Why do you say that?" But Kit's queries only

reached Ursa's back as he galloped off to scout what lay ahead.

* * * * *

North by east they rode until they were high in the Eastwall Mountains, surrounded on all sides by rocks and slopes. On the third night they stopped early. Kit picked up a distinct air of anticipation as the others sharpened weapons and checked their equipment. The horses also received special care; Radisson made sure they were amply fed and watered.

Droopface made a haricot stew that they all gulped down hungrily. Afterward, he retreated some distance from the others and read his favorite book, slobbering over the pages until he fell asleep the way he always did, sitting upright. Radisson wrapped himself in his blanket and lay down on the ground near the fire. Ursa and El-Navar were studying a piece of parchment—obviously a map—taken from one of El-Navar's pockets, and carrying on a low debate.

After some time, El-Navar came over to where Kit was sitting. "Let's get to work. I'm going to cut your hair." He took his short, double-edged blade out and ran it over a rock, watching her.

"Why?" she asked in surprise, raising her hand protectively to her head. "Isn't it short enough?"

Kitiara heard Ursa grunt with amusement as he turned to his bedroll. It was the first characteristic laugh out of him in several days, albeit at her expense.

"It has to be shorter yet," explained El-Navar, "and I need to collect some for tomorrow. Tomorrow's the day the . . . *plan* goes into action, and you are going to have to look more like a certain man."

"Gwathmey's son?"

El-Navar didn't answer, but Kit let him come closer and comb her hair.

"Ah," rhapsodized El-Navar. "You have beautiful hair, Kitiara. Black as midnight. Pity we must chop some of it off." He began to cut at it, pulling off small bunches and placing them in a tin bowl. "But it's necessary."

El-Navar seemed surprisingly practiced at the task, cutting delicately, particularly at the nape of her neck. Kit shuddered involuntarily as he placed his strong hand on her neck to bend her head forward, but it was not an unpleasant sensation. He worked in silence for a long while.

Kitiara was lulled by his touch, which was as gentle as it was assured.

"What is Droopface always reading?" Kitiara asked.

"Oh," said El-Navar as he worked. "It's some book he picked up in a market somewhere. Magic tricks and potions. I can't read for beans myself. He thinks he's studying to be a mage. He has managed to teach himself a couple of simple spells that do come in handy. I expect we'll see some of his expertise tomorrow."

El-Navar was meticulous. He worked for a time on her bangs, shortening almost up to her hairline. And as he worked he stared right into Kit's eyes. She was startled to realize his eyes weren't as hard and metallic as they first appeared. She could see through them, to their essence, which was lush and sensuous. His breath was hot and aromatic, suggestive of faraway lands.

"But," continued El-Navar, "Droopface has no real affinity for magic. It is all stunts and illusions. If you ask me, magic is a plague sweeping Krynn, and there are too many people trying their hand at spellcasting who ought to be doing something else with their lives."

"Tell me this," asked Kitiara, changing the subject, "who is Gwathmey's son, and why are we so interested in him?"

The Karnuthian laughed lustily, baring his white teeth, shaking his curly snake hair and sending the gold hoop into a frenzy of motion. "You don't give up, Kitiara," he said, taking a few final snips of her hair, "but you will know everything soon enough. Not yet. Not tonight. . . ." His voice was a rich, soothing purr.

The sky was tranquil. The other three men appeared to have fallen asleep. Clouds hid Lunitari, though Kit could still tell that the red moon was full.

"Done!" The Karnuthian stood up, reached into his pack, and pulled out a piece of cut glass which he proffered to Kitiara.

She examined herself and found a curiously new face with a wide expanse of skin at the forehead and temples, framed by sideburns and a neatly trimmed cap of black hair. The effect did make her look for all the world like a young gentleman.

El-Navar placed select tufts of hair into a small pouch. "We will finish off the mustache in the morning," he said.

"Mustache?"

"You are to be the decoy, Kitiara," said El-Navar. "We are not after Gwathmey's son. More precisely, we are after what he is carrying. When we attack him, you will lead his guards on a merry diversion. From a good distance, you will look almost exactly like the young fellow."

El-Navar strode to Radisson's horse and took something out of his saddlebags. "Radisson was going to play that part, but your appearance was fortuitous. We can use him closer to the action. Here, try these on," he added, tossing a small bundle of clothing at her. "Make sure they fit."

Kitiara took them and went behind a tree. The costume consisted of leather breeches, a brocaded shirt, and an expensive vest. A jacket finished the ensemble. The outfit fit a little loosely, but Kitiara made do and came around the tree for El-Navar's appraisal. He was cleaning his blade with water. When he looked up at her, his expression was almost startled. Slowly he sheathed his blade and stood up to gaze more closely at Kitiara.

"Yes," he said, with obvious satisfaction.

She frowned at him. "I feel silly. Can't I do something more important?"

"You'll be doing something very important," said El-Navar. "Do not fear."

"How much of a fortune is the duke's son carrying?"

"Tomorrow, Kitiara," El-Navar replied, with good humor. "Tonight, get some sleep."

Kit stole another glance at herself in the piece of glass; if she had to admit it, she liked the way she looked in these luxurious clothes. As she angled the mirror, Kit caught El-Navar gazing pointedly at her. Suddenly she discovered herself trembling. Kit held his gaze for several long seconds before bringing the mirror down.

"I like it," she said, turning to meet his glittering eyes.

Kit handed the mirror back to the Karnuthian before going behind the tree to change again. She had managed to slip out of the leather breeches and was just unbuttoning her shirt when El-Navar's voice came to her in an enchanting whisper.

"It will be cold tonight, Kitiara," El-Navar said. "I would share my bedroll with you."

She came out from around the tree, half undressed. "Say what you mean," she said evenly.

"Come to me," El-Navar replied.

For some reason she could not have put into words, Kit glanced over to where Ursa slept. His back was to her. She could not see that his eyes were wide open, that their expression was stony. But he lay still, apparently asleep. Without further hesitation, Kitiara went to El-Navar.

Chapter 7

The Decoy

Kitiara had a dreamless night. When her eyes fluttered open, she stretched and yawned. Then, with a start, Kit realized the sun was bright in her eyes, and she jumped up, clutching the blanket to herself, embarrassed.

She was the last one awake. Radisson, who was tying something to his horse, smirked at her. Droopface was already astride his mule, with its pouches, pots, and pans, looking more alert and purposeful than he had for days.

Her face burning, Kit slipped behind some bushes to change into her gentleman's garb. She could hear Radisson chuckling, and Ursa saying something to him. Radisson muttered something else, and Ursa told him to shut up. Furiously she fixed her costume and came out from behind the bushes, ready.

Ursa came over, glaring. He reached into his pocket and got out a bushy swatch of Kit's hair that had been affixed to a strip of muslin. With some paste he stuck the makeshift mustache under her nose, roughly enough that she winced. "Yes," Ursa said approvingly, appraising her mannish disguise.

Among them all hung an air of tension that had been absent before, when their mission had not been so immediate. And where was El-Navar?

She spotted the sinewy Karnuthian on his white stallion, atop a rise some distance away, shading his eyes and looking off toward the northeast. El-Navar was slumped in the saddle, almost humpbacked, reverting to his strange daytime languor. He did not even so much as glance in Kit's direction.

She realized that she was staring too hard at the Karnuthian and that Ursa was watching her carefully, so Kit turned her face sharply toward the mercenary.

"Why didn't you wake me up sooner?" she demanded angrily.

"Why didn't you wake yourself up, sleeping beauty?" piped up Radisson from his horse. Droopface gave an uncharacteristic guffaw.

Kitiara took a step toward Radisson, her hand reaching for a knife that was not there—indeed, she was unarmed, and on her costume there were no belts or loops for weapons.

"You had a good rest," Ursa said tersely, stepping in front of Kit to block her. "There was little for you to do anyway. Now, let's hurry." He looked at the sun, already midway through its morning arc. "We don't want to miss our . . . *appointment.*"

Kit couldn't help but glance again at El-Navar, but the Karnuthian hadn't budged, still hadn't even looked toward her. He seemed as if he were sleeping, or dead, as if only his eyes were alive, searching the horizon.

Damn your soul, Kitiara thought coldly.

She made sure Cinnamon was all right while the others

waited. Then she pocketed Gilon's small carving knife, just in case. In a matter of minutes Kit climbed onto her father's chestnut mare and rode out last in the mercenary band, their sparse column stretching out for a quarter-mile. Today El-Navar was far in the lead, still hunched in the saddle, never looking behind him as he rode.

* * * * *

They rode hard for about an hour and were now in steep, rocky territory that led into the Eastwall Mountains. Kitiara reckoned they were about an hour from Silverhole, and that the road they could see at intervals, below them to the right, was the main one that took several days to wend around this perimeter range. She had never been this far north, but knew from crude maps that Silverhole was at the foot of the range which became, farther upcountry, all but impassable except at select spots.

After riding for a short time, they entered a maze of gorges and ravines. They maneuvered closer to the main road, and then, up ahead, El-Navar gave a signal. He pointed off to the east, dismounted, tied his horse, and melted into the rocks. Radisson and Droopface rode on, waiting near El-Navar's horse. When Kitiara, too, began to move forward, Ursa grabbed the reins of her horse and pointed up and in back of them, toward a sharp incline.

"Up here," he said, turning his gray. Kit followed him for several minutes, heading directly up the slope. Ursa kept going to the east, with Kitiara following, until they reached a ledge that jutted out over the area, offering a good view of a place where the main road took a sinuous bend through the rocks. No longer could she see El-Navar or his horse, nor either of her other two comrades.

Ursa gestured for her to be as quiet as possible. He tied his horse and crept to the edge of the overlook. Kitiara followed his lead, advancing slowly on her hands and knees until they were both peering over the side. There was no one in sight below. Ursa gestured for her to follow him back, and she did, until they were near the horses.

"This is the place," said Ursa in a low voice. "Here's what you do. . . ."

Quickly Ursa reviewed her part in the plan. Kitiara still had not gotten over the humiliation of the morning, and her face showed resentment as she listened. Though she now knew what her part was in the scheme, no one had bothered to tell her what her share of the take would be when it was all over. Or what the job was all about. El-Navar had told her last night just to do her part and forget about everything else. But she was tired of being left out of all the important decisions.

"What if something goes wrong?" Kit asked Ursa. "What if I need to . . . help . . . or rescue you?"

Ursa's face was taut, more so than ever now that the deed was close at hand. He had been very ironic and amusing when she'd first met him, but there was none of that in his steely look now.

"If something goes wrong," snapped Ursa, "you run away. You have a simple job: Do your part and don't get caught. Stay ahead of your pursuers, don't let them get a good look at you. Double back and meet us. That's all you have to do. If you do that much, you'll be doing fine."

Kit said nothing, her lips pursed.

"If something goes wrong, remember, you don't know us and you were never here."

He clapped Kit on the arm and mounted his horse. Turning the horse, he looked over his shoulder at her. His expression relaxed and for a moment there was something of the former Ursa in his dark eyes, something genial and warm. "Luck," he said to her, waving as he rode off.

*   *   *   *   *

Another hour passed. There were few trees up this high to shade Kitiara. The sunlight reflecting off the rocks was blinding, the heat almost palpable. Kitiara heard only the sounds of occasional birds and animals, and she looked down below so long at the spot where the road snaked into a bend, seeing nothing, that her eyes began to swim with dots. She felt as if she was in the middle of a swirling snowstorm, a whiteout of all color. She wanted nothing more than to close her eyes, lie down, and go to sleep, but she remembered what El-Navar and Ursa had said. She had to stay awake and do her part.

Then she heard approaching sounds, and immediately crouched low. Tensely Kit eased forward on her hands and knees, until she could just see over the precipice. Surely they would not be able to spot her, with the unrelenting sun in their eyes. But she took no chances and stayed low.

Kitiara could see a stretch of the pebbly road as it appeared among the jutting rocks. After the road continued for several hundred yards, it disappeared back into the rocks, before once again winding into full view. She watched the first stretch of road carefully, knowing that Ursa and his mercenaries waited behind the wall of rocks that concealed the narrow, second bend.

With no warning, a man on a horse appeared at the head of the road. He was dressed in fine armor that shone like silver in the sun. He was helmeted and carried a short lance with a plume of purple feathers. Obviously wary, he moved slowly into the open area, his horse, a magnificent sorrel, prancing nervously. But the helmeted leader did not break pace, and close behind him followed other men and horses.

By the gods, there were more than a dozen of them, fully armed and armored. Some were dressed in colorful regalia, others plainly. The armored men carried a variety of estimable weaponry, while the others, probably estate workmen, carried spears. They looked like a formidable bunch, and they outdid the four waiting to waylay them in number and arms.

Alarmed, Kitiara wondered if she should somehow signal Ursa and the others. Did they realize how many men they would be up against? Had they plotted all along to overcome such odds?

Kit uttered a low gasp as she spotted a figure riding in the center of the group, on a pale roan which was the most beautiful of the horses. Strapped to his ornamented saddle was a small decorated chest that, Kit guessed, held the object of their mission.

This horse's rider was young, slender, mustachioed, with short-cropped black hair. He carried no weapons. He wore a black gentlemen's vest and white lace blouse, and even from overhead, at a distance of several thousand yards—*especially* at a distance of several thousand yards—Kitiara saw how he might be mistaken for herself.

She ducked even lower to the ground, and with trepidation saw that the first of the riders had vanished beyond the bend. The rest of the retinue followed, one by one. For what seemed like long minutes—more likely it was long seconds—there was a tension-charged silence. It would take the riders roughly five minutes to emerge from the bend, Kit guessed. Yet the silence went on until Kitiara thought she would scream. It was as if everything, the birds and animals and the wind too, had stopped. Kitiara craned her neck, but could see nothing.

A quick series of loud reports rent the silence, not quite explosions, but terrible noises that jolted Kit's nerves. Following this, there spiraled up from the ground a cloud of dust and smoke. The cloud did not quite reach where she was perched, so she could look down on it from above. It was a strange color, a pearly white that seemed almost transparent in the sunshine, yet small particles of pitch black swirled around within it.

As she gaped, the air in the cloud crackled and each of the small black particles burst apart. From within them, as far as Kitiara could tell, a thousand black crows emerged, cawing and shrieking and flying in a mass so dense and terrifying that Kitiara shut her eyes and thrust her arms in the air to ward them off. Whether they were real or illusory, she did not know, but when she opened her eyes again after several seconds, they had entirely disappeared. When she looked down, she saw that the pearly cloud had disappeared, too.

During the occurrence, Kit was vaguely aware of screams and cursing and the noise of close fighting below. She thought she heard Ursa shout something. She heard groans and the cries of dying men, and hoped that one of them was not El-Navar.

As she looked on, several of the armored men and estate workmen rode from the bend into view, halting in apparent confusion as if something they had been chasing had suddenly vanished. Two or three of them were wounded and bleeding. The young gentleman was conspicuously absent from their midst, and Kitiara quickly gauged that about half of their original number was gone.

How Ursa and his men had escaped, if they had escaped, Kitiara did not know, but this was her cue to act.

"Ho there!" she shouted in as gruff a voice as she could manage. She stood up on the cliff so that she was clearly visible to those below and waved her arms. Kitiara could tell from their upturned faces that they were confused by seeing their lord and master so high up and far away. "Up here!" she called. "Hurry!"

Then Kit whirled out of view, jumping onto the waiting Cinnamon. After listening for a moment, she was satisfied to hear a clamor of voices and then the sounds of hooves pounding on the road. She knew it would take them a while to make the climb.

She spurred Cinnamon up a crude, twisting-turning path that wound up the mountainside to still higher ground. Branches whipped Kit across the face. She scraped her legs on the sharp rock outcroppings. Cinnamon stumbled once, and Kitiara had to get off and pull at her bridle to get the mare going again. Small animals darted across Kit's path. A hawk flew upward, shrieking annoyance.

After a few minutes, Kitiara dismounted and, breathing hard from the exertion, found another overhang that afforded a good view of the terrain below. She waited. Shortly, the band of armed riders and estatemen moved into sight. They looked around, looked over the edge, and looked up. Seeing nothing, they began to argue amongst themselves.

"Hey!" Kit stood up again, gestured elaborately, and saw the men's surprised, suspicious faces as they spotted her. One of them shouted something at her, which she couldn't make out.

"They're up here! I took one prisoner. The others—"

Kitiara thought that a good touch, breaking off as she spun out of view. She listened a moment and heard them arguing again. She knew that one or two of them might drop back, but even if the others were no longer convinced that she was their young lord, they couldn't pass up the possibility that catching her would lead them to the other perpetrators.

As Kit remounted Cinnamon, she heard the horses below snort and whinny before starting again in her direction, up the rocky incline. She looked around and chose another, even more narrow, precipitous path slicing upward. She could zig and zag in these low mountains forever, and eventually lose the ones who did not turn back. All she had to do was stay well away from Silverhole and not get lost.

* * * * *

Several hours later, and a dozen miles to the northeast of where she had started out, Kitiara was satisfied that she had left her pursuers behind and no longer had any reason to be cautious.

She stopped beside a small stream and splashed welcome refreshment into her mouth, then poured several tin cups of the cold water over her head. Cinnamon bent her head to drink alongside her mistress. Kitiara yanked off her mustache and tossed it into the bushes. Allowing herself a brief rest, she lay on her back and basked in the rays of the sun, now descending in the sky.

Kitiara figured she had about two hours of riding, straight toward her destination, before she would be back at the rendezvous spot. That should be well before nightfall.

Indeed, it was almost two hours later that Kitiara approached the previous night's campsite. She was clinging to the saddle, sore and weary, much more exhausted than she had thought she would be. Cinnamon, too, was no longer moving with ease, but was almost plodding along the forest trail.

As she neared the rendezvous, Kit was startled to see, lying strewn before her on the trail, an assortment of debris that included ripped clothing, smashed weapons, some coins and jewelry, and pieces of broken wood she recognized as fragments of the treasure chest that Gwathmey's son had been carrying with him. She also noticed markings that led off the path.

Warily Kit dismounted and, drawing her knife, advanced slowly into the undergrowth. Here, she saw that bushes and twigs had been trampled underfoot, and these clues led farther into the dense woods. Stooping low, Kitiara followed the trail. It was now nearly twilight, yet she was fully alert, breathing fast, ready.

At last Kit came upon a trampled form face down in the dirt, sprawled full-figure, as if it had been running and been knocked down, but with such force that it could never get up again. Taken aback, she stopped and took a moment to glance around, seeing and hearing nothing.

Cautiously, she proceeded closer. Then, with growing horror, Kit flipped the body over. She gasped when she recognized the person as being a ringer for herself—the young nobleman with his short black hair and thin mustache, Gwathmey's son, the man she had impersonated. He was quite dead.

Worse than dead. His front torso was torn to bits, with pieces of entrails hanging out and blood congealing around every wound. It looked as if he had been clawed by some ferocious monster, and then, Kitiara winced at the thought, half-eaten. Only his serene, youthful face, white as snow, appeared untouched.

This was the first time Kit had ever seen a dead person so close. This was the first time she herself was partly responsible. She felt no sorrow, no pity, only shock. And fright.

Stumbling backward, Kitiara lost all orientation. She turned, ran, fell, got up, ran again—wildly, in circles, pushing branches out of the way with one arm while the other shielded her eyes. She couldn't find her horse. She couldn't breathe. She couldn't see anything in the swiftly falling darkness. Kitiara stumbled again, and this time did not get up. Lying there, she fell asleep.

Kit lay on her back, her face to the sky.

She dreamed of a youthful face, pure and beautiful, that did not seem to belong to its mangled body, a face that looked remarkably like her own.

* * * * *

A cracking noise sounded in the undergrowth, and Kit felt the presence of something. Even before she woke fully, Kit knew that she was no longer alone.

She tried to sit up, but a hand on her chest pushed her back, and when she opened her eyes she was looking up at Ursa. He put his fingers to her lips, whispering, "Shh. Keep still." He was on his haunches, bending over her, but his eyes darted back and forth among the trees.

It was pitch dark, well past midnight. The air had cooled. Kit saw that her horse and Ursa's were tethered nearby. She couldn't see very far through the trees. Her own fast breathing sounded loud in Kit's ears.

After long seconds, Ursa relaxed his hold and permitted Kitiara to sit up. Disoriented, she tried to remember what had happened, how she had got here: Oh yes, it all came back to her. The ambush, the decoy escape, doubling back, and finding . . . the mutilated body of the young nobleman.

Although Kit had probably only slept a few hours, she felt revived. She was no longer afraid; in fact she felt almost confident. As she looked around for the others, Ursa rose and began making a small fire. She could see now that they were in a slight bowl of land sided by rocks and bushes. A good concealment. Ursa must have carried her here, and found Cinnamon.

"Where are El-Navar and the others?" she asked.

"Waiting somewhere," said Ursa, his back to her. The tone of his voice indicated some worry. He busied himself making broth—putting water from a canteen into a big tin cup, adding some stuff from canisters in his pack, and then, with a forked stick, heating the contents over the fire.

Kitiara moved near the fire and sat down so that she could see his face clearly. "Were you followed?" she asked anxiously.

"Were you?" Ursa asked. His tone was noncommittal.

"I lost them hours ago," Kit said a bit proudly. "First, they thought I was . . . you know, just like you said they would." Her face darkened at the recollection of the slain nobleman. If Ursa noticed the hitch in her voice, he didn't interrupt.

"But then," Kit continued, "they chased me around the hills for a time. I stayed just far enough ahead of them to make them think they were going to catch up." She couldn't help chuckling a little. "After I tired them out, I made a wide circle and headed back here, where you said you'd meet me. Then . . ." Her voice trailed off.

"Here," said Ursa, wrapping a rag around the tin cup and handing it to her.

"What is it?"

"Doesn't have a name," Ursa replied.

"It's good," Kit said after taking a sip. It tasted like strong tea, but more nourishing than that. From the flavor of the broth, it was a mixture of roots and powdered fish. Kitiara hadn't realized how hungry she was.

"Uh-huh," was all Ursa said. She waited for him to say something else, but he just sat there, watching her for several minutes, until she had drained the cup.

"Where are the others?" she asked again.

"Waiting somewhere," he repeated.

"You said that," Kit pointed out, getting angry.

He stared at her for a long minute. "They're not coming," he said, "and I'm going, shortly."

"What do you mean?"

"Look, they didn't even want me to come," Ursa said flatly. "I came to make sure you were all right."

"Why?" she demanded. "What do you mean? What's happened?"

He looked at her again for a long time before answering. He stood and started to pace, before facing her. "I guess you have a right to know."

"Know what?"

Ursa sat down again, watching her reaction. "The dwarves in Silverhole are building a mountain road. The convoy we robbed was carrying a half-year's salary, in advance, for their labor. Fifty dwarves, some humans, six months of excruciating labor—enough gold and silver to make the four of us rich for ten, maybe twenty years."

"Five of us," she corrected tersely.

He let it pass.

"The road," Ursa continued evenly, "was going to link two feudal estates on opposite sides of this particular mountain range. Without the road, it takes weeks, sometimes months, to travel from one estate to the next. A straight route would cut the time to a week, ten days at most."

"So?" wondered Kitiara. Why was he telling her all this?

Ursa sighed. "Well, Kitiara, if you would listen once in a while instead of cutting in . . . It's always good for a mercenary to know more about a job than simply when to fight or what to steal. Like how and why they're doing it. Why do these two estates need a direct road at such expense, and how do we come into the plan?"

Kitiara had to agree that made sense. She relaxed her tone. "OK," she said, curious. "Go on."

"On the far side of the mountain lives a rich vinegrower whose fields are tended by minotaurs captured in foreign wars. The vinegrower is known as Lord Mantilla, although he is about as much a noble as I am a bard of Silvanesti. The minotaurs are bought at great expense at slave auctions. This vinegrower has a daughter, named Luz, who, on one of these auction trips, met a young nobleman with whom she fell in love. The young nobleman lives on the other side of the mountain. His father is a proud forester whose family has ruled a wide swath of land around here for generations and whose son is the jewel of his existence. He is a true nobleman, a former Knight of Solamnia called Sir Gwathmey."

"I see," said Kitiara, her eyes widening. Yet she didn't see at all. This long nighttime tale reminded her of the kind her father used to tell, the ones that used to lull her asleep. But she wasn't sleepy and she was certain that Ursa was getting to some point.

"No, you don't see," said Ursa, although with more kindliness in his tone than before. "Not yet. The vinegrower had worked for the forester as a young man, but was paid badly and accused of stealing foodstuffs from the main house. After he left in a furor, he made his way across the mountain and founded his own fortune, beginning a new life. The worst thing in the world would be for his daughter to marry his enemy's son, and so he was anxious to break the marriage contract.

"But he had to do it without letting his daughter discern his role, because she is headstrong and would have insisted on having her way in spite of him."

"Hmmm." Events were beginning to add up.

"It so happens that Radisson has a brother who works as a household entertainer for Lord Mantilla. Radisson's brother was asked to make contact with a group of mercenaries who would waylay the payroll shipment, thence stopping the progress of the mountain road, which was being built as part of the marriage accord. Such was the value of the payroll that the forester will not be able to finance his road again for a long time, if ever. The dwarves will stop working when they hear news of the robbery, and no other self-respecting road gang will make the mistake of taking on the task. No road, no marriage."

"Did you get the payroll?" asked Kitiara, a little confused.

"Yes," answered Ursa grimly. "Three of their men were killed, but none of us was even injured. We managed to capture the nobleman's son and make our escape under the smoke screen of magic that Droopface concocted. Then, you led the rest of the guards on a merry chase in the wrong direction. That much went well and as planned."

"Then why aren't we celebrating. What's wrong?"

"Something we hadn't counted on," said Ursa, his mouth curling bitterly. "There was a spell on the payroll chest. We couldn't open it. Droopface tried everything he could think of, but his magic is limited and is more in the category of illusion than actual prowess. We tried everything to convince the nobleman's son, name of Beck, to tell us the secret of the magic. But Beck Gwathmey proved an arrogant fool who wouldn't tell us anything about the chest or stop taunting us with his plans to imprison and execute us."

Ursa stood now, his back to her again, his voice lowering with tension.

"I saw his body," Kit said softly.

"That wasn't planned," said Ursa harshly. "That was El-Navar, who couldn't control his temper."

"El-Navar?" began Kit wonderingly.

Ursa spun and grabbed her by the shoulder. "He's a shape-shifter, you idiot! Don't you know anything about Karnuthians? Why they're never seen in these parts? They can turn into blood-crazed panthers—can and do, especially at night. That is their essence and their true nature. They can't swim, are terrified of water, and never cross the oceans. But El-Navar was captured in his native land and freighted by ship across the great waters. On the continent he escaped from his handlers, and I met up with him. Most of the time he can manage when he turns into a panther. He is a good comrade. But sometimes it just happens. He changes into his beast form, and . . ."

Kitiara was speechless. Her eyes were glazed as she struggled to fathom the fact that El-Navar was a panther shape-shifter. That explained the strange dichotomy between his behavior in the daytime and at night.

"El-Navar," Ursa continued, "got so worked up that, before our eyes, he transformed himself and attacked Beck, clawed and devoured him. It was incredible. I have never seen anything the like. It was over before we could think what to do. I'm not sure we could have done anything, even if we had tried."

Ursa paused now, his voice choking. "The funny thing is," he added after a time, "the spell on the chest was broken. Whatever the magic was, it was linked to Beck's life. With Beck dead, the spell ended. We were able to get inside the chest, grab the silver and gold, and get away from that nightmarish scene as quickly as possible."

Kitiara was silent, thinking. Now she understood. "And El-Navar?"

Ursa whirled angrily on her. "Forget El-Navar," he said to her, glaring. "El-Navar ran off. We caught up to him. By the time we did, he was . . . human again. Don't be worrying about El-Navar. You're behaving like a lovesick cow."

"It has nothing to do with love," Kit declared vehemently, standing up so that she was face to face with Ursa.

He met her eyes. She didn't flinch. After a moment, he stepped back and sat down wearily. "El-Navar is fine," he told her more calmly. "They are waiting, miles from here. None of them wanted to take the chance of coming back to the rendezvous."

"Terrific," Kitiara snorted, sitting down again. "So I'm the only one who still considers me part of the group."

"I came back," said Ursa deliberately. He raised his eyes to meet hers, and she nodded her gratitude.

There was a moment of silence. They were surrounded by blackness and looked at each other across the small fire.

"Still," he added meaningfully, "it's bad business. Nobody told us to kill Beck. Sir Gwathmey will have a price on our heads, and I'm not sure how Lord Mantilla will take the news. If he's smart, he'll say and do nothing. He detests the Gwathmey bloodline. But the whole episode may, eventually, lead back to him. And what El-Navar did may point to a Karnuthian among us, and mark any in his company."

"So?" asked Kitiara.

"So," responded Ursa, "I'm sure the best thing for us to do

would be to split up for a while, get far away from this part of the world, and lay low. Let some time pass. See what happens."

Kitiara thought about that. "All right," she agreed. "Give me my share. I was only planning to join up for this one job, anyway."

"You don't understand," said Ursa, standing up and moving toward his horse, fiddling with the saddle and reins. He turned to look at her. "You were never one of us. We only used you to make the plan easier, to free up Radisson to help us with the main attack. You're not getting any share."

"What?" Kit leaped to her feet and lunged toward him, pulling her knife. But Ursa moved even more quickly and grabbed her wrist. He bent it backward until the knife was next to her face. With his other arm, he slapped her hard across the face. He jerked the knife out of her hand and pushed her away.

"They wouldn't let me give you a share," he said, half-apologetically. "Even if I wanted to."

The look on Kitiara's face was pure fury. She made another move in Ursa's direction, but he waved the knife in front of her, and she backed off.

"At least I came back," he declared between clenched teeth. "I came back to see if you were all right. The others wanted to ride on."

"Thanks for nothing," Kit said, spitting the words. She looked around for another weapon, something she could grab and throw, anything, but it was a standoff.

Ursa watched her for several seconds, until he was convinced that she had no recourse. Then he turned toward his horse, unstrapped a long bundle wrapped in scrim cloth, and tossed it on the ground at her feet.

"What's that?" she asked contemptuously, barely looking at it.

"Open it," he said.

Cautiously, Kit stooped down and worked the strings and wrapping, revealing a scabbard bound in tooled leather. She unbladed a short sword: bone grip, etched, thick blade, the hilt and pommel ornamented with tiny, brilliant stones. It was as magnificent a sword as she had ever beheld.

"It's yours," said Ursa. "It's worth as much as a good horse."

"Why me?" Kit asked suspiciously, handling it.

"Beck's sword," Ursa said matter-of-factly. "Obviously of personal significance, maybe a gift of heritage. The only thing we would dare do with it is bury it. You can take it back to Solace, which is far enough away. You're the last one to figure in on this mission. Nobody knows you were with us. You're safe—but I'd keep it wrapped and out of sight for a long while yet."

Ursa waited for her response. Kit gazed with satisfaction at the sword in her hand, but when she looked back up at Ursa her eyes were hard and uncompromising.

"You had to come back here anyway, to bury Beck," Kit said accusingly.

Ursa's face looked stubborn. "Maybe," he said. He waited, but when Kit said nothing else, he started to mount. The minute his back was turned, Ursa knew he had made a mistake.

The mercenary felt a sharp tip cut into his back. Blood trickled from the wound.

"Not so fast," Kitiara said with a hiss.

He turned around slowly, the sword in Kitiara's hands prodding him. Now the sword tip moved up to chest level and again nicked his skin.

"Thanks for the sword," Kitiara said. "Now I want my fair share."

"Don't be crazy," Ursa said tersely.

Kit gave the tip of the sword a little nudge, opening up another small wound. "I don't have it with me," Ursa said through gritted teeth.

"Then let's go get it," Kit insisted.

"They'll never give it you," warned Ursa. "They'd kill you, and they'd let me be killed by you, if need be, without a second thought."

"Too bad for you," said Kitiara. She gave the sword another push, and Ursa's blood flowed freely. Yet as Kit did so, the mercenary astonished her by reaching over with amazing speed and grabbing her sword by the blade. She hadn't noticed before—idiot!—but his hand was gloved in heavy leather. And though the sword cut sharply into the hide, Ursa was able to grip the sword firmly and push it away before Kit could react.

Then, her attention diverted, Ursa kicked upward, catching Kit fully in the groin. As she buckled, he kicked even higher with the other leg and caught her in the chin. She felt a snap and collapsed, bobbling the sword. Ursa gave Kit one more vicious kick in the side before she lost consciousness.

Ursa stood over her, quickly bandaging his hand in some cloth torn from his tunic. The wrapped hand looked blood-soaked, but in reality the cut was not very deep or painful, and Ursa knew it would heal. The look on his face was more of anger than anything else. His eyes were cold and unforgiving.

He picked up Beck's sword and, with some difficulty, wrapped it up again in its elaborate covering. Kitiara was motionless.

Ursa shuffled toward his horse and rose stiffly into the saddle. He was about to stick Beck's sword back into its niche in his pack, when he glanced again toward Kitiara and had a change of mind.

"Here," he said to no one in particular, his voice heavy. He tossed the sword into the dirt, next to her crumpled body. "You earned it, Miss Kitiara," he added as he turned his horse away.

Chapter 8

Stumptown

Kitiara struggled awake, feeling as if she had been drugged. The throbbing pain that came a moment later made her wish she was still asleep. The memory of her nasty confrontation with Ursa flooded her mind.

Anger tugged her to her feet as surely as if a rope was pulling her up. Brushing off her clothes, Kit noticed a long, thin bundle laying at her feet. Beck's sword, she realized. Ursa must have left it. Little enough for my trouble, she thought. The image of El-Navar, his diamond eyes and black hair like writhing snakes, flickered across her mind. There had been that too, a rite of passage that she no longer had to anticipate with either curiosity or trepidation.

The dusky morning light revealed ugly bruises spreading across Kit's jaw and neck. She touched them gingerly. Well, she thought to herself, they can't leave the daughter of Gregor Uth Matar in the dust.

Kit picked up the sword and strapped it to her back before untying Cinnamon and hobbling alongside her horse, tracking Ursa's hoof prints. As she might have guessed, after about a half an hour of painful walking, the search ended at a stream where the tracks vanished. Ursa was too practiced a mercenary to have not made an effective escape. Kit knew she would never pick up his trail and, if she did somehow, it would vanish again somewhere down the line.

Standing there, Kit realized how hungry she was. She bent to the water and drank deeply. Then, with a few encouraging words to Cinnamon about the likelihood of a warm, well-stocked stable at the end of the day, she stiffly mounted her horse and set off—to where, she had no idea.

Silverhole was ten or twenty miles to the north, but she didn't dare go there; the men who had been chasing her would certainly scout that place as a likely hideout. But Kitiara figured there would be smaller settlements, feeding off the road builders, directly to the south and west.

By midday Kit found herself in the southern foothills and felt safe. Silverhole was a half-day's ride distant. She was on the edge of territory where the forest dwindled and the land rose sharply into miles of knifelike ridges. Farther to the west, the terrain became barren and inhospitable. Not even mercenaries would seek to escape in this direction, she thought confidently.

Kitiara approached a small group of dwellings. Not much of a town, it was more a hastily thrown together assemblage of tents, huts, and shacks, with the occasional timbered building. Stumptown, a lettered sign read, no doubt because the trees hereabout had been leveled by lumbermen, and all that remained were scarred stumps. A motley assortment of people moved about on muddy, makeshift streets. Still, there was at least one food and drink establishment, Kit saw, and she was ravenous.

Of course there was a slight problem in that she didn't have any money.

As Kit drew closer, she saw a sign proclaiming: Piggott's Hospitality. The place was large enough, though the wood was weathered and the paint peeling. The windows were dingy where they were not cracked or boarded over. The single midafternoon customer—an ancient, grizzled dwarf—wobbly ascended the wooden front steps, looking as if he had just emerged from a barrel of soot and ash.

Nothing like the well-being and hospitality that emanated from Otik's inn back in Solace, Kit reflected, feeling a momentary pang of homesickness. She shook her head.

"Must be my aching body and empty stomach taking over," Kit muttered to herself as she dismounted and led Cinnamon around to where she supposed the kitchen entrance must be.

After tying her horse to a post, Kitiara secreted Beck's sword among some bushes. Squaring her shoulders, she knocked on the door, determined not to appear to be a beggar. A fat man with a thick, slack jaw, wearing a grease-stained apron, answered. Taking his time, he looked Kit up and down. One of his ears was clotted and misshapen, no doubt the souvenir of an altercation.

"Well, you look a little worse for wear, m'lady. Lover's quarrel was it? I likes 'em sassy, meself, but not too lippy. Now, what can I do for you?"

The man hadn't budged from the doorway. His considerable bulk filled the frame, blocking Kit's view of the interior. The smells wafting out, while no comparison to Otik's famous fare, were tempting enough to make Kit fight down the immediate revulsion she felt for this oaf and reply civilly.

"I'm passing through your town and have lost my purse along the road. Is there some work I could do in return for a meal?"

The man's attitude toward Kit took on a more calculating edge. "Know your way around a kitchen, do you?"

Kit, who had been hoping for some more physical chore, got a sinking sensation in her stomach, but hunger impelled her. "Yes, I can wash dishes, and in a pinch I can cook."

The man startled Kit by grabbing her arm and yanking her inside the door. "I do the cooking, m'lady, but if you can wait tables and wash dishes you can pitch in. The fellows who work here need all the help they can get. We don't get many ladies helping out, cuz the ladies in this town don't waste their time with kitchen work. They've turned their talents to more profitable ventures, if you know what I mean."

He threw his arm familiarly around Kit's shoulders and steered her toward one corner of a long table in the middle of the messiest kitchen Kit had ever seen. Dirty dishes, pots, and pans covered every available space. A gigantic black iron cauldron filled with something or other bubbled away over the fireplace, splattering into the flames and onto the hearth. Spilled water, grease, and all manner of foodstuffs glinted on the floorboards under which ran a shallow crawlspace. Gaps between the boards allowed most of the spillage to run off below. And from the rustling she heard beneath her feet, Kit surmised that none of it was going to waste.

"Piggott's the name, as in 'Piggott's Hospitality.' Hey, Mita, get the new girl some of that stew you're burning," Piggott yelled to a slightly built teenage boy skulking in the corner.

He turned back to Kit. "Work the dinner shift, and we'll see how it goes. One bowl now, all you can eat afterward. Them's my rules. If you work out, we'll see if I can think up anything else for you to do." He leered at her meaningfully before heading toward the doorway that led into the public room and tavern.

"What about my horse?" Kit called out after him. "She's tied up in the back."

Piggott paused to glance over his shoulder at Kit. "If you want me to feed your horse too, then count on staying through breakfast tomorrow. I'm not running a charity. One way or another—" he winked lewdly at her "—you'll have to pay for what you get."

Kit was too tired and hungry to shoot him the insult he

deserved. She sank wearily onto a bench at the table. The boy named Mita brought her a bowl of some stew, setting it down in front of her. Kit spooned it up hungrily even though it was so hot it burned her tongue. It was tasty, though.

Mita hovered at the edge of the table. He had yellow hair that bristled like cornstalks, a pockmarked face, and a pink slab of a tongue.

"Well," Kit said after several mouthfuls, "if you're waiting for me to tell you how good this is, it's decent enough, but could use more pepperoot. My father always said, when in doubt, add pepperoot. And Piggott is right. You've burned it."

Seemingly disappointed, the boy's pink tongue disappeared, and he turned away silently. As he walked toward the hearth, Kit noticed that he limped slightly. For some reason, she was reminded of Raistlin and immediately warmed to the boy. It makes more sense to have him as an ally than an enemy in this place, Kit thought reasonably.

"My name's Kitiara," she called after him, her tone more congenial. "You aren't that clodhopper's son are you? I hope not. I'd rather be his slave than his kin."

Mita turned and cracked a wan smile. He was almost as grubby as the kitchen surroundings, but his smile was sweet and genuine. "I get paid a little, and my meals. I stay in the barn."

"Tonight," said Kit, returning his smile, "the barn'll be my home, too."

She returned to her stew, and for the next several minutes gulped the rest of it down. Mita went out to tend to Cinnamon for her, and when he returned, Kit was already getting started, dumping dishes into an empty wooden tub.

"Start filling this with water from the well out back," she ordered. "Carry two buckets at a time if you can. We've got to get organized here."

Mita hesitated for a minute, as if deciding whether to challenge Kitiara's assumed authority. He was about her age, maybe a year or two older, in fact.

Just then the rumble of voices from the public room grew louder as people began arriving for supper. Mita shrugged his shoulders, picked up two buckets, and went out the door.

Soon Piggott was yelling numbers through the door, and Kit and Mita were doing their best to keep up. There was only one dish served every night, always some variety of stew, and the numbers signified how many bowls needed to be dished up. It wasn't long before Mita and Kit were filling up bowls whether they had time to clean one beforehand or not.

"Don't worry, nobody expects cleanliness-and-godliness when they eat at Piggott's," Mita advised Kit good-humoredly as he hurried in with a dirty bowl, wiped it with a dirtier towel that dangled from his waist, and spooned in a helping for the next customer. "Leastwise they don't if they live around here. If they do mind, they're probably just passing through and won't be back anyway. This is the only place for miles around that serves hot food."

Dashing in and out of the kitchen, ferrying empty and filled bowls of stew, Kit hardly had time to look around the public room. A bar and counter stood at one end of the place, near the kitchen door, where Piggott filled drinks and took orders. Along the floorboards stood tight rows of colored bottles—a fixture in lowlife Krynn bars—and at eye level, cheap, framed watercolors of snowy mountain peaks and cascading waterfalls were hinged to the walls.

The clientele consisted mostly of dwarves, plus a few grime-covered humans. Most were miners or loggers; some were from the road crew, which was obvious by their heavy-stitched clothing, backpacks, and belts of implements. The noise was shrill, and as she passed by the tables, Kitiara could make out only snatches of excitable conversation.

"It's a ploy, some kind of damn trick, if you ask me. . . ."

"They say Sir Gwathmey's son was himself killed. . . ."

"I still don't believe it, and I won't believe it till I spit on the evidence. . . ."

"You drink any more of that stuff tonight, and you'll be asleep and wetting your own pants. . . ."

"Are you going back to work. . . ?"

"What do you take me for, Aghar? I won't be gulled. . . ."

Kitiara pricked her ears as she moved easily among the grumbling customers, for nobody was paying much attention to her. And nobody was looking to tie a young woman into the crime—or hoax, some said—they were all steamed about, the hijacking of the road gang payroll. The road builders among them had already packed and made plans to head home.

"Somebody made off with a fortune," Mita said when the dinner rush was over and they had a chance to talk. "The dwarves think it's all a stunt to deceive 'em into working for free a little longer. Dwarves are shifty and suspicious types," he added knowingly, "and they don't like to be made fools of."

"Anybody hurt?" asked Kitiara innocently. At least, she hoped the question sounded innocent.

"Just a nobleman's son," shrugged Mita. "The robbers killed him but good. Made it look like a wild animal, though, which is one reason why the dwarves smell something funny. One thing's for sure, dwarves don't work on credit, and that road's never gonna get built now."

"Won't Piggott's business suffer?" asked Kit.

"Some," conceded Mita. "At first. But seems there's no end to dwarves and travelers. And if you want to get hot food and strong drink and—" he lowered his voice a little apologetically "—female company in these parts, you've got to come to Stumptown."

Kit and Mita had served helpings of stew until the black iron cauldron was almost empty, at which point, Piggott had announced that the kitchen was closed. By that time, the crowd in the public room had already thinned out considerably.

"Don't get much of a crowd after dinner time," Mita confided as he limped around the kitchen, stacking empty bowls to be cleaned. "Piggott waters his beer, and the place t'other side of town doesn't."

"What place across town?" Kit asked. "I thought you said this was the only spot to get hot food?"

"It is that," said Mita, lowering his voice again. "The other one is, well, you know . . . what Piggott was talking about before. Women what sells themselves to men. Even dwarves, if they can pay."

Mita's cheeks were flushed. Kit looked at him scornfully, not the least bit offended or embarrassed.

Mita busied himself with banking the fire. Piggott, out in the public room, had fallen asleep. Only one or two customers remained, nursing their tankards. Piggott was sprawled on a table, snoring obscenely.

"Never mind him," said Mita to Kit, who stood at the door to the big room, observing the fat proprietor. "He has a tendency to wake up just as the last customer leaves, and then he usually locks up. We can go now. We got a dwarf, name of Paulus Trowbridge, who comes in most mornings to clean. He didn't show up this morning, which is why the place was worse than usual. Come on, I'll show you where to bed down."

Mita led Kit out back where there was a small, sturdy building, less than a barn but more than a shed. Cinnamon was stabled inside, and there was some extra room. The mare whinnied softly when she caught Kitiara's scent. Clean hay was stacked against the wall, and Kit saw that Cinnamon had plenty of water, too. She was grateful to Mita for his thoughtfulness.

"This is it. I sleep in that corner. I added some layers to the wall so it keeps the wind out better." Mita rummaged around in the hay and pulled something out. "I see you have a blanket. Here's an extra. It's not much, but you'll need them both to keep you warm."

Numb with fatigue, Kit took the worn blanket and added it to her own gratefully. She was too tired to care much where she lay down. She trudged over to the corner opposite Mita's, plumped up some straw, and felt herself falling asleep even before her head hit the ground.

* * * * *

Kitiara had climbed into a tree. From her hiding spot she watched, transfixed, as El-Navar in his panther form ripped open Beck Gwathmey's body. Suddenly the sleek, black panther paused and looked up, directly at Kit. His gleaming diamond eyes invited her down, to partake. . . .

She woke with a start, hay dust in her nose, Mita kneeling down and gently shaking her. "I let you sleep as long as I could, but Piggott's going to be up soon, and if you're gonna stay, then we have to get ready to serve breakfast," he told her.

Kitiara shook off the dream and, rubbing sleep from her eyes, slowly stretched. Peering through the doorway behind Mita, she saw by the quality of the light that it was barely past sunrise. She rose crankily and brushed the straw off her clothes.

"Hurry!" Mita insisted, limping off toward the back door.

Kit resolved to stay through breakfast at least. She had no money and no immediate plans. Piggott's place seemed like a magnet for all kinds of road flotsam, and she might pick up some valuable information and new companions. She decided to try and work out some deal with the horrid man.

Kit almost changed her mind when she entered the kitchen and experienced one of Piggott's foul moods. He was cursing in several dialects, knocking over stacks of dishes, and kicking at the table. A young dwarf—young for a dwarf, that is—was trying to ignore the innkeeper's temper while methodically stacking pots, pans, and dishes, well out of Piggott's immediate reach.

Piggott caught sight of Kit, seemed about to say something, then thought better of it. Instead, he huffed and puffed out into the back courtyard, where he could be heard screaming at the chickens.

Mita slipped in the back door a moment later with an armful of wood for the fire. Kit went to help him.

"What was that about?" she asked in a low voice as together they stoked the flames.

"Road project's officially shut down," Mita whispered back. "Most of the dwarves have gone back to Thorbardin. Just like I predicted."

"Foreman had a mile-long bar tab, included him and his eight cousins," the dwarf, who was scrubbing dishes, tossed over his shoulders. "Left in the middle of the night, conveniently neglecting to pay up. Name of Ignius Cinnabar. Real tinpot on the job. Drinks half a barrel in his one night off, and his cousins just as much—each."

The dwarf was wearing patched coveralls that absorbed the water and slop splashing onto him. He had long silver hair tied in a ponytail behind his neck. His eyes were light brown. If stubby and arrogant, he was quite handsome for a dwarf.

"Sooner or later he'll be back," the dwarf said. "Ignius is honest; his faults lie elsewhere. He'll pay his due, but maybe not for months. Meanwhile, Piggott can fume all he wants."

Kit looked at the dwarf, and Mita took the cue to introduce them.

"This is Paulus Trowbridge. He's been here longer than me, off and on, and I've been here for going on five years."

Kit heartily shook the dwarf's hand. His grasp was more powerful than she expected and matched the strength that shone in his face.

"I was over at Silverhole when they broke camp," said Paulus by way of explanation. "They had been shorted, so they couldn't pay any bills even if they cared to. But try telling that to Piggott. He thinks the whole world is out to cheat him. Especially—" he spat on the floor for emphasis "—dwarves."

He went back to cleaning and stacking dishes, but talked to Kitiara and Mita over his shoulder as he worked.

"Did they catch the ones who did it?" asked Kitiara, as nonchalantly as she could manage, her heart beating fast.

"Nah," said Paulus, "and they won't. They're long gone

from hereabout. And even the ones who know, who saw them and maybe can recognize them again, they're gone too. The guards and the estatemen, they scattered but fast. They got to answer for their own failure, and the daughter what was gonna marry the young nobleman once the road was finished, she's posted a big reward for all accomplices, dead or alive. They say she's holed up in a tower somewhere, stark crazy with grief."

"Enough small talk!" snapped Piggott, who had come in the back door without them realizing it. He glared at Paulus. "You, get those dishes done and stop your dwarven chatter. Mita and Kitiara—if you're planning on dining off my generosity this morning, get to your chores. The customers are already arriving."

Sure enough, there was the sound of clomping from the dining room, signifying the arrival of customers. Paulus showed an indifferent mask to Piggott's hostility and turned to his work. Mita and Kit began to run around the room, preparing food and readying servings.

Within minutes, things were better organized, in part because Kit was not shy about giving orders. "Paulus, don't stack dishes so far away from the tub," she told the dwarf. "Move them closer. And see if you can find a different tub for the pots and pans."

The young ponytailed dwarf did as he was told, eyeing her with faint amusement.

"Mita, this is how you should beat biscuits." Kit took the bowl away from the kitchen helper and gave an expert demonstration. "And make sure the oven is hot enough before you put them in, or it won't matter if you mixed them right, they still won't turn out."

This was the type of work that Kit detested, but her years of virtually running the Majere household had left her with more than a few organizational and culinary skills. Anyway, if she got things running right, there would be less actual work for her to do.

Just then Piggott bustled into the kitchen, somewhat mollified by a good turn-out of breakfast customers, but ready from habit to explode. His eyes showed his surprise. Kit pulled the fat proprietor aside.

"After the rush, I'd like to talk to you about staying on here for a while *and* for a price."

Piggott, surveying the improved organization in his kitchen, nodded.

Mita, overhearing the request, smiled to himself.

* * * * *

Piggott agreed to pay Kit a small amount every week, in addition to room and board for herself and Cinnamon.

Bringing some order to the chaotic kitchen proved well within Kit's capabilities. Mita showed himself to be a willing and able apprentice cook. And Paulus Trowbridge, stoic about his chores, was a good worker. With a smile and a joke at Piggott's expense, Kit could keep both kitchen helpers in good humor while prodding them to move faster.

The money did not add up to much, but if Kit was going to be forced to return to Solace, at least she wouldn't have to slink back, penniless. Lying in the barn at night after a tiring day, Kit often found herself thinking about her home, and more particularly, her twin brothers. She wondered how Raist was doing in the mage school and whether Caramon was watching over him well. She savored these weeks away, but she had almost made up her mind to go back.

If Kit had had any idea where her father was, she would have gone there, or at least in that direction. During her first days at the inn, Kit found many excuses to go out into the dining room where she always looked over the crowd carefully, watching for a familiar face—Gregor's, or even Ursa's. There was never anyone she had seen nor met before. Now and then a grizzled warrior or roving Knight of Solamnia wandered into the place. Kitiara always contrived to wait on their tables. And if she could get a word in edgewise, she asked them if they had ever heard of a particular someone, the legendary mercenary, Gregor Uth Matar.

Some had heard of Gregor, or at least they thought so,

but no one had any information that was reliable or up-to-date. After a while, Kit stopped asking.

At first Kit overheard much talk about the ambush of Sir Gwathmey's payroll expedition. Bits and pieces of information as well as unfounded gossip kept travelers and the locals buzzing. But the upshot was that none of the perpetrators had been identified, nobody arrested or captured. The dead man's fiancee, across the mountains, had offered an astronomical sum—people said it was three times the amount of the robbery—for revenge against the murderers. Lady Mantilla had turned to dark magic, it was whispered, and employed a veritable army of spies and mages, as yet to no avail.

Kit stuck close to Piggott's place; indeed, she had little time or interest in poking around Stumptown. She figured it was wise not to attract attention. Beck's sword remained hidden among some bushes where no one ventured.

After a while, the rumors died down, until nobody talked about the payroll robbery anymore. Kit gave up hope of ever tracking down Ursa and getting her fair share of the booty. The episode seemed increasingly distant to her. Without the responsibility of caring for her half-brothers for the first time in years, and with a little change in her pockets, Kit gloried in her independence.

The companionship offered by Mita also helped make her time pleasurable there. She regarded the lad as the equivalent of another younger brother, though in age he was her peer. Although she suspected that Mita saw her more romantically, Kit was thankful he never said anything nor acted on that mistaken impulse. They slept within yards of each other every night, platonically, comfortable in each other's company.

One hazy afternoon when they were together in the courtyard, searching for eggs laid by Piggott's hens, Kitiara asked Mita why he limped.

"Don't know really," he said, averting his eyes because she had raised a delicate subject. "I always did. I used to live not too far from here with my grandmother. She tended a herd of goats to help keep food on the table. When I used to ask her how come, she wouldn't tell me. She'd just shake her head and look away, sadlike. Piggott said he supposed a big goat of hers must have stepped on my leg one day, 'cause of this."

Mita pulled up his pant leg to reveal a curved imprint on his lower right leg, the one he favored. Kit peered at the scar, but wasn't at all sure it looked like a hoof mark.

"What did your parents say when you asked them?"

"I didn't ask. Didn't ever know 'em. First I remember, I was living with Grandma."

Kit was standing close to Mita, and when her eyes met his, she had the oddest sensation he was going to try and kiss her. But the moment passed. How different from El-Navar's bold assurance, Kitiara couldn't help thinking to herself.

* * * * *

Piggott was not quite as gentlemanly as Mita, and more than once the fat, greasy owner had planted himself squarely in front of Kitiara, leering and saying something offensive. But Piggott never pressed his point when Kitiara brushed him off. He knew she always carried a small knife on her, concealed inside her tunic.

The one time Piggott had leaned too close, his beery breath hot in her face, Kit had slipped the knife out and pressed its tip against his prominent gut. "Well, aren't we rough and ready," Piggott had cracked, but the menace was gone from his voice, and his eyes darted around nervously as he looked for a way to retreat without losing face.

Piggott's mood was habitually foul. At times he would cuff Mita on the back of the head and berate him; or if the dwarf, who was part of their alliance, happened to drop a plate or come in late, Piggott would dock everybody's pay.

One morning, late in the summer, Kitiara woke having made up her mind to leave. Not because of Piggott, really—she could handle him—but her prospects for finding adventure in Stumptown seemed dim. She had enough money; she'd had her time away from Solace; so now she would return home.

Right away she told Mita, and he astonished her by saying that he would go with her. "I'm sick of Piggott's bullying," he declared. "I've got quite a bit of money saved up, and I'm going with you."

"What about your grandmother?" Kit asked. "Won't she miss you?"

"Oh, she died three years ago," said Mita matter-of-factly. "That's how come I decided to move in here and work for Piggott in the first place."

Kitiara said that, no, she was going home to help take care of her brothers, Mita couldn't come and stay with her, and he wouldn't like Solace anyway. Mita responded that he would go with her partway, then, and turn south toward Haven somewhere along the road.

Kit shrugged. Mita grew so excited about it that Kitiara caught some of his mood and became enthusiastic, too. Together they scurried around the barn, beginning to organize and pack their scant belongings.

Later, inside the kitchen, before the breakfast customers showed up in force, Kitiara and Mita were whispering about their plans, laughing, when a hand clapped Kitiara on the back. She turned to see Paulus giving her an unaccustomed glowering look.

"Let me in on the big secret," said the ponytailed dwarf, his eyes shifting between Mita and Kit.

They told him they were getting ready to quit, and Paulus astonished Kit further by announcing that he would quit, too, and go along with them. And when Mita split up with Kitiara, Paulus would keep heading south with the boy. "I can't wait to see that fat buzzard's face when we tell him," grinned Paulus.

Only minutes later, all three of them got that opportunity, when they cornered Piggott and informed him they were leaving after breakfast. The beefy innkeeper flushed a dark shade of crimson and erupted in expletives. He yelled and screamed insults at them, and they hurled their own insults back. Then Piggott switched tactics and plaintively entreated them to stay, at least for a couple of days, to give him time to find new kitchen workers.

"How can you leave today?" he pleaded. "You, Mita. How will you travel? You don't have a horse!"

"I'll buy one," Mita said proudly. "I have enough money saved up to buy three or four."

"No," said Paulus grandly. "Let me buy you one, friend. I have enough money for a dozen!"

"Kit, where's your gratitude? Mita, I've been practically a father to you. Paulus—"

Their laughter cut off his futile pleading.

Piggott changed his tack again, his face taking on a sly cast. He tugged at his cauliflower ear. "I'll tell you what," he said. "I'll give you twice your normal weekly salary, if you stay for two more nights. That's all. Just to let me make some arrangements. Twice your salary. After that, no hard feelings."

Kit, Mita, and Paulus exchanged looks. That offer was too good to pass up, and, in any case, they could use the time to gather supplies and prepare for their journey.

"Done!" said Kit, offering her hand to Piggott. He took it coolly, wiped his own on his apron afterward, then brusquely told them all to get back to work.

Two days later, the night before they left, Piggott counted out two week's salary, a tidy pile of coins, into each of their outstretched palms. The disagreeable man had said almost nothing to them during their extended time, and he was not around when the trio set out early the next morning, before sunrise.

Kit felt good to be riding Cinnamon again, after all this time. She carried only the few simple things she had arrived with, her purse of earned income, and Beck's sword, which she had retrieved from its hiding place. The sword was still wrapped, but Paulus's glance indicated that he guessed that Kit was carrying some prized weapon strapped across her back.

Mita was riding a palomino he had purchased from an old forester, and Paulus was astride a small pony. Both horses were draped with bundles and bags, some of which bulged and others of which conspicuously jingled. Where Mita had squirreled all of his trove away while they were living together in the backyard shed, Kit could not figure. She realized she was gawking at her two companions.

"Saved it all up," beamed Paulus, noticing her wide-eyed stare. Mita nodded with a big grin. Kit shook her head, then spurred Cinnamon forward.

Laden so, they rode slowly. They only covered twelve or thirteen miles from Stumptown, heading roughly south-west through the low mountains and dense forests, before making an early camp for the night.

The three of them argued over who should make dinner, and Paulus—as the least likely candidate—won. To Kit and Mita's surprise, the clever dwarf cooked up a delicious fry-ing pan meal of twice-sizzled eggs and sausage bits. The other two were amazed that Paulus had contented himself all that time at Piggott's place as a lowly dishwasher and kitchen helper, without volunteering his hidden culinary talents.

All were in a buoyant mood, laughing easily and swap-ping stories about themselves, as Lunitari emerged from be-hind a cloud. The wind shifted, a slight breeze came up, and Cinnamon whinnied. So innocent of all treachery were the trio that none of them realized anything, until Kit looked up and saw that three figures stood just outside their circle of light, waving weapons.

Immediately Kit and Paulus jumped up. "Don't move!" shouted a vaguely familiar voice. That one belonged to the largest of the three shapes and the one deepest in the dark-ness. Despite the moonlight, Kit could make out little about this cloaked and hooded man. At least, he had spoken in a man's voice.

One of the other two figures slid forward, waving a short sword. His hood had fallen back, revealing black hair, pointed ears, and a face painted with exotic designs. Wild elves, Kit thought to herself. She had seen very few in her time, and indeed had a prejudice against the entire elven race, believing they were not as forthright as dwarves or as innocuous as kender.

The Kagonesti with the short sword hurriedly patted each of the three travelers down. On Paulus he found a dagger and a small pegged cudgel, and, on Kit, her concealed knife. He missed the bundled sword, which Kit had taken off and lashed unobtrusively to Cinnamon, under her saddle blanket. Mita, who had risen, half-stupefied, was found to be unarmed.

Another of the brigands went to the horses, where Mita and Paulus had unloaded and stacked their accumulated wealth. He was Kagonesti, too. The two elves spoke back and forth in their own tongue, which was unknown to Kit, while the third, larger figure stood silently—nervously Kit thought—in the background.

Paulus glanced at Kit, but she shrugged, not sure what to do. Kitiara began edging backward, toward her horse.

The Kagonesti with the short sword shouted what was obviously a warning at Kit, and Mita looked over at her, alarmed. But the figure in the background called out something to the Kagonesti, in heavily accented Elvish. It sounded to Kit distinctly along the lines of, "Don't worry about her."

The Kagonesti with the sword backed toward his fellow elf, watching the three friends carefully, holding his sword-point in front of him. Kit was able to take a few more steps backward toward Cinnamon. As the Kagonesti reached his confederate, he turned half away from the prisoners to help his fellow finish searching the saddlebags.

Kit made her move. She whirled behind Cinnamon, slid out the concealed sword, and worked desperately to take off its tight wrapping. She heard the third man—she was sure now that he was not a Kagonesti—shout something and rush forward, wielding a wicked, curved knife. Peering over the rump of her horse as she unwrapped the sword as fast as she could, Kit saw the big one lumbering toward her, followed by one of the Kagonesti. Paulus had dropped down to the dirt. Mita just stood there, mouth open, seemingly frozen in terror.

Kitiara confounded them by charging. She came at them from the other side of Cinnamon, her sword finally at the ready. There was a gasp from the big man, and he stepped back. The Kagonesti kept coming, so Kit leaped into the open, away from her horse.

As she did so, Mita seemed jolted into action, and with a keening war cry that took everybody by surprise, made a running jump. Despite his limp, he managed to land on the back of the big, hooded figure, who dropped his knife in astonishment. With his arm around the man's neck, choking him, Mita pulled off the hood, revealing none other than their fat, scabrous former employer.

"Piggott," Kit spat in disgust. She should have guessed.

His tongue was protruding, and Piggott was doing his best to whip around and throw off his assailant. But Mita was hanging on and had the good sense to use his free arm to pound the fat innkeeper's bad ear. Piggott was shouting and cursing unintelligibly.

Things happened so fast, then, that Kitiara found it hard later to reconstruct everything in her mind.

The first Kagonesti had reached her, and she was fending him off with feints and short, quick attacks with her sword. He was a capable fighter, but Kitiara's sword, unsheathed, was intimidating. It caught the moonlight and sparkled in her hand, and she could tell that the Kagonesti, although he stood his ground, was worried by it.

The other elf had also rushed forward to help his cronies. As he reached the almost comical struggle that was going on between Piggott and Mita, the innkeep spun around. The Kagonesti lunged forward and stabbed poor Mita in the side. The boy cried out, lost his grip, and slumped to the ground.

Kitiara saw all this only out of the corner of her eye, for she had troubles of her own. The Kagonesti worrying her had proved resourceful. He had managed to back her against a tree, but had also managed to stay out of the way of her increasingly wild slashes. Now she had nowhere to retreat, and he was closing in.

Running to his side came the other Kagonesti, shouting in their incomprehensible language.

Piggott was just standing up and catching his breath, when from underneath him thrust his own knife, hard and fierce, deep into the underside of his fat belly. The awful man screamed out in agony. As Piggott gaped downward, his best kitchen knife slit the front of his stomach, up to his chest bone. Gripping its hilt was Paulus.

The first Kagonesti made the mistake of looking over his shoulder at what was happening, and before he knew it, Kitiara had lunged forward and stabbed him, deeply and with finality, through the heart.

Now Paulus came running over, carrying a big rock from the campfire in one of his bare hands, the knife in the other. The look on his face was fearsome.

The second Kagonesti had stopped, angled around, and now was holding both the dwarf and the young woman off, pointing his sword in front of him. He was clearly panicked.

Slowly Kitiara and Paulus closed in. With a surprising movement, the elf darted toward them, his sword threatening. When they took a necessary step back, he whirled and vanished into the bushes so quickly that they could barely react.

Kit and Paulus stood there for long seconds, looking after him, hearing and seeing nothing. At last, the dwarf dropped his weapons.

After stripping their corpses of valuables, Kitiara and Paulus left Piggott and the Kagonesti to the forest predators, but they buried Mita as best they could, under a shallow mound of branches and leaves.

"He was foolish," said Paulus, standing over the grave, his voice trembling with emotion.

"No, he was brave," said Kitiara.

They rode south for two more days, taking Mita's horse

and all of his belongings with them. On a high ridge, where the mountains cleaved and two roads went off in opposite directions, they decided to separate. Kit had urged Paulus to take all of Mita's things, but he wouldn't hear of it. She herself had no appetite for the leavings of her friend's life, so on the ridgetop they removed everything from the boy's palomino, then let the horse go free.

The ridge overlooked a deep narrow valley, and one by one Paulus threw all of the carefully packed bags and bundles as far as he could, out over the steep sides into the canyon. They could not hear them hit bottom.

"Seems a waste," said Kit.

"His life was a waste," answered Paulus, looking off.

"Where are you heading?" asked Kit as she got back on Cinnamon and prepared to leave.

"I dunno," said Paulus, getting on his horse. "Somewhere different, I know that."

"Will you do me a favor?" asked Kit solemnly. "Don't tell anyone about, er, all this . . . but especially, my sword." She reached down and patted the valuable weapon. The wrapped blade was looped to the saddle she had taken from Piggott's horse.

"I won't," said Paulus, his eyes meeting hers. "And I won't ask why."

"Luck," she said.

"Luck!"

Paulus was the first to turn away, his demeanor as nonchalant as when they had first met. Kit sat there, astride Cinnamon, and watched the handsome, ponytailed dwarf as he disappeared down the smaller trail that led toward the main road west. After a time, she galloped off in the direction of Solace.

Chapter 9

Home Again

After several more days, Kitiara reached Solace. It was late summer, and the branches of the majestic vallenwoods made an emerald canopy overhead. The familiar smells spurred Cinnamon into a trot. The horse didn't need any help finding the way back to her old stall in the shed beneath the Majere cottage. Kit fed and watered the mare, then, mindful of Ursa's warning, took Beck's sword and buried it under an unassuming pile of hay. Later, she would sneak the weapon up to her room.

With mixed feelings she climbed the spiral stairs to home.

It was almost meal time. Kit knew that her whole family would probably be home. Just as she was about to enter, the door swung open. Caramon threw himself on her, squealing with excitement.

"You're really back! Raist was right! He said you'd be standing there if I opened the door. I bet him a bag of rock candy that you wouldn't be, but I'm happy to pay up."

Caramon grabbed Kit's hand and pulled her into the center of the room. Rosamun's door was almost entirely closed, and Gilon was absent. Though the late afternoon was warm, Raistlin was sitting in a chair pulled up close to the hearth. A book lay open in his lap. Curiosity, admiration, resentment, and a little petulance mingled in the look he gave Kit.

"I didn't expect to see you back so soon. Was your journey a worthwhile one?" Raist asked her gravely.

Kit grinned. Same old Raist. "Let's say it took some unexpected turns. Judge for yourself how worthwhile."

Caramon, sensing the imminent handing out of presents, began hopping up and down at Kit's side. "Oh, she brought us something. It better be good; you've been gone all summer."

With a flourish, Kit pulled two small packages out of her bag. Despite his desire to appear cool and collected, Raist hopped off his chair and ran up to Kit. She gave the first package to Caramon. He tore off the crude wrapping and exclaimed loudly over the sturdy short sword she had brought him.

"It must have been so expensive!" crowed Caramon, turning it around in his hand admiringly.

In truth, Kit had taken the sword off the dead Kagonesti, but there was no reason for Caramon to be told that. "Watch you don't cut yourself," she admonished.

Raist unwrapped his smaller package more slowly, but seemed equally pleased with his set of leather vials.

"Now, those were expensive," Kit said, winking at Raist. The dead Kagonesti had contributed those, too.

As each boy was examining his souvenir, Gilon walked in the door carrying herbs and other foodstuffs, appearing harried. He looked at Kit in surprise, then followed that reaction quickly with a grin of genuine warmth. Having his arms full, he was able to avoid the awkwardness that typically passed between them over whether or not to embrace.

"Well, the adventurer returns! You must have grown two inches in the last couple months. Welcome back, Kit."

Indeed, she had grown up over the time, physically and otherwise. Gilon could see that Kit carried herself with, not just adolescent swagger, but true assurance. And while someone who looked at her fleetingly might still mistake her for a boy, anyone whom she engaged more closely with her crooked smile and laughing eyes would not.

Gilon dumped the food he was carrying onto the table. Just then, Rosamun shuffled out of their bedroom, a glaze over her eyes. Her face didn't show recognition of Kit, nor anyone else in the room. Her hair was uncombed, and she'd obviously slept in her clothes.

Kit frowned. Gilon hurried over and led her mother back to the bedroom, speaking to Rosamun in soothing tones. The twins, occupied with their new possessions and probably inured to the ghostly appearances of their mother, didn't take much notice.

Gilon strode back into the room. "I'm afraid it will be a while before we eat," he said to Kit apologetically, "and the meal won't be much. I don't have your knack in the kitchen."

A cosmic conspiracy seems determined to keep me in the kitchen, Kit thought to herself. "Sit down, Gilon," she said with a sigh. "I'll do the cooking. I haven't gotten out of practice, especially in the last few weeks."

As she prepared a homecoming repast, Kit regaled Gilon and the twins with selected stories from her exploits. In these, Ursa became Trubaugh—she thought it wise to disguise as much about him as possible, including his name—a mysterious man she had met at the spring festival, who swore he knew where her father was. He agreed to lead her to him, far to the northwest, if she would cook for him and his gang of ruffians. When it turned out that he was luring her up there for more nefarious purposes—here she wrinkled her brows to imply that these were motives best left unspoken—she relieved this Trubaugh of some of his purse and left him and his hapless gang in the middle of the night.

"Good for you!" said Caramon approvingly.

"Yes, he deserved worse," chimed in Raistlin.

"What about Gregor?" asked Gilon hesitantly. "Did Trubaugh really know anything? Or was it all a lie?"

"As false as everything else about Trubaugh," said Kitiara, shaking her head sadly.

After leaving Trubaugh, Kit continued, she had made her way through perilous mountain trails until she came upon a congenial settlement of miners and lumbermen called Dragonshead. Better than Stumptown, she thought to herself with the pride of creative deception.

The inn there was a jovial place, and for many weeks she had a job and friends. Piggott became a hilarious buffoon, and the motley crew that frequented his inn all played comical supporting roles. She left out all mention of their true names and the dark side of her experiences. Gilon and Caramon laughed heartily at her inspired version of events, but Kitiara caught Raistlin gazing at her thoughtfully.

Caramon, who was normally easy to gull, asked a zillion innocent questions about the time she had spent away, and Kit found herself squirming to think of plausible replies.

"C'mon, didn't you fight anybody when you were gone? I bet you did. Who? Was it this guy Trubaugh, or somebody at the inn? What weapons did you use? Did you win?"

Kit just smiled and tousled her brother's hair. "Don't be so dramatic, Caramon. Do I look battle-scarred?"

Caramon seemed crestfallen at her disclaimer, while Gilon and Raist regarded her skeptically.

"What about you?" Kit asked Caramon, deftly changing the subject. "Have you been practicing with your sword? And how has mage school been, Raist?"

"Well, I haven't had anyone to practice with, but I was pretty good to begin with," bragged Caramon, "Y'know that fancy lunge and parry you showed me? I can do that easily now. I'll show you after dinner, OK?"

"And mage school?" Kit persisted.

Raistlin looked down at his plate. Kit saw that Gilon was

observing Caramon's twin solicitously.

"I already know more than some boys who have been studying with Morath for a year," Raist responded in a low voice.

"Good!" exclaimed Kit enthusiastically. "And what about friends? Are you making any?"

"I don't really have much to do with the other boys there," he answered, fixing his gaze on his plate.

Kit's eyes met Gilon's. She mimed a shrug of unconcern. "They're probably all spoiled little bookworms," Kit declared. In her view, there were far more important things than being the most popular boy in the class.

Gilon left the table to try to coax Rosamun into eating something. Kitiara remained seated, joking with the twins, basking in their attention. When Gilon returned, unsuccessful at his mission, it was Kit's turn to leave the table, but only for a moment. She returned carrying a small pouch, which she emptied on the table in front of Gilon, creating a small pile of copper and silver coins.

"I don't know how long I'll be staying, but I want to pay for my room and board while I'm here. This should cover it."

The twins crowed at the sight of the coins. It was more money than they had seen in their lives. Gilon was momentarily speechless.

As he began gathering the coins from the table, the big woodcutter finally spoke, with evident emotion. "Thank you, Kitiara. This will help."

Kit had relished the gesture, and she did want to help out. But she suffered a twinge as she watched Gilon count the money. She had spent rather too freely on the journey home, enjoying a soft bed at a roadside inn on more than one night. Giving those coins to Gilon left her almost flat. It meant she was a little more stuck in Solace than she would have liked.

Oh well, Kit thought to herself. I've left once before without anything saved up. I can do it again if needs be.

That night, Kitiara climbed the ladder to her sleeping loft

and surveyed her old quarters. What once had seemed, if not exactly grand, then at least luxuriously set apart from the rest of the house, now looked cramped and dingy to Kit. Deeply tired, she stretched out on her straw pallet and received confirmation from yet another source that she had grown in the last few months, for her ankles overhung the edge of the bed by a good two inches.

In the cottage below, Kit heard Raistlin toss and moan in his sleep. The boys had stayed up past their bedtime and were overtired when they finally did go down. That often meant nightmares for Raist. Kit listened as Caramon roused himself to climb into bed with Raistlin and comfort him.

A rhythmic shuffling noise came from Gilon's and Rosamun's room. When Rosamun was in one of her wandering trances, Gilon actually had to put a cuff around her wrist and loop her to the bedpost some nights. Rosamun would pace back and forth alongside the bed, muttering weirdly to herself all night long. Such was obviously the case tonight.

Home, sweet home, Kit thought to herself. Well, she was glad to be back in Solace—temporarily. Her mind raced ahead to ways she could keep her stay short, but sleep overtook her before she could think of anything.

* * * * *

Waking up was hard business. Kit stretched on her too-small pallet. From the whispered conversations that drifted up from below, she surmised that Gilon and Raist were preparing to leave for the long walk to Poolbottom and that the rest of the household was still asleep. It was early, just after sunrise, when she heard them slip out the door.

Kit waited a moment to make sure they were gone before grabbing some clothes and climbing down from her loft. When she reached the first floor, Caramon was up, leaning on his elbows, regarding her with a sleepy smile.

"What about school for you, Caramon? What time to you have to be there?"

"I have to leave in an hour, if I go. When Mother is having one of her bad spells, I often stay home to make sure nothing happens to her. What's for breakfast? Usually father leaves me something."

Kit found a piece of bread with honey lathered on it that had been set aside in the larder which, she noticed, was not particularly well-stocked. She made a slice for herself and picked out some other food for her and Caramon's breakfast.

"What are we gonna do after we eat?" asked Caramon eagerly. "Want me to show you that lunge-and-parry?"

"Don't gobble so fast," Kit advised her little brother, who had started to bolt down his food. "I have to eat, too, then before I do anything I have to make sure Cinnamon has food and water. After that, maybe."

"I've been using your wooden sword while you were away, the one Gregor left you," said Caramon, chattering exuberantly. "I hope you don't mind. It's good for practicing. I've outgrown it, that's for sure—especially now that I've got a real sword."

Kitiara reached across the table and cuffed him on the ear.

"Ow! What's that for?" asked Caramon.

"For being stupid," Kit replied. "Keep the real sword at home until you're bigger. If there's one thing that my father taught me, it's don't show a sword unless you're ready to use it. And you won't be ready for some years. Meanwhile, a wooden sword is fine for a runt like you."

"Aw," said Caramon, chastened.

"Why, Kitiara, you're back."

Kit started at hearing her name and turned around to see Rosamun standing in the doorway of her and Gilon's bedroom. Her mother had woken up, smiling and lucid for the moment. Her skin seemed to hang on her bones; she looked withered before her time.

Neither Rosamun's spectral appearance nor her mood shift seemed to make much impression on Caramon, who happily skipped over to his mother for hugs and kisses.

"Yeah, isn't it great. She came back last night before supper. She brought me a real sword, Mother, a valuable one."

Caramon took Rosamun by the hand and led her toward the kitchen area. He dropped her hand now and ran to a high-backed ashwood armchair whose surface had mellowed to a satiny patina: Rosamun's chair, crafted by Gilon's handiwork. Caramon pushed it near the window into a pool of sunlight. Rosamun sank down into the chair and rested her head against its back, evidently wearied by the simple task of crossing the room.

Kit saw how fragile Rosamun's state was. Caramon would not be going to school today. "Would you like me to heat some water for tea, Mother?" the boy asked.

Rosamun smiled vaguely. "That sounds fine, dear."

Caramon grabbed the kettle eagerly. Kit could tell he wanted to show off to her how he could make tea all by himself now.

As Rosamun sipped a mug of tea, Caramon proudly showed her the sword Kit had brought him. As he knelt by her side, she stroked his golden brown hair. All of her mother's rapt attention was on the boy; though Kit had been gone for weeks, Rosamun barely noticed her daughter. The longer Kit stood there, ignored, the more irritated she became at the cozy domestic scene from which she was excluded.

"Well, Caramon?" she interrupted brusquely. "Are we going to practice our swordplay or not?"

"You bet!" he said, jumping up.

"Get my sword, too, will you?" she asked him.

Caramon reached under his bed and retrieved both Kitiara's old wooden sword and the small-handled one that Gilon had carved for him. As the would-be warrior waved both blades in the air with glee, Kit glanced at Rosamun, who was sunk in her chair, a look of hurt on her face.

"First we have to check on Cinnamon," reminded Kit. "I'll give you some lessons in taking care of a horse. That's a good thing for a warrior to know."

Caramon raced out the door without a backward glance at his mother.

* * * * *

Caramon and Kitiara practiced for hours. Kit used her old wooden sword, feeling childish, but she knew better than to bring out Beck's sword and let Caramon, much less anyone who happened to be passing by, get a look at it. Caramon wielded the sword Gilon had made for him, which was shorter than hers, but heftier. Both toy weapons were sharp enough that it hurt when they made good contact.

The sister and brother went at each other hard, down by the shed. Kit had to admit that Caramon had improved by leaps and bounds. What he lacked in technique, he more than made up in agility and determination. She could whack and stab him, but she couldn't back him down. Frowning with concentration, his hair stuck to his head with perspiration, the plucky six-year-old was beginning to tire. So was Kit, but neither would surrender.

"Let's go down by the lake," proffered Kit as an olive branch.

Not far from their home was Crystalmir Lake—Crone Lake, the kids sometimes called it, in reference to the legend of a witch who was believed to haunt it. Now and then the crone was spotted by a fisherman who'd had too much to drink, or a gnome traveler who, having heard the legend, would sit on the banks of the lake for two or three days, brandishing a See-Through-Virtually-Anything Aquascope.

"Sure thing," said Caramon, taking off in front of her. Kit easily passed him at a lope.

The shore was mossy in parts, sandy in others, the lake placid. Sticks, leaves, dead bugs, seaweed, and lily pads had washed up on the shoreline.

For an hour they explored the beach, stopping frequently to turn over big rocks and skip smaller ones across the surface. Caramon waded into the water, trying to catch crawfish that eluded his stubby hands. Kit laughed as he screamed epithets at one of them that had managed to pinch his fingers. When her brother fell backward into the water and came up sopping wet, she laughed all the harder.

Up on the bank, Caramon was wringing water out of his shirt and Kit was lazing on her back, marveling to herself at how quickly she was becoming bored by old, familiar Solace.

"Kit?" Caramon asked, strenuously squeezing his shirt.

"Yes," she answered dreamily.

"You ever seen the crone?" he wondered.

"What crone?" she asked back.

"The Crone Lake crone."

"Oh," she said, her eyes closed. "That's just a story they tell to little boys and girls to scare them."

"That's what Raist said," said Caramon in a small voice.

Afterward, they went back to the house, checked on Rosamun, who was napping, and decided to take Cinnamon out for some exercise. As Kit readied the mare, she turned her back on Caramon, who was idly scuffing his feet and poking around in the shed.

"Kit! What's this? You've been holding out on me. Where'd you get it? It's wonderful!"

Kit turned back to see Caramon swaggering with Beck's sword. Furious, she snatched it away from him and quickly wrapped it up again. Then she thrust it farther into the straw, behind a pile of field stones.

"Never mind where I got it," she said fiercely. "Nobody must know I have it. Understand? Nobody! On your honor as a warrior, promise to forget about it." She stood over her little brother intimidatingly.

"Aw, why?"

Kit raised a hand.

"OK, OK. I promise."

* * * * *

Later they rode. Kit sat behind Caramon, her arms encircling him, and they shared the reins. Guiding the chestnut mare beyond the forest into the tall grass, they rode for several hours, crisscrossing the open country, laughing and almost falling off. How good the wind felt!

By the time they returned from riding, it was approaching late afternoon, the time when Raist was expected home. Caramon told Kit that some days his twin stayed late and slept overnight at Poolbottom. A number of the students there came from far greater distances and boarded at the mage school, so there were good accommodations. But Raistlin preferred to walk the long way home most days. When Kit asked why, Caramon looked thoughtful while he replied.

"He doesn't have many friends there. He told me they call him the 'Sly One.' I think it's because he's smarter than all the other students. He's always the first to finish his assignments, and he's the best at remembering spells." Caramon paused for a moment, looking at his feet and kicking a stone as he walked along. He was frowning.

"Morath doesn't seem to like him much, either. The master mage thinks up a lot of extra work for him. That's the only time Raist stays overnight, when he has too much extra work to finish."

Caramon stopped on the walkway near the Majere cottage, fists clenched at his sides. "I know I ought to help him, but I don't know how. I know I got to worry about Raistlin and Mother, when you're not around. Father tries, but he works from sundown to sunup just trying to keep food on the table."

At that moment Kit was proud of little Caramon. Wasn't he just like her in some ways? Hadn't she been only seven when Gregor had left her alone with Rosamun? And at eight, hadn't she taken on almost all the responsibility of caring for the twins?

Just then Raistlin appeared in their path. His clothing was ripped and disheveled. One eye was already swelling shut, and his upper lip was bleeding.

"Who did this to you?" Caramon demanded.

Raist, his lower lip trembling, pushed past them into the cottage without saying anything. Inside, Rosamun fell on him instantly, exclaiming and weeping. She sat him in a chair and wiped at his lip and scratches. Caramon paced up and down in front of the door, swearing revenge. Kit stood off to one side, watching everything anxiously.

Afterward, Rosamun retreated to her room, and Raistlin and Caramon started quarreling.

"If I had been with you, this never would have happened," said Caramon, puffing out his chest.

"Don't be ridiculous. This is between me and—"

"Caramon, calm down," Kit commanded. "Now, Raist, tell us what happened. I think we can all agree that any revenge devised by all three of us will be three times as sweet as anything you can concoct by yourself." Her tone brooked no argument.

"I was on my way home from school, on the outskirts of Solace where there's that stand of young trees," Raistlin began slowly. "I had just entered the shade of that grove from the bright sunlight, and my eyes were still adjusting to the dimness so I'm not sure exactly what happened. But someone or something pounced on me from above at the same time that I tripped, I think over a rope drawn tight across the path. I hit my face on some rocks as I fell down, which is how I got the cut lip.

"Before my head had cleared, my hands and feet were tied up. I saw who was tying me—it was Dune Wister. His brother, Bronk, was with him. They made fun of me for being a magic-user. They looked in my pockets for anything of value. There wasn't any gold or silver, of course, but they took the pouches you gave me, for holding my spell components, and they filled them instead with . . . bat dung. They ran off laughing, and it took a while for me to get untied."

For an instant Raist looked as if he were about to cry, then he fiercely blinked back the tears.

"Those scum!" Caramon exploded.

"Quiet!" snapped Kitiara.

"Dune and Caramon are in the same class at the village school," Raist continued. "Dune's just like his brother, a pint-sized bully. Every time he sees us, he makes a crack about Mother." Raistlin's voice dropped a notch in the telling.

"Tell her about the last time," urged Caramon.

"The last time," said Raistlin, shooting a glance at his brother, "I was ready. We haven't learned many spells at Poolbottom yet, just some simple illusions. There was one that only called for dried beetle wings, which are easy enough to get, so I was carrying some with me. So as soon as Dune started saying something about Mother, I had Caramon pin him down and I made the spell. Every time he opened his mouth to say something, bugs fell out." Raistlin and Caramon grinned at the memory.

"Bugs?" repeated Kit.

"You know, beetles and ants, centipedes and flies. Dune couldn't open his mouth without spitting out bugs. The spell was supposed to last for a couple hours, so I don't think he had much fun teasing anyone the rest of that day."

Despite his scratches and swollen lip, Raist looked slyly pleased with himself. Caramon, though, had stopped grinning. "We ought to settle this my way," he declared vehemently, "We're three against two. Bronk and Dune won't dare jump Raist again."

Raistlin glared at his twin, but Kit spoke first.

"One good brain is worth more than a dozen stout warriors," she said emphatically. That was one of Gregor's maxims, and the twins had heard Kitiara repeat it before.

"Come here," she said, drawing her younger brothers close in a huddle. "I have an idea."

*   *   *   *   *

The sun had just risen when Kit slipped the note under the door. She hoped that, as the oldest, Bronk was up first to help with the chores. If Aureleen had been right all those months ago, Bronk wouldn't be able to resist an invitation from Kitiara, even if what little common sense he had told him the circumstances were suspicious.

My heart's beating quickened when I saw you the other

*day. Meet me at the end of the path to Crystalmir Lake to-
night at dusk.*

Affection, Kitiara

Pleading aches and pains from the previous day, Raist
stayed home from Poolbottom. Gilon raised his eyebrows
at the excuse, for Raist had always been eager to go to
school, even on days when he'd had a raging fever. But
Gilon was preoccupied with his own concerns, and Raist's
acting job convinced him.

After solicitously serving the twins breakfast, Rosamun,
her strength depleted, dozed in her favorite chair.

Kit, Raist, and Caramon spent the day coming and going
on mysterious errands. After one final whispered confer-
ence between the three of them in the late afternoon, Kit
disappeared with a bundle under her arm. Not one of the
three came home for supper, and Rosamun became very
worried.

"Don't fret," said Gilon, when he returned to the cottage.
"They must be up to something." He stroked his wife's white
hair soothingly. But Gilon was worried, too.

Kit had found a vantage point on a hill overlooking the
path down to the lake and was keeping watch. As she expected, Bronk showed up a good hour before sunset, nervously checking the area for any traps. He made a more
thorough job of it than she would have guessed, then settled
down on a stump at the edge of the sand leading down to
the water.

Bad luck. Earlier that day the twins had tethered a line to
the far side of that exact stump, burying it under the sand
and running it down into the water. Kit didn't want Bronk
to start poking around the stump, so quickly she shrugged
out of her tunic and leggings, then unrolled the bundle from
home.

A gauzy, flowered dress, one of Rosamun's old ones, fluttered in the lively breeze. Kit regarded the garment with
some distaste, then slipped it on. The rich colors set off her
dark hair.

Bronk had started to idly dig into the sand with the toe of

his boot. Kit looked up the path toward Solace. No sign of the twins, yet she had no choice but to begin the charade.

Making certain Bronk did not see her, Kitiara hurriedly crept around to the back of the hill where she had been perched, then stepped away onto the path. Fortunately, he caught sight of her right away and stopped his idle digging.

She sighed with relief. "I'm so glad you came, Bronk," Kit murmured. "I didn't think it was going to be so dark on the path down here."

Bronk mistook her sigh for a flirtatious gesture. When she glided closer to him, Kit could see that his mouth was hanging open. He was definitely off his guard.

"Gee, I, uh, I . . . what's all the mystery, Kitiara?" he stammered, thrusting out his chest and striking a virile pose.

"Well," Kit began, "it's just that I haven't seen you for an awfully long time."

"You've been gone," Bronk said, sounding a little miffed. He glanced around nervously. "Everybody wondered where you went. Nobody knew for sure. Not even your brothers, I don't think. Where'd you go anyway?"

"What does it matter?" she said, lowering her head. She tried some sniffling. "It's all over anyway."

"What's over?" he demanded to know.

"What does it matter?" Kit repeated mysteriously. Sniffle, sniffle.

Bronk sidled over and clumsily put his arm around her shoulder.

Where were Caramon and Raist? How long was she going to have to put up with this dunce and keep him dangling around this tree stump!

"Well," Bronk said petulantly, "I'm glad you realized the error of your ways. I always thought that us . . . that is, you and me . . . I mean, even if I don't like your dumb brothers, I always thought that you and me could be friends. More than friends."

This had been a long and almost articulate speech for Bronk. He seemed winded and confused, as if he had said more than he'd meant to. Again his eyes darted nervously around. Then Bronk gave Kit a tentative little squeeze.

"What do you mean, 'more than friends'?" she asked ingenuously, batting her lashes. Where were her darn brothers? But Bronk, preoccupied with his next move, didn't notice the tension in her shoulders.

His arm tightened around her shoulders. Kitiara smiled up at him, hoping he wouldn't notice she was gritting her teeth.

Please! She couldn't take much more of this.

Just then, the sound of boys' voices reached them, coming from the path.

"What's this?" Bronk asked with considerable irritation.

The voices grew louder, until Kit and Bronk could make out some of the words.

"You'll eat those words," Caramon was saying.

"My brother would never—"

"See if you believe your own eyes." That was Raist.

Bronk had dropped his hand from Kit's shoulder and was looking at her with revived suspicion. When he finally realized that it was Dune's voice he was hearing, along with the twins, he grew agitated.

"Say, what is this?" he said, shoving Kitiara's shoulder.

Dune came around the bend. He was wedged between Caramon and Raistlin, almost being propelled forward by the twins. His eyes grew big when he spied his brother standing next to Kit.

Dune was a thick-witted little boy who worshiped his bully brother. Caramon and Raistlin had told him that Bronk was secretly romancing Kit. Dune couldn't believe that his brother was wooing the very girl about whom Bronk had said so many terrible things. On a bet, the twins had brought the boy to Crystalmir Lake to sneak up on the two supposed lovebirds and prove the romance.

"Bronk!" Dune cried in dismay.

"It's a dumb . . . rotten . . ." Bronk sputtered a few more words, but they were unintelligible.

Kit had intended to maneuver everyone closer to the water, but decided she had better act right away, while Bronk was momentarily unnerved. She edged around the stump and pulled on the hidden rope.

Nothing.

She pulled again, harder. This time she could feel something give on the other end.

Kitiara signaled Raist, who was hanging back. He stood ready in his best spellcasting stance.

After a few murmured phrases from Raist, the surface of the lake near the shore where they stood began to bubble and seethe. The odd noise captured Bronk's and Dune's attention. Immediately, the two brothers lost interest in their private drama. They froze, their eyes riveted to the lake.

"What's that?" Bronk whispered fearfully to Kit.

Good. They've forgotten all about Raistlin.

Dark plumes of smoke and fingers of flame erupted from the sandy banks. The surface of the water roiled, and a huge shape began to emerge.

With the smoke and the dim light, it was difficult to see exactly what the shape was. A thing, a creature, manlike but much larger, with wet tendrils of slimy plants clinging to its sides. Suddenly its empty eye sockets blazed with orange fire, and its upper limbs began to sway, making it appear as if the horrible creature were moving toward shore.

"It's the crone!" Caramon whispered near Dune's ear.

"The crone!" shouted Dune in fright. "It's the crone!"

Screaming in terror, Bronk and Dune fell over each other scrambling up the path. Their yells continued for several minutes before fading into the distance.

Kit, Raist, and Caramon collapsed on the sand, laughing. They were distracted by a loud hissing sound coming from the water. When they looked up, they saw the garish shape slowly collapsing in on itself.

"I wondered how long those sheep bladders would hold air," Raist said, suddenly thoughtful. "I was worried when we had to force that contraption into a cage and sink it underwater, whether it would deflate and not be able to float when Kit released the lid."

"You were worried!" exclaimed Kit, between fits of laughter. "Bronk was about to try and kiss me!"

"Did you see them take off?" Caramon asked, his face flushed and eyes bright. "It'll be a long time before either of them look in our direction."

"It'll be a long time before they can look each other in the eyes," Raist added solemnly.

"Of course," Caramon felt compelled to add, "I could have beaten them fair and square, if you had let me settle it my way." He struck an injured pose. "But that was fun," he admitted after a moment. "Good job, Raist."

"You built the 'monster'," Raist said.

"Let's leave this junk here," Kit said, standing and surveying the collapsed creation. "Bronk and Dune are bound to slink back and investigate in the safety of daylight. Then they'll see what it was that scared them—birch bark, an empty ale barrel, sheep bladders, and old rags. That's the witch of Crone Lake."

They all laughed again.

"Tomorrow we'll spread the story, right?" exulted Caramon. "That'll teach 'em."

"No," said Raist.

Caramon looked perplexed. Kit nodded understanding.

"Let them wonder why we don't tell people," said Raist wisely. "Let them wonder when we are going to start."

The three of them laughed, reliving their glorious trick on Dune and Bronk all the way back to the cottage, where even Kit was delighted to discover that Rosamun had made vanilla pudding.

* * * * *

Kitiara had itched with restlessness from almost the moment she'd returned to Solace. Yet as the days grew shorter and fall approached, Kit lingered in the Majere household. Before she knew it, another winter had come on, then spring again, then another summer.

Kit wanted desperately to leave, but she didn't have very

much money and no real destination in mind. There was no word of her father, and she was so far away from Silverhole that she didn't expect to hear any news of Ursa. And she knew that the mercenary would never come back to her part of the world again.

For the most part, her days revolved around Caramon and Raistlin, but the two of them were so busy with their individual schooling, both were so much older and self-sufficient, that there was less for her to do.

Rosamun's health went into another stage of deterioration, and most of the time she had no idea that Kit was even living there, as before, up in her small loft. Rosamun had so weakened that she was bedridden for weeks at a time, and easy enough to look after. Bigardus came to the house several times a week, at Gilon's bidding.

Kit's old friend Aureleen Damark had developed womanly affectations and a steady boyfriend, Ewen Low, a militia cadet. When the two teenage girls got together, they fell easily enough into their former pattern of giggling conversations. But Aureleen's mother did what she could to see that Kit did not receive many invitations to visit.

Another winter approached. With the onset of colder weather, Kitiara got into the habit of frequenting Otik's in order to keep an eye on parties traveling through Solace.

Chapter 10

A Proposal

Though Otik Sandahl had only been proprietor of the Inn of the Last Home for about fifteen years, the reputation of his place had already spread throughout Abanasinia. Travelers made a point of stopping over in Solace in order to sample the specially brewed ale and spicy fried potatoes Otik served. The innkeeper himself was another inducement. His round eyes and equally round belly bespoke an enjoyment of life he worked hard to share with his tavern's clientele.

The current renown of the Inn of the Last Home was the more remarkable because of its reputation under the previous owners. These were a married couple, hill dwarves, whose sour dispositions seemed to taint everything from the ale they served to the generally inhospitable atmosphere travelers felt the second they entered the inn. The smells from the kitchen were enough to offend a gully dwarf— well, almost.

Maybe the root of it was their dissatisfaction with having to live quite so far above ground or the unending irritation about their clan's exile from the mountains. Whatever the cause, their marriage degenerated into cold stares and public bickering, even as the inn itself crumbled into disrepute.

One day the husband got up earlier than the rest of Solace, packed a meager bag of belongings, and left town. Nobody missed him, least of all his wife, who sold the inn to the next traveler on the road—Otik Sandath—for "a kender half-penny," according to local wags. Where Otik was coming from, or going, was the subject of some speculation, but whatever his plans had been, Otik had reached that stage in life where he wanted to travel less and to settle down more. In any case, it was a happy happenstance. Otik had found his natural calling.

His first task was to give the inn a thorough cleaning and lovingly polish the vallenwood floors and furniture to perfection. Then he set to work in the kitchen. Of his spicy fried potatoes Otik would say only that the recipe had two basic ingredients: potatoes and spices. "If it don't fill you up, you don't have to pay up," Otik was fond of saying. Soon no one doubted his word.

Not quite as famous, but every bit as tasty, were other dishes he had learned to prepare on his travels—braised trout cheeks, duck liver pudding, buck stew, and cranberry surprise.

His traveling days were also reflected in the decor of the inn's common room. He decorated the walls with various mementoes, curios, and anything else that had caught his fancy during that time. And he kept expanding the collection. Despite protests from his customers, each year Otik insisted on closing up the inn for one month—not really trusting anyone else to run it in the proper manner—and indulging what remained of his wanderlust.

Otik was determined to see as much of Krynn as he could

in his time and he journeyed far afield. A rough map behind the long bar, paid in barter for a meal by a kender, showed X-marks for all the places he had visited. Otik always returned with one or two souvenirs. Once it was a fearsome minotaur battle axe. Another time it was a finely embroidered scarf, elfish in origin.

On his first day back, Otik would produce these curios with a great flourish for his regulars and anyone else who happened to be stopping over at the inn. Then he proudly added the objects to his decor, fussing over exactly the right way to display them, with plenty of advice from his patrons.

By now, the Inn of the Last Home was a veritable museum of objects from the disparate Krynnish cultures. This collection was one of the reasons Kitiara both liked and disliked hanging around the inn. She would stare at the different objects and daydream about whence they came, the things they had witnessed. But eventually those daydreams always led Kit back to the fact that she was stuck in Solace, far from any excitement. At that thought she might bury her head in her hands and groan in frustration, stalking out of the place, not to be seen around the premises for a week or so.

But Kitiara always returned. Too young to have a taste for Otik's ale and too cash-pinched to afford his hearty fare, she rarely bought much, just sat alone at a table and sipped one glass of pear juice for hours at a time. Her favorite spot was in a corner near the front door so that she could have first look at the travelers who climbed the long, winding stairs up to the treetop inn. One of them might have news of her father. One of them might be able to alleviate the tedium of Solace.

Kitiara had stayed in the treetop community far longer than she had expected when she first returned from her adventures with Ursa and Stumptown—more than two years. She had waited in vain for a likely group of travelers to latch on to in order to leave again, ones that looked to be on their way to something more interesting than the next village.

At first, Otik hadn't really liked having such a young girl

hanging about, but he grew to tolerate Kitiara—the main reason being he had given up trying to keep her out. If he escorted Kit out the front door, she edged in the back. If he watched both doors, somehow she slipped in through one of the windows. When she seemed gone for good and he had forgotten all about her, he would turn around and there she would be, sitting near a window, paying him not the least attention.

Truth to tell, Kitiara was not bad for business. In the right mood she could play jackdaw with the best of them. She was a patient listener to stories of the road, and every inn needs its good listeners as well as its good storytellers.

And Otik was at heart a gentle soul. He didn't begrudge Kitiara time away from her home, which he knew was dominated by Rosamun's sickbed. When there were no other customers, Otik would even strike up a conversation with Kit. He liked to talk about the origins of his souvenirs, occasionally taking one down from the wall and letting Kit caress it. She listened avidly to Otik's little histories, gaining an education about the world that couldn't have been obtained in school. The innkeeper treated Kit kindly, just as, years later, he would treat Tika Waylan, the orphaned daughter of one of his barmaids.

It was plain to Otik that Kitiara would not be pining around his bar for long. At sixteen years of age, she was already shedding the gangliness and rough-edges of adolescence. Her face had emerged into an arresting angularity, narrowing from high cheekbones to a determined chin. The lower half of Kit's face was softened by full, rosy lips. Her dark eyes were fringed with glossy lashes whose midnight color matched the cap of black, curly hair she continued to wear in a boyish cut.

Careless of her appearance, she favored close-fitting tunics and leggings because they allowed her freedom of movement, seemingly unaware that they also showed off her natural grace and a slender figure that had begun to curve appealingly. Now, on the occasions she and Aureleen wandered through the marketplace or walkways together, appreciative stares were as likely to be directed at Kit as at her conventionally pretty friend.

Yet any man who tried to flirt with Kit met a prickly response. As far as she could tell, most men wanted much more than they gave back, and Kitiara didn't like that equation, even when it applied to her brothers—though, thank the moons, at eight years old they already seemed fairly able to take care of themselves. Raistlin's magic studies were progressing well and occupied most of his waking moments. When Caramon wasn't skipping school to practice his swordplay, he was tagging around after Gilon.

As if she had conjured him up with her thoughts, Kitiara looked out through the front door Otik had propped open on this warm afternoon and saw her high-spirited brother running up and down the walkways outside the inn with a group of friends. He and another boy began mock-jousting with two long sticks. Caramon was obviously stronger and more agile with the stick, but, laughing, he let his friend best him and threw up his hands in mock surrender. Kitiara frowned. That boy had inherited too soft a nature from Gilon.

A moment later, Caramon turned up at the inn's entrance.

"Hey, Kit, wanna buy me a glass of pear juice or some of those good potatoes Otik serves?" he said with a grin that even Kit in her current ill humor found difficult to resist.

But, as was her custom when he tried to set foot in the inn, Kitiara pounced on Caramon and tossed him out before even Otik could react.

"Any more potatoes and you'll be too larded up to lift your sword. Now get going or you'll be late to meet Raistlin on his way back from Poolbottom!"

Shooing Caramon out the door, Kitiara noticed two strangers climbing the stairs that ended at Otik's doorway. That was not odd in itself, but these two strangers were as mismatched a pair as Kitiara had ever laid eyes on. Kit returned to her seat to await their entrance.

Within a few moments, they were standing inside the front door, surveying the room. One was a behemoth, his hair braided in a dozen strands that fell down his neck to brush his shoulders, his head massive but with eyes tiny as bugs, sunken in fleshy sockets. Six and a half feet tall and, Kit guessed, three hundred pounds, he was tented in a great swath of multi-colored clothing. Her glance went immediately to his weapons—a scimitar, a knife, and a knobby short club, all slung conspicuously around his formidable girth. Over his back he carried a great wooden trunk, which he now flung down on the floor and pushed to one side. He said nothing, but his eyes glared around the room, alighting briefly and without interest on Kit.

He was accompanied by a man who was even more curious for the fact that at first glance Kit might have thought he was a woman. This other one was tall—though not so tall as the giant—and slender, with alabaster skin, jet-black hair, and azure eyes. He was dressed in a tunic of sea blue, with a tooled belt cinching his narrow waist, weaponless, and carrying a leather pack that he dropped wearily to the floor on top of the trunk. He's not much older than me, Kitiara thought, perhaps twenty. As he walked up to the bar, she noticed that he was wearing an unusual pendant with a dazzling green stone around his neck. Along with this uncommon piece of jewelry, Kit was astonished to notice a scent. He obviously was wearing some perfume or oil.

The man carried himself with tremendous dignity, and she realized that he must be someone of privilege and station. More than that, he had a definite aura of gentility and sophistication unlike all the roughnecks and common folk she was used to. Kit had never seen such a man. Any traces of bad humor vanished from her face. Her eyes were alert, her expression intrigued.

"Is lunch still being served?" asked the man as Otik bustled out from the kitchen to greet them.

"A late lunch or an early dinner," Otik said cheerfully. "It's all the same to me. Set yourselves down, and I'll be happy to accommodate."

Being well-traveled, the innkeeper was not as struck by their appearance as Kitiara. He rightly judged the young man to be a well-born noble from Northern Ergoth, accompanied by his slave.

"I am Patric of Gwynned, and this is my manservant Strathcoe," said the man. "I am told by everyone I have met that I should be sure to try your spicy fried potatoes."

His voice was forceful, accustomed to being obeyed. He continued to hold Kit's interest.

Patric's comment about the spicy fried potatoes brought a smile to Otik's face. "Some ale?" asked Otik. "Ale goes good—"

"Fresh water, please," Patric said, cutting him off. "Then, perhaps, some wine. You do serve wine, don't you?"

This last was said as Patric appraised the common room, taking in the sign over the bar that read, Healthy and hearty fare for the citizen and wayfarer.

Otik's face clouded over at the stranger's implication that he ran anything less than a first class establishment. "Of course we serve wine," he said, letting a note of displeasure creep into his voice. "And what would you gentlemen like to eat besides spicy potatoes?"

"Just potatoes, for now," Patric said pleasantly. Clearly he had decided that he would test the mettle of Otik's cooking before ordering anything else.

Vaguely insulted but holding his tongue, Otik hurried off to prepare the order. As he did, the two men looked around and chose a big table near Kitiara.

She had been watching them intently, but shifted her gaze to the window, feigning disinterest, as soon as they moved toward her. Yet she sensed that the younger man was distinctly aware of her presence. She, Patric, and the slave called Strathcoe were Otik's only customers, and an unusual silence prevailed in the normally convivial inn.

"Hey, Kitiara! I'm bored." Caramon stood at the threshold again and was beckoning loudly to his sister. "It's too early to meet Raist. Can't we do something like go down and look at the horses in the stable?"

"Later," said Kitiara sharply, waving him out the door.

"You're not doing anything," the eight-year-old protested,

putting on his best pleading look.

"Later," said Kitiara, glaring at him.

It was a look and a tone Caramon knew better than to cross. Sulking, he backed out the door.

As he did, the stranger called Patric turned and looked directly at Kitiara. Their eyes locked. Kit shivered, feeling an intensity in his gaze that she hadn't encountered since— well, since her dealings with El-Navar. Flustered, she looked away, annoyed with herself for doing so. She forced herself to raise her eyes and found Patric still watching her. This time Kit returned his steady gaze. Finally he broke the tension by acknowledging her with a nod.

"Will you indulge us by sharing our table?" he asked. "My servant is not much for conversation, and we have been on the road for many weeks."

"Yes," Kit said, surprised to find herself eager to join them. Otik, coming around to the table with a pitcher of water and two goblets, raised his eyebrows in surprise, gaining a sideways dirty look from Kitiara in response.

As she went to their table, Patric stood and bowed slightly from the waist, then pulled a chair out for her. His slave, arms folded imperiously, did not acknowledge her presence with words or gestures. Yet up close, under these circumstances, Kit did not find him so imposing.

Otik returned to the kitchen and came back a moment later with two plates of fragrant potatoes. He set them down on the table with obvious pride.

"Anything for you?" Patric asked Kitiara, but she shook her head at Otik, who retreated to the bar where he could keep an eye on his guests.

The young noble tasted a few small mouthfuls of his food, sipping water in between. The man-mountain slave evinced no such delicacy. He set to work, noisily and with evident satisfaction, on his plateful of potatoes.

"These are quite good," Patric said to Kit with an apologetic smile, as if entrusting her with a great confidence. "And certainly Strathcoe has no quibbles. I think I will order some more food and drink. I fear I have ruffled the innkeeper's feathers by my hesitation. Perhaps this will smooth them. Are you sure you can't be tempted?"

"No, no thank you," Kit said, striving for a nonchalant tone. "And don't worry about Otik's feelings being hurt. Nothing really upsets him except a kender trying to leave without paying his bill."

As Patric called Otik over to the table to order a bottle of the local wine and some buck stew for his servant, Kit cursed herself for feeling so tongue-tied in the presence of the young noble's glib charm.

For a while the only sound at the table was the slurping and chewing of Strathcoe, whose eyes darted back and forth between the two of them as he devoured his food.

"You must forgive Strathcoe," said Patric. "He was not properly raised, but he has many sterling qualities. His bad ones are, at worst, amusing." He smiled.

Patric sipped his wine before speaking again. "He can't speak, poor wretch. My father had his tongue cut out for some bad behavior—I forget what. He was demoted to serving me. He is quite loyal, a good fighter, and a stalwart traveling companion. Although he can't speak, we communicate very well. I tell the jokes, and he laughs at them."

Kitiara looked at Strathcoe skeptically, but the big man had obviously heard and understood everything Patric said, because he bobbed his head up and down enthusiastically with a big smile spread across his face. It changed his aspect entirely, so that for a moment, before the smile disappeared, he appeared almost a jovial bear.

Patric smiled also, looking directly at Kitiara. "You know our names. What is yours?

"Kitiara Uth Matar, daughter of Gregor Matar." Kitiara spoke the name proudly, color rushing to her cheeks. Then she smiled, lopsidedly as ever.

"From far away I have heard of Otik's potatoes and of his ale, although ale is not to my taste," said Patric, looking intently into her eyes. "But I had not heard that the young women of Solace were so beautiful."

Kitiara caught her breath, and her color deepened. Never

before had she been so aware of the smudges on her face and hands. Such talk from the men who filled Otik's place Kitiara had heard often, but the words had been spoken roughly, half-jestingly, and she had turned them aside in kind. She searched her brain for something to say, yet no words came.

Perhaps sensing her discomfort, Patric dropped his glance and changed the subject.

"We have been on the road for nine weeks. It's a ritual of travel I undertake every year. This year we have been gone longer than expected. We are now on our way to the coast, where a ship is waiting to take us home. Gwynned is on the western coast of the island of Northern Ergoth."

Kit knew where Northern Ergoth was, of course, but she was not so sure about Gwynned—at least a month's sea crossing, she was sure of that. "What do you look for on your travels? Adventure?" Kitiara asked eagerly.

"No, no," said the young noble hurriedly. "Sometimes adventure comes, unbidden, but I don't look for it. I look for . . ." For the first time, Kitiara saw him search for words. "For edification, for peace, for . . ." He hesitated again. "For escape."

Kitiara considered what this well-born young man needed to escape from, and what it must be like to travel at will, without worry of expense.

"Oh, you are an adventurer. I can see that," Patric continued, idly fingering the pale green pendant around his neck. "I don't think badly of it, but why do people seek adventure? Usually, for riches or power. Where I come from, my father is the ruler of a vast territory. I am his heir. In time I will have riches and power. I am in no hurry for them, and in the meantime I have no thirst for adventure."

He sat up straight and thrust his chin forward at this last statement, as if defying Kit to find fault with it. As if someone in his life did, she thought to herself.

Meeting no challenge in her eyes, Patric looked down, suddenly reflective.

Throughout his brief soliloquy, Kitiara's attention had

been drawn to his green pendant, which was webbed in a delicate silver filigree and spun in constant motion on its chain. She couldn't put a name to the stone, but it was exquisite. Probably very valuable, she thought.

"You admire my chrysanth," Patric said, naming it for her.

"It's very beautiful," Kitiara admitted.

"The fact that you like it shows that you have superior taste. It belonged to my mother, and before her, to my mother's mother."

For a moment, Patric fingered the necklace again, pensively. When he dropped it, he looked up, invigorated. He grinned at Kit, and she grinned back.

"Our travels have been arduous this year, and I would like to rest before the last leg of my journey home. Solace seems a hospitable place. If we stayed, could I impose on you to show us some of the local sights?"

Strathcoe grunted, set aside his plate, his heavy-lidded eyes lowered to watchful slits.

"Strathcoe agrees that it's a good idea," said Patric.

Kitiara had to grin. "How can you tell what he is saying?" she teased.

"I told you, we communicate well," Patric said rakishly. "It's a talent I have with people who are strong of heart." Impulsively, he reached over and grabbed Kitiara's hand. "Will you be our guide?"

Kitiara blushed again. Her hand tingled in his warm, moist grip. Then she pulled it away and stood up from the table.

"If you want to take your chances on accommodations at this fleabag, suit yourself." Here she cast a sidelong glance at Otik, who started sputtering protests and shaking his finger in her direction.

Barely able to keep from laughing, Kit continued. "And I don't know what sights you expect to see in Solace," she said, shaking her head with mock seriousness and looking at Patric, whose eyes had not left Kit's face. "But I'll be your guide," she finished softly.

Across the table Strathcoe nodded and beamed.

Kitiara pushed back her chair and strode toward the door, conscious of Patric's eyes on her.

"What time?" he called out after her.

"Not too early," she replied over her shoulder.

All the way home Kitiara pondered the young noble in the sea-blue tunic. He was a man who obviously had led a soft, privileged life—the kind of man she normally would disdain. Who knew if he could even wield a sword?

Yet something about him had touched her. His intensity? His vulnerability? His obvious liking for her? She wasn't sure. Kitiara just knew that she was looking forward to meeting him in the morning.

Her ruminations took her all the way back to the cottage. She opened the door to more than the usual chaos.

The smell of burned food filled her nostrils. Rosamun was crying out in the adjoining room, but Kit could hear her aunt intercede in soothing tones. Her mother's unmarried sister, a nervous sparrow of a woman named Quivera, had been staying with them to care for Rosamun, who seemed to spend most of her time hallucinating these days. Kit was relieved of the burden of her mother somewhat, but Quivera paid little attention to the other needs of the household.

Caramon was standing by the stove, holding a tray of something blackened beyond recognition.

"Kitiara, I've burned the biscuits," Caramon complained. "What are we going to eat?"

Kit sighed and closed the door behind her.

* * * * *

There was not much to see in Solace, but the days spent with Patric and Strathcoe offered a pleasant respite to Kitiara. Once the local sights were exhausted, they would just meet in the morning and wander off aimlessly, always in good spirits.

She escorted the two visitors through the elevated walkways, around the town square, to the shores of Crystalmir Lake, even riding with them to Poolbottom, showing them the curious school inside a hill and bragging a bit about her brothers, Raistlin the precocious mage and Caramon the budding warrior.

Patric proved a good listener, his courtly manners warming to a more familiar attitude as the week wore on. At times he would reach out and touch her cheek or ruffle her curls, murmuring softly, "Kitiara Uth Matar."

Kit found herself craving this contact, growing very still under his hand, only to have Patric turn away, as if made uncomfortable by his gesture. Always after a few moments of awkwardness, the trio would resume their easy camaraderie, with the ever amenable Strathcoe providing ballast to the situation. He proved a genial giant who, Kit learned, smiled and laughed as much as he grunted and groaned. Strathcoe seemed to find everything amusing, especially the conversation of his master.

Patric and Kitiara were discreet in the questions they asked each other. Kit revealed only a measured portion of her past. In Solace, everyone knew that Rosamun would never get better, that Kitiara was the daughter of that poor madwoman and might herself be cursed with a streak of wildness. But Patric had no reason to know or care; and with him, she emphasized her father. She told him she was the daughter of Gregor Uth Matar, a consummate warrior and kin to a proud if distant family.

From him she learned of an imperious father, a mother he idolized, and a waiting mantle of responsibility and authority for which he didn't always feel equipped.

*   *   *   *   *

On what was to be the last night before Patric and Strathcoe resumed their journey home, the three planned a moonlit picnic on the shores of Crystalmir Lake.

The night was perfectly cloudless, with both moons shining brightly in the sky and all the world latticed with beams and shadows. They set up their feast on a knoll overlooking the water—cold meats, wine, bread, and fresh fruit packed by Otik.

After dinner, Kit and Strathcoe had an entertainment planned. She went into her pack and pulled out a wrapped sword, the magnificent weapon from the long-ago ambush of Beck Gwathmey, which she had secreted these past two years. When she unwrapped it and held it before her, Patric's eyes gleamed with surprise and pleasure at its beauty.

"That is wonderful," he exclaimed. "What do you plan to do with it?"

"Well, first, I must best the servant," Kit teased. The big, long-tressed man was holding his sword in a pose of mock ferocity. As soon as she finished speaking, Kitiara and Strathcoe set to in a match of mock swordplay. At the end of which, with many grunts and groans, Strathcoe winked at Kit and fell to the ground, clutching his heart.

"Now the master must defend himself," Kitiara said, pointing her sword toward Patric so that it glinted in the moonlight.

"Not me," Patric protested with amusement. "As you see, I carry no weapons. That is Strathcoe's business, though the cur has fallen down on the job."

Strathcoe, sitting up and gurgling with his version of laughter, tossed Patric one of his weapons.

Kitiara observed that the young noble caught the sword handily enough. With a flourish, she saluted him. Patric hesitated, then responded in kind. Soon they were engaged in the thrust and parry of swordplay. Patric frowned in concentration, but handled the sword well. Yet Kitiara was more agile and decidedly more skilled. After a few minutes she stepped back and raised both hands, laughing. "I'm vanquished," she said, bowing her head in mock surrender. She felt Patric step closer and looked up to find his gaze locked on hers. Impulsively, she stood on tiptoes and kissed him full on the mouth. This time he did not pull away.

Strathcoe diplomatically retreated to the bottom of the knoll and soon fell asleep, but Patric and Kitiara sat with arms entwined, staring out over the lake and talking, long past midnight.

As dawn approached, Patric disentangled his arms and removed the pendant from his neck and held it out to her.

"It's yours."

Kit drew back, not sure what this meant. "No."

"I would be lying to you if I told you it was worthless," Patric said, "but the value is mostly sentimental."

"All the more reason why I can't take it," said Kitiara.

"All the more reason why you should," Patric said firmly. He draped the amulet around her neck.

Kitiara opened her mouth to say something else in protest, but Patric waved away her words. "We will make it a trade," he said softly. "Something of yours for something of mine."

"But I don't have anything," Kit began, then she stopped. Her eyes fell on Beck's sword. It was the only thing of true value that she owned.

"Take this," she decided impulsively, though it was truly the most prized of her possessions.

"It is too wonderful, and as you saw—your generous defeat notwithstanding—I have little use for a sword."

"I think it is a fair exchange," Kit said determinedly. "Strathcoe approves," she added, pointing toward the bottom of the hill where the servant lay, snoring contentedly and loudly.

Patric had to laugh. He took her hands in his own, gazing steadily at her. "Kitiara Uth Matar," he murmured dreamily. "I want you to come to Gwynned with Strathcoe and me."

Instantly, without having to think it over, she said yes.

"I'll run and pack my things," Kit told him, "and sneak away."

At that Patric frowned. "What about your father and mother?" he asked with genuine concern.

"I told you, he's my stepfather, not my father, and my mother is too ill to have any understanding of the outside world. Half the time she doesn't know if I'm alive or not."

He placed his hands on her shoulders. "I don't want you

to run away without telling them," he said. "I want you to ask their permission to go away with me. . . ."

Her eyes showed that she did not understand.

"And get married."

Kitiara's eyes bugged out in astonishment, astonishment and something else. She couldn't conceal a shiver of distaste. Traveling with Patric and Strathcoe would be fun, an adventure, but the last thing she wanted to do in her life was get married, even to someone she felt as drawn to as she did to Patric. Images of Rosamun, of Aureleen's mother, women who had no life outside their homes or independence from their men, flooded her mind.

"Kitiara," Patric said quickly, "I don't want you to say yes or no now, and I promise never to pressure you. The voyage to Northern Ergoth is a long one, at least four weeks, and you will have plenty of time to think about my offer. Take all that time, and more if you want it."

"But," said Kitiara, groping for words, "I don't know if I could ever get married. Especially not now. There is too much . . ."

Kit looked at the handsome young man sitting next to her and felt confused. No one had ever extended her the consideration and courtesy he had. No one had ever made her feel the way he did now, looking deeply and approvingly into her eyes.

"Don't worry about it now," Patric said hastily. "We have only just met, but we will get to know each other better. When you return to my country, you will be treated like royalty. Everything you ask for will be yours. You will have food and clothes and slaves to do your bidding. You may find that very appealing."

Indeed, Kitiara thought to herself, I might. "Why me?" she asked.

Strathcoe had roused himself and was making grumbling noises as he stretched and glanced up the hill. The sun had peeked over the horizon and turned everything pink and orange.

Patric sighed deeply. "Because," he said wistfully, "I think

I love you."

Kitiara noticed that Strathcoe had stopped his noises and was watching them intently. Until she opened her mouth she didn't know what her answer would be. "All right," she said, not sure precisely what she meant.

* * * * *

Kitiara was a little annoyed that Gilon was the one who seemed most genuinely saddened that she was going away, perhaps forever, though she downplayed the "forever" part. Loudly enough for Patric and Strathcoe to overhear, she advised Gilon to keep her loft for her at least until he heard that she was happily settled in Northern Ergoth.

"I hope that you will be happy, Kit," said Gilon with feeling as she gathered a few belongings and prepared to leave. "But if not, I hope that you return to us, for we will miss you."

Caramon and Raistlin certainly gave no hint of that. This early in the morning, Caramon was still lying sleepily in his bed, tangled up with the blanket. "G'bye," he mumbled before rolling over.

Raistlin, of course, was up, already engrossed in some thick, tattered book. He sat on a stool in a far corner of the cottage's main room. He looked up when Kit gave him a parting peck on the cheek, glancing first at her, then at Patric and Strathcoe who were standing respectfully by the door, then back at Kitiara.

"You'll be back," he said, lowering his eyes again to his book.

Well, she thought to herself, he and Caramon are mere children. What did I expect, an eloquent farewell?

"You must say goodbye to your mother," insisted Gilon stolidly.

Kitiara flinched. "She won't even understand what I'm saying."

Gilon shrugged his big shoulders and stepped outside again to wait, motioning Patric and Strathcoe to come with him. Patric glanced back at Kitiara expectantly as he closed the door behind him.

Rosamun was not asleep. She lay on her rumpled bed in a state of half-consciousness, eyes staring at the ceiling. Her hair had evidently been brushed by Quivera, who was out at the shops, and it lay around her pillow in a white halo. Rosamun breathed softly through parted lips that were pink and puffy like flower petals.

Kitiara regarded her mother coldly, then approached her as quietly as possible. At Gilon's insistence, she had scribbled a letter, in case the time ever came when Rosamun regained lucidity. Kitiara rolled it up and tied it with one of the hair ribbons Quivera kept for Rosamun. She laid it at her mother's side.

Dear Mother,

I have met a young gentleman who has asked me to marry him. We are traveling to Northern Ergoth, to Gwynned where his family reigns. I will be rich and will be able to send you and Gilon and the twins money.

Love, Kit

Kit knew it was a paltry message, but it was all she could muster for this woman who had alienated her father and whose weakness had kept Kitiara a virtual prisoner in the cottage.

As Kit hovered for a minute near the bed, she thought she noticed a pale light flickering in her mother's gray eyes. But nothing else.

Then, as Kitiara turned to go, Rosamun's right hand suddenly reached up and grasped her near wrist. Rosamun held her tightly, and Kitiara was surprised at her frail mother's strength. Rosamun moved her lips, but no words came out. Her eyes stayed open but unfocused. After several minutes, Kitiara pried away her mother's fingers and lay her hand gently back down on the bed.

Outside, Patric and Strathcoe were waiting next to their horses. Gilon had saddled Cinnamon for Kitiara. A pack mule stood patiently with Patric's great trunk strapped to its back. Strathcoe, his weapons in obvious display, marched about importantly, tying and rearranging bundles. His main audience was Caramon, who had finally woken and now stared in awe at this mountain of a man.

Solemnly Patric shook Gilon's hand, then Caramon's, before mounting. Kitiara nodded at her stepfather, then ruffled Caramon's hair before getting on Cinnamon. When she looked back she saw Caramon waving extravagantly, the sun glinting off his golden hair. Behind him, Raistlin stood in the doorway, still as a statue.

Kitiara had one last thing she wanted to do before leaving. She asked Patric and Strathcoe to wait at the town square while she spurred Cinnamon to Aureleen's. Her friend cried when she heard the news, but recovered rather quickly.

"A nobleman! Wait until I tell my mother. I always told her she underestimated you," Aureleen said teasingly. "Is he handsome?"

Kitiara found herself blushing as she nodded yes. "I have a feeling this is the sort of adventure even you might like," she teased her friend back. The two young women hugged. "You can write me care of the Alwiths of Gwynned," Kit called out over her shoulder as she climbed down to her horse.

By midmorning they were on one of the roads that led north from Solace through flat farm fields. They had to ride north and a little east to avoid the highest points of the Kharolis Mountains and reach the bay where Patric's ship waited.

At first Kitiara felt a little dazed with the speed of events, but by late afternoon she had settled into the rhythm of the journey and was thoroughly enjoying herself. The three of them were companionable travelers. More than that, at last she had escaped from Solace and its humdrum routines. And they were heading north—north, the direction in which her father was last seen heading.

After passing through croplands, they reached rolling green hills, then steeper terrain as they crossed the tail end of the Kharolis mountains on the way to the coast. There were only a few small communities, and these they skirted, because, as Patric said, he was done with traveling and anxious to start home. From other wayfarers they heard reports of a two-headed troll, who was terrorizing the region, but they saw nothing of the beast.

Each day, an hour or two before they camped for the night, Strathcoe would leave Patric and Kit, returning with a hare or some other wild game that he prepared for their evening meal. His cooking was surprisingly good. After dinner she and Patric would usually sit arm in arm and talk, enjoying the attentive audience provided by Strathcoe.

Under the starry sky, Kitiara often wondered if the passionate kiss she and Patric had shared that night at Crystalmir Lake would be repeated and pursued further, but strangely, it never was. Strathcoe was never far from the two of them. And like her father, Patric could outlast her with his tales. More than once she woke in the morning without remembering having fallen asleep.

Five days after leaving Solace they neared the bay where Patric's sloop waited. From a rocky promontory they caught their first glimpse of the Straits of Schallsea. Kitiara had never seen such a large body of water, blue and white-capped, extending as far as the eyes could see.

They followed the coastline west for another day before coming to the edge of the bay where they spotted the ship, the *Silver Gar*, anchored offshore with sails furled around her three masts. Strathcoe pulled a large brass whistle from one of their bags and blew a long high note on it to announce their coming. Colorful flags signaled from the forecastle that they had been seen.

As they approached the ship, sailors hanging from the riggings shouted out a lusty cheer in Patric's honor. Clearly he's a popular lord, thought Kitiara. Many of the men cried out Strathcoe's name as well, she noted. Movement below deck, along the sides of the ship, drew her attention. Poking their horned heads out through some of the shore-side portholes, minotaurs also watched the travelers' arrival. These bestial slaves would pull the oars when the winds were still.

Already several of them had been winched down in a boat to row to shore and bring Patric and the others back. Kit noticed a barge on the beach that would be used to transport the horses to the ship

When they finally climbed on board, Kitiara also noticed a group of elegantly dressed men and women sitting to one side of the deck. They alone did not greet the new arrivals, although the expressions on their faces indicated that they were relieved to be nearing departure.

"We take some passengers along," explained Patric to Kitiara. "It defrays expenses and helps maintain good relations between my father's estate and nearby lands."

Just then a man strode toward them, moving gracefully with the roll of the ship. He was dressed in leather and braid, and wore a close-fitting striped cap. His face was dominated by a formidable hooked nose and a merry grin. He looked like a man who could be counted on in a fight, thought Kit, but she noticed he carried no weapons. Instead a compass and a looking scope hung from his belt. This was obviously the captain of the *Silver Gar*.

"Greetings, Patric and Strathcoe," he boomed out, vigorously shaking hands with each of them in turn. Then his eyes took in Kitiara. "And who is this beautiful young lady?"

"Kitiara Uth Matar," she announced, stepping forward to take his hand.

"My betrothed," Patric added smoothly, ignoring the frown Kit sent his way.

Rather than shake her hand, the captain bowed deeply at the waist and kissed it.

A look of wonderment came over Kit's face. The captain's manners were as good as his master's, although Kitiara had the impression steel lay beneath his velvety exterior.

"La Cava," he said flamboyantly as he straightened up. "At your service, m'lady." His eyes registered some delayed impulse. "Uth Matar?" he asked.

Kitiara nodded eagerly. "Perhaps you have heard of my

father," she said quickly, "Gregor Uth Matar. His reputation is known far and wide. . . ."

"As?" asked La Cava, letting go of her hand but keeping his eyes on her face.

"As?" Kitiara repeated, puzzled.

"Why, his reputation as what?" asked La Cava evenly.

"Oh," said Kitiara, flustered. "As a great soldier of fortune. An incomparable warrior. A man of honor and integrity."

"Yes, of course," said La Cava. He pondered the name for a moment, before his face assumed a polite mask. "No," he said, "I haven't heard of him."

Patric drew La Cava to one side and whispered in his ear. The captain nodded in response. "Lurie!" the captain cried out.

A tall, bony man with blotchy skin rushed up to the captain's side, his expression obsequious. Dressed in leather shorts with a bare chest, he was obviously one of the mates.

"Lurie," commanded Patric, "give my betrothed my personal quarters and put me in the adjoining room with Strathcoe, the one across the hall. Bring out my mother's trunk and make sure Kitiara has everything she needs—oils and perfumes, the finest clothing."

As Lurie listened, he bent his neck at an angle like a bird and darted sharp, curious eyes in her direction. When Patric finished, Lurie extended a bony forearm to Kit. "Follow me, my lovely."

Kitiara was about to protest—she hardly needed to be spoiled—when Patric touched her on the arm gently and said, "Go now. I will join you for dinner."

Kit shrugged and grinned. As she was escorted below by Lurie, she knew several dozen pair of eyes were fixed on her. Indeed, she felt like royalty already.

* * * * *

Her cabin was in the gallery below the deck, with wide portholes that showed an expanse of sea. A comfortable looking bed, a chest of drawers, and a small writing table were built into the cabin's walls. Lurie watched Kit nervously as she walked around and touched things. It was as if she had to be sure they were real, that this wasn't a dream. When she finally turned to dismiss the captain's mate, he held up his hand in a gesture, bent down, and pulled a case from under the bed.

Lurie unsnapped the lock, and Kit could see that the trunk was carefully packed with all variety of fine clothing. Lurie, seeming to know just what he wanted, reached into it and drew out a yellow silk dress that had a low neckline and long billowing sleeves.

"Very pretty," he said, grinning and winking. "Pretty dress for lovely lady."

Kit snatched the dress from his hands, but she couldn't help but smile. It was all a little ridiculous, especially Lurie with his bent neck and birdy mannerisms. She had never seen, much less worn, such a dress. But as she took it in her hands and felt the softness of the fabric, Kitiara reveled in the luxury of it.

"Try," said Lurie.

Kit held it up against her body and saw that it would fit as if made for her. Lurie, his gaze curious, gave her an encouraging smile. He opened the door of a built-in closet, revealing a full-length mirror.

Slowly she approached the mirror. The person in it seemed not to be herself, but some princess. In the reflection she could see Lurie back out the door, his eyes taking one last look at the beautiful betrothed of his master.

"Set sail!"

With its canvas snapping in the wind, the sloop got underway.

Chapter 11

The Silver Gar

The afternoon heat blistered the deck, relieved only occasionally by a slight breeze. Lurie and Strathcoe had paired off midship, making a contest of throwing knives at a puppet figure tied to one of the masts.

"Bad throw, bad throw, dearie," said Lurie, clucking his tongue and shaking his head as he ambled up to the puppet. Once his back blocked Strathcoe's view, Lurie surreptitiously pulled the knife out of the target's dead center and moved it an inch or so to one side.

His gargantuan opponent stormed up to the mast. Strathcoe cast Lurie a suspicious look, then grunted and pulled out his knife with such force that the puppet came loose and dangled upside-down on a string. Then he circled his arm, as thick as a vallenwood branch, around Lurie's waist and lifted him up against the mast, miming that the captain's mate could be the new target.

"No, no, no, no. Not with your aim. Captain La Cava, he need me to sail. If Lurie get hurt, whole ship be hurting, especially captain," Lurie proclaimed indignantly.

Lurie could afford to brag. La Cava was down below, napping. The captain liked to take the helm at night, alone under a starry sky while everyone else slept. He caught up on his sleep in the afternoon.

Patric, too, was below. He had settled down in his cabin to write in his journal and had waved away Strathcoe, who otherwise would have stayed at his master's side.

All the other passengers had retreated to their cabins, chased there after lunch by the midday sun. Even most of the crew had made themselves scarce. Only two or three sailors remained above deck. The minotaurs pulled at the oars to keep the ship moving, but did not exert themselves. The sky was hazy with reflected light, the water a deep, sapphire blue. The bow of the ship was pointed north by west.

Driven from her cabin by boredom, Kitiara climbed on deck in time to observe Strathcoe's forcible persuasion of Lurie. After almost two weeks of land travel with Strathcoe and a week on board the *Silver Gar* with Lurie, she knew them well enough to see that the quarrel was not serious. A fundamental camaraderie underlay their every activity.

"Hey! You two look like you need someone with the wisdom of the gods to settle this, and I want you to know that I'm available," Kitiara called out, grinning as she approached.

Kitiara had never been on any body of water larger than Crystalmir Lake, but she had taken to life at sea. During the first day or two she had thoroughly explored the ship, adapting to the sea swells and moving with her customary agility.

After watching Kit and answering perhaps her hundredth question, La Cava had decided she could be of some use. He had permitted Kitiara to help with some of the shipboard tasks—taking down the sails, climbing the rigging to untangle lines, and even having a turn at day watch in the crow's nest. The sun had toasted her skin to a warm golden tan, and the physical activity had added more sinew to her slenderness.

The paying passengers gaped and sniffed at her as she clambered around, trading jokes and insults with the crew. La Cava indulged her the way a father would a spirited child. Slowly, most of the sailors, who were unaccustomed to a female behaving as their equal, grew to regard her as such, respecting her willingness to try anything.

Kit found Patric's reaction difficult to decipher. She often felt his eyes on her as she moved around the ship. At times he seemed bemused by her energy and physicality, at other times proud, almost possessively so, of her and the admiration she attracted from the sailors.

In other ways, though, Patric had drawn apart from her. The longer and farther they sailed, the more protracted became his moods and silences. Kit could not figure out what preoccupied him.

Only at night, when they dined with La Cava, did Patric become animated, telling story after story about Gwynned and his family's estate, and other tales from the region. With looks and gestures, he included Kit in the embrace of his storytelling. Afterward, though, when they would walk up on deck, he spoke less freely and rarely touched her. Their kisses, which she usually initiated, were oddly chaste.

She shook these thoughts from her mind as she greeted Lurie and Strathcoe. "Show me how to do that," she asked them.

They nodded, and Lurie handed her the thick-handled knife they were aiming at the makeshift target, a foot-high straw icon of a hobgoblin. Kitiara hefted the knife in one hand, feeling its weight as she squinted at the target, about ten yards down the deck. With her other hand she shielded her eyes from the glare of the sun.

Kitiara had handled plenty of knives growing up, but she had never taken much target practice, nor actual training with a short blade like this. Gilon's knives were practical ones better suited for butchering meat or carving a table leg than for fighting.

Strathcoe grinned encouragingly at her. He, Lurie, and Kit had become almost friends, a surprising development considering that Strathcoe could not utter a sentence and Lurie had his own idiosyncratic way of expressing himself, not always making sense.

"Here," said Lurie, "hold it this way." He put his arm around her shoulder and laid his hand over hers, showing her how to grip the knife with the fingers splayed along the length of the handle. Then he made a sideways, whiplike motion. The knife flew from her hand, missing the puppet target by several inches and embedding itself in a rain barrel that, fortunately, was empty.

Strathcoe mimed disgust at Lurie for failing to impart a piece of vital information to their pupil. He ran forward to pull the knife out, bringing it back to Kit. Strathcoe made an elaborate point of wiping both sides of the blade on his trousers before handing it to Kit. She glanced at Lurie, puzzled, because the blade had not been wet.

"Strathcoe, he says, 'keep it dry,'" interpreted Lurie.

"Why?" asked Kitiara, as she readied for another try.

Strathcoe made some indeterminate, strangled noises, ending with his characteristic grin. "Truer aim," said Lurie matter-of-factly. "Water bends the knife. Dry goes in deeper, too. Always dry before big fight or after each throw. Very dry, best."

This time Kitiara tried the throw by herself. A roll of the ship set her off balance at the last moment, and the toss went astray, clattering to the deck a couple of feet from the target. Exuberantly, Strathcoe hurried to retrieve it.

When the big slave got back, he showed her his style of grip and throw. Strathcoe's fingers tightened over the handle. His body tensed as he whirled in a half-circle—despite his bulk, Kitiara was struck by the grace of his motion—and the knife flew from his hand in a blur. An instant later, she saw that the blade had cleaved the chest of the doll target.

Lurie sauntered over to pull it out, came back, and, as he readied his own throw, cast a scornful glance at Strathcoe. It was as if Patric's slave should have been ashamed of himself for showing off. "Score a mark," said the captain's mate drily.

* * * * *

Lurie served as Kitiara's willing guide to all the workings of the ship, the better, she suspected, to avoid his regular duties. At just over one hundred twenty feet from stem to stern, the *Silver Gar* was not a particularly big ship. Still, there was an abundance of things to see and explore. The only room barred to Kit's investigation was La Cava's private chamber. The captain kept his cabin locked when he was not there, and Lurie, who had a key, dared not trespass. Kit's cabin, and Patric's, were near the captain's, in the stern.

The other passengers were quartered forward of the stern in ten or so cabins that were smaller than Kit's, but beautifully appointed. One day she and Lurie explored their small section. Several of the doors were open to allow for any wisp of a breeze. Ever curious, Kit glanced inside the cabins when she could and saw each was outfitted with oak paneling, plush velvet cushions, and elegantly functional furniture.

In one, she also saw a plump, veiled lady wearing a woolen dress despite the heat, reclining on her bed and breathing heavily. The young boy traveling with her was doing his best to keep her cool by waving a large peacock feather fan. Both were dressed absurdly for the hot weather, and Kit almost had a mind to say so. But Lurie gave her a nudge, and she moved on.

Through another doorway, Kitiara glimpsed a pale elf, pointed ears showing through longish white-blond hair, sitting on a stool and staring out a window at the sea. Although he sat with his back to the doorway, Kit had the impression that his eyes were closed. She heard murmuring, some kind of incantation it sounded like, from his direction. Next to her, Lurie shifted his weight impatiently and brushed up against the doorway, making a sound that caused the elf to turn sharply. He had such a frown on his face that Kit involuntarily took a step back and hurried on.

On another day, Lurie guided Kitiara down to the hold where a dozen chained minotaurs rowed their oars, during periods of calm, to a rhythmic sea chant. One of La Cava's men watched over them constantly. Still, Kit knew they were treated relatively well, eating the same rations of food and water as the sailors and rich passengers.

Kit stared at them, fascinated, remembering the first time she had seen a minotaur close up. That had been with Gregor before the battle against Swiftwater. These carried no weapons, of course, but their hulking, hair-covered forms awed her nonetheless. Their sharp horns looked deadly. Their huge eyes seemed to stare ahead at some fixed point invisible to mere humans. Despite the chains that bound their feet to the floor, they exuded an aura of power essentially untamed.

They also exuded a powerful stench. Lurie pulled out a handkerchief and covered his nose with it.

"They seem," said Kitiara, searching for the right words, "almost regal. Like they should be the ones in the cabins and we all should be down here rowing."

"Sometimes," said Lurie, holding his nose, "they act up. Then, they trouble. Mostly, they work hard, do their job. But stink. Very stink."

"Yes," Kitiara had to agree. "Very stink."

* * * * *

After a week at sea, Patric and Kitiara received an invitation to dine with the captain on the occasion of his birthday. Unlike most nights when they ate in the ship's dining room, this time they were privileged to be invited to La Cava's quarters.

Patric had seemed particularly remote that day, and in an

effort to please him Kitiara planned to dress up for the occasion. She dug through his mother's trunk and chose a white dress that left her shoulders bare. The diaphanous material swirled gracefully around her figure down to the floor. She wore the chrysanth pendant Patric had given her and fluffed her hair out. When he knocked at her door and she observed his reaction, Kitiara knew she had chosen well.

"A beautiful vision," he murmured.

For his part, Patric was dressed in a uniform that must have been worn, at one time, by his father, for it fitted him a bit loosely. It was braided at the shoulder and hips and decorated with family emblems. At his waist, Kit noted with some surprise, was the sword she had given him, its precious stones winking in the cabin's light. He looked, Kit decided, thoroughly dashing. Impulsively, she embraced him and was pleased to feel his warm response. Hand in hand, they crossed over to La Cava's cabin.

Kit didn't know what she expected, but what she found were richly furnished quarters displaying a mixture of fastidious good taste with unruly evidence of a life spent at sea. La Cava had shelves lined with books and the occasional piece of driftwood, drawings framed on the wall alongside colorful navigational maps. Through the doorway into his sleeping chamber, Kit saw that his bed was covered with a finely sewn, multicolored quilt. In the sitting room, where they were to eat, a pedestal occupied a place of honor. Draped around it was a gray-green tentacled creature, the size of a large dog, with bulging eyes and razor-sharp spines covering its body.

"That thing got washed aboard during a storm," La Cava said when he noticed Kit eyeing the creature. "Wrapped itself around the helm. Those tentacles and spines shoot poison, and I had to fight it to regain control of the wheel. After I killed it, I had Lurie preserve the thing. It's not often I come that close to losing a fight," he said, winking at Kit.

La Cava, too, had dressed handsomely in a fitted short jacket and dark pants, with a red sash tied at his waist and a red and white striped scarf knotted around his neck.

With a small bow, he invited Kitiara and Patric to be seated across from each other at a wooden table set with china and illuminated by candles. La Cava seated himself at the head of the table. The three of them smiled at each other a little awkwardly in this unfamiliar situation.

Any tension was relieved by Figgis, the ship's cook, who made a show of carrying in a tray of cooked pigeon, birds Kit had seen earlier in the day, caged among some of the other food supplies. The resourceful Figgis was followed by a small cabin boy who could barely balance a tray heavy with pieces of fish, marinated kelp, nut pudding, and dried fruit.

Ample portions of wine from the captain's private stock loosened them up as the evening wore on. La Cava was in good temper, but as usual spoke little, always choosing his words judiciously. Patric had warmed to the special occasion and ensured there were no gaps in the conversation. He talked expansively, telling story after story in a way that reminded Kit of the week they had spent together in Solace. Patric could be a bit of a bore, Kit acknowledged to herself, but he certainly was the most handsome man she had ever known—after Gregor, that is. She grinned at him beguilingly over the table.

"So my mother says . . ." It was past midnight, and Patric was in the middle of a long tale about how his father had tricked his mother into marrying him. La Cava was listening politely, though he no doubt had heard this one more than once before. Kit could tell that the captain was growing tired.

" 'I can't marry you, Alwith, I am betrothed to another.' 'Well,' says my father, 'either I will kill your betrothed or myself. I won't be unhappy. You may choose. Him or me.'

"Needless to say, it seemed an impossible choice. Both were handsome, both were from good families, and both would do anything to win her, for she was the fairest of the sisters in her family and stood to gain a fortune when her father died.

"Alwith counted on the fact that Maryn, my mother,

would speak to her favorite—a kender—and ask his advice. Now, this kender, name of Sampler, not only made maps for my mother's family, but also acted as soothsayer for Ravetch, my father's chief rival. Sampler was as honest as most kender and actually believed he had a modest gift for predicting the future. Maybe he did, maybe he didn't. It doesn't matter to what happened.

"When my mother told Sampler about my father's threat to kill either himself or Ravetch, Sampler did what any normal kender would do, he ran and told Ravetch. Kender have certain talents, but keeping a secret isn't one of them. Now Ravetch—though equal in looks and breeding—was not as brave as my father, nor as smart. Immediately he grew frightened and asked Sampler to read his palm. Sampler, no doubt caught up in the drama of the situation, predicted that someone was bound to die, but which of the suitors it would be, he couldn't be sure. He would know afterward, but not necessarily beforehand.

"Ravetch was willing to do anything to marry my mother, except die. And he wasn't going to take any chances. So he disappeared, leaving a note saying he had been called away on a hobgoblin-hunting expedition far to the north. The expedition took nine months. When he returned, Maryn and Alwith were already married. And, with only minor awkwardness, Ravetch switched his attentions to one of Maryn's sisters."

"What happened to Sampler?" asked Kitiara.

"Oh, he's still around," answered Patric merrily. "Still my mother's friend, but every bit my father's too. They say that shortly after telling Ravetch's fortune, Sampler turned up with an extraordinary amount of gold coin in his purse one day, which he of course promptly spent. Does the usual kender nonsense for a living, and still tells a fortune now and then. He's quite a character. Famous in Gwynned."

Kitiara and La Cava laughed appreciatively. Then the captain stretched to get up, signaling that it was time to go. He bid them good night, bending over to brush the back of Kitiara's hand with his lips. Kit flushed with—what? Pleasure? Embarrassment? She slipped her arm through Patric's as they left the cabin.

Neither of them felt like ending the evening right away. They went up on deck and gazed out over the black water coated with phosphorescence, shimmering in the moonlight. The night was serene, the only sounds made by the ship cutting through the waves. Patric disengaged himself from Kitiara and walked far forward, his hands clasped behind his back. Kit would have lost sight of him but Beck's sword caught the moonlight, glittering.

A wave of frustration swept over Kit. What was the matter with Patric that he was so moody nowadays? Kit felt her ardor cool. And as it did, she cast aside the role she had been trying to play, that of Patric's fiancee. She knew, then and there, such was not to be her fate.

Patric turned and walked back toward her. "I'm going below," he said softly. "All of a sudden I am very tired." Indeed his voice sounded cracked and weary. Any sign of his earlier good humor had faded.

Kitiara gestured that he should go ahead without her. She wanted to stay on deck a little longer.

It wasn't until several minutes later that Kit heard a sound and realized there was someone else on deck. Peering forward, Kit saw the elf whom she had noticed in the passenger quarters. He was standing on the forecastle, braced with his back against a mast, facing her. Even at that distance Kit had the distinct feeling that the elf had been watching Patric and her, and that in his eyes lurked something threatening.

* * * * *

The next morning Strathcoe reported to La Cava and Kit that Patric had come down with the flux. For two days he remained in his cabin, seeing no one but his faithful servant. As this was the case, and Strathcoe's communication abilities were limited, Kit learned very little about Patric's condition. On the third day, he was back on deck for his morning stroll, a trifle wan and dispirited, but otherwise apparently none the worse.

Yet both knew there had been a shift in their feelings toward each other. Kit resolved to talk to Patric about how she might get back to Abanasinia once they landed at Gwynned, but the young noble evaded her. He began to take evening meals in his cabin, alone with Strathcoe. When they chanced to pass on board, Patric's eyes would not meet Kit's.

At the same time, the weather had also changed. Clouds hung like gray stones in the sky, and days passed without a glimpse of the sun. Yet the temperature remained stupefyingly hot. A great storm was apparently threatening, but it hung always on the horizon, never breaking.

With Patric alienated from her, Kit spent more time alone, or with Lurie and the other sailors. She enjoyed their rough competition and would challenge them to knife-throws or races to the top of the rigging. Although she was smaller than the men, she proved herself more than their equal at those feats, often beating Lurie and the other champions among them. She sometimes felt La Cava's eyes on her during these times. Kit sensed he understood what had transpired between her and Patric better than she did, but he said nothing.

Lolling on the deck many afternoons, when work dwindled and the games often stopped, Kitiara found herself thinking about where she would go next. She considered returning to Solace, remembering Raist's prediction that she would be back soon enough. Kit wondered what was happening to her brothers. They were so young—Raistlin so vulnerable, and Caramon so foolish. Yet she knew they had, of necessity, become remarkably self-sufficient. Well, she had done her best. Let the gods smile on them. She would return sometime, but not right away.

In her heart, Kitiara wanted to continue traveling and resume her search for her father. But years had passed since she had received any even vague indication of his whereabouts—somewhere in the North. Where would she begin to look?

Late one night, unable to fall asleep, Kitiara came upon La Cava and Lurie together on deck. She perked up when she saw them. She had been meaning to trap the ship's enigmatic captain into a conversation. There was a certain subject she wanted to pursue.

Now, she marched right up to them. As La Cava tried to move away, Kit boldly stepped in front of him, blocking his path. A slight smile played on the captain's lips. He nodded some signal to Lurie, who moved away from them but remained on deck, idly gazing out at the sea. La Cava himself stepped back from Kit and relaxed his stance, letting her know that she had his attention, for the moment.

"What is on your mind, Miss Kitiara?" asked La Cava in that elegant but mildly ironic way he had of addressing her.

"Captain," she said directly, "the day we met—"

"Yes?" La Cava raised an eyebrow.

"I had the distinct impression that you had heard of my father. Gregor Uth Matar."

"I said otherwise."

"You said otherwise, but as I say, I had a distinct impression."

Her chin was set determinedly, and her eyes blazed. Yes, the more she had pondered it, the more she felt that La Cava knew something about her father. His face had betrayed something, but perhaps he hadn't wanted to mention anything in front of Patric.

La Cava reached into his pocket and withdrew a pipe. From his other pocket he took out a pouch of tobacco and deftly tamped it into the pipe's bowl. Putting the pouch away, he brought out a stone and flint and struck it sharply. In the flare of light, Kit could see what she knew was behind La Cava's cavalier facade, a ferocious personality reined in by age and wisdom.

La Cava turned and leaned against the railing, drawing smoke from his pipe. He, too, looked out across the sea— the mirror image of Lurie, down the railing several paces. Sailing men often find comfort or inspiration by leaning against a ship's railing and staring at the sea.

Kitiara took this as an invitation. She drew closer to La Cava and leaned against the railing too. Only Kit was looking up at La Cava, not out at the sea.

"I had a distinct impression," she repeated for the third time.

"You are most persistent, Kitiara," said La Cava, turning his head slightly to look at her. His tone had softened and had dropped some of its formal politeness. "Stubborn, really. You are determined to get something out of life, but you have no idea what it is you want. Stubbornness is a quality I admire, but I think it is important to know what you want."

"My father . . ."

"Forget about your father for a minute, girl," declared La Cava a little sharply. "What is it you want? What is it *you* want?"

"What do you mean?" asked Kitiara, puzzled.

"You are not going to marry Patric," said La Cava a little scornfully. "You're too smart and strong for that fellow. He could never tame you. I could tame you, but I'm too old to be interested and too smart to try. I would rather live in peace, have my little ship and my tobacco. I am not looking for anything more. My time of adventure is done.

"But what about you, Kitiara? What are you looking for?"

Now it was Kitiara's turn to glance away. Down the deck she knew that Lurie must be listening and overhearing some of La Cava's words. She liked Lurie. Even so, she was flushed with embarrassment because La Cava's words had pierced her.

After a long silence, she spoke softly. "I don't know." When La Cava said nothing, another long silence ensued. "I want to be . . . recognized. I want to be more than just an ordinary girl from Solace. I want to travel and do things and fight important battles. I want to be . . . someone. No, that is not right. I want to be myself, Kitiara Uth Matar, and become rich and powerful. *Rich and powerful.*"

La Cava took a long draw from his pipe. "You well may," he said evenly.

"About my father," she persisted.

La Cava sighed deeply and turned to face her so that she could read his eyes. "Your father," he repeated. "Your father is famous in some parts of Krynn, unknown in others."

Kit waited for him to continue, and it seemed that he did so with some effort. "I have never met him nor seen him, nor do I know anyone who has. But I have been everywhere that a ship may go, and I have heard of Gregor Uth Matar and his exploits, and—" here he paused "—of his fate."

Kitiara's breath caught in her throat. "What of him?"

"It is not a happy story, and I do not make a habit of recounting gossip or folklore. It very well may be untrue."

"Tell me anyway," she insisted.

Another deep sigh, and the ship's captain turned his face back to the sea. "Up north there is a region called Whitsett that has been in a perpetual state of war, dating back almost a century. Some call it a civil war, others a blood feud between two rival families, both of them wealthy and privileged and able to sustain great losses. Your father, Gregor Uth Matar, has a certain reputation for master tactics, and some time ago he gathered under his command a mercenary band of one thousand raiders who were utterly ruthless."

"Go on."

"It is said that your father brought his army to Whitsett and offered their services to either of the two rival families. Indeed, his raiders were auctioned off to the highest bidder. I do not know anything of the two sides of the conflict, but the story is told that one of the lords deliberately underbid, so that Gregor and his men were pledged to his family's longtime archenemy. Then this lord made a secret pact with a small faction of Gregor's men, offering them twice that amount to doublecross their leader."

"Treachery!" exclaimed Kitiara.

"Aye, treachery from men whom he had treated fairly," said La Cava. "But his was a business built on money, not loyalty. Of course, I repeat, this is only what I heard. I myself cannot vouch for what is true. You hear a lot of things on your travels, and stories like this get made up as well as embroidered—"

"What happened?" demanded Kitiara. "What happened to my father?"

"From what I hear," said La Cava, more softly, "Gregor kept his part of the bargain, encircled the army he had been paid to defeat, and vanquished them easily. His client's army marched in to sign the surrender, and he was lulled into complacency. At a certain signal, the traitors in Gregor's raiders rose up, slew the chief rival and his generals, as well as . . ."

"Yes?" demanded Kitiara.

"As well as Gregor and those few of his devoted retinue."

Kitiara could hardly breathe. Her throat constricted and tears welled up in her eyes, but she would not permit those tears to flow. She had to grab the ship's railing for support. She could see nothing, feel nothing, think of nothing but Gregor. Her father. Dead. Betrayed.

"Traitors," she spat. "Traitors."

"Aye," said La Cava sadly. "If true."

"Then that is where I will go!" she cried. "I will go to Whitsett."

"If you must," said La Cava. "But according to the story that I heard, the traitors divvied up their riches and disbanded, dispersed to the far points of Krynn. No two of them together. No one of them heard of, since—"

"I'll find them," insisted Kitiara, her voice strangled. "I'll hunt every last dog of them down, if it takes me a lifetime."

"If you must," said La Cava resignedly. He turned to go, touching Kitiara warmly on the shoulder. "If you must." She was oblivious to him now.

When, a moment later, she looked up, La Cava was gone and Lurie was standing there, his neck bent characteristically, a sympathetic look on his birdlike face. Kitiara could say nothing for a long time, just stood next to him as minutes passed. Her emotions boiled. Despite her furious bravado, she now was more confused than ever as to where she should go, what she should do. Her father, dead. Betrayed.

Finally Lurie broke the silence. "Tell you something," he said matter-of-factly.

"What?"

The captain's mate leaned back against the railing and watched her reaction. "About Patric."

"What about him?" Her tone was almost sullen.

"Others," he said. "Other ladies he was going to marry. He brung them on board too."

"What others?" Lurie had her attention now.

"Oh, two or three others, before you I mean," said Lurie. "About one a year. We sail around. He gets off, goes wandering. Strathcoe goes with. Not me. I wait with the captain. Time goes by. He comes back. Always with a new lady he's going to marry. Only he never don't."

"He doesn't? Why not? What happens to them?"

"Nothing happens to them. We send them back, afterward."

"Afterward?" Kitiara had to clench her teeth to avoid screaming in frustration. What was he trying to say? Lurie meant well, but his speech was maddening.

"Patric starts out," continued Lurie, "plenty happy. New girl. Everything good. But . . . as we getting closer, he getting nervous. Confused. Tense. Changes his mind. Bride not so especially perfect. Maybe he don't want to get married after all. Not so hasty."

"He loses his nerve," murmured Kitiara, beginning to understand. "He doesn't really want to get married."

"Not exactly," replied Lurie. "He worries about his mother, father. Especially mother. Big important lady. Very fancy. Looks down on everybody. Nobody good enough for Patric. Everybody got too many faults. Patric afraid to go against Lady Maryn."

Kitiara was silent, infuriated, absorbing this latest intelligence. If Lurie had a mind to help Kit forget the fate of her father, he had succeeded. At least for the moment, Gregor Uth Matar had been banished from her thoughts, replaced by Patric. Maybe she never had any real idea of marrying the idiot, but he had a lot of nerve, stringing her along.

"The closer he gets to home," added Lurie consolingly, "the more he makes up different mind. Not get married this time. Wait till next trip. Find new lady. Better lady. Please mother."

Furious, Kitiara thrust her chin out. "He won't get the satisfaction of turning me down," she declared hotly, brushing past the astonished ship's mate and heading for her cabin.

Lurie opened his mouth to say something, but Kit had already vanished below. Suddenly Lurie was alone on deck, overwhelmed by the dark sky and glittering stars and the vast, roiling ocean.

The captain's mate was left with the distinctly uncomfortable feeling that the conversation had ended rather abruptly and that he had said something to offend Kitiara. What could that be? He had only done her the favor of telling her the truth.

*   *   *   *   *

Tossing and turning past midnight, Kitiara couldn't sleep. All she could think of was what Lurie had told her. Her mind seethed with scenarios that would permit her to teach Patric a lesson.

The storm that had been threatening for days broke out in the darkest hour of that night. Great booms of thunder and furious lightning ushered in a slashing downpour. The lightning lit up the sky in streaky flashes and threw horrible shadows across her cabin. The wind built to a pitch and waves crashed over the bow.

The ship erupted in shouts as sailors rushed to take down the sails and do what they could to keep the ship on course. In her state of mind she had no impulse to get up and help. Lying in her small bed, Kitiara listened to the ship creak and groan under the punishing wind and waves.

She sat bolt upright. There was a sound at her door, a scratching and muffled knocking that was not part of the symphony of the storm.

Getting up, she bundled her blanket around her and crept to the door, opening it a crack. Strathcoe's face pressed heavily into the opening. He was trying to say something, but Kit could barely see him much less interpret his garbled sounds. When she opened the door wider, he fell into her cabin as if he were drunk. She turned to give him a piece of her mind, this bloated dunce who, all along, had been in on Patric's charade.

Strangely, Strathcoe had slumped over her bed, as if bending to look for something. She grabbed him by the shoulder and savagely twisted him around.

"What in blazes," she began, then stopped in midsentence. He collapsed to the floor, and the look on her face turned from one of anger to shock. Quickly she bent down and cradled his neck with her arm.

Poor Strathcoe looked up at her for a moment, and his lips tried to move. Out of his mouth came not words but a bubble of dark red blood. Kit looked and realized his throat had been neatly and mortally slit. As she watched, his eyes fluttered shut.

Horrified, Kit dropped his head onto the floor, stood up, and swiftly donned some clothes. She looked around for a weapon of some sort. The only one available was one of the knives she had practiced with on deck. Strathcoe was unarmed and evidently had been taken by surprise while still in his night shirt.

Again Kit opened her door a crack and cautiously peered out into the corridor. From above deck, she heard loud yelling and the sounds of sailors struggling to save the ship. In the corridor, there was nothing, no noise and no person.

In this part of the ship were only three cabins: first hers, then as she headed farther away from the stairs, the captain's, then Patric's. She edged along the wall and neared La Cava's quarters. The door was shut, but she kicked it open and whirled inside, holding the knife up.

As her eyes swept the room, she realized her arm was shaking, and she had to make a strenuous effort to quell her nerves. Nothing. Nobody. La Cava was obviously up on deck, working to steady the ship through the storm.

An explosive noise made her start, but it was only the loudest thunderclap yet. The storm was not abating.

Back out in the corridor, she made her way slowly to Patric's cabin, afraid of what might lurk there. Crouching, she came around the corner to see that his door was slightly ajar. With one arm extended, Kit pushed his door open, and waited for some reaction. Again, nothing.

Crouching lower, so that she was almost on her hands and knees, Kitiara crept around and through the door, ready to spring or roll. Seeing nobody, she stood up. It was then that she noticed the outline of a body, covered with a bloody blanket, lying on the bed. Before Kitiara pulled the blanket off the head, she knew that it was Patric. He lay in a stain of blood that continued to spread from a wound in his chest. It was clear that he, like Strathcoe, had been taken by surprise and stabbed while he was sleeping.

Her senses buzzing, Kit went to the door and surveyed the corridor again; as before, she saw and heard nothing. Closing the door, she took a good look around Patric's room. There were no signs of a struggle, no evidence that might reveal who had slain Patric and Strathcoe.

She could see that Patric's immense traveling chest was still here, his pouches of belongings, everything that might tempt or lure a thief. For a moment, she sat down on the edge of Patric's bed, dazed and confused. Why would anyone sneak in and kill these two? What possibly could be the motive, if not robbery?

Her eyes drifted to Patric's face, livid with death but otherwise unmarked. He had probably died without waking. She felt only the merest twinge of pity for him.

For a moment, Kitiara thought of another young noble cut down in the prime of his manhood, several years before. She had never met Beck Gwathmey, but could he have been so very different from Patric of Gwynned?

Decisively, she stood and looked around. Patric's death meant that she had to leave the ship as soon as possible.

After her reaction to what Lurie had told her, she would be suspected in his killing. Kit had no desire to test the limits of La Cava's mercy.

Quickly she rifled the pockets of Patric's well-made clothing, finding identity papers that might be useful. These she stuffed into her blouse. Kitiara grabbed some of Patric's clothes and wadded them into one of his medium-sized traveling bags. She tugged and tinkered with the lock of his massive chest, then tried to break it open with the handle of her knife, but it barely showed a mark from her efforts. Happily, Kit found a small bag of gems in the heel of one of Patric's spare boots. This, too, she stuffed into the bag, which she finally tied over her shoulder.

Dropping to her knees, Kit found Beck's sword under the bed, wedged between a plank and the wall. She took it out, made sure it was padded with covering, and strapped it across her back.

Last, Kit went over to where Patric was lying, removed the necklace she was still wearing, and draped it on his body. Fair's fair, she thought to herself. And she didn't want that reminder of him and his mother.

Stealing out into the deserted corridor, Kitiara listened to the continuing chaos up on deck and realized that the time to act was now, when the storm was at its peak and people were distracted.

Kit took a deep breath and climbed the stairs as inconspicuously as possible. Men were dashing back and forth, tying ropes and shouting directions at each other. The ship was lurching violently, and Kit was thrown to the deck once or twice before she gained her balance.

Thunder crashed and lightning split the sky. The bolts illuminated, for a brief instant, La Cava at the helm. The captain screamed orders to a phalanx of his drenched crew. Kit was correct in guessing that nobody would notice her in the midst of such turmoil.

Often stumbling, Kitiara made her way to the bow of the boat. The shoreline was, at most, ten miles away, and Kit thought she had a good chance of making it, even in the storm.

A glance at the sky told her that the thunderheads were breaking up. The worst was over.

Stripping off her boots, Kit stuck them in her pouch, then made sure that everything was tied tightly to her body. She climbed up on the railing and, without glancing backward, jumped.

The cold, turbulent waves hit her with the force of solid stone, nearly knocking her out. But before Kit's brain could go numb, she was already swimming, a speck in the water moving slowly but inexorably away from the ship.

"Man overboard!" was the last thing she heard.

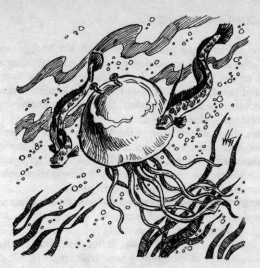

Chapter 12

Washed Ashore

The storm sucked all the light and color from the sea. The waves looked black as they crashed down on Kitiara, again and again. She struggled to keep her head above water. Her arms flailed until they were numb.

Hours passed.

Weighted down by the sword strapped to her back, Kit could barely summon the strength to kick her legs. Her whole being felt waterlogged. Kit had swallowed so much seawater that she retched violently as the waves rolled over her, not for the first time that night.

Luckily, Kitiara had managed to grab hold of a small wooden barrel that whirled past her in the water. Its buoyancy was the only thing keeping her afloat now—that and her determination not to let go of it.

The storm raged much longer than Kit had guessed it would when she jumped overboard. She had long ago lost sight of the ship, but had no idea whether she was still pointed toward shore or how far away the shore was. Although the storm had subsided, the cloud-darkened sky did not offer any hint of dawn.

Kit's cheek rested against the barrel's rough timber. Her tongue had swollen so that it felt twice its normal size inside a mouth that was parched of all moisture. Her lips were rimmed with salt residue. A bone-tiredness overtook her. Kit's eyes closed. She didn't care anymore.

Instantly, images of Crystalmir Lake flooded her mind, its surface glittering with sunlight, waves lapping at the shore, a day peaceful and perfect. . . .

A hundred stinging needles jolted her awake. Her leg screamed in pain. Something was attacking her. Kit could see little beneath the waves, but she gritted her teeth and kicked hard at whatever it was.

Kit came in contact with something cold and slimy. Twisting around, she could barely make out a silvery-white gelatinous mass that had broken the surface.

As she stared, the thing—two arm's widths across and one high—drew closer. While her attention was diverted, more needles raked across her back. She kicked hard again and saw two elongated shapes, red-brown with chocolate splotches, slither away from her under the water.

Then she realized it was a giant jellyfish accompanied by sentinel eels. Kit was on the menu for breakfast!

She gazed in horror at the quivering jellyfish, hovering some feet away. Two milky eyeballs protruded on stalks in front of the beast. The stalks probed forward, while the bulbous body swayed in the water.

Kit watched as the two eels cut through the water on either side of the shimmering hulk, heading straight toward her. Lurie had told Kit about these sentinel eels who often traveled with jellyfish. Their job was to herd prey into the mass of tentacles by relentlessly attacking them with their hundreds of tiny, razor-sharp teeth.

This time the shock of their attack almost made her lose her grip on the barrel. The eels had wrapped themselves around one of her legs, pulling her down. With all her might Kit resisted, but her brain reeled from the biting pain. By the time her senses cleared, the jellyfish was upon her. It loomed over her, smothering her, sucking her toward its soft, purplish mouth.

Kit let go of the barrel and dove under the tentacled mass, as deep as she dared. She came up, her lungs bursting, behind it.

The two eels were still attacking her leg, but she had a moment to reach down and pry one of them off. It squirmed in her grasp, trying to fasten its rows of tiny teeth on her arm. She lifted the eel out of the water and, with all of her strength, twisted it up into a knot and tore it in two sections. The two parts writhed in the water, spewing blood.

No sooner had Kitiara done this than the other eel detached itself from her leg and swam over to feed on its mate.

She had no time to congratulate herself. The huge jellyfish was upon her again, this time wrapping its tentacles around her legs and back, shooting venom into her. Her sword was of no use; Kit couldn't get at it in the water. And the weight of the jellyfish was pulling her under, even as it dazed her with its poison.

One of its stalks glided before her eyes, probing her. Desperately she reached out and was able to touch one of the sea creature's milky eyeballs. The stalk thrashed frantically. Kitiara was rocked with pain, yet she managed to close her fist around the eyeball and squeeze.

The soft, pulpy thing exploded in her hand, sending a spray of blood and ooze through the water. In that instant, the beast wilted, its will or strength sapped. Before Kit knew what had happened, the slimy creature had withdrawn, swiftly gliding backward and vanishing underwater.

Bits of quivering slime covered her. The pain was already receding. But Kit was quickly losing consciousness from exhaustion.

"Curse Patric for getting his throat slashed and curse the heavens for the wretched storm!" Kitiara weakly shouted, somehow comforted by the sound of her own voice.

Kit's heart leaped at the thin dark line she glimpsed to the west. Land!

The barrel floated by. Her legs pumping, Kit reached out and caught hold of the bobbing wood. She held on with what little strength she had left as the current carried her toward shore.

*   *   *   *   *

Kitiara woke to a relentless thirst and the blazing mid-morning sun. She was dazed and sore, but alive.

Picking her head up off the sand, she saw that she had washed up on an isolated stretch of beach. Just as well, considering that the waves had torn at her blouse until it was now little more than scraps held together by threads. Her pants had survived the storm only somewhat better.

Sitting up groggily, Kit took stock of her resources. Beck's sword was still lashed to her back, luckily. But the small pouch of gems and identity papers grabbed from Patric's cabin had been lost in the struggle at sea, as had the bag containing her boots and extra clothes. A quick inventory of her pockets turned up a few coins, nothing more.

Kitiara poked through the debris tossed up on the beach by the storm: assorted timber, a battered ship's lantern, pieces of frayed rope, a dead cat, a single boot, and something that looked like the chewed-up head of one of the eels that had attacked her. Nothing was of interest to Kit except for a worn leather vest. It must have belonged to a sailor not much bigger than she, and fit her fairly well. When Kit donned it and rearranged the shreds of her blouse, she looked almost presentable.

A rumble from atop a boulder-strewn cliff made her think there was a road above the shoreline. Barefoot, she climbed the rocks.

She was right: a road. Kit saw an open wagon approaching from one direction and flagged it down. The driver, obviously a farmer, pulled over in neighborly fashion, but he eyed her warily. She was a sight in her piecemeal garb, with the sword-shaped bundle that she carried on her back.

Kit gave him her best crooked smile. "Shipwrecked," she said. "I'm going wherever you're going."

He hesitated before smiling. "Hop in," he said, motioning her up on the bench seat alongside him. "You look shipwrecked all right, although I reckon it's a more interesting tale than that."

She climbed in eagerly, saying nothing else to satisfy his curiosity. He seemed to take no offense, and the wagon started moving again.

Kit noticed a water canteen on the seat next to the driver. Thirsty as she was, she could not keep her eyes off it. Without a word, the driver handed it to her.

As she was drinking, Kit appraised her savior. A black hood pulled up over his head to protect him from the sun contributed to a sinister first impression. On closer inspection, however, Kitiara saw kindly eyes in a weather-beaten face.

He caught her looking at him and smiled again. "Name's Rand," he said. "I just came from the market at Vocalion. If that's where you're headed, I won't be going back for a couple days, but you're welcome to come home with me for the time being. I'll feed you, maybe even find some decent clothes for you. Won't be the first almost-drowned sailor I ever rescued."

Rand gave her a friendly wink. "All I'll ask is a little help around my place."

Kit found it hard to put on a convincing expression of joy. Working on a farm, even for one or two days, held no attraction for her. On the other hand, food and fresh clothing sure sounded good.

"Vocalion's only a half day's ride," Rand continued, unimpeded. "It's smaller than Eastport, but it has good shops and facilities, and you should be able to find a job to tide you over. You could probably walk there in a day, if you don't want to wait for me. On the other hand, I'm not such bad company for a few days.

Rand kept up such a steady stream of talk that Kit didn't have to say much in response. His virtual monologue gave the young woman a chance to think about what she would do next. Eastport was out of the question; she knew that the *Silver Gar* had been planning to put in there. That meant she may as well give this place—Vocalion, did he call it?—a try.

*   *   *   *   *

It turned out that Rand lived by himself—a widower—on an isolated farm. "My castle," he had proclaimed as they pulled up in front of a low-slung farmhouse built into the side of a hill. After three days there, Kit would have said it was anything but.

Sod covered the roof, which meant that dust sifted inside constantly, especially when Rand's goats climbed up there to do some grazing. The interior was dark, but Kit came to regard that as a half-blessing, for Rand wasn't too tidy a housekeeper.

Still, Rand kept a well-stocked larder. He was also generous with its contents, which included not only goat's milk and cheese, but all variety of meat and fruit in season. In addition to raising goats, Rand brewed a tasty mead in a shed near the barn. Its local popularity meant he could always barter for something he didn't care to raise on his own.

"I tell you what," he had said that first day, after watching her wolf down bread, cheese, an apple, and two helpings of cold mutton. "If you'll stay to help me get this latest batch of mead barreled, I'll send you on your way with a few coins. It'll only take three days. You don't want to go to Vocalion as a beggar."

Kit suspected what Rand really wanted was a listener for his chatter, but she had already made up her mind to stay there for a couple of days before heading on to Vocalion, so she agreed. She had learned to be a good listener, or at least how to appear to be a good listener, at Otik's.

In truth, the three days passed swiftly. Not only did Kitiara feel rested when it was time to leave, but Rand was more than generous with the handful of coins he counted over to her.

As soon as his newest batch of mead was barreled, the farmer prepared to take it—and Kitiara—to Vocalion.

"You're lucky," Rand told her over supper the night before they were to leave. "Tomorrow's the last day of the famous Vocalion Wooden Weapons Annual. Famous in these parts anyway," he chuckled. "Folks come from miles around to watch it and make bets."

"Wooden Weapons Annual?" Kit asked, amused.

"Only wooden weapons," said Rand, slurping some mead. "That way nobody dies. Well, hardly ever. Best man wins."

Kit was only half listening. What fun was a tournament without weapons? Sounded just like something dullards would think of.

"The tournament goes on for seven days. If you win the first day, you fight two matches the second, and so on for the other six days. One defeat and you're eliminated." He shook his head. "By the seventh day only the best fighter is left—usually this chap by the name of Camium. On the seventh day he has to fight six more fresh challengers, one at a time, before winning the prize. But he always does. Camium's been champion for eleven years straight."

"What's his secret?" Kit asked.

"No secret," said Rand. "Just a ruthless cuss. Best man going on twelve years."

"Why do you keep saying 'best man'?" Kit asked with an edge of irritation.

"Just a figure of speech," answered Rand, oblivious to her annoyance. "Although females are barred from the competition, of course. Fortunate for them too," he slurped some mead, "because Camium is no gentleman."

Kit's interest was piqued. "What's the prize?"

"Oh, didn't I mention," added Rand, "a bag of gold, guaranteed, plus one coin out of ten from the bets."

"And tomorrow's the seventh day, you say?" she asked, her eyebrows drawing together.

"Yep. You should go. Women ain't barred from betting."

* * * * *

It had taken them a lot longer to load the wagon than Kit had expected, for Rand was painstaking in his preparations. It was midmorning before they had departed the farm, and late afternoon before they caught sight of the town. Rand's massive chestnut farm horse strained against the harness, pulling the wagon to the top of a crest overlooking a turquoise bay. Kit caught her breath. She knew little of this part of Krynn, but she was surprised to discover such a scenic outpost.

Most of Vocalion's buildings appeared to be made out a uniform white stone that reflected light. On the landward side, a wall interrupted by guard towers and gates protected the town. Several ships bobbed in the pretty harbor.

As they drew closer, their wagon entered a line of carts and foot traffic headed toward Vocalion. Kit's fingers drummed impatiently against the wagon seat. "Here, I'll just jump out," Kitiara said suddenly, gathering up a sack that held her sword, a few extra clothes Rand had given her, and some food she had packed.

"Thanks for everything, Rand," Kit added.

Rand barely had time to register his surprise before she had fled down the road ahead of him. "Luck, Kitiara," the farmer called out.

After walking for several minutes, Kitiara entered the town proper and fell in behind two broad-shouldered fellows whom she judged to be members of the local guard because of the common insignia on their helmets and breastplates. The crowd parted somewhat for these two, and Kit was able to move swiftly in their wake.

Snippets of their conversation floated back to her.

"Have you heard? How's Camium doing today?" the stockier one asked. "The tournament must be nearly over."

"What's the suspense?" replied his companion. "Camium hasn't lost a match in years."

"What a fighter! Did you see the contest against the minotaur? Camium had the brute on his knees after thirty minutes, but the minotaur still wouldn't concede—you know what a proud race they are—so Camium had to club him senseless. After the beast was unconscious, there was no question as to the winner!"

The guards turned onto a side street, leaving Kit on her own. She was all the more determined to get to the tournament before it was over, if for nothing else than to have a glimpse of this Camium, whose reputation intrigued her. Posters for the Wooden Weapons Annual dotted the streets, pointing to the north end of town. Dodging around people, she raced in that direction.

The Vocalion coliseum was small but impressive, a circular, arcaded building that stood above the low-slung houses and drinking establishments that surrounded it. The outside was thronged with scores of people, all talking and laughing. But from inside, Kitiara could hear the roar of hundreds, shouting and cheering and swearing.

Kit pushed her way up to a betting stall.

"What're the best odds on one of Camium's opponents?" she asked an unsavory character with a red, bulbous nose.

"Where have you been, girlie?" the bet-taker replied with a sigh. "It's the last fight, and nobody's betting against Camium. Camium's not even winded. It'll be over in a matter of minutes. Save your money."

That took her by surprise. She stepped away from the booth and looked around disappointedly, spotting the coliseum entrance.

The noise from inside swelled. Well, she had come this far, she might as well catch the last few minutes of the event. Kitiara was about to head toward the entrance when she spotted a side door ajar.

Slipping through it, Kit found herself in a narrow, darkened hallway leading to the waiting room where the contestants prepared for their matches. Entering the room, she could see a young boy with a broom, a brush, and a huge, wooden bucket. He was scrubbing at what looked like darkened patches of blood.

At the far end of the room another shorter and narrower corridor led to a small doorway that was filled with bright sunlight. Through the doorway Kit could just see two indistinct figures, somewhat eclipsed by the glare, circling each other outside in the arena. The crowd was cheering and jeering.

"Who's that?" The boy had looked up and was squinting at her. He was a thin, scrawny boy of about eight, probably an orphan jobbed out for the tournament.

"I was sent, er, to help," said Kitiara quickly.

"Oh," said the boy cheerlessly. "Here." He tossed her a hard-bristle brush. "Pitch in anywhere. There's blood and dirt to go around."

Kit caught the brush handily as she angled near the door for a closer look. A small, squat shape was doing his best to ward off the windmill blows of a big, well-proportioned figure. Both wielded thick, heavy clubs. Huh, thought Kitiara, looks like a real mismatch for Camium.

She noticed, as she glanced around, that all manner of wooden weaponry hung in the room. Clubs, wooden maces, stout poles, wood hammers, even hoopaks—the favored weapon of kender throughout Krynn—lined the walls for contestants to choose. Kit stashed her bag behind a bench and pretended to scrub at one of the walls.

The bristles of the brush were like tiny wooden spears and, thought Kit, could probably make their mark on steel. She peered down the hallway toward the match. Kitiara didn't see how the little fellow could last much longer against the blows of Camium.

The thundering noise overhead told her that she was probably directly under the crowded bleachers.

"That's Camium's last victim, is it?" asked Kit.

The boy looked up again and shrugged. "Unless somebody else wants a beating," he said tonelessly. "That's the fifth today. Camium's getting such a bad reputation they could only talk five into it. Well, last year it was only four, so I guess there should be no grumbling." He went back to his work.

Some in the arena crowd had started to boo, and looking down the corridor out through the door Kit could see the two figures rolling around in one tangle. Obviously the fight was winding down.

Kit was thinking fast. This was a chance—even if it was a chance to get her skull cracked—that she couldn't pass up.

She spied a small leather helmet and strapped it snugly around her head, tucking in the few curls it didn't cover. She went to the wall and selected a long, rounded stick called a besom, slapping it on the ground a couple of times to be sure it was sturdy.

Kit had passed for a man once before. With the leather vest she had picked up beachcombing, the rough tunic and pants and heavy boots that she had got from Rand, she could do so again. Kit rubbed some dirt on her face and hands.

The boy had put down his scrub brush and was looking at her with new curiosity. "What do you think you're doing?" he asked. "You wouldn't stand a chance. You're a—"

In a flash she was next to him, fumbling in her pocket. "Here," she said, handing him a few of her coins. "Go make a bet on the last contestant. Me. And forget what you saw."

"But—"

Kit raised her stick and ominously cracked it against the floor. "Go!" she yelled, "and thank your gods I don't do worse!"

As the boy vanished, running, Kit heard a brief silence outside, followed by a unanimous roar. The match was decided. Kitiara turned and sprinted toward the square of light.

The crowd gave a sharp collective intake of breath, then let out a welcoming cheer for the newcomer.

From the darkness into late afternoon glare it took a couple of seconds for Kitiara's eyes to adjust. She stood in the sand arena, with fifty rows of benches climbing up its sides, all filled with common people whose eyes were now trained on her. They were shouting and gesticulating, but clearly pleased about the prospect of one more match.

In the center of the ring, Kit was taken aback to observe, lay the battered body of a tall, powerful-chested fellow. A comparatively pint-sized guy perched atop the body's motionless chest.

The little guy was wizened and ancient, with a balding pate and long, curly salt-and-pepper beard. She could see that he was no taller than her chest and that he was bowlegged. His nose had been smashed so many times it flattened out in several directions.

The fighter was a dwarf. He was beaming victoriously and finishing off a tankard of ale. Seeing Kitiara, he flung the tankard aside and hopped off his fifth victim's chest. Then Camium Ironbender, the champion of the Wooden Weapons Annual going on twelve years, stood professionally and gave Kit a rather formal bow from the waist.

* * * * *

After about five minutes of fighting Camium Ironbender, Kitiara understood why he had ruled the Wooden Weapons Annual for eleven years. After about ten minutes, she'd had enough of the match, but the trouble was, Kit had to surrender in order to lose and it was against her code to surrender. The fight could end one of two ways, it seemed, with Kitiara either unconscious or dead.

From the tenacious way he fought, it was clear Camium Ironbender would be happy to oblige either alternative.

After about thirty minutes, Kitiara could barely stand on two wobbly legs, could barely see out of two purpled eyes, could barely lift her besom stick in order to make a swing at the grizzled dwarf.

The dwarf didn't move much. He was more than willing

to stand and take Kitiara's blows, as many or as fast as she could land them. It was almost a matter of pride for Camium Ironbender, it seemed, to get a whack on the chin or a conk on the head without so much as wincing. Kitiara tried thrashing his knees for a while, but his legs proved just as obdurate as his skull.

Throughout it all, he let her circle him, barely moving from his planted stance, watching her cannily. Kit had a good reach on Camium and could strike almost at will. She wielded her thick besom stick—half again as long as she was tall—almost like a sword, but he took all her best shots with a grin, which fueled the crowd's approval.

As for Camium, he carried an ugly, knobby club, pitted with holes and blemishes. He lugged it on his shoulder, almost nonchalantly, although it was as long as he was tall and probably half as heavy. He swung about once to Kitiara's every five or ten strikes, and seemed to do so with great reluctance, as if he didn't want to hurry things up.

But his scoring average was high, and his blows landed with powerful force on her legs, chest, shoulders, and face. He was probably more than ten times her age and no taller than Caramon, but the little dickens sure could fight. Right before she passed out, Kit was thinking that there had to be some way to stop him.

The crowd booed fiercely as she crumpled into the sand, face first. Camium went to a large tap that had been set aside for him along the arena wall, and drew a tankard of ale. He drank long and hard, watching the three judges absently.

Three citizens in official robes sat on a high tier, observing Kit's sprawled and motionless form. They were not anxious to end the spectacle prematurely. The crowd continued its booing.

Good-naturedly, Camium went over to Kit and tossed a tankard of ale over her head. She jumped up, looked around confusedly, and beat a retreat from the arena down the narrow corridor to the weapons room.

The crowd was evenly divided between booing and

screaming merriment. Camium, shaking his head with amusement, turned back toward the ale tap.

Thus he did not even see Kitiara as she ran back into the arena in a straight, furious path toward him. The crowd's surprised reaction alerted the dwarf, but Camium did not know what to make of an opponent who was waving a huge, banded bucket and bristle brush. His jaw was down, and so was his knobby club.

Before Camium could make a move, Kitiara had leaped on his shoulders and brought the bucket down on his head, smashing the bottom out of it and driving it down so that it girdled his chest, pinning his arms. The momentum of her attack knocked the dwarf down momentarily, and Kit took the bristle brush and raked it over his face, pulling most of the right side of his beard off before getting stuck in its tangles.

Such a yowl the crowd had never heard. And never such a noise out of the mouth of Camium Ironbender. Silence gripped the arena as Camium struggled to his feet, still girded by the bucket. His face was red with mortification.

He struggled to break the bucket, but its iron bands held.

Kitiara had yanked his club away and now she clunked him on the head as hard as she could, again and again, a half-dozen times. The dwarf tottered, spun, tottered some more, but would not fall.

Kitiara swung the club as hard as she could, striking him across the face. Camium lurched to the right, danced a few steps, tottered again. But he would not fall.

Camium's eyes had puffed shut. He could not move his arms. The bristle brush dangled from his beard. Blood seeped from under the bucket, from places where Kitiara had torn away skin with her blows.

Still Camium Ironbender, champion of the Wooden Weapons Annual for eleven years, would not fall.

Kit doubted that he was even conscious. She had respect for the old dwarf and didn't want to hurt him any worse, nor embarrass him any further in defeat. Raising her eyes wearily, she looked to the judges in mute appeal.

Conferring hastily, the three officials raised their arms to signal a draw and an equal sharing of the prize.

The crowd erupted.

Camium swayed.

Kit slumped to the ground.

*   *   *   *   *

A couple of hours later, hours crowded with healers and well-wishers, Kit was left alone on a stone bench in the weapons room, working her jaw back and forth painfully.

Alone except for a tall, furtive stranger, his face shadowed by a cowl, who had been lingering to catch her by herself. He didn't worry her. If she could fight Camium Ironbender to a draw, she could handle whatever was next.

Even so, the man's voice took her by surprise. "You're making a career out of posing as a man," the stranger remarked, standing over her.

"Ursa!" She spat out his name bitterly, jumping up. She looked around for her choice of weapons.

"Whoa!" Ursa Il Kinth said, looking over his shoulder warily. "Not so loud."

She made a move. He grabbed her arm, but gently. "You've had enough fighting for today," Ursa urged quietly.

He let her arm go. Kitiara stood her ground, her eyes flashing. All weariness had vanished, replaced by a surge of energy. "I owe you a whipping going back years!" Kit said angrily.

He sat down and pulled off his cowl, shaking his long, tawny hair free. Kit had time to grab a weapon—and did. Her bag with the sword in it was across the room. The studded cudgel she hefted would have to do.

She waited for Ursa to make a move, but he just sat there, staring up at her with his dark, glinting eyes.

"Yes," he said at last in a somber voice. "That was bad business all around. You owe me a whipping, and I owe you your share of . . . of that job."

"Where is it? Don't think you'll get away this time without giving it to me!" She jabbed him in the chest with her cudgel.

Halfheartedly, he pushed the weapon aside. "Don't be a fool," he said. "You're better set than me now." Instinctively she patted the half purse of gold in her pocket, Ursa's eyes watching her a little wistfully.

"I owe you something," he continued. "I don't deny it. But I'm glad to see you. Can't you see that? Even though you did cost me a fair slice of what little money I was carrying." He grinned sheepishly. "Like everybody else, I had made my bets on Camium."

She snorted unsympathetically.

"It took me a while to recognize you. But eventually I couldn't help but see through the poor disguise of someone who first taught me the virtues of wooden weapons as a girl," he said in his best teasing manner. "You weren't such a bad fighter even then, but you're damned impressive now, I have to admit. What are you doing in these parts anyway?"

Kit scowled, softening. In truth she was a little glad to see Ursa with his roguish grin. He seemed sincere, if a trifle low-spirited. "You first," she said, lowering her cudgel. "What are you doing in these parts?"

"I've got a job," he said, brightening. "Me and Cleverdon—yes, he's still with me. Not the others." Ursa's face clouded over. "I'll tell you all about the others later. Now what about you?"

She didn't see any reason to hold back. Kit told him, briefly, the story of her mock betrothal to Patric, her sea voyage, his mysterious murder, and her escape overboard. It already seemed like years ago.

"The *Silver Gar!*" Ursa exclaimed. "Everybody in the crowd was talking about that ship. It put into Vocalion just this afternoon for repairs. It sits in the harbor even as we speak. The talk is that the captain is in a state, for he must sail back to home port with the dead body of his lord."

The news stunned Kit. "If the *Silver Gar* is here," she put in excitedly, "that means I might be able to get Cinnamon back."

"If what you tell me is true," Ursa said, "you had better be careful."

"True . . ."

"I tell you what," Ursa said. "Join up with me, and I'll get Cinnamon back for you somehow."

Kit was about to object when he put up his hand. "And in good time I will pay you back what I owe you," the mercenary promised. "You may as well trust me on that."

* * * * *

Ursa's tall, stooped companion waited for them in an unsavory section of the waterfront. Droopface—she could think of him by no other name—evinced no surprise, no reaction whatsoever to Kit's presence in their midst after two years. For her part, she wished that she could take her sword—or something—to the traitor, but Ursa's whispering restrained her.

If she had to admit it, with silent resignation, Kit was comfortable with the idea of working with these two again.

"There it is! I see it!" Kit exclaimed. The *Silver Gar* was docked at a pier right off the waterfront, a gangplank leading up to it. She thought she spotted La Cava stalking around on deck and pulled her companions into the shadows of an alleyway.

"There's the captain. My advice is not to run afoul of him, whatever you do. I think he's your match, and then some," Kit said to Ursa.

The young woman peered around the corner again and saw several of the passengers returning up the gangplank. No sign of Cinnamon, who was probably being cared for below.

"Our horses are stabled on the edge of town. You and Cleverdon get them and take them to the edge of the marsh just north of here. Cleverdon will know where I mean."

Droopface nodded silently.

"Wait for me there," added Ursa. "I'll join you as soon as I can. If Cinnamon can be sprung, I'm the man." Some of his old cockiness had returned.

Droopface shifted, and Kit got up to go with him. Ursa put a hand on her arm. "Wait, Kit," he said. "How about that purse?"

Her mouth opened to protest.

"For bribes," he grinned, "and other operating expenses."

With a sigh she felt in her pocket and handed it over. Ursa was right: she might as well trust him. And she hadn't had any illusions about holding onto her gold for very long anyway.

The three of them moved out of the alleyway between two buildings, Kit and Droopface going off in one direction, Ursa melting into the crowd in the other. After they had split up, a cloaked figure emerged from a nearby doorway, gazing after them. If Kitiara had looked back, she would have recognized the dark elf from the *Silver Gar*.

Chapter 13

The Slig's Lair

Kitiara and Droopface had been waiting at the designated rendezvous, on the edge of a reedy marsh ten miles east of Vocalion, for almost two days. At first Kit was patient, but as time wore on she grew restless, worrying that something had happened to Ursa.

Their makeshift camp was concealed by a cover of tall fireweed and sawgrass, away from the main road. All around them was a sparsely wooded lowland plain dotted with ponds and ice. To the north Kit could glimpse a snow-dappled range of mountains.

During their wait Droopface had said little, as was his wont. If the tall, stooped, lugubrious one was at all worried by Ursa's absence, he did not show it. He had reverted to his usual self, stoically reading his tome of magic, his lips moving soundlessly as he occasionally slobbered over the pages.

At last, when it seemed as if her nerves were about to burst from the waiting, Kit heard a clatter of hooves and then the sounds of several horses that had left the highway and were pounding in their direction. She realized that Droopface must have been more concerned than he let on, for he had stood up and was fidgeting expectantly.

Ursa hove into sight, and Kit's heart leaped when she saw the horse that was trotting behind his own. "Cinnamon!" she cried joyously, and rushed forward to untie her father's horse and give Cinnamon an unabashed hug. "How did you get her back?" she demanded of Ursa. "How—"

Even as she asked that question, Kit became aware of another rider close on Ursa's heels, pulling up on a skewbald pony. This new arrival had long, free-flowing sandy hair entwined with feathers and was wearing a painted leather vest and chaps. Yet what took Kit most by surprise was that the stranger was a young woman.

This female addition to the group dismounted gracefully. She was rather short, almost pygmy-like in stature, but obviously limber and strong. She eyed Kit, fingering the dagger thrust into her belt.

"It wasn't easy," bragged Ursa, tying his horse as he gave a rippling laugh. "That ship's captain, I think he wanted to keep your horse as his own. Cinnamon was getting the royal treatment. They kept a constant guard over her, and I could barely get near her without raising suspicion. I learned, however, that she was taken off ship, twice daily, for a walkabout. I figured the ship would only be in port for about a week. That gave me time to arrange an old trick."

Turning back toward Kit, Ursa realized that she was staring hard at the new woman, who met her look coolly.

"Oh," said Ursa, enjoying his little surprise. "This is Colo. She's been riding with Cleverdon and me for several months now. Colo, this is Kitiara—I told you about her."

"You didn't tell me about Colo," said Kit tersely.

The other stood her ground.

"Colo's stealthy," enthused Ursa, "and good in a fight.

Ask Droopface."

Droopface, who had sat back down, murmured his assent.

As Kit weighed this information, her face relaxed. "Kitiara Uth Matar," she said, proffering her hand in a greeting.

Colo declined the hand, raking Kit over with a glance before hurrying off and squatting a few feet distant from the three of them with her back to the campsite, busying herself at something. Peeking over her shoulder, Kit could see that the diminutive female mercenary was engaged in throwing a cup of stones and bones, poring over their configuration.

"Not very friendly," Kit grumped, albeit good-naturedly, to Ursa. The mercenary had sat down on a rock near the fire that she and Droopface had started. Kit poured herself some tea from a container that had been warming over the low flames.

"It's not your fault," said Ursa, his eyebrows furrowed. "She's convinced we're under an ill omen."

"How cheerful."

Ursa began to unpack his bedroll. "Just a run of bad luck," he said, his mouth set in a hard, thin line. "It started four months ago, when Radisson was killed and El-Navar disappeared. We've been on the run ever since. Haven't been able to get back into things. She thinks we're being followed."

"Followed?" asked Kit. "By who?"

"Whoever it was, we lost them," boasted Ursa confidently. "We've been zigzagging between places and covering our tracks. Our luck is starting to turn. Isn't my liberation of Cinnamon proof of that?"

"What about Radisson—and El-Navar?" Kit felt compelled to ask. "You haven't told me what happened to them."

He sat on a rock opposite her. Kit noticed that Droopface had set down his book and was listening intently. Colo was paying them no attention, her back still turned, consulting her oracles.

"We were outside a small nothing village, across the channel and three hundred miles southwest of here. Radisson went into town with El-Navar looking for some drink and—" he watched Kit's reaction "—female companionship. They went into a tavern called the Double Shiner. Everybody knows about the place, an old standby for wayfarers in those parts. They should have been safe there. We were forty miles from any enemies, forty miles from our last job."

"But there had been signs," ventured Droopface solemnly.

Kitiara was so surprised to hear the sad-faced mercenary speak so adamantly that she nearly dropped her tin cup into the fire. Ursa, reaching over to pour himself a mug of tea, nodded at Droopface's comment.

"Yes. Somebody or something had been following us. I don't know who or why. There were strange birds in the sky and unfamiliar noises at night. I thought it was wiser to stay clear of people, stick together. But Radisson wanted to get away and have some pleasure, and El-Navar said he would go with him." He paused, frowning. "They ought to have been safe. Radisson can outwit most regular people, and El-Navar has the strength of a half-dozen."

"What happened?" asked Kit anxiously.

"Don't know," Droopface shook his head ruefully. "Don't know."

"When they didn't come back," continued Ursa, "we went into town to look for them. The Double Shiner had been leveled—destroyed. It was almost as if it had been uprooted and ripped to bits and sucked away somewhere, so that the ground was littered with its remnants.

"Everything was gone but its center post, from which dangled Radisson's body. He wore no clothing. His eyes had been dug out, and over his body were scribblings done with a knife point. A thousand little cuts and holes and markings all over his body."

"And El-Navar?" Kit tried to keep her voice even, while in her mind flashed memories of the sinewy Karnuthian. She remembered his deep, mellifluous voice; the hair like writhing snakes; the gentleness of his touch; the power of a panther that lay dormant within him.

"Gone too. Vanished. No evidence of his death or any clue as to his whereabouts. Colo there—" he indicated the female mercenary, preoccupied with her soothsaying "—is an able tracker. She could find nothing."

"Even if the townspeople could have told us anything," added Droopface, "they wouldn't. They were too afraid to talk."

There was a long silence after that remark. Ursa swirled his tea. Droopface got up and went over to his pack, preparing to go to sleep. Colo gave Ursa a sharp look, then went to her horse and unstrapped her bedroll.

"As I was saying," said Ursa, ignoring Colo and taking one last sip of his tea before tossing the dregs on the ground, "our luck is changing. We haven't encountered any difficulty for weeks, and now we happen upon you." He flashed Kitiara one of his old brisk grins. "Grown up some and even more skilled as a fighter than I remember."

She had to grin back.

"It will be good to work together again," he finished.

"What's the job you mentioned?"

"It's not much of a job, but it'll bring a fair price. A slig is terrorizing a community just forty miles north of here, someplace called Kimmel."

"What's a slig?" asked Kit.

"Oh," Ursa laughed. "A slig is a rare experience. You'll find out soon enough. Here—" he kicked some twigs and branches onto the fire "—you take first watch. Wake me up to relieve you."

She noticed that he made up his bedroll close to Colo, who was already asleep.

* * * * *

For a day and a half they progressed northward into hill country, following scrawled directions that Ursa fished out of his pocket and consulted at intervals. They gravitated to lesser roads and dirt paths until, in the late afternoon of the second day, they came to a rushing river that they followed upstream in the direction of a small farming village named for the leading family, Kimmel.

The late autumn days were blustery, and the nights at this altitude increasingly cold. But the weather stayed dry, and Kit liked the snap of early winter.

Kitiara had to admit she felt strangely comfortable being with Ursa and Droopface again. Ursa had his swagger back, and she enjoyed his bragging about exploits. Droopface, with his long, inscrutable silences, reminded her of poor, inarticulate Strathcoe; he had become just as companionable, too. Kit wondered about the fate of El-Navar, but she couldn't coax either of her old partners into talking about the Karnuthian any more.

Colo was a strange sort, militant and masculine in some ways, but flirtatious and feminine in others. She seemed to carry no grudge against Kitiara. The first night on the road she performed a wild dance by the firelight that made them all hold their sides for laughing. She always rode in the lead, because Ursa said she had eyes that could see far into the distance.

The place where they eventually arrived was less a town and more a number of hill farms that had clustered together for community and protection. The locals had pooled their resources to hire mercenaries to slay a slig that had been roaming the area, stealing food and terrorizing the women at night. Some citizens had tried to battle the slig, but this one was a ferocious rogue male, detached from his tribe. He was tricky to track and even more perilous to corner.

It was in Vocalion that Ursa heard the good people of Kimmel had chipped together and were offering a fair sum, with proof of the creature's demise.

For an hour, the mercenaries met with representatives of the citizenry led by the constable, a cowardly fool who seemed eager to foist the responsibility for taking care of the problem onto someone else. Ursa presented his credentials, and they in turn affirmed the amount of the reward. The general whereabouts of the nuisance was well-known. The slig dwelled somewhere among the sandstone cliffs that bordered the river, near where the forest ended.

That night Ursa and the others camped away from the town, as was their habit.

Ursa was in a gregarious mood. Around the campfire he told stories about the time he rode with a company of upright Knights of Solamnia, pretending to be one of them until he was drummed out of their regiment for his drinking and womanizing. Like a lot of his stories, you couldn't tell if this one was entirely true, but Kit laughed along with Colo and Droopface.

They made up their bedrolls early. Colo went off into the darkness to take first watch. Lying side by side on their blankets, Ursa and Kit stayed awake, passing back and forth a jug of local mead that had been bestowed on them by the grateful citizens of Kimmel.

"Sligs are tough kin of hobgoblins," Ursa told Kit, preparing her for the morrow. "Whatever you do, don't get in the way of its venomous spittle. The spittle can't kill you, but it'll burn your skin and make you wish you were dead. Their eyesight is poor in daylight, but their aim is good at night or in caves."

Eventually they drank the jug down to the bottom. The drunken Ursa made an emphatic point of telling Kit that the reward for killing the slig would be shared equally—four hundred pieces of gold, or one hundred pieces each. He was doing his best to make up for his past transgression.

The highland cold was harsh. Following Ursa's example, Kit pulled her blanket around her ears. As she was falling asleep Kit knew, even though she could only see his eyes, that Ursa was watching her with a roguish smile on his lips. His crooked smile was not so unlike her own.

* * * * * *

The afternoon of the following day they rousted the slig from a tree roost along the forest edge. Colo had spotted its tracks and been stalking it since late in the morning. Kit had never seen such a thing. It was six feet tall with a horny hide of burnt-orange; a stubby tail; big, pointed ears; and a long, thin snout lined with wicked-looking fangs.

Ursa was right; the slig's eyes were worthless, narrow slits, and this specimen had no stomach for fighting when the sun was still high in the sky. The slig loped away from them with little provocation.

The horses could not easily pursue the slig in this densely wooded area, so they picked a spot to tie up their steeds and then proceeded on foot. The slig seemed to be toying with them, picking his way through rocks and trees, staying just barely ahead until one of them managed to catch up, then turning to take a dangerous swipe at the closest follower.

Colo was the most nimble of the four, and she rushed ahead, leaping over bushes, pushing through thickets a short distance behind the slig. She carried a spear that she had made that very morning by lashing her best knife to a pole. Crude though it was, the spear might pierce the slig's hide. First Colo had to get close enough to throw it.

Stopping to catch her breath on a small rise, she turned back to the others. Ursa and Kit were only minutes behind her; trailing laboriously in their wake was Droopface.

Kitiara carried Beck's sword. Recognizing the weapon when Kit had unsheathed it earlier that day, Ursa had shared a conspiratorial smile with her.

"Hurry up!" shouted Colo. Just as they spotted her, the diminutive warrior-woman turned on her heel and seemed to tumble forward. They heard her screaming and shouting, but could no longer see her. Kit reached the rise first, but luckily Ursa was following closely and managed to grab Kit before she too plunged into the pit trap on the other side of the slope.

Looking down, they saw Colo at the bottom of a sharply angled, slimy hole in the ground, about fifteen or twenty feet deep. She was on her feet and staring up at them with a vexed expression.

"Are you all right?" shouted Ursa.

"Nothing broken," she yelled back. "But the bottom of this pit is crawling with lizards. Maybe poisonous ones. I've killed a few and the others are staying away for now, but I don't know for how long. Get me out of here!"

Kitiara looked ahead and saw the slig, not far off, watching them. The creature opened its huge mouth and let out a bizarre, elongated, hiccuping roar, before turning to lope away.

"It's laughing," said Ursa, touching Kit on the shoulder. "The pit trap is a joke it's played on us. Of course," he added more somberly, "it would circle back to eat her later on. Good," he said, looking up. "Cleverdon."

Droopface had lumbered up and stood, hands on his hips, taking stock of the situation. He carried a length of strong rope, which he quickly unspooled to the bottom of the pit trap. Colo eagerly grabbed hold of it and, after some minutes of exertion by the others, was pulled to the top. When she finally emerged she was covered with mud and a thick, yellow slime.

Cursing her own stupidity, she splashed water from her canteen all over her body and wiped herself off with strips torn from her cloak. The others waited as Colo purged herself of the slime.

"It could have been worse," commented Ursa philosophically. "Sligs have been known to dig pit traps that go down fifty feet, and the bottoms are sometimes covered with sharpened sticks. I'd say you were lucky."

"Funny," said Colo, finishing up as best she could, "but I don't feel lucky."

The others bit their tongues to keep from laughing at Colo's appearance, knowing the tracker didn't think it was very amusing. They had lost precious minutes, and the slig was out of sight. Yet it didn't take long for Colo to pick up the thing's traces, and soon the four of them were again close on its trail. They took more care this time to avoid the pit traps that occasionally gaped in their path, blended into the terrain with vines and weeds.

By late afternoon they had tired the slig out with their relentless pursuit, and the creature had done what they hoped it would, retreat to its lair, a cave that had been scooped out of a sandstone ridge behind a waterfall. The light inside was feeble, and no doubt the slig felt unconquerable there. It sat on its haunches, staring out through a curtain of water, roaring its defiance, as the four mercenaries regrouped below.

Ursa had a plan. In his pack he had prepared a bundle of pitch-soaked branches, which he now handed over to Colo and Droopface. He announced that they would distract the slig with bright fire while he and Kitiara endeavored to get a jump on the beast and kill it.

"Why Kitiara?" complained Colo. "I've been with you longer than she has. I have more experience."

Kit was about to say something in her own defense, but Ursa spoke sharply. "You are clumsy with a sword," he said. "She is better. That is the only reason I picked her. Bring along your spear. You will be farther away from the slig and may get a chance to use it."

Kit couldn't restrain a smirk of pride. Ursa turned to leave, but thought of something else. "Remember what we talked about," Ursa added to all of them, "sligs are abnormally intelligent. This one will be listening to us as we attack it, trying to guess our strategy. Speak to each other as little as possible. Talk directly to the slig instead. Distract it with speech. Confuse it with words."

Despite herself, Kit was impressed by Colo's bravery as the female mercenary climbed the cliff face next to the waterfall and crept dangerously close to the mouth of the cave, holding a flaming branch in front of her. Colo stabbed it into the dark hole. The slig jumped out at her, roaring, but would not confront the fire. Shortly it retreated deeper into the cave.

Droopface, ever prudent, stood on an outcropping to one side of the opening. He, too, waved his torch back and forth in circles, yelling and chanting nonstop to keep the monster's attention.

With the slig distracted, Kit and Ursa circled, unnoticed, until they hung precariously to slippery rocks above the cave's entrance. At a signal, they dropped in. The slig wheeled on them, knocking Ursa down and opening a gash in his shoulder. His sword fell to the ground, but Ursa managed to jump up and retrieve it, then scurry to one side of the cave. Kit had retreated to the other, her back against the wall.

The slig stood between them, its slitlike eyes darting around nervously. Nor could it forget the two humans at the mouth of the cave, waving sticks of fire and shouting at it. Smoke was filling the cave, making breathing difficult.

"Ursa!" cried Kit, concerned.

"I'm fine!" he shouted. Ursa was inching around toward the rear of the cave, behind the slig.

"Awm fawm!" screamed the slig. *"Awm fawm!"*

It's imitating Ursa's speech, thought Kit, even as she made her move, charging with Beck's sword held in front of her.

As she did, the creature agilely leaped to one side, so that Kit had to stab sideways, then back far away from it. No longer could she spot Ursa, who was lost in the dark recesses of the cave. Colo, meanwhile, had crept forward on her hands and knees, holding up her burning torch.

The creature threw the tracker a scornful glance, then focused its attention on Kitiara. Its eyes fastened on her, and she was transfixed by the feverish white pupils. Kit held her sword threateningly, but she wondered if she could make her legs move if she had to.

Droopface shouted out a stream of words, and the slig's face twitched, his attention momentarily distracted. But before Kit could recover, the slig had turned back and once again fixed her with its sulfurous gaze.

"Look out!" was all Kit heard before being bowled over by Colo. As Kit tumbled head over heels, she realized that the slig had squirted a stream of its venomous spittle toward her. But Colo, pushing Kit out of the way, had been splattered instead. Now the tracker was screaming in pain and rolling over and over on the dirt floor of the cave.

Getting to her feet unsteadily, Kit barely had time to comprehend Colo's predicament before the slig attacked. With one swipe of its great, hook-clawed arm, it knocked her hard to the ground. As she fell, Kit dropped her sword, which skittered away from her.

Lunging toward Kit's prostrate form, the slig suddenly halted and gave a terrible yowl. It instantly whirled around, and Kit, scrambling away, saw that its short tail had been lopped off and was flopping on the ground. The slig hopped around on its hands and clawed feet, screaming in agony.

Ursa danced around in front of it, thrusting his sword at the creature. His tawny hair was tossed back, his dark eyes glinting with determination.

Droopface, who had sneaked onto the lip of the cave, stepped forward and heaved a big net over the creature.

The slig threw back its head, crying out fiercely, trying to shake the net off. Droopface immediately fell back out of sight, clinging to the rock ledge. The slig seemed off balance without its tail and careened toward Ursa, making desperate but powerful swipes with its thick, muscular arms.

Kit glanced over toward Colo, who was bunched up on the ground, shivering and moaning. Not much to be done there, not now. Kitiara scuttled toward her sword lying in the dirt and managed to grip the hilt.

Ursa had not backed off, and Kit was impressed by his strength, his courage, his resolve. The slig made furious charges at the mercenary leader, but Ursa gave no quarter. Then the beast stumbled, and Ursa rushed in, plunging his sword deep into the slig's side. Black ichor poured out.

The slig swung recklessly and smashed Ursa in the face. Yet the mercenary held onto his sword and, with a superhuman effort, pushed it in even deeper. As he did so, from behind them both came Kit, at a running leap, thrusting her own weapon deep into the right calve of the slig. She immediately pulled her sword out, then plunged it back into the beast's torso.

The slig lurched backward so abruptly that Kitiara lost her grip. Swaying and falling face forward, it knocked over Ursa, pinning his right leg. Hurrying to the fray, Droopface helped Kit pull their leader out from under the dead creature.

After a moment Ursa sat up, a shaky grin on his face. A bloody gash ran across his shoulder, and his face was bruised and raked with scratches. But he flexed his leg without much pain and managed to stand.

Across the cave, Droopface was already tending to Colo. He had stripped off her clothes and was rubbing her body with one of his unguents. Her moaning had subsided, although every once in a while she yelped in pain. Rolling in the dirt had not been just a reflex; Colo had slowed the effects of the spittle with her actions. Kit knew, from Ursa, that a slig's venom stung like an army of bees, but if treated swiftly, could be counteracted.

The ugly slig lay twisted and motionless in a dark pool of ichor, its stench filling Kit's nostrils. Looking down at it, she asked, somewhat breathlessly, "What now?"

"We cut off its head to prove we killed it," said Ursa.

They got to work with their swords, she and Ursa. It was hard slogging, for the slig's plated orange hide and corded neck muscles made it like cutting through stone. Only out of this particular stone poured a fetid black mess of blood and innards.

After toiling at the grisly task for some time, Ursa stood up wearily, the job done. He had secured a rope around the slig's head so they could lower it from the cave without having to carry the heavy, dripping trophy.

Kit went to Colo, who sat on a rock. Her skin was all red and blistered, and she was naked except for a coating of ointment and the blanket that Droopface had draped loosely around her.

"Thanks," said Kit awkwardly. "If it hadn't been for you . . ."

Ursa came over, too, and grinned down at Colo. "The pain will start to go away in a couple of hours," he said, then added, "if Cleverdon knows his stuff."

Even under the adverse circumstances, Kit was struck by Colo's lithe, sensuous figure. The female mercenary didn't show any false modesty. Colo didn't draw the blanket any more tightly beneath their gaze. She looked up sulkily at both of them, settling her disgruntled face on Ursa.

"Slime and spittle," she muttered with a curse. "It hasn't been my day."

*   *   *   *   *

They rigged up a crude pulley and lowered the bloody head of the slig, the size and weight of a boulder, onto the ground below the waterfall. This took some time. It was past dusk and darkness was descending swiftly. Ursa dragged the slig's head several hundred feet into a small clearing and dropped the rope.

"We may as well camp here tonight," said the mercenary, rubbing the wound on his shoulder ruefully.

"What about the horses?" wondered Colo, who was still draped with a blanket.

"I'll get them," said Droopface, setting off in the direction from which they had come.

"I'll help," volunteered Kit, starting to follow.

Droopface waved her off and disappeared into the dark woods.

"He'll be all right," said Ursa.

"What about, er, that thing?" asked Kit, indicating the slig's gruesome head.

"Oh," said Ursa, "it isn't going anywhere." With some effort he lifted the bloody trophy and stuck it on the end of a short, thick branch thrusting out of a nearby tree. It dangled there, askew, like some grotesque pumpkin-face.

"It'll give the owls nightmares," said Colo with a shudder.

"It'll sure keep the crows away," added Kit with a grin.

Ursa laughed heartily. They were all exhilarated after the successful fight. Ursa whistled as he bandaged his shoulder, then started a fire. Colo was feeling better already and insisted on donning some clothes and scouting the area for food. The wild berries she brought back augmented the meatsticks that Ursa carried in his pack.

After eating, they set to work cleaning their blades. Colo

was looking for more ointment and rummaging in Droop-face's pack, which he had left behind. Kitiara had just finished wiping her sword and was wrapping it in some big, dry leaves when Ursa spoke.

"Wonder where Cleverdon is," he said quietly. "He's been gone pretty long."

Before one of them could answer, a voice rang out in the woods and furtive noises encircled them.

"Stand where you are," said the voice.

Kit noticed that the small clearing had been invaded by a dank mist seeping in from the perimeter, billowing and growing in size. Out of the mist stepped a dozen men, two or three in ordinary tunics, the others elaborately armored from head to toe. These dozen said nothing, just stood there, shifting their weight. The armored ones wore flat-topped helmets with small eye slits and breathing holes. They were weighted down with an array of weapons, including ornate maces and battle-axes, as well as more conventional crossbows, shields, daggers, and swords.

Ursa made a move toward his sword, which was propped against a rock, but as he did so several nets flew out of the mist and wound themselves around him. They fell about him so tightly that he lost balance and toppled over into the dirt.

Two of the armored men clanked forward and hoisted Ursa between them. He could barely move, much less put up a fight. Kit struggled against her impulse to try to help him. Before he was gagged with a strip of leather Ursa managed to shout out, "Forget me! Save yourselves!" His face was taut and pale with fear.

A pair of the other men marched forward and grabbed Kitiara and Colo, tying them together with their backs to each other. Colo struggled and kicked, but all she got for her efforts was a hard jab in the side. Kit's mind was racing, trying to think—who were these new foes? What could she do to break free?

The guard closest to Kit was so thoroughly shrouded in steel that she could not tell if what lay underneath the metal was human or spirit. The one watching over Colo was not armored and looked more commonplace—a burly, bearded peasant with a chiseled face and glowering eyes.

Now Kit saw that three other men had materialized from the mist to join the original group. They were the leaders of this business, she realized. Two were elves, or half-elves, Kit guessed by how they held themselves, while the third was a dark-robed mage who stood apart from the others, his eyes glowing with concentration, lips moving, hands fluttering.

"No. Untie the black-haired one. She comes with us," said one of the elves, pointing to Kitiara. "Kill the other."

"What is her connection?" asked the other elf.

"She had the sword," said the first elf. "Let her answer for it."

He stepped forward, his eyes sweeping the area. Beck's sword, newly wrapped in leaves, lay at Kit's feet. In the darkness it was camouflaged. The elf, frowning and taking a step forward, did not see it.

Kit got a good look at him. It was the dark elf who had been watching her on board the *Silver Gar*. Somehow he had picked up her trail and followed her. But why?

"We must find it," the dark elf said tersely.

The mist surrounding them was now so thick that Kit could no longer see more than a dozen yards ahead of her. She could hear Ursa grunt as he was dragged to his feet. Colo whispered at her back.

"Get ready!"

Ready for what?

The peasant guarding Colo drew his curved dagger.

The mist was almost suffocating. But something more, it began to pulse and swirl, and then to swirl faster, creating a wind that whirled at terrific speed. A low, almost whining noise built to a din and then into a deafening roar. A roar so horrendous that Kit's one thought was not to escape but to break her bonds and clasp her hands over her ears. Leaves and branches broke off and flew past her. Debris whacked her in the face.

Through it all, strangely, she heard the low murmuring of the mage.

Kit felt her feet lifted off the ground by the force of a powerful current. She heard someone's sharp groan, then the sound of a body hitting the ground. "Now!" Colo shouted in her ear.

All of a sudden, Kit was cut free. She bent and groped for her sword hilt. Grasping it, she started toward where Ursa had been—Kit could no longer see him. The whirlwind knocked her off the feet, flattening her on the ground. Colo grabbed Kit from behind, and when she tried to get up again, the tracker held her down on the ground.

"Don't be a fool!" Colo screamed into her ear above the roar. "Stay down. Roll this way as fast as you can!"

Kitiara could just barely make out the female mercenary in front of her, rolling and crawling and snaking to the right.

Suddenly the maelstrom exploded in full force, sweeping everything up into itself. Even as Kit tried to follow after Colo she was being sucked back toward the clearing and worse, pulled aloft. Her fingers clawed into the dirt. Futile. All manner of things boiled past her, ascending—weapons and horses and flailing bodies.

The slig's head.

"Grab on!" yelled Colo.

Kit could see that the diminutive warrior had dropped into a small ravine and was clinging with one arm to a giant root. With her free hand she grabbed Kit's ankle. The force of the gale was such that both women's bodies were linked in a line, fully extended.

Kit heard the cries of men all around her. She had to close her eyes against the dust and dirt flying into them. She had to gasp painfully to draw a single breath. Through it all she felt Colo's steady grip on her ankle.

A rock hurtled up and hit Kitiara square in the temple, and she blacked out. The last thing she heard—or thought she heard—was a violent explosion.

Chapter 14

Mantilla Vale

Kitiara woke up, cold water splashing on her face.
She was lying on her back on the banks of the river and
looking up into the face of Colo, who was crouched beside
her, water cupped in her hands. Kit gave a start as
everything—the slig hunt, the ambush, the destructive
gale—came back to her.

"Shh!" whispered Colo.

Kit propped herself up on her elbows. This didn't look
entirely familiar. "Where am I?" she asked.

"About half a mile from where we were," said Colo, still
whispering.

"How. . . ?"

"I had to drag you! Now be quiet or you'll give us away!"

In a daze Kit heard distant tramping in the underbrush,

muffled voices arguing, horses riding off. After what seemed an eternity, the noises tapered away, and she and Colo were surrounded by silence.

"What—" she began anew.

"Quiet," ordered Colo, placing her hand over Kit's mouth for emphasis. "Sleep now. In the morning . . ."

They went behind some rocks. Colo covered Kit with a layer of branches and leaves so that she couldn't be easily seen and then made a similar blind for herself. As she fell asleep, trying to piece together what had happened, Kit was aware of Colo's watchful eyes peering out from the camouflage.

* * * * *

Kit woke early the next morning. Colo was on her haunches next to her, throwing her dice and bones and muttering to herself.

They were on the edge of the woods, near the bend of the river where the four mercenaries had first begun tracking the slig the previous day. Obviously, the menace had passed, for Colo had no compunction about being spotted.

"Who were that bunch? What did they do with Ursa?" Kit asked insistently. "Will you please tell me what has happened? Why did that mage summon a whirlwind?"

"I don't know," Colo stopped her soothsaying and answered grimly.

"How did you—*we*—manage to escape?"

Colo smiled slyly. "When they came upon us, I had my hand in Cleverdon's bag and was able to grab one of the poison blow darts that I knew he carried. It was tiny enough to fit into my hand and slip in my mouth. I waited for the right moment, when the stupid man who was going to kill me reached for his weapon. I spit it into his face. The poison is fast-acting, and in the confusion we were able to get away. Some of them tried to find us afterward but couldn't, because I dragged you downstream."

"Where are they now?"

"I think they have given up," said Colo. "Now it's our turn to look for them." She had walked to the riverbank and bent over to sip some water from her hands. "Drink some," Colo advised. "It'll be good for you."

Both drank their fill. Colo thought it best if they were to stay away from the river during daylight, and double back to the site of the whirlwind by a roundabout way through the forest.

They had one sword—Beck's—which Kitiara had managed to hold onto during the entire episode. Setting off through the brush, they took turns with it now, hacking away undergrowth wherever their path was impeded.

After a short but grueling press through the forest, Kit recognized the general vicinity where they had tied the horses the day before. There were majestic trees with yellow leaves and some clearings dotted with bare rock. Coming into one of the clearings, she and Colo stopped dead in their tracks at the sight that awaited them.

Cleverdon—Droopface—hung from a tall tree, his body stark naked, covered with cuts and oozing pus and blood. The look on his pathetic face was almost peaceful, but his eyes had been dug out. They lay on the ground at his feet where some birds had pecked at them.

Beneath him to one side was faithful Cinnamon, staked out on the ground and horribly flayed. She lay on one side, her flank skinned so that her innards lay exposed, rotting in the sun. Droopface had been killed before he'd been hung, but Cinnamon had died slowly, tortuously bleeding to death while woodland scavengers feasted on her.

Kitiara couldn't bear to look at the sight. She fell to her knees, covering her face with her hands, fighting nausea.

Colo crept forward, looking around warily. Reaching Cinnamon, the tracker gave the dead horse a hard kick, raising nothing but flies. Likewise she gave Droopface a push. Though the sad-faced one swung back and forth crazily, there was no other movement or sound. Cleverdon had been dead for many hours.

Confident that no one else was around, Colo stalked

back to Kit and shoved her in the back.

"What's that for?" demanded Kit hotly, jumping up to face Colo with a hard-set jaw.

"Because we don't have time for that schoolgirl stuff," Colo said angrily.

"That was my father's horse," said Kit softly.

"So what? Who's your father?"

"Gregor Uth Matar," Kit said dejectedly. Her father seemed farther away now than ever.

Colo looked surprised by this information. "The one Ursa rode with?"

"Ursa!" responded Kit, even more astonished than her companion. "What do you mean? He never said anything about riding with my father."

"I don't know," said Colo guardedly. "Maybe I'm wrong. I have a knack for getting names mixed up."

"Tell me what you know." Kit pushed her.

"I don't know anything," insisted Colo. She stood chin to chin with Kitiara, not in the least intimidated.

Although Kit wanted to fight it out, she also had to admit that she trusted Colo, who had saved her life—twice so far. Perhaps Colo was honestly mistaken. Anyway, how could Ursa have ridden with her father and never mentioned it?

"We don't have time for this anyway," Colo repeated.

"What do you mean?"

"They killed your horse, but not the others. That means three horses might be running free in the woods. We have to find at least one of them if we are going to stand a chance of catching up."

Kit thought a moment. "If the raiders didn't take them, the horses would have followed our scent and ended by the waterfall and the slig's cave. That means if we keep going in this direction we stand a good chance of running across them."

"Right," said Colo, setting off again through the woods. Kit looked over her shoulder at Droopface and Cinnamon. Colo turned around. "Coming?"

"Yes," said Kit, hurrying after her.

After another two hours of slowly making their way, they came upon the knoll within sight of the waterfall, the same spot where they had made camp, and been attacked, the night before.

The sight that greeted them was even more eerie than the one in the other clearing. Trees were bent and twisted, even uprooted. The ground had been swept clean of rocks, leaves, and everything else. Over the site hung a strong, gassy odor.

There was no evidence of Ursa or the slig's head or the guard whom Colo had killed, no evidence of anyone or anything from the day before. The place looked not destroyed, but strangely emptied.

"What does it mean?" asked Kit, unnerved.

Colo was stomping around, trying to pick up a trail of something. "Powerful magic. Evil magic. I think they were after Ursa and, for some reason, you. When they captured him, they spirited him away—somewhere. That great cyclone was a magic wind. It took him and everything else away."

"A powerful mage must be his enemy," said Kit wonderingly. She was thinking about what Colo said, and wondering why anyone would be after both her and Ursa.

"Or somebody with enough money to hire a powerful mage," added Colo thoughtfully. Suddenly she cocked her head. "Did you hear that?"

"Hear what?" asked Kit.

"There it is again!" shouted Colo and took off, sprinting through the forest. Kit had to run as fast as she could, leaping over branches and rocks, to keep her in sight. They burst into a clearing, and there was Droopface's mule, calmly munching grass. The mule shied away from them, but Colo grabbed it. Stroking its head soothingly, she jumped on and then extended an arm down to Kit, pulling her up.

* * * * *

It took them all afternoon, traveling in ever-widening circles, to pick up a trail, although they did not understand why there were signs of only two horses, heading west.

After another hour it grew dark, but Kit and Colo kept going. They only had Beck's sword between them, so Kitiara wondered not only who they were following, but what they would do when they caught up. Long past midnight they saw a campfire ahead. They dismounted and crept forward on their hands and knees.

Once they got closer, Kit saw that it was the two dark elves, who were bickering. Closer still, Kit could make out some of the words. She realized they were arguing over her—"the shadow girl," as one of them put it—and which of them was to blame that she had absconded.

"If you had done it my way—"

"You agreed!"

"Well, it will be your job to explain."

Colo put a finger to her lips and circled to the right. Kit had no idea what her plan was, but she held the hilt of her sword firmly, waiting for some signal.

Colo emerged from behind the elves, leaping at them with such breathtaking speed that Kit was taken aback. The tracker carried a big rock. She flung herself on the back of one of the dark elves, bringing her rock down on his head with a sickening crunch.

Even as she did so, Kit sprang out of hiding and rushed ahead with an impromptu battle cry. The other elf had jumped up and grabbed a dagger. Now he rushed toward Kit, but she had the advantage of surprise and a longer reach. She knocked his blade out of his hand with one swipe of her arm, then plunged her weapon into his chest. He fell dead.

It was over in a matter of seconds. Kit saw that Colo was stripping the weapons off her unconscious victim, attaching a knife and various pouches to her belt. She looked up at Kitiara with a confident grin.

"What now?" asked Kit, wiping her sword blade.

Colo sat down on a log and took a bite out of the haunch

of venison that was roasting over the fire.

"We wait," she said, gesturing to the elf she had downed, "until this one wakes up."

* * * * *

Eventually, the dark elf groggily came to. His expression hardened when he saw Kit and Colo standing over him. He squirmed to sit up. Colo had bound his hands and feet, and tied a rope around his neck, then to a tree branch, so that he could not move very far without cutting off his breath.

It was the elf Kitiara remembered from the *Silver Gar*. For the first time Kit could see him close up, with his almond-shaped face, large, pointed ears, and haughty expression. The dark elf refused to show any fear and, struggling to stand, stared at them insolently.

Colo matter-of-factly hit him across the face, drawing a streak of blood from his lip. There was a long pause, and the dark elf slowly bared his teeth in a bitter smile. Colo hit him again.

"Where is he? Where did they go?" she demanded.

"Far away from here," he answered tightly.

"How?" she asked.

"Magic wind."

Colo nodded to Kit.

"Why didn't you go with them?" she asked.

"Because we lost the girl," he said, indicating Kit.

Kit's eyes widened. "You were following me on the boat, weren't you?" she probed.

"No," he said. "That was accidental. I wasn't following anyone. Then I noticed the sword that Patric was carrying."

"You killed him!" Kit said fiercely.

Now Colo was listening with wide eyes, trying to add it all up.

"I killed him," the dark elf said, "and I was going to steal the sword, but I was interrupted. The sword disappeared, and I realized you had taken it. I thought you had drowned, but after your horse was stolen, I began to figure it all out.

It wasn't Patric I should have killed, it was you. Who are you anyway?"

"Kitiara Uth Matar," she said proudly. "What is that to you?"

His face showed that it was nothing to him. He had never heard her name before.

"What do you want with Ursa?" Colo took up the questioning again.

"It is not personal with me," the elf said arrogantly. "My mistress has paid well for him. She would pay more for you."

"Who is she?" Kitiara demanded.

"Luz Mantilla. A lady who wants revenge on the persons who murdered her beloved."

"Lady Mantilla!" exclaimed Kit.

"You have heard of her," the elf said with satisfaction. "She is a crazed person who has the money to employ the services of dozens of mages, spies, and assassins. Her life is devoted to finding the mercenaries who waylaid and murdered her fiancee, an innocent nobleman. There were five of them. We have only ever been able to name four. We don't dare return without the fifth—and that is you, Kitiara Uth Matar."

"Return where?" asked Colo.

The dark elf spoke with an almost sinister glee. "To a small, once-thriving kingdom on the other side of the Eastwall Mountains, now a land of rubble and death and dark magic. A hellish place. I have never been there. Kraven there—" he indicated the dead elf with an unsentimental nod "—he was the contact and the purser."

There was a long, heavy silence.

"I think I know where," said Kit to Colo.

Colo pulled her aside so that they could speak out of range of the elf. They squatted in the moonlight, speaking in low tones. Colo's face was serious. "So you know something about this, after all?"

Kit waited a moment before speaking. "It was one of Ursa's jobs. I tagged along and played a part to trick the pursuers. From what he told me, the job was botched and this Beck, a young nobleman, was killed."

For an instant Kitiara flashed on that night—the memory of Beck, his lifeless face and mutilated body.

"You didn't get the money?" asked Colo.

"Well, *I* didn't get the money," said Kit with wry bitterness, "but the others did, Radisson, Droopface, Ursa and—" her voice faltered "—El-Navar. They cut me out of the payoff and rode off without me. Ursa gave me this sword as a 'reward,' Beck's sword." She indicated the sword in her hand, whose tip was restlessly prodding the ground.

"Then?" asked Colo.

"Beck Gwathmey was pledged to be married to a gentlewoman on the other side of the mountain," Kit continued. "A road was being built to seal the marriage. When he died, everything fell apart. I got stuck in a place called Stumptown for several months and heard a lot of gossip about what happened. Luz Mantilla went insane, people said, and murdered her own father. He had planned the ambush to prevent the marriage. She vowed to track down the hired killers. Nobody ever knew I was part of that business."

"Except the other four," Colo said.

"Radisson must have died before telling," Kitiara mused. "Nobody knows what happened to the Karnuthian. And now Luz has Ursa. . . ."

"Where is this place?" asked Colo.

"Across the channel, then a week's ride, hundreds of miles, through not one but several mountainous areas."

"The magic wind must have taken them there."

Kit said nothing. Both of them glanced over their shoulders at the dark elf. He stood there, knotted in rope with a tight loop around his neck, staring hatefully.

"They don't know your name yet, that you were part of it," mused Colo.

"Unless Ursa tells them."

"If he is still alive."

"That was so long ago," mused Kitiara. "Three years. I had almost forgotten. Except . . ."

"Except what?" Colo looked deeply into her eyes.

Kitiara averted her glance. "Nothing," she said.

Colo got up and took a long draw of water out of a tin cup by the campfire, watching the dark elf. He laughed and spat in her direction. She went to their two horses and meticulously riffled the saddlebags, pulling out a few precious items—a heavy purse, some dried food, and a crumpled map that she held up with satisfaction for Kit to examine.

"What are you going to do?" asked Kit.

"What do you think?" replied Colo with annoyance. "I'm going to ride after Ursa. What about you?"

"I—I don't know," said Kitiara.

"Don't you owe that to a man who made love to you?"

"What do you mean?" said Kit, flushed.

"Ursa," said Colo. "I owe him that much. Don't you?"

"I never made love to Ursa," declared Kitiara angrily.

"You're lying."

"No."

Kit met her eyes. Long seconds passed. Colo had just started to turn away when Kit made up her mind.

"I'll come," she declared.

Colo pulled out the dagger she had taken from the dead dark elf and handed it over to Kit. "What about that one?" asked Colo pointedly. "He knows your identity now."

Kitiara hesitated just a moment before taking the dagger and walking to the prisoner. The tall dark elf stared at her, his eyes sour. "Don't expect me to beg," he said coldly.

Kit grabbed him by the hair, yanked his head back, and slit him across the throat. He died without another word.

"That's for Cinnamon," she murmured. And for Patric, she added to herself.

She pulled the knife out and wiped it on her leggings, then handed it back to Colo, meeting her eyes. Kit chose one of the two elven steeds, Colo the other. Both were strong black animals. Droopface's mule, which had served them well, was set free.

In spite of the late hour they bounded onto their horses and rode off.

*   *   *   *   *

With feverish speed they headed south and east toward one of the seacoast villages north of Vocalion, where Kit would not be recognized. The dark elf's crude map showed them the most direct route back to the deep valley stronghold of the Mantilla family in the Eastwall Mountains. But first they had to make the crossing of the channel to Abanasinia.

Reaching the coast in the morning, they settled in a sleepy town named Conover, whose harbor was filled with vessels of all types. Taking care not to call attention to themselves, Kit and Colo climbed the gangplanks of a dozen ships, trying to book passage for themselves and their horses. But sea travel slowed during cold months, so most of the ships were moored for the season. And no captain was willing to carry them for the amount of money they could spare.

At the end of a frustrating day on the waterfront, Kit spotted a broad-bottomed cargo ship anchored out in the harbor, away from the dock. They rowed out to speak to the captain, a barrel-chested seaman who was in transit with a delivery of furs and wool. He agreed to take them on condition they pitch in as deck hands, for he was short one sailor, and reckoned two females might make up one man.

Colo was ready to grab him by the throat, but Kit acted first. "Done," she agreed, shaking his hand on the bargain.

His ship, the *Fleury*, left early the next day. The week's sail was an agony to Kit and Colo—not the hard work, which at least used up the time, but the slowness. When not occupied with duties, they paced the desk ceaselessly, saying little, finding it difficult to sleep.

When the *Fleury* finally reached the coast, the crew lowered them and their mounts into the waves. Rather than wait to be ferried, one by one, on the loading barge, they swam ashore.

They were at the far edge of Abanasinia and knew from the map that they had to travel west and north, around the spur of the Kharolis, before turning south toward the peaks of Eastwall.

For six days and six nights Kit and Colo rode, sleeping for only an hour or two each night, then rising before dawn to take the saddle again. Stopping periodically only to gulp strong tea and gobble down some dried fruit, they made good time, driving their horses hard. Colo set the pace. She was a natural rider and perhaps had the strongest animal at the outset; but Kitiara was never far behind.

On the third afternoon Kit's horse collapsed at full gallop, and by the time Kit had staggered to her feet, the animal was in its death throes. They had to double up for a few miles and then stop to buy another horse from a farmer.

On the fourth morning, Colo's horse was not able to get up, and she had to put the sword to it. Again they doubled up until a few hours later when they stopped at a roadside smithy to buy another steed.

As they made distance the sky turned gray and the cold alternated with drizzle and fog. In the morning, patches of ice dotted the ground and, as they moved away from the coast to higher elevations, a light carpet of snow. At times the snow covered the ice, making treacherous going for the horses.

The weather seemed intent on breaking their speed. When it wasn't snowing or drizzling, it was foggy. The damp seeped into their bones. On top of being exhausted and saddle-sore, almost numb from the exertion, they could not rid themselves of the constant chill, even in the sunlight.

Kit had never been this far north and seen this vantage of the Kharolis. She was in awe of the peaks that stretched on for miles in the distance, filling the horizon—great, jagged ribs of brown and purple clumped with snow.

By the sixth day the landscape had become more familiar as they entered the northwest slopes of the Eastwall range. According to the elven map, they could follow an elusive course here, winding through trails and ravines and small valleys, into the fiefdom that was Mantilla Vale.

The way was quite treacherous, slicing up rocky country around big, toothy peaks and steep gorges, through hewn foot trails and barely passable areas, at times doubling back and rounding on itself. The horses had to pick their way slowly at times. Other times, Kit and Colo had to dismount and walk alongside their jittery steeds. Still, the map was precise, and they ate up ground.

Eventually the twisting rocky ground took its toll on one of their horses, which stumbled and ruined a foreleg. They had no choice but to finish off the suffering animal and share a single horse again. Kit and Colo were close enough to their destination now that, if necessary, they could travel the final miles down into Mantilla Vale on foot.

On the afternoon of the seventh day, they came to a snowy crest with a ribbonlike waterfall. The crest overlooked a deep, irregular valley that, from the distance, was obscured by a thick, yellow mist. Charted on the map was a narrow trail down the gentle slope.

Kit had never felt more drained. Every bone ached, her eyes were bleary, her clothes torn and dirty. Colo, standing beside her, gazing out over Mantilla Vale, looked no stronger. Indeed, as they stood there, without making a move toward their destination, Colo slumped to her knees.

Realizing they needed to rest and regain some of their strength, Kit and Colo decided to camp for the night on the ledge. As it was not yet dark, they had a leisurely amount of time in which to tether their horse and make camp. They oiled and dried and laid out their weapons. With melted ice and snow, they managed to clean up a little, which helped them to feel refreshed.

Colo built a small fire behind some rocks so that its glow could not be seen even from the valley. When night fell, they could glimpse nothing in the valley below and, even stranger, nothing in the sky above. It was a night for neither moons nor stars. Only empty darkness.

At first the two companions spoke little to each other. Weary but thoughtful, they sensed they were on the verge of something—something that they might or might not live through. With food cadged along the trail, Kit prepared a meal, but hungry as they were, they were too wrought up to eat much.

After a long time Colo began to speak. What she told Kitiara was how she had met Ursa. It was only nine months before. He was traveling with Cleverdon alone, through Southern Ergoth, at a particularly low point in his adventures. According to Colo, Ursa was dressed shabbily and scrounging for any kind of work.

At an inn on a highway where Colo had stopped for the night, she was accused of cheating at cards—which, indeed, she had been. Ursa, too, was in the game, saying very little and playing very well, although he was losing steadily, mostly to Colo herself. Yet he took her side in the argument, and when a yokel drew a knife on Colo, Ursa responded in kind, at some risk to himself. The two of them, with Droopface, backed out the door and got out of town one step ahead of a mob.

Once safely away, Ursa told Colo that he knew all along she was cheating and demanded half of her earnings. They had been traveling together ever since.

"I didn't know he was much for playing cards," mused Kit. What she really meant was that she didn't realize Ursa would stoop to such a tame way of conniving some money.

"I think he can do a little bit of everything," said Colo admiringly.

After that, Colo lost energy and, before long, fell asleep.

Feeling restless, Kitiara walked to the edge and looked out over Mantilla Vale. The map said the family manor was in the center of the small, oval valley, roughly five miles down and another five to the west. She stared hard in that direction. The dire blackness gave up no clues. No light pierced the valley.

Kitiara wondered about Ursa Il Kinth, whether he was still alive and how, when she stopped to think about it, he had loomed so importantly in her life thus far.

For the first time in many weeks Kit found herself wondering about Caramon and Raistlin, too, about how they were faring. Caramon would be growing bigger and stronger and bragging about his skills. Raistlin was probably growing more inward, silent, and clever. Kit felt certain he was every bit Caramon's equal, but that his abilities would show themselves in a different way.

She hoped she would see her twin brothers again sometime. But tonight, she was not so sure that hope would ever be fulfilled.

As for herself, Kit felt that she was finally living a life her father would understand. Looking out over the valley, thinking ahead to the next day, she silently mouthed the maxim she had heard Gregor Uth Matar repeat many times: The sword is truth.

*　*　*　*　*

Beneath the thick, yellow mist, the road leading to the Mantilla castle bore evidence of waste and apocalyptic calamity. Carts and wagons lay abandoned with broken wheels. Farms were half-burned, the fields charred. Tools, equipment, clothing, furniture, and household objects were scattered along the road.

A pall hung over the land. No familiar babble of birds or animals, no sounds of people broke the eerie silence. No wind disturbed the unearthly mist that did not lift or waver.

They rode, Kit behind Colo, on their only horse, fidgeting with their weapons. At first they rode cautiously, but seeing no one, they picked up speed.

As Kit and Colo drew closer to the castle, the first bodies began to appear. People hanging from blackened trees. Skeletons in the field. Scorched bodies, as well as pieces of bodies, lying where they had fallen, in gullies and on top of each other. Some were obviously months dead, others relatively fresh and putrid.

"Look!" cried Colo, pointing to one dangling from a tree.

Kit nodded as she recognized a soldier in the full armor of the unit that had surrounded them two weeks earlier. It was one of that troop, or certainly one who had belonged to that troop at one time. And he was only the first of many from that armored militia, brutally slain, whom Kit counted as they passed.

The spectacle was more terrible than either of them could have anticipated. Kit had never dreamed such unspeakable horror, and she had to steel herself to endure it. Colo's eyes looked straight ahead, but she too was reeling with disgust.

They passed a section of land that was sprinkled with upright corpses hanging on poles like scarecrows. Their faces suggested gargoyles, distorted grotesquely; some of them were ancient and rotting, some of them newly slain. These were all mages, and some had signs hung on their bodies. One of them, covered with cruel wounds, had a board slung around his neck:

This mage failed my purpose and paid the price—Luz Mantilla

"The mage," whispered Colo, pointing.

"Yes," said Kit, recognizing the robes of the one who had performed the magic cyclone that had whisked Ursa away only two weeks before.

Still they spied no living soul.

Now they caught sight of the towers of the castle. But something was wrong. The towers were crooked, distorted, some parts smashed to the ground. Only a needle spire in the center of the mass rose high into the sky above the yellow mist. This one tower seemed separated from the rest, an island adrift in a sea of rubble.

It was as if the fist of a god had smote the castle down, shattering it and driving it underground in several directions.

Closer on, the yellow mist became even more oppressive and it was impossible to see very clearly things more than a few yards away. All of a sudden a monolith of brick and rubble jutted up before them, ending the road and making a blockade. In the middle of the jumble of stone was a maw framed by timber that showed descending steps. They could ride no farther.

Except down. The stone steps led into a passageway. No

sentries barred their way. Light flickered ahead.

"This way?" questioned Colo.

"Either that or turn back," said Kit.

"We've come too far already."

Kit nodded, but took a moment to check her weapons. In one hand she wielded Beck's sword and in the other she carried a copper dagger that she had taken from one of the dark elves. She glanced over at Colo.

The tracker had two swords taken from the elves, a short blade, and a coil of rope. Kit's companion had risen at first light, painted her face and braided her long, sandy tresses with feathers. Now Colo tied up the horse and turned to lead.

Kit felt a rush of warmth for the diminutive female, who was the very opposite of a homebody such as her mother. Colo was one of the most truly admirable women she had ever encountered.

Without speaking to each other, Kit and Colo began to inch down the stairs and through a long stone corridor that stretched endlessly in front of them. Torches set high along the walls gave what little illumination there was. The women stuck close to the walls, staying clear of the center in case of traps. They scuttled a few feet at a time, weapons alert, feeling for side passages.

At times the stone corridor eased downward, other times it buckled and elevated slightly. Unseen creatures scurried out of their path. The tunnel was damp; water trickled somewhere. Unpleasant fumes hissed through cracks in the walls. At times the way was so dark that Kit and Colo could see very little, except the outline of the other against the opposite wall.

After a time they came to a large, high-ceilinged chamber that was better lit, but seemed half caved in at one end. There were four exits—five, counting the one from which Kit and Colo had entered. They branched off in four forward directions that, with the entrance, made up a star shape.

In the center of the room was a high mound of bodies,

heaped on each other like firewood. Some were propped up whole, seemingly alive, frozen in mid-gesture; others were mere skeleton parts. There were dozens, maybe hundreds of corpses, with skulls white and rotting, clothes in tatters, body organs everywhere, and rats darting in and out of openings.

Kitiara gave a gasp and brought a hand to her mouth, while Colo involuntarily stepped closer to her, gaping at the sight.

"What?" Kit shuddered.

"Breathe shallow," said Colo firmly, steadying Kit with a hand on her shoulder.

They shuffled closer to better see the gruesome death heap, to look for any evidence that Ursa was among the dead. Suddenly a ghost of a man sprang up from the middle of the pile, all yellow skin and bones and leer, wispy white hair and goatee, dressed in fetid, flapping rags.

Colo and Kit separated in an instant, their weapons up and flashing. But there was no other movement in the room, and the old coot seemed more daft than dangerous. He was leaping from foot to foot, chattering to himself. In his hand was an iron ring of rusty keys.

"She has come! I be free! Which one is she? Maybe I be seeing double. After all this time, I be free!" babbled the old fellow.

"Stand still," ordered Colo. "What are you saying, grand-father?"

"Here! Here!" The man proffered the hoop of keys.

Kit gingerly outstretched a hand and took the ring. The metal was lime-encrusted.

"I think he's dotty," said Kit acidly, still looking around warily.

"Who are you old man? What's happening here?" Colo demanded again. She sheathed her sword and belted her knife, perhaps to reassure the codger.

The old man had leaped close to Kit and Colo, and now pranced in a circle around them, conversing merrily with himself. His long, white hair shimmered like cobwebs. He kept pointing off in various directions.

"The Great Lady, she says I can go when you come. I been loyal. Last of the loyal, that's me. I been keeping the jails for many years. Many, many years. I'm all that's left. Except—" he bit his tongue and lolled his eyes "—except the Iron Guard." He halted his dancing nervously and said loudly, "Except the Iron Guard. I don't forget thee, no sirree. I pay homage to thee." He bobbed his head spasmodically.

"Take," he said, indicating the keys. "Yours now. I go! She promised." He gave a little wave and started off.

"Wait!" cried Kit fiercely, grabbing his arm and gesturing threateningly with her dagger. "Where is the lady you speak of?"

He turned to regard her, stroking his goatee. "Five tunnels there be," the old man said thoughtfully. "You will find her by traveling the right one, I do believe. Which one? I do not speculate. Myself—" he looked fretful "—I have not laid eyes on the Great Lady for many months now. She leaves me alone. That is my reward. Others not so lucky. Advise extreme carefulness."

He bent and whispered conspiratorially. "I seen the Iron Guard, though. They come and go. Go get visitors. My job," he said with a proud chuckle, "is to take care of the visitors. Only," he beckoned Kit closer with one thin, yellow finger, "two left. Tch-tch."

He put the finger to his lips. "The Great Lady is very angry," he added knowingly. "Shush," he said, swiveling to cut off Colo's question. "I risk my life telling you this."

The old man swaggered around, his chest puffed out. "She up in tower somewhere, very angry. Everyone fail, everyone disloyal. Big killing." He tilted his head toward the death pile in distaste. "Not me. I'm very trustworthy. I keep the keys! I be loyal!" he bragged.

"Which way?" demanded Colo in exasperation.

He stroked his goatee. "Yes. That is the question. I used to know the answer—" he gave a shudder "—before. Before." He wheeled slowly, seeming to ponder each of the exits, his eyes rheumy. "I forget," he said plaintively. "Which way is out?"

Colo jerked a thumb over her shoulder toward the stone corridor where they had entered.

In a blur the gibbering old man pushed past her and darted into the tunnel. "Gods bless you!" he shot over his shoulder as he disappeared out of sight. "I be free! Free!" For several minutes they could hear the echo of his footsteps, trailed by his chortling.

Kit held Colo's arm. "Let him go," she said. "He's harmless."

"Maybe he's a spy," said Colo.

"No doubt," said Kit. "But Lady Mantilla knows we're here by now. We're stuck with the problem of fighting her, one way or another. He's nothing to us."

Kit adopted an almost amused expression. She held out the moldy ring of keys. "What about these?" she asked.

Colo took the ring in her hand and made a fist, crumbling one of the ancient keys into bits. "I don't think they'll be of much use," she said drily.

Turning back to the huge chamber, Kit and Colo were greeted once again by the grisly tableaux of death. With somber expressions, their eyes swept the timbered doorways leading out, assessing their options. One was obstructed by fallen rock. Otherwise they looked like identical holes of darkness.

"Well?" asked Kit.

"I think we should stick together," said Colo. "I didn't like that talk about the Iron Guard."

They looked again, uncertain. "Well, we needn't worry about that one," Kitiara said, pointing to the exit that was obstructed with rock and debris. "And we know that behind us is the way out," she continued, indicating the tunnel behind them, "or at least the way in. We may as well start there." She pointed to the tunnel farthest to her left. "We can work to the right from there."

Colo nodded. Looking down the tunnel's expanse from the mouth, they could see even less well than before. This way was more dimly lit than the first one. Kit and Colo stuck close to the walls at first, inching along, weapons low and ready. After a time, hearing and seeing nothing, they could go more quickly.

At first, although the torches in the walls were set farther apart, the tunnel appeared the same—empty, damp and noxious. As they went on, the torches began to diminish in number and appear at greater intervals. Kit and Colo began to stumble over fallen timber, wide crevices, and loose rock; smelly vegetation hung from the low ceiling, and vines and roots grew out of the walls, latching onto the women as they passed. The stone corridor rose and fell slightly, angled and veered.

"We'll probably end up back where we started," offered Kit wearily after a time.

The unrelieved tension as much as the effort of trudging through the dank tunnel made their shoulders slump, their faces shiny. Kit had sheathed her sword and was using her knife to hack away at the tough spider-webbing and vines that slowed their progress. Colo, on her side of the tunnel wall, had glided ahead.

All of a sudden the tracker pricked up sharply. "What's that?" Hurrying to catch up, Kit heard a strange furtive noise, a low whooshing and thrashing. Squinting ahead, they could not pinpoint its source. "Careful," Colo warned.

As they moved farther down the stone tunnel, more alert now, the sounds grew and subsided. Bursts of smacking were followed by intervals of silence. Still they could make out nothing ahead. Both had their weapons poised, edging forward stealthily.

Kit was a few steps ahead of Colo, peering hard into the murk, when abruptly she slipped and slid forward as if down some steep chute. She screamed and let go of her copper knife, managing to close the fingers of her left hand around a thick, knobby root. With her other hand she held onto her useless sword.

She dangled in space. Below her she could see nothing, just a dark, bottomless chasm.

But she heard a tremendous roar, followed by the swishing and thrashing of some creature far below in a pool of water. The reek that wafted upward stung her nose.

Shouting, Colo uncoiled her rope. She came forward as far as she dared, so that she could just make out Kit's fearful face. The tracker missed her first throw. The second time, Colo got too close and lost her footing, almost falling forward herself. The third time, Kit managed to swing up her arm and grab onto the rope with the hand that was also clutching the hilt of Beck's sword.

The snarling monster let out another roar from below.

"Just hold on. I'll pull you up!" Colo shouted out between gritted teeth.

The rope cut into Kit's hand, and a trickle of blood ran down her wrist. She could barely hold on to the rope and Beck's sword at the same time. Colo's strength was remarkable for someone her size, but even so it took her long minutes of strenuous hand-over-hand pulling to raise Kitiara up over the steep edge.

Crawling forward, Kit rubbed her wrist ruefully. Colo was stretched out with fatigue. It was several minutes before either of them could speak. They could hear the roars and thrashing of the water beast below. No doubt the creature was disappointed by Kit's narrow escape.

"Definitely not a slig," Kit remarked at last.

"No," said Colo, sitting up. After a moment, she added wryly, "Now we're even anyway."

They rose slowly and began their way back. They could hurry but even so, it was some time before they re-emerged into the chamber of death. Two clear tunnels remained to be explored.

Kit figured it was already past midday, and they were hungry. They shared their modest provisions in the presence of the victims of Luz Mantilla's lust for revenge. They were almost becoming accustomed to the grotesque surroundings.

Sprawled on some rocks, Colo spoke. "As I see it," she said sensibly, "if each of the two other tunnels takes as long to explore as that one, we will be underground all day and far into the night. And even then, we may not have found what we are looking for."

"I was thinking the same thing," responded Kit cautiously.

"I don't want to spend two days in this hellish place," said Colo, looking around warily.

"Nor do I," admitted Kit.

"We should split up. Each take a tunnel. If nothing pans out, meet back here."

"Agreed."

"Take it slowly," urged Colo. "Carefully. Watch out for traps and . . . the Iron Guard."

"Don't worry," said Kit with her crooked smile. "I won't make the same mistake twice."

They stood and clasped each other's shoulders. Kit realized she had grown fond of the tracker's company. Colo's eyes shone with similar feeling.

Turning first, Colo made for the far tunnel and disappeared into its entrance. Kit waited for several minutes, but heard nothing other than her companion's receding footfalls. Then, with trepidation, Kit headed toward the last tunnel.

* * * * *

After about ten minutes Colo's tunnel became virtually impassable for all of its debris. Not just rock and timber, but junk and clutter. Perhaps, the tracker debated with herself, this stone tunnel was no longer in use, and she ought to turn back and hook up with Kitiara.

The tunnel was littered with objects—rusted pieces of armor, clumps of smelly clothing, stained rugs, broken pottery, old farm tools. Webbing and moss hung down from the ceiling, tangling with her hair. Spiders and bugs as big as saucers dangled over her head. She could hear rats and other small creatures skittering into their hiding places as she passed.

"By the gods," she muttered, using her sword to sweep

away the webs. "I must have got the worst of the two choices."

After almost an hour of wending forward, Colo came to a dead end, a slagheap of stone, timber, and assorted junk that formed a veritable wall, stretching up to the ceiling. She was about to turn back when she noticed a pinprick of light showing through from the other side. When she got down on her knees to peer through the tiny hole she could see that the tunnel continued with less impediment on the other side of the mass.

With a sigh she took her sword and jabbed at the opening, working at hollowing out a wider egress. When it looked big enough to crawl through, Colo wriggled in head first and found that, with some effort, she could snake forward. After crawling on her belly for some minutes in this fashion, she was well coated with dirt and slime and dust.

Holding her knife in front of her, she found that she could chip away a path. She progressed a couple of feet at a time until she came upon a particularly large rock, whose jagged, down-slanting edge blocked any further advance. After some time she managed to pry it loose, but when it dropped out, she could feel the weight of the slagheap above her creak.

Colo thrust herself forward as quickly as she could, considering how narrow the burrow was. But there was a tremor, and behind her, just before she was able to push out the other side, the rock and junk pile collapsed, crushing her left ankle.

"Damnation," Colo screeched, trying to twist her head to get a look at her foot. The pain was excruciating.

She managed to corkscrew around and, lying on her side, poke her sword around near her foot. With some twisting, she was able to work her foot out of the mess. She had just yanked it free and lurched forward when the entire blockade started to tremble and groan.

Colo rolled forward as it came crashing down.

The dust and noise settled. Propped up a safe distance away, rubbing her bloody, mangled ankle, Colo looked back and observed that the entire slagheap had flattened out, so that now there was easy passage over it.

Ahead of her was another section of tunnel, relatively clean and lit with torches, angling sharply to the right. Her ankle was hurting badly, but it was twisted, not broken, and Colo could put some awkward weight on it.

She tore off a piece of sleeve and wrapped it around her foot, then hobbled forward, using the wall for support, dragging her crippled foot.

As Colo followed the angle of the tunnel, she realized that she was in a sort of underground jail, with rows of cells on opposite sides of the sconce-lit corridor. The cells were mostly empty, with old bones in some, twitching rats in others. As she continued on, she counted at least one hundred of the stone pens, each the size of a horse stall. She pulled herself along by the bars to steady her balance.

Up ahead the tunnel veered to the right again and beyond the bend she could hear some vague noise. She thought it might be another creature like the one in the pit, and her first impulse was to scan the floor and make sure she was not about to plunge into another camouflaged trap. But this noise was different, more subtle, a padding and shuffling, followed by throat-clearing noises.

Human breathing!

She limped forward, clutching her sword, and peered around the corner. What she saw, a short way up ahead, was a narrow flight of stairs leading upward to the right and a cell larger than the others that was set into the far end of the tunnel. In the cell paced Ursa Il Kinth, wearing only a pair of pathetic leggings.

"Colo!" he cried out, grabbing the bars, when he spotted her.

"Ursa!" She rushed forward as best she could, alternately hopping and dragging her injured foot.

Coming closer, she could tell that Ursa was badly battered, thin, and weakened. His face was heavily bruised, cuts streaked his bare chest, and his shoeless feet were swollen and blotched with purple. Inspecting him sorrowfully, dged blade.

n the panther, screaming its rage, hurled itself
the interior bars. Even at the distance of several feet,
ld feel the hotness of its breath. She was so startled
attack that she fell back. The powerful animal paced
nd forth in frustration, eyeing her, swishing its long,
tail.

ld this really be the alluring Karnuthian with whom
d first made love? For long minutes she stared at the
flecting on that seemingly long-ago time.

nly Raistlin were here, he would have an idea what to
itiara thought to herself.

n as she thought of Raistlin, her eyes drifted to the
vhere the steep winding steps led upward. With a sym-
tic backward glance at El-Navar—who was still pac-
iriously in the wooden cage—she began the climb.

Colo became aware that he was gazing likewise at her, foc-
using on her injured foot, whose make-do bandage had
turned dark red with blood.

Their eyes raised at the same moment, and Ursa could
not help but give a barking laugh, so kindred were the pity-
ing expressions each wore on the other's behalf.

It is good, thought Colo, he has not lost his humor.

"What happened to you?" Ursa asked.

"A sort of cave-in, back in the tunnel," she indicated. "But
it's nothing. I won't win any races today, but I can walk on
it. What about you?"

"Hungry. Sore. Weak." His dark eyes gleamed. "Alive!"

Unlike the other cells, his space was lined with two rows
of thick, iron bars; a firm shaking of the set that was closest
to Colo proved they would be hard to break. A water
trough with a muddy trickle ran between the two rows of
bars, separating Ursa and Colo by roughly a dwarf's height.

Glancing around Ursa's cell, Colo could see only two
wooden buckets, no cot.

"One pail for water they give," said Ursa grimly, noting
her searching eyes, "and one for what I give them in return.
Believe me, there's no way out."

"Are there keys?" she asked, cursing herself for having
left the rusty ring behind. Only the inside row of bars
seemed to have a door, a heavy slab of metal that did not
show any lock.

"Pah!" he snorted. "The door is opened by some magic,
and the only person who can open it is 'the Lady.' "

"Lady Mantilla?"

"Yes," Ursa said. "She is crazed and dangerous. Kitiara, is
she . . . is she with you?"

"Yes," Colo answered nervously. "Searching another of
the tunnels."

"You must find her and warn her," said Ursa urgently.
"She is in line to be killed. The only reason I've been kept
alive is that I haven't told the Lady who Kit is or where she
can be found."

Colo glanced over her shoulder, and down at her bloody,

mashed-up foot. She was wondering how she would find Kitiara and how fast she could retrace her steps. "What's up there?" Colo asked, indicating the narrow steps leading upward.

"I'm not sure," Ursa answered, also glancing down at Colo's foot caked in blood, reading her mind. "It's where *she* always comes from."

When Colo met his eyes again, her look was decided. "This place seems practically abandoned. Is anyone else here—any mages? We encountered an old man who spoke of this Iron Guard. . . ."

"She has a retinue of guards," said Ursa tersely. "They are formidable. As far as mages, she has a new one every week. They don't last very long."

Colo handed over one of her swords, hilt first, through the bars, and shifted toward the stairs. Ursa pushed his face against the inner bars.

"I tell you, Colo, she is dangerous and insane."

"I can be dangerous too," the small woman said with a brave wink, slowly starting to ascend the stairs.

* * * * *

Kitiara was exploring her tunnel. It was adequately lit, but there was nothing to mark the way except for loose rock and human debris. The corridor became almost tedious in its sameness, and Kit was able to go quickly, displaying the only weapon she had left, Beck's sword.

After a time, the tunnel made a turn to the left, where a small flight of steps led down to another level. Seeing nothing threatening, Kit cautiously took the steps. The ceiling was so low here that Kit had to stoop or scrape her head. Indeed, as the corridor continued on, the ceiling tamped downward.

At last Kit was forced to get down on her knees and crawl forward. There seemed no danger other than the obvious one of getting stuck.

The ceiling's height was beginning to concern Kit when,

ahead of her, she saw the tunnel
Creeping around the corner she saw
the ceiling shot up once more, an
opened up to another small flight of
steps led into a more clean and spacio
And at the end of the corridor stood a
like structure that gave off distinct p
sounds.

Kit hesitated. What could it be? Sho
find Colo?

First she would investigate.

Kit glided slowly forward. The light
she could see that the huge box struct
heavy black velvet.

As Kit drew closer, the noises grew lou
tent roars that made her tremble. But not
interfere with her. Standing in front of th
was roughly square and twice as high as
noticed narrow, winding stone steps, le
ward, etched into the left wall behind the

Edging forward, Kit extended her swor
rope on one side and made a swipe at it.

She leaped backward as the black
swooped upward and then swirled to th
the cage—for that is what it was, a gigant
And in the cage prowled an animal as large
it was beautiful, a black panther.

El-Navar!

If Kit recognized the Karnuthian in his
Navar showed no recollection of her. As s
drapery was lifted, the animal leaped agai
ing sharp teeth as big and white as cand
were blazing. Its coat had a wild sheen.
mouth.

Actually, there were two sets of bars, on
er, which gave Kit the advantage of tryin
without getting her arm chewed off. Mac
cane, the bars did not budge and only yiel

Chapter 15

Love Lost

"Come in," a voice said. "I've been expecting you."

Kitiara pushed the door open wider and stepped boldly into the room.

She was in a large circular hall at the top of the only tower of Castle Mantilla that had remained intact through the years of madness. Kit could not see much around the perimeter—the room was dark with only a small number of windows, which were curtained. In any case, it must have been night outside.

In the center of the room, in a straight-backed chair under a cone of pale light, whose source Kit could not discern, sat Lady Mantilla. Although Kit could see the woman plainly, she wondered if her foe could mark her, in the shadows, as easily.

Formally arrayed behind Lady Mantilla were the vaunted Iron Guard—four of them, to be precise. They were garbed from head to toe in heavy armor, with mere slits for eyes, nose, and mouth. Each held a jeweled sword. They stood almost ceremonially, as still as statues. Indeed, Kit wondered if they could move at all.

Sitting to one side, on a faded throne, was a stout mage whose vermilion cloak concealed his features. He also did not move, but seemed to stare at Kitiara reproachfully. As she moved into the room, Kit tried to keep him in her line of vision, wary of his magic.

The room was preternaturally cold and dry. When Kitiara took a step, the sound crackled across the space.

"Come in, I say," cackled the voice. "Time is short. *Your* time is certainly short, at any rate. You'll be dead soon enough."

Her hair was long and white, the tendrils knotted and ratted, cascading over her shoulders and almost down to the ground. She had pink eyes and deathly pale, bluish skin, except for bright, rosy cheeks. Luz Mantilla couldn't have been much older than Kitiara, but she gave the impression of an ancient sea hag.

The Lady—for that was the name by which her servants knew her—was dressed in a white lace gown that was ripped and torn, with one sleeve missing entirely. It was, or would have been, Kit realized, her matrimonial gown. She gripped the armrests of her chair tightly as she leaned forward, staring hard at Kitiara.

Kit had remained along the perimeter, beginning to circle the room and take stock of its defenses. The room may have been splendid once. Now it was disgusting, layered with dirt and grime and excrement.

Black velvet covered the walls and furniture, adding to the dark atmosphere. In one corner stood a four-poster, neatly made up, albeit dusty and cobwebbed and perhaps never slept in. A glance above her told Kit that the ceiling of slate and timber was in an advanced stage of rot.

The walls were hung with gilt-framed paintings and once-grand tapestries in faded oranges and purples. Glancing at one of these works, that of a moon-faced maiden sitting at the foot of a regal gentleman, Kitiara found herself looking at Lady Mantilla as a young innocent, before she had been ravaged by time and tragedy, and probably by dark magic.

"Yes," said the voice that fluttered out of the decrepit woman's mouth, "that is I. Then." With a wave of her hand she indicated the painting that Kit had been staring at. "My father, too—" her voice suddenly dripped contempt "—before I killed him, of course. He was my first victim. He was behind the whole nasty business, you know. He thought he knew what was best for me. I had revenge on him for the sake of my beloved."

She leaned on the chair and peered at Kit.

Kit stopped circling and took a step toward the woman, trying to get a closer look, while at the same time angling nearer to the stout mage, who seemed to regard her with stony, hate-filled eyes.

"Before he died," Lady Mantilla continued in a bored voice, "my father was good enough to tell me that Radisson's brother had set up the, uh, episode that resulted in the death of my—" here her voice faltered "—my beloved. That one died rather abruptly. I would have preferred to let him suffer a little more. Of course I was a novice in these matters at that time."

She tilted her head back and gave a long, trilling laugh that would not have been out of place at a royal costume ball, save that it was tinged with madness.

Kit wondered what she ought to do. She didn't think she could defeat four of the Iron Guard, plus the mage and the crazy woman, yet it was too late to go back and get Colo. And strangely, no one had made a move toward her. She was edging imperceptibly—or so she hoped—toward the mage, who sat there, cloaked and hooded, inscrutable.

"It was easy to connect Radisson to his brother, but it took a little longer than I hoped to track Radisson himself down. I got lucky. He was with the panther-man. El-Navar, I believe is his name?"

Kit controlled her voice. "Why didn't you kill El-Navar, as you did Radisson?"

The lady's brows furrowed. "I'm very upset about that. That the strange man could turn himself into a panther was something I didn't anticipate. In that form he is evidently protected by some ward, and I cannot communicate with him. Or kill him. Believe me, I tried. I tried! I've got the obnoxious beast caged underground. I'm still deciding what to do about the nuisance."

Kit had maneuvered close enough to the mage so that she was able to act, bringing her sword up in a swift arc and, in a flash, down again. She severed the man's right hand, which fell to the floor. Yet no blood flowed from the limb and, incredibly enough, the mage did not even move a muscle, did not so much as wince.

Lady Mantilla shrieked with laughter. "Oh, my dear," she cackled, "you have been worrying about that idiot mage. He is number seventy-three, the latest of those who have been employed to assist me. I killed this one days ago, as I have killed them all for their failures and artifice. After a while I pick up their tricks, and they bore me with their airs."

Kit held herself in a guarded stance, wondering if she looked as silly and confused as she felt.

The Lady's voice shifted into a lower, baritone register. Despite the ominous tone, there was a hint of anguish. "You don't know what it's like," Luz Mantilla said to Kit, "to lose someone you love. To dream your life with someone else, and to lose that dream. To be left alone. All alone. Alone!" She gave up any pretense, and sobbed with her head in her hands.

Kit studied the quartet of armored guards who stood behind the lady. She could not make out their eyes or any other indication of their humanity. Through their narrow slits they seemed to regard her coldly. Were they also dead, like the mage, or simply empty shells of metal?

As if reading her thoughts, Lady Mantilla's head snapped up. With a bony finger she traced a contour in the air. The

quartet of knights began to spin and move with such grace
and agility that Kitiara was astonished. The only noise they
made was the clanking of their equipment. They did not go
toward her, but instead, in some choreographed maneuver,
moved toward the perimeter and took up prearranged positions at four equidistant points around the room. Kit noted
uncomfortably that she was the focus of their pattern.

Holding both her knife and sword in front of her, Kitiara
did her best to look threatening.

Lady Mantilla's face shone. Her rotting yellow teeth were
bared in a smile. "You are wondering about my Iron
Guard," she said with almost a wink. "They are more alive
than my mage. Well, only half-alive, or *half-dead* to be
sure, but I like them better that way. I only have four left,
more's the pity. I think I've been rather hasty with the rest of
them. But the important thing is—" she made a clucking
sound and put a finger to her head "—the important thing is
they are created so that they will do anything for me—even
die at my bidding. They are exceedingly loyal about that,
dying I mean. Shall I demonstrate? Zierold!"

One of the armored men took a step forward, his armor
creaking. Kit braced for a challenge, but Lady Mantilla said
airily, "Jump out a window for me, will you, Zierold?"

The heavily armored Zierold went to one of the windows
curtained with velvet. With ballet-like moves he hoisted
himself up to the ledge, turned to salute the Lady, then,
without an utterance, hurled himself out the opening.
There was a long moment of silence, followed by a muffled
crash. Lady Mantilla positively squealed with glee.

Good, Kit thought, one less. She shifted her position
slightly so that none of the remaining three Iron Guard
stood directly behind her.

"Yes," continued the Lady, "it was easy to catch up with
Radisson and El-Navar, but a little harder to find that
sneaky Ursa. He seemed to disappear, be swallowed up. He
separated from Cleverdon for a while. We followed Cleverdon, but then he managed to lose us as well. They donned
disguises, camped in the outlands, traveled hundreds of

miles outside of my purview.

"I found out all I could about Ursa. I had spies and agents everywhere. He never visited the same place twice and always managed to stay one step ahead of us. But in the end I came to know more about him and his habits than his own mother did, and I knew I would eventually track him down."

She shifted tone, velvety now, like her curtains. "To find out who you were proved harder than locating Ursa, my dear," the Lady cooed. "Radisson didn't have a chance to tell me before he died, and El-Navar does not converse very well as a panther. I know from the eyewitnesses that five people were involved, but I never considered that one of them might be a woman. Not until, purely by chance, one of my operatives was traveling on a boat and spotted my beloved's sword. But even then, we thought it was this fellow, Patric. Of course he claimed to know nothing. But he had to be killed anyway. Just to be on the safe side."

While the Lady was preoccupied with her tale, Kitiara had edged closer, until she was only a few dozen paces away. With her next step, Kit entered the cone of pale light that enveloped Luz so that, for the first time, the wretched woman could get a clear look at her. And as she did, Lady Mantilla gave a gasp.

She shrank in her chair from horror. Kit was so startled by her reaction that she froze, then took a step backward, retreating into the shadows. Then Kit realized that to the deranged Lady, she, with her short hair and fighting garb, must still resemble Beck Gwathmey.

Kitiara stepped back into the glare, Beck's sword glinting in the light.

"It is you, then?" whispered the Lady. "It is you! You have the sword."

Behind her Kitiara could hear the clanking of the armored men as they began to move again. She took another step closer.

"The sword I gave to my beloved . . ." the Lady moaned plaintively. "His betrothal gift. He was carrying it with him when he was . . . *assassinated*."

"I had nothing to do with that," Kit said truthfully.

The expression on the Lady's face changed. She bent over and gave a shiver, then straightened up. Her face contorted with fury. "You will die for your part in it," Lady Mantilla screeched. "You will die! Die! I have sworn!"

Kit could hear the armored men clanking behind her. She lunged toward the Lady, holding out her sword so that the crazy woman was trapped against her chair.

Close up, Kitiara could see that Lady Mantilla's face was deeply creased with lines and garishly made up with white powder and rouge. "Call them off," Kit said tersely.

"You can't kill me," the Lady countered. "I've been dead for a long, long time. Ever since that day."

"Call them off," Kit repeated, bringing the tip of the sword up to the Lady's neck, glancing nervously over her shoulder. The three remaining guards were gliding closer to her, moving to a different rhythm, slower, more cautiously. Yet they still came forward with that peculiar grace that, despite their heavy armor, they were able to muster. They had formed a tighter triangle now, with Kit in the center, and were gradually closing in.

"Tell me your name!" the lady hissed.

"Kitiara Uth Matar!" Kit proclaimed.

All of a sudden, she heard a low sliding noise that she could not account for, then a high-pitched cry; from behind her, out of a door hidden behind a tapestry, charged someone she had almost forgotten—Colo.

The tracker was clumping on one foot, but made the short distance before anyone could react. She leaped gamely onto the back of one of the Iron Guard, wrapping herself around his neck and trying in vain to find a spot without leaden protection to plunge in her knife or sword.

Kit's attention was diverted for all of three seconds, yet by the time she had turned back to Lady Mantilla, the woman had gone from the throne. She stood in another part of the room, cackling. Kitiara didn't have time to ponder this failure, however, because she heard more clanking and wheeled just in time to see the danger, ducking beneath the swing of one of the Iron Guard.

Twirling like a dancer, this Iron Guard leaped behind Kit and aimed another blow at her head. She raised Beck's sword up in time, and their weapons smote each other with tremendous force. The superior strength of the armored guard drove Kit back and smashed her up against a wall. Reeling, she stabbed upward with her knife, striking only metal.

Colo was faring no better. She was riding the broad back of the Iron Guard who careened around the room, knocking into furniture and walls in an attempt to dislodge her. She hung on stoically, her weapons futile, screaming curses at her enemy.

The third Iron Guard seemed momentarily unsure as to what he should do. He stood closer to Kit and her struggle, but Colo and her opponent covered a lot of ground, swooping and stumbling around the room. This third opponent took tentative steps toward Kit, then whirled and took a few steps toward Colo.

From one side of the hall, Lady Mantilla watched the melee with relish, shouting derision at Kit.

As if in reply, Kitiara feinted with her sword, then suddenly went limp. The Iron Guard, thrusting forward, was not able to break his heavy momentum. He crashed his helmeted head into the wall, and by the time he was able to turn around, Kit had slithered out from under him and was back near the center of the room.

Although somewhat dazed, Colo finally had figured out that her sword was of no use. She let it drop to the floor. Then, with her legs still wrapped around the guard's chest, she reached around with two hands and stabbed her knife upward into the exposed eye-slots of the Iron Guard. An unearthly wail of anguish filled the room. He dropped to his knees, clawing at his eye-slots, as Colo held on and drove the knife home repeatedly.

Kit's antagonist was coming hard at her again, and she backed up, dodging and feinting. Suddenly the Iron Guard took a step back and surprised her with a graceful, almost hypnotic gesture that did not involve his sword arm; he swept some object off a table, some decorative ceramic, and hurled it at her. It smacked Kit neatly in the chin. She buckled and then straightened, bleeding and wobbly.

"Kit!" Colo called out, breathing hard.

Kitiara managed to look over to her and give her a reassuring nod. But as she did, Colo was distracted for too long a moment. The third Iron Guard, who had been circling for a vantage behind her, found his opening and drove his sword into Colo's back. Her face froze, and she slumped to the floor.

At the same moment, the Iron Guard with a knife stuck in his eye-slots collapsed into a twisted clump.

Kit gave a cry. Turning her back on the guard who had been stalking her, she vaulted across the room to the other side, straight toward the one who had stabbed Colo. The Iron Guard watched her charge with—surprise? Fear? Caught without his sword, which was still embedded in poor Colo's back, the armored man struggled to pull his knife out of its sheath.

Kitiara knocked him over backward with her momentum, straddling his chest. The armored man flailed at her. But Kit swung the hilt end of Beck's sword at his face, hard and fast, again and again, pounding the mask into a dented, twisted shape.

The Iron Guard clawed at his mask, choking and strangling.

Kit got up and, as gently and swiftly as she could, pulled the sword from Colo's bloody back and rolled her friend over. Colo's mouth and eyes were open. Her face was pallid.

"Colo . . ." Kit tried to say something. She had no time to think of appropriate words, though, because she heard clanking. She looked up just in time to roll away from the last Iron Guard, who had heaved himself at her.

His sword fell and hers skittered away, knocked from her grasp by the narrow escape. He had a knife still; Kitiara had no weapon. He lunged at her, but she grabbed his mailed wrist.

They wrestled and writhed across the floor, spitting and cursing into each other's faces. She was only vaguely aware of Lady Mantilla, crouched and hovering several feet behind her, hissing words. The Iron Guard weighed twice what Kit did. It was all she could do to keep him from crushing her.

They bowled over furniture as they rolled to the middle of the room. The struggle took its toll on both of them, but Kitiara was losing strength more rapidly. Finally the guard shook off Kit's hold and managed to get on top of her, raising his knife high. Desperately Kit twisted her head to one side. She felt the Iron Guard's dagger graze her skull and break its point on the floor.

Her left hand groped around on the floor, coming up with nothing. Her right hand reached out and touched the point of Colo's sword.

The Iron Guard was frantically trying to pull out his other knife when Kit swung the tracker's sword and smacked him in the head with its hilt. The blow knocked the guard off balance and caused him to drop his second knife.

Kit jumped up and stumbled backward. She managed to steady herself as the Iron Guard rose to his feet. Now she was the one with a sword, and he was weaponless.

Her opponent glided backward toward a wall. Kit wrapped both hands around the sword's hilt, lowered her head slightly, and charged, thrusting upward at his helmet. Her aim was good. The sword ran through his mouth slit. The guard was effectively pinned against the wall, groaning and twitching.

Kit felt spent; her clothes were torn, nicks and bruises covered her body. It took all the effort she could muster to pull out her sword. The Iron Guard slid to the ground.

Kitiara turned toward Luz Mantilla. She had returned to her chair in the center of the room, encircled by the cone of pale light.

Kit picked up her own sword and approached her warily,

scanning the room for other enemies or magical devices. The Lady observed her with a smirk.

"Pity about your friend," oozed Lady Mantilla. "Colo? Was that her name?"

The Lady made a subtle hand gesture that, if she had not known about such things from Raistlin, Kit might not even have noticed.

Kitiara had come within a few feet of the Lady, but now found herself unable to get any closer. Some sort of force field, something like an invisible wall, stopped her. Stooping, Kit felt around with her hands to try and determine where the barrier started and ended.

"I lost a friend once," said Lady Mantilla in her baritone. "The only dear friend I ever had. The only person I ever loved, who ever loved me. Now you know how it feels, Kitiara Uth Matar."

Kit realized, with a shiver of apprehension, that the force field did not protect Lady Mantilla. It was surrounding her. Kit could move only a few feet forward or backward or sideways. The wall rose so high over her that she could not feel its top. She was caught like a spider in a jar.

Looking at Luz Mantilla, Kitiara noted that the Lady's eerie gaze rested on the sword in Kit's hands. Where the sword moved, Lady Mantilla's eyes followed.

"My beautiful sword," said Lady Mantilla in a low moan, stroking her white, tangled hair abstractly. "My precious gift of love. I should like to have it back. I should like to have it as a . . . memento."

"You will get it back, witch," murmured Kitiara, "right through your heart."

"What did I ever do to you, Kitiara Uth Matar?" the Lady crooned mournfully, her eyes following the sword as Kit shifted it from one hand to the other. "What did I ever do to you that you would help kill my beloved?"

Kit said nothing.

"I don't understand you," said Lady Mantilla. "Now that I know your name, I am even more mystified by your behavior. By your allegiances."

Kit stared at her. "What do you mean?"

"Your name—Matar. Your father was Gregor Uth Matar?"

"What do you know about my father?" asked Kit, her confident tone wavering.

"I told you I gathered a long file on Ursa," said Lady Mantilla, almost petulantly. "I told you I found out all about him—where he had been, what he had done, how he operated."

"What are you saying?"

"What am I saying?" repeated Lady Mantilla. "I mean to say, how can you be in league with the turncoat who betrayed your own father?"

"What!"

Lady Mantilla's eyes revealed complete astonishment. "You don't know," she murmured. "You really don't know. . . ."

"What trick is this?" Kit took an angry step toward the lady. Futile. The invisible barrier stopped her.

Lady Mantilla tilted her head back and gave a long, high-pitched shriek of laughter. "It was in Whitsett, far to the north, four years ago. Ursa was part of a force of mercenaries that fought a climactic battle under the leadership of your father. Gregor's men were successful, and when the contest was over it was Gregor who set the terms of surrender. Surrounded by his loyal entourage, he waited in an open field as the other army rode in to relinquish its arms.

"What your father didn't know was that among his own men there was a faction that thought he did not fairly divide the spoils of his victories, who thought that he was growing rich at their expense. Among them was a man, a first lieutenant who until then had ridden faithfully at Gregor's side. He organized the faction in a secret conclave. They pledged to betray Gregor. This group, under the leadership of Ursa Il Kinth, helped to fake the victory and conspired to arrest Gregor at the peace council."

"Liar!" Kit shouted, but the accusation was half-hearted. The tale Luz told was very similar to the one that Captain La Cava had told Kit aboard the *Silver Gar*. Perhaps the

Lady had heard the same story and is embellishing it now to set me against Ursa, Kitiara wondered hopefully.

"No," cooed Lady Mantilla, reading her thoughts, "not a lie. Too terrible a truth to be a lie, don't you think? Ursa's men surrounded your father, bound him in leather straps, and delivered him to the other side. Ursa took twice the purse your father had agreed to, apportioned it among the conspirators, and then they split up. Your father was led in chains to the dungeon to await his beheading. What a coincidence that his daughter would turn out to be partnered with his traitor!"

Again Lady Mantilla tilted her head back and let go with screeching laughter. The cackling went on for several minutes before, strangely, it disintegrated into choked sobs.

Kit's head reeled. She clenched her fists and buried her face in them. As she turned away from the lady, a tremor went through her body. She dropped Beck's sword.

A rustling made her look up. Lady Mantilla, her face changed, her composure almost placid, had stood. She was pointing toward the door behind the tapestry where Colo had entered.

There was a moment of silence.

Kitiara made a quick movement and kicked Beck's sword, which lay at her feet, over to her captor. Lady Mantilla stooped to clutch it fervently. As she did, Kit heard a sibilance—the release of the force field. She dashed toward the tapestry door.

Behind her, Lady Mantilla, a strangely serene smile on her face, sat down again, fondling the sword of her beloved.

* * * * *

Kit bounded down the steps, only to come face to face with Ursa, who was squatting at the far end of his cell. The mercenary leaped up excitedly and grabbed the first row of bars.

"Kit! Where's Colo? Can you get me out of here?"

For a minute, she couldn't say anything, just stared at Ursa, remembering when she had first met him, entirely by chance, and how, in unexpected ways, he had marked her life. He looked more dead then alive now; so did she, probably. Yet his eyes gleamed at her. Through it all, he'd kept that likeable, roguish aspect.

In other circumstances she would have been drawn to him, far more than to El-Navar. Yet she knew what Lady Mantilla told her was true, and at this moment she hated Ursa with all her heart.

"What's the matter?" he asked when she did not respond immediately. "Did something go wrong?"

Kit leaned her back against one wall, and slid to the ground, exhausted. "Colo is dead," she said simply.

"Dead!" He seemed genuinely shaken. "First Radisson, then El-Navar, Cleverdon, too, I suppose. Now Colo . . ."

"El-Navar isn't dead," she said in a flat tone.

"No?"

"I've seen him. He's in another of these tunnels, changed into a panther. He didn't recognize me. Lady Mantilla said she tried to kill him but couldn't."

"You've seen her then! You've bested her." That old grin of his.

"No," Kit said dully. "She bested me."

"But," said Ursa, bewildered. "You're still alive. How—?"

She stood up. "I gave her Beck's sword. That's all she really wanted—the sword that you took from Sir Gwathmey's son . . . and gave to me."

He thought about that for a second. Then Ursa cocked his head and gave a laugh that, in spite of his ragged appearance, bespoke strength. "Good. Now, can you get me out of here?"

She looked at the cell without much enthusiasm. "I can't," she said, "and even if I could, I wouldn't."

"Why not?" he asked, confused again.

"In return for the sword she told me the truth—about you."

"What truth?" he scoffed.

"That you betrayed my father."

His eyes widened. Ursa opened his mouth to say something, but thought better of it. He turned, walked back to the wall, scuffed at something, and returned to the bars. His face had hardened, become wary.

"You believe that, I suppose," he tried.

"Shouldn't I?"

He shook the bars desperately, to no avail, and a craven note crept into his voice. "You've got to get me out of here, Kit," he pleaded. "You've got to help me. You can find a way."

"I want to know this. Why did you do it? Why?"

His eyes rolled. "Don't be naive, Kit," he said dismissively. "It was business. Business! It was money. It had nothing to do with your father. I happen to have liked your father."

"You were his friend!"

He shrugged and put on a smile. "Not much of one."

She glared at him. "You led him to his death."

"But he didn't die!" Ursa protested. "He was condemned to die, yes, a month and a day after he was seized, but I put aside some money for the jailer. I'm certain he got away."

"Another one of your lies."

"I didn't wait around to find out," he said stubbornly. "I can tell you that, not only had I turned on him, but some of his men had to be put to the sword. But Gregor didn't die, I'm sure of that. Not Gregor. He always had the luck of a kender."

"You expect me to believe that, after you admit you betrayed him?"

"I didn't betray you," he argued. "I didn't betray you. I was beaten, starved, but I didn't tell her your name. I didn't tell her that you were in on it."

"Pah!" she spat. "You didn't tell her because you wanted to save your own skin. If she knew who I was, she wouldn't have had any further use for you. She would have killed you instantly. You would betray anyone."

"Not you," he said, his voice cracking.

*   *   *   *   *

In the circular room of the high tower, Luz Mantilla sat in her chair and gazed upon the painting of herself in a far-away place and time. She held the sword of Beck Gwathmey, whom she had loved, and lifted its blade high in the air, turning it and examining it in the cone of pale light. She had forgotten all about Kitiara and El-Navar and Ursa and all the rest—about everybody and everything. She only thought about Beck, dead, gone these many years, waiting for her. Somewhere.

She clasped the hilt and turned the blade around until it was slanted down. Then, with a joy that she had not felt for a long time, Luz Mantilla drove the point into her heart.

*   *   *   *   *

Kit was staring at Ursa with hate-filled eyes when a low rumble shook the stone corridor. The first row of bars to his cell vanished before her eyes, and the innermost door clicked open.

Kit blinked. Ursa, too, was slow to react.

Kit's eyes went to the sword that Colo had left for him, but Ursa was closer than she and had already bent to grab it. Now he stepped through the door and over the line where the bars had been.

Kit took a step back.

"Get in," he said, waving the sword toward the cell.

She didn't move. "How will you lock it?" Kitiara asked scornfully.

That gave Ursa pause. He scratched his head. "I guess I'll have to kill you," he said matter-of-factly.

He rushed her, but Kit was a better fighter than when they had first met, when she was but a girl. She grabbed his wrist and kicked upward, cracking his arm. As weak as he was, he slammed her backward, each of them struggling for control of the sword. His face was up against hers, but it was the face of Gregor Uth Matar that swam before Kit's eyes. She felt a surge of adrenalin.

"Just like before!" Ursa tried to joke as Kit jerked the sword away from him and slammed him across the face with her elbow. He fell on his back, off-balance, and looked up at her in amazement—just in time to see Kit lodge the sword in his chest.

He tried to stand, but collapsed onto his side. With his free arm, Ursa reached up to Kit, fell back, and died.

For long seconds, Kitiara looked at him, feeling revulsion yet also some pity. She could not bring herself to yank out the sword. Weaponless, she ran back down the tunnel.

* * * * *

Later—it could have been hours, days or years, for she had lost all sense of time—Kitiara stumbled out of Castle Mantilla.

The mist was slowly lifting.

A body lay near the entryway in a pool of blood. It was the dotty old jailer, trampled and clawed. He had not gotten away fast enough. Looking down in the dirt, Kitiara saw the tracks of the old man's murderer, the prints of a huge panther.

El-Navar was free.

She could barely lift her legs. She moved as if she were slogging through quicksand. Her head was on fire. Her muscles felt dead. One arm hung at her side, limp. Luckily, her horse was still alive, waiting for her.

El-Navar had left a clear trail. For a moment Kitiara considered following him, but the tracks led south. She struggled to climb up on the horse and, barely conscious of what she was doing, turned the animal north. North was where she was headed, to find news of her father.

Epilogue

Nobody in Whitsett could tell Kit for sure what had happened to Gregor.

The journey there took nine weeks—across the Eastwall Mountains to Newsea, a stopover at the Island of Schallsea, then onward to the middle reaches of Solamnia, the region of Throt.

Across uninhabited mountains and inhospitable waters, frigid wetlands and snowy steppes, woods whipped with wind and eerie cries, high grasslands encroached upon by sheet ice.

She arrived in the middle of the winter. She came alone.

Kitiara found that Whitsett was very much changed. Whitsett was the name of a community, one not much bigger than the village terrorized by the slig, but also the name of the loose federation of homes and farms located throughout the surrounding basin of land nourished by the tributaries of a wild river. The two estates that had been at the center of the feuding almost four years before had dissipated. Now they were melded into the federation, which was honorably ruled by a high official agreed upon by all families, who made decisions of commerce and justice.

The two local lords who had started and escalated a war between their followers had died in the intervening time, one of natural causes, one by violent means. Their lieutenants had scattered. Once the leaders were dead, the two opposing sides saw no reason to continue old animosities, and the peace that was made had lasted.

The jailkeeper from those years had been hung for corruption; the jail had long since burned down, and a new one had been built. There had been three changes of officialdom since. No one in authority could name anyone connected with the long-ago sentencing to death of a mercenary named Gregor Uth Matar.

Although few could claim to have known Gregor, they mouthed various contradictory legends about his fate in Whitsett.

The nephew of the jailkeeper of that time told Kitiara, "My uncle was hung not for corruption but for complicity in letting a certain man go. This was a charge made against him by his enemies. Actually, he had doublecrossed the prisoner and pocketed the money. The real reason he was hung is that he cheated his superior officer out of his share of the crooked money. As for the prisoner himself, this Gregor, feh, I believe he died on the gallows."

A village elder told Kit, "There was to be a mass hanging that day. Not just your Gregor—ten, twelve men. But they say that one was discovered missing, too late, and that this one had been shown a secret underground tunnel. . . ." But the man was unable to prove the existence of such an underground escape.

A third man who claimed he had watched the climactic battle from a hillside said, "I heard they arrested the wrong man. This Gregor, he was a canny one. He suspected the plot against him and put another man in his clothes. The false Gregor was seized and beheaded, while the true Gregor evaded discovery and vanished from these parts."

Nobody could back up their version of the hearsay. Worst of all, Kitiara could find no one to blame, no one to hate, no one to kill for the sake of her father.

After three weeks in the vicinity, a bitterly disappointed Kitiara left Whitsett, not a jot wiser than when she had arrived.

* * * * *

For more than seven years Kitiara Uth Matar wandered the North, as much in quest of adventure and riches as for any word of her father. She learned nothing more about Gregor. If he was somewhere, she deduced, it was no longer North. But she gained much in the way of wealth and experience.

Little that is certain is known of her wanderings.

It is said that Kitiara sought out some paternal relatives, in the heart of Solamnia, hoping for some news of her father. They knew less than Kit; Gregor had not been heard from for many years, and they did not welcome her inquiries. Consequently, Kit's stay in those parts was both short and unpleasant.

It is said that, for a long time, Kitiara journeyed in the company of two men, both humans and expert swordsmen. They roamed the wilderness, preying on solitary travelers. Both of her companions were in love with her, and one of them killed the other after a drunken argument, only to wake up the next morning to find Kitiara gone.

It is said that Kitiara lost a wager in a roadside inn and was forced to serve the whim of a bounty hunter seeking fugitive minotaur slaves. He took advantage of her debt to him and enjoyed making her perform lowly tasks, such as wiping and polishing his boots. But he had some attractive qualities, and she did relish tracking minotaurs and improving her wilderness skills in the bargain. In any case Kitiara was merely biding her time, and after six weeks won the wager back. For an equal period the bounty hunter came under obligation to her.

For a time Kitiara rode as a scout and defender of trading caravans that had to pass through hobgoblin country on their way to the far frontier. She distinguished herself, according to eyewitnesses, in numerous skirmishes and ambushes.

For at least two months, it is said, Kit adopted a pseudonym and joined with Macaire's Raiders in the northwest— the outlaw band under the leadership of Macaire, the wily half-human known for swooping down on small settlements and isolated farms, always eluding capture. The female who rode at Macaire's side during this time, rivaling him in her fearlessness, fit Kit's description. Her sobriquet was "Dark Heart."

How much of this is true, how much of it folklore, is uncertain.

However you add it up, months and entire years of this period are entirely blank as to where Kitiara was and what she was doing. Perhaps she was operating under an alias. Perhaps she was laying low somewhere.

During the first three years of her travels she returned home at least twice, keeping her visits very brief, giving her family some money from her adventures. But without making a conscious decision in that regard, she had let four more years go by without passing through Solace or hearing word of her kin.

About seven years after the time she had killed Ursa, Kit was stopping over in a mill town, west of Palanthas in the region of Coastlund, staying in an inn, when she was approached by a kender.

This kender was the same Asa who made regular stops in Solace while on the road throughout Krynn, harvesting and vending herbs and roots. He augmented his income with, among other specialties, the sideline of courier.

How he happened upon Kitiara is quite unknown. But

kender do have their ways.

The kender handed Kit a sealed paper from Caramon, earning, for his troubles, not the tip he fully expected, but a scowl and a stare until he went away. The letter said:

Dear Kitiara,
This kender says that if anyone can find you, he can, and so I have given him six coins to do so. Kender are sneaky but honest, so I hope he does, and soon.

I am writing this letter by hand, but Raistlin is telling me what to say. He would write it himself but he is fatigued from exertions in the course of trying to make our dear Mother feel better as she lies dying.

Firstly, let me say that we have been overwhelmed by tragedy lately. Our poor, beloved father, Gilon, is dead.

It was a dreadful circumstance, and I do not think it could have been avoided.

It seems he was chopping down a tree as a storm was threatening, and he ought to have stopped. For the wind came up strong in an unexpected direction and blew the tree down on his leg, mashing it and pinning him. He could not move out from under it.

Perhaps because of the storm I did not immediately hear Amber barking outside the door. I was surprised that Gilon was not with her. Raistlin was at mage school, and I was watching over Rosamun. I hurried to follow Amber, but it took me at least an hour to get to the place where Gilon was trapped.

Not knowing what was wrong, I did not have the proper supplies, and it took me another hour to get Gilon loose and to rig a crude sled to bring him back (for, needless to say, he could not walk).

By now several hours had passed since the accident. His leg was black with blood and infection. He was quite delirious.

The cleric said his leg would have had to be cut off anyway, if he hadn't died of pneumonia, because of all the time he was in the cold wind and rain. He died coming back. I didn't even know that he was dead until after we stopped.

We are very sad. The house is not the same.

Raistlin said I did the best I could.

The news had a shattering effect on Mother. Oh, Kit, it was terrible to tell her. Raistlin said he would.

It has now been some weeks. Mother is pale as death itself, barely clinging to life. Raistlin has become very adept at potions and is easing her pain.

(I have become very good at my sword work, and I wish you were here so that I could try some moves on you.)

But she will not live much longer, and I wish you were here to help us. If the kender finds you with this letter, I apologize for its length. But if you are able, I wish that you would come.

Your brothers,

Caramon and Raistlin

Kit put down the letter. Her legs were up on the table. Her tankard of ale went untouched as she sat there, frowning in thought.

Truth to tell, now and then Kitiara wondered about Solace—about home, her old friends and enemies there, Gilon, her brothers, Rosamun.

The letter was an excuse to go back. Within an hour she had paid up her bill and saddled her horse, loading it down with presents and riches.

* * * * *

The plump woman crossing the road was so surprised by the horse that suddenly galloped past, splashing mud on her clean white uniform, that she only had a moment to look up at its rider.

A lean, muscular young woman, dressed in fine leggings and a shiny breastplate, rode in the saddle, her unruly, black hair whipping in the air and a deep scarlet cloak flapping behind her.

Minna shook a fist at the arrogant rider, then patted the

hair on the top of her head. She did not recognize Kitiara
Uth Matar, and Kit did not notice the old midwife.

At the Majere cottage, the scene was a mixture of joy and
sorrow. The boys greeted Kit warmly. Boys! At sixteen,
they were already young men. Raistlin was tall and weak-
bodied with a wretched cough—but he regarded his half-
sister warmly. Caramon was robust and squeezed Kit in a
bear hug until she sternly told him to put her down.

Both of them were agape at her armor and finery, at the
sturdy roan she rode, and at the parcels that weighted it
down. She had brought money to pay all outstanding debt
and several gifts for each of them.

The happy homecoming was tempered by the tragedy
unfolding in the interior of the cottage, where Rosamun
was dying. She looked like a pale wraith. Her small room
was lit with candles, and her faithful sister, Quivera, was at
her bedside. Quivera gave Kit a nervous nod when she at
last entered.

Rosamun had little or no comprehension that Kit had
come home.

Kit took to sleeping in Gilon's bed to be close-at-hand in
the final days. Yet the days stretched on, and Rosamun did
not die. She did not open her eyes, she never got out of bed,
and her breath came in weak spurts. Still she did not die.

Kit saw Aureleen down at the market one morning. Her
old friend glowed with health, but she was married now
and had two little children in tow. A handsome, stocky
peasant carried her purchases, giving Kit the eye while tugging at Aureleen. They moved on quickly. The old friends
had little to say to each other.

Kit spent an afternoon out horse-riding with Caramon.
The oldest twin was much changed—not only bigger and
stronger, but more sensible. Gilon's death had matured
him. Now, when Kit looked in her half-brother's eyes, she
thought of her stepfather, how much his son looked like
Gilon, and how Caramon had Gilon's stolid good nature.

In other ways, too, Caramon was different. Kit noticed,
with amusement, how he snuck away some late evenings to

keep an appointment with one of the local girls down by Crystalmir Lake.

Kit stayed up part of most nights with Raistlin, who had taken on the responsibility of caring for Rosamun during the darkest hours. The visions Rosamun once suffered had faded, but she was still wont to toss and turn, moaning. In this pitiable fashion Kit's mother expended the only energy she had.

Unlike Caramon, Raistlin was not talkative—the opposite, in fact. But in his case, Kitiara had learned to listen for the silences, and the time they spent together at Rosamun's bedside, even under the difficult circumstances, renewed their kinship.

Rosamun's sister stayed with them most of the time, helping out during the day and, at night, sleeping in the big room curled up on a pallet by the fire. A nondescript woman, Quivera gave them a wide berth, and for Kit it was as if she did not exist.

Solace seemed smaller and duller than ever. The house was caught in a limbo as tedious as it was terrible. Before she came, Kit had some idea in her head about making peace with Rosamun at last, but her mother was so far gone that she couldn't respond to words. And Kitiara wondered what it was that she ought to have said to her mother, anyway.

With a passion Kit wished it were all over. She didn't feel in the least guilty about her desire.

Five weeks to the day after Kitiara arrived back in Solace, Rosamun died. Raistlin was alone with her, and he woke the others with the news. That morning, Kitiara said she wouldn't be staying for the funeral which, by Solace tradition, would be three days hence.

"Stay," pleaded Caramon.

"That's all right," said Raistlin. "Go."

In their own way both of them understood.

Even as Rosamun's body was being cleansed and wrapped in linen, Kitiara was beneath the cottage walkway, seeing to her horse. She came up to say goodbye and to give each of her brothers a small leather pouch of carefully selected gemstones worth enough money to see to their worries for more than a year.

"Thanks," stammered Caramon.

Raistlin's eyes showed his gratitude.

"Use them well. They were hard-earned," Kit said, with a wink.

Then, at the last moment, she remembered something and ran back inside and up the short ladder to the space in the back of the cottage where she had lived her girlhood, such as it was.

Things had been moved around, and she had to explore a little before finding the loose board in the wall she was looking for. She reached in and took out a child's wooden sword, smaller than she remembered it and covered with grime. Carrying it, she went out, never sparing a glance into the room where Quivera toiled over the body of her dead sister.

Kit stuck the wooden sword among her possessions before riding off. What use she had for it would be hard to say. But a wooden sword was the only thing of Solace Kitiara cared to take with her, a memento of Gregor Uth Matar. Not that she ever thought about her father any more. Nor about Patric or Beck Gwathmey or Ursa Il Kinth. All that was behind her.

The Dark Horse Trilogy

By Mary H. Herbert

Follow the heroes of the Dark Horse Plains as they forge the destiny of their medieval world . . .

Valorian
Prequel to the best-selling *Dark Horse*, *Valorian* is the epic story of the sorcerer-hero who unites the horse clans against the tyrannical Tarnish Empire.
ISBN 1-56076-566-6
Sug. Retail $4.50

Dark Horse
Gabria, a young woman turned sorcerer-warrior, seeks revenge upon the vile sorcerer responsible for the massacre of her clan.
ISBN 0-88038-916-8
Sug. Retail $3.95

Lightning's Daughter
In the sequel to *Dark Horse*, Gabria and her people must conquer a magical creature bent on destroying the Dark Horse Plains.
ISBN 1-56076-078-8
Sug. Retail $3.95

TSR BOOKS

FORGOTTEN REALMS®
Fantasy Adventure

THE LONG-AWAITED SEQUEL TO THE MOONSHAE TRILOGY

Druidhome Trilogy
Douglas Niles

Prophet of Moonshae   Book One

Evil threatens the islands of Moonshae, where the people have forsaken their goddess, the Earthmother. Only the faith and courage of the daughter of the High King brings hope to the endangered land.

The Coral Kingdom   Book Two

King Kendrick is held prisoner in the undersea city of the sahuagin. His daughter must secure help from the elves of Evermeet to save him during a confrontation in the dark depths of the Sea of Moonshae.

The Druid Queen   Book Three

In this exciting conclusion, the forces of the Earthmother are finally united but face the greatest challenge for survival ever.